SCOURGE IN THE WOODS

ISBNs:
979-8-9902205-0-8 (eBook)
979-8-9902205-1-5 (paperback)

SCOURGE IN THE WOODS

Haydn Boyce

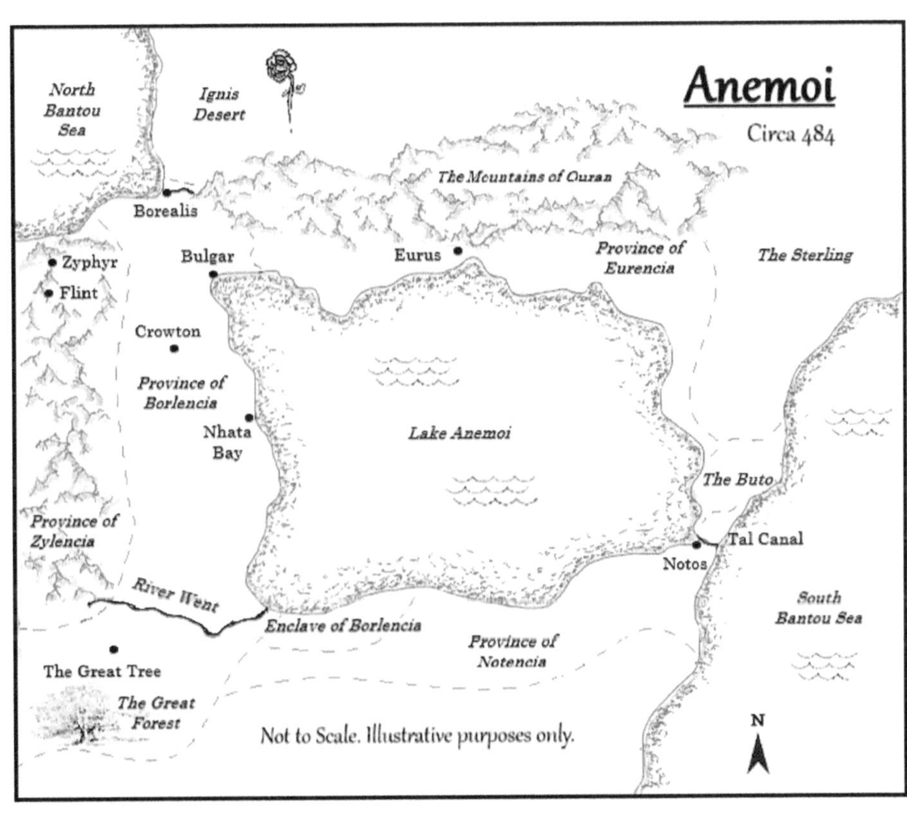

Anemoi
Circa 484
North Bantou Sea
Ignis Desert
The Mountains of Ouran
Borealis
Zyphyr
Flint
Bulgar
Eurus
Province of Eurencia
The Sterling
Crowton
Province of Borlencia
Nhata Bay
Lake Anemoi
The Buto
Province of Zylencia
Tal Canal
River Went
Notos
Enclave of Borlencia
Province of Notencia
South Bantou Sea
The Great Tree
The Great Forest
Not to Scale. Illustrative purposes only.
N

CHAPTER 1

Septembrix 13, 476; city of Borealis, province of Borlencia—Carolus's thick shoulders slumped. He withdrew his gaze from the horizon, the possibility of defeat written in his eyes, and looked to his wife.

"How long?" Alya repeated. Taller and stronger than your average Borlencian woman, Alya was still dwarfed by the lean, sinewy man who stood before her.

"Not long. Three, maybe four hours. They'll be at the North Gate before nightfall."

"Who are they? Why do we only see their banners on the horizon now, and with no warning from Nasdir?" Anger swelled inside her. "And what of the caravans or the desert outposts? How can we be so blind to an army of that size?"

"Alya, listen to me—" He tried to interrupt.

"The other garrisons." She breathed in desperation. "Send riders. Erzse can have the western garrison here in less than a week. Let them fall against the walls whilst reinforcements come."

"Alya! Riders have been dispatched to the cities in the east and Zyphyr in the west, but it takes days to mobilise and march, let alone deliver the message. Not to mention the other garrisons are unlikely to commit without combined strength. You know this better than most. No, as far as I'm concerned, we're on our own, and if that army does breach the walls, the odds will be stacked against us three to one. For both our sakes, you must leave the city before they reach the gates."

"And what of you?" she choked, already aware of the answer. "What chance do you have against seventy-five thousand? You'll need me. The city will need me. I must stay and fight."

Even with the heavily armoured garrison, the absence of the fleet and ground reinforcements out of reach meant they faced an impossibly difficult battle. To Carolus, a senior minister of Borealis and the commander of its garrison, only a miracle or a complete fluke could halt the city's demise.

He pulled her close. "All that matters now is that you and Xander are safe. Ricard will take your battalion, and you'll leave with the civilians through the South Gate. I've already given the instruction." He paused. "Don't seek shelter with Erzse. If Borealis falls, Zyphyr's too close for comfort."

"And the rumours?"

"They're just rumours, nothing more. Sister or not, if there were any substance, the courts would've dealt with her." He spoke carefully. "So please, let this topic be done."

Alya stared up from his chest, her dark hair splayed across her bronzed shoulders, and she locked her green eyes with the dark, omniscient jewels reflecting her pain. Softly, she stroked her hand across his lips and angular cheekbones. As he had a mother from Borealis but a father and childhood from beyond the Ignis Desert, his brown features were more akin to the desert people than the soft, tanned features of the city's natives.

She sighed as the tear in her heart grew with anguish. "I will take Xander to Nhata Bay. My great-aunt, if she still lives, has a cottage there. I can't think of a safer place right now…and, Carolus, please don't leave me waiting."

He smiled, sadness in his eyes. "I won't. Now where's our daughter?"

CHAPTER 2

Xander hugged the shadows as several transcribes scurried by. It was one thing to toy with the guards in the gardens and quite another to break into the Parliament Palace through the drainage system. Of course, this was not her first incursion, and oblivious to the danger that approached the city, she felt only excitement for the challenge presented by the unusually large number of guards, politicians, and servants in the palace corridors.

Her ears perked up at the metallic clank of armour from a nearby room. Eager to continue, she brushed the dark curls from in front of her flecked green eyes and peered around the corner. Nobody! For luck, she fondled the dark-grey metallic trinket in the pocket of her mother's green commander's jacket and then sprinted down the corridor, all the while trying not to clip the intricate tapestries, vases, and ornately decorated murals that so often captivated her deep-seated curiosity.

At nine years of age, Xander had light-brown features that carried the angularity of her father's, though her physicality could have been a tidy blend of both parents. With the height and athletic prowess of boys several years her senior, she made quick work of the lengthy corridor and its ancient collection, and after rounding the next corner, she nimbly dashed behind the nearest vase before the armoured congregation at the opposite end of the hall could spot her.

She frowned. Putantis's door was only a couple of metres to the right, but it would be nearly impossible to reach without being caught. Still, unwilling to cede defeat, she slowed her breath and used the trickle of the many palace cascades as an elixir for her nerves. About ready to make for it, she froze.

Soft at first, the intrusion grew in intensity and menace. The walls, the floor, and even the antique vase all hummed with its vibration. The timed thumping of the war drums was foreign to her mind, and accompanied by the ominous glow of the twilight sun and a growing chorus of terrified screams suddenly emanating from the city below, it was both eerie and troubling. With the guards distracted by the unannounced terror on the horizon, she rushed the door.

"Xander," Putantis said in shock, looking up from his desk. He was a scrawny, middle-aged man with the crooked posture and soft, spotty cheeks of one unaccustomed to physical exertion and sunlight. And his expression conveyed none of the joy one would expect from the man when in his element. Devoid of space for all the clutter of books, maps, and artefacts, his office was a treasure cove of history and information and in need of a good clean. "What are you—"

She walked over and lifted her hand to reveal the trinket.

"Oh!" His worried demeanour relaxed a touch as he lifted her hand. "What have you got here?"

"Putantis, what's that noise? I've never seen the palace this frantic, and just now I could see the guards fearful of what the horizon brings," she said, confused.

He looked up at her. "It's an army, my dear Xander. We do not know who they are or where they've come from. We are therefore at a loss as to why they are here, but from what one of our scouts was able to report, these soldiers that number fifteen battalions approach our city with heavy siege machines. I'm afraid that the evident reason for their sudden appearance can only be hostile in nature." Then, like a crow to polished silver, he peered back at the trinket with curious eyes. "So what do we have here?"

"I found it under the City Temple. I don't understand. If they march on the city, why are you still here? Why are all the people still here?"

"My dear, with only several hours' warning and no founded confirmation until a short while ago, we have been left hanging at fate's doorstep. And as for myself, well, I'm an elected minister of the city. I cannot just up and run," he said as he examined the trinket. "Fascinating!" His weathered face brightened in awe.

"Something ancient?" she blurted excitedly, her worries momentarily forgotten.

"The worn-down remnants of an old boot buckle. Couple of hundred years old, I would guess. I joke, my dear, no need to frown." He rubbed his thumb over the piece, his expression pensive. "Truly fascinating. It would appear you have found yourself one shard of a grander object. And look, these arbitrary lines and dots could be text or code, or simply decoration. Without the other shards, though, I couldn't tell you with any certainty."

"Putantis!" Alya shouted from the doorway, startling them, her relief evident. "I see you've found my daughter. Ah! And with her, my jacket."

Wonderous admiration took Xander as she beheld her mother. Alya's silver-plumed helmet and light-blue breastplate were as if they had been taken from a book on the legends of Anemoi, and the round silver shield and ancient sabre she carried were her flagrant reminders on the cruelty of war. The girl's eyes fell to the green broadleaf insignia etched beautifully onto her mother's breastplate alongside the city's emblem, the Rose of Anemoi. Symbolising the spirit of life born out of the ancient forests of Anemoi, the broadleaf was unique to Alya's family legacy, her own family legacy.

Then suddenly, quite unable to recall having ever seen her mother in full battle armour, her marvel vanished, thwarted by the gravity of what was to come dragging her violently back into the present.

▲ ▲ ▲

As the duo exited the palace into the main courtyard, the courtyard Xander had made every effort to avoid during her incursion into the sprawling building, Xander was struck with the sheer number of gathered commanders and their captains. Soldiers scrambled with maps, weapons, and orders, and the usually tranquil square of sand-coloured walls and flowered balconies now played the part of the chaotic war room. The magnitude and nature of the situation were apparent. Located on the northern side of the river atop the highest centrally located hill in Borealis, the palace was ideal for defence and command if the situation arose.

"Alya, over here!" Ricard beckoned from amidst a group of heavily armoured soldiers. A foot shorter and a generation wiser than the typical soldier, Ricard's reputation as the "Battle Ox" and as Borealis's most interesting man was a reputation earned. An immigrant from afar, he was Carolus's most trusted confidant. Xander ran and jumped into his burly, tanned arms. "Good to see you, kiddo," he chirped, his silver-bearded features mirroring her affectionate grin.

"And you."

He put her down and turned to Alya, and any hint of ease evaporated.

"Carolus has passed on instruction for the city to be evacuated by ship, but with the majority of the galleys out on expedition, we've had to commandeer a portion of the merchant navy," he said with regret, clearly aware of the ransom the merchants would force on the city as compensation.

"And the South Gate?"

"Two thousand horsemen have been spotted south of the river. We figure they're heading to the South Gate to block the evacuation," he said, to Alya's shock. "Meet Carolus at the City Temple. Waste no time. I'll recall the small army he's got looking for you and the kid."

"Thank you, Ricard," she said with growing worry.

"He'll be fine, Alya. I'll bring him back to you once we've rid the city of this horde. Then we can open a bottle of Borealis's fine wine and break bread," he said, and turned back to his soldiers.

▲ ▲ ▲

The perpetual bustle that defined the streets of Borealis had not lost any of its stir, although the atmosphere of the city's citizens had soured into one of confusion and fear. Street vendors packed wares in haste, soldiers barked evacuation orders and instructions, and family members called desperately for loved ones.

As the pair raced along the river towards the City Temple, Xander longed for the imminent threat to be vanquished and for a return of the jubilant feeling that usually accompanied her strolls through the farmers markets. Days when the calls and chatter of street merchants and their customers calmed the nerves. And the assorted scents of fruits, jams, meats, and deliciously warm breads invaded the senses and accentuated the beautiful tapestries of colourful streets and exotic trees. With an extensive network of underground sewage and drainage systems, Borealis was absent the rotten odours that characterised cities tainted by open-air sewers—a true pleasure for locals and visitors alike.

At the top of the temple steps, it was only through recognition of the insignia on Alya's armour and the commander's jacket Xander wore that the captain of the fifty-strong retinue of soldiers blocking the entrance permitted them access into the temple, a not-so-odd encounter given the circumstances.

Built as homage to Anemoi and the spirit of life rather than any particular religion, the City Temple was a behemoth of a structure as ancient as the city itself, and its dull colour was in stark contrast to the brightly coloured buildings adjacent. Xander's gaze fell on the lone figure standing before the large wooden altar, both mere specks against the columns thicker than the most ancient of trees. There was an army on the doorstep, and her father was not usually one for spirituality, so she was baffled as to why he lingered in here.

"Carolus!" Alya called as they neared.

He turned around, and his solemn expression relaxed into one of relief at the sight of his wife and daughter. "Let me guess: she was with Putantis," he said as he embraced them affectionately, though his features hardened as he withdrew. "This retinue of soldiers will escort you down to the port. Help them and the others ensure an orderly evacuation, then make sure you're on the last ship out. They'll accompany you. That's an order."

She nodded sadly.

He pulled them back into his reach, his grip tight. Xander could sense the uncertainty and fear in the man she always thought immune.

He sighed. "I must head to the North Gate now. The bulk of the troops have amassed in preparation for the primary attack. I've split one of the five battalions, twenty-five hundred men each to guard the East and South Gates," he said, more to himself than his wife, irritated at the lack of available information on the enemy's whereabouts.

"They've split their siege weapons?" Alya asked.

"We're not sure. The last report we had was of the horsemen to the south. None of our scouts have reported back since. We're in the dark," he responded wearily, daunted by the fight ahead. "I've sent a scout ship to our fleet with news of the attack." He looked solemnly at Alya and spoke softly. "I gave the captain a letter for Lawrence if the worst were to happen."

He picked up his spear and the broad shield depicting the Rose of Anemoi and led them back into the city, sadness and dread etched on their faces.

CHAPTER 3

Night had fallen, and still the streets teemed with panic-stricken civilians and soldiers. As if on cue, raindrops descended onto the crowds, and the wet streets began to hinder them. Squads of soldiers marched towards the northern wall and appeared to be nothing more than small islands of shiny metal against the flood of city dwellers herding carelessly towards the port. Over the constant hum of the war drums, the guardsmen shouted to the civilians to drop their belongings and make haste.

Built to slow attackers and provide staged defence in the event of a breach, the city's maze of alleys, courtyards, and defensive walls was as aesthetically pleasing as it was a hindrance; even to the locals, it made an obstacle of any rushed evacuation. As the pair and the retinue of soldiers finally entered the square that adjoined the river and port, it became nearly impossible to move amidst the crush of people, and with only two or three merchant ships moored in sight, there was nowhere to go.

"I don't understand. Where are the rest of the ships?" Alya called to a nearby guardsman as she used her shield to keep the press of the crowd off her and Xander.

Blindsided by the commander's question, the guardsman fumbled for words. "Timing, Commander. With such short notice, we're still bringing in merchant ships from the mouth of the river," he bellowed, for the crowd's sake as much as Alya's.

She turned to her assigned captain in disbelief at the desperately slow progress. Even with the short notice, the evacuation should have been well underway. Just as she was about to speak, the incessant hum of the drums stopped, and with it, the clamour of the crowd until only the pitter-patter of raindrops against the cobblestoned street and the soldiers' armour filled the square. Xander, still in shock at the speed of the events, matched Alya's quizzical look. Silence wasn't a suitor for the approaching storm.

The crowd fluttered nervously as the first warning flares reached above the North Gate, mere dots on the horizon against the backdrop of the night sky, a signal that told of an enemy at the walls.

▲ ▲ ▲

The sound of the explosions pierced at its inception and eventually subsided into a repetitive, dull ringing of the ears. The whips of the blasts were so violent that they shook not just the city's foundations, but also the minds of the hardiest warriors. In horror, the evacuees, packed ever so tightly against the river, stared in disbelief at the debris tossed into the air from the North Gate. The night sky shone bright with fire and death, and fear quickly erupted across the square as the crowd overwhelmed what few guardsmen there were. A mad scramble for the too-few moored ships rapidly ensued.

Alya barked orders at the soldiers, a calmness exuded, and on command, they moved frantically through the crowd towards the ships. It was then that the second set of blasts exploded, not from the walls, but from the merchant ships at the mouth of the river—huge explosions that left little doubt in all their minds that death had cornered them. Without hesitation and moments ahead of the crowd, Alya grabbed Xander's hand and dragged her hard out of the square, kinship betraying duty. Slowly but surely, the mass of bodies swarmed in their direction.

Not more than two blocks from the maddened rush and crush of people, Alya pulled Xander close and spoke quickly but clearly. "We must get out of the city. Our only chance is to head for the South Gate and down along the coast towards Nhata Bay. Nhata Bay—remember this name, Xander."

"Why are you—"

"If anything happens to me, Xander, you must find Nhata Bay. When there, ask for Evia. You'll be safe with her."

Xander nodded unquestioningly, but the look of desperation on her mother's face, visible even through the dark, unsettled her.

Utter chaos and confusion enveloped Borealis, and the distant echo of metal on metal and panicked shouts played in tune to the renewed chorus of the drums. The duo pushed hard through the narrow streets and over one of the gated bridges to the south side of the city, where the sound of battle lacked the ferocity and confusion of the northern melees. Both with enviable endurance, they were winded by the rush of the chase, and as they rounded a corner onto the main road in view of the South Gate, Alya halted, her mouth agape. The immense gate had been breached, and the soldiers' desperate fight to expel the multiplying attackers was a visibly futile affair.

"We're trapped," Alya gasped in hopelessness. "Maybe we can try for the East Gate," she muttered, more to herself than to Xander.

"What about the temple?" Xander said, her eyes beckoning hope. "Come on, we can hide in the catacombs."

"How in Anemoi…ah, your treasures. Come on then. Let's go before these vermin turn their attention to us," she said as the last pockets of resistance evaporated in the melee ahead and the unknown enemy started in their direction.

The duo could feel the predatory presence on their rear, their armour black, their skin dark, and their shoulders broad. Chased through an eternity of dimly lit alleys littered with carts, cargo, and hastily strewn produce, they gradually lost ground to their pursuers. Though the sights of the same gated bridge and the rapidly forming line of riflemen beckoning them through brought renewed hope, Alya understood the futility of the lone volley. The two did not remain and had made only a short distance when they heard the spent volley and the subsequent cries of the overwhelmed riflemen.

With the shadowy pursuers at the bottom of the temple steps, Xander pulled Alya into an open-air courtyard that splintered off behind the main altar in the temple. A plain shrine to the rear was sparsely illuminated by several braziers on the wall, and a small, barely visible burrow peeked from the ground in the corner.

They both turned to the rush of footsteps that echoed from the main chamber, and that betrayed the impossibly large number of pursuers that had joined the hunt.

"Xander, you must leave now."

"What?"

"Now!" Alya scolded.

Reluctantly Xander made for the burrow and was barely inside when an intoxicating allure invaded her senses. Alya's anger and desperation for her daughter's safety had warped into an overwhelmingly powerful bloodlust—it was a ruthless desire to kill that Xander swore she could feel permeating through her own body.

As she peered into the courtyard where her mother stood, her eyes widened in awe as the lone figure bravely staring down the scourge drew her sabre and lifted her shield with a smirk that goaded. Not wanting to disappoint, the masked assailants rushed their beckoner.

Alya had blistering speed and a strength Xander had only seen from the burliest of men. She whipped her sabre in a controlled frenzy and severed throats and limbs with ease. She felled half a dozen within moments of the attack, but as they continued, driven by a reasoning beyond the girl's comprehension, Xander felt only dread. Then, quite suddenly, the attack wavered and stopped in its entirety. The soldiers withdrew several paces, and in entered a warrior wearing a black mask with gold stripes. Slim in build but powerful in presence, he drew a savage-looking sword more akin to a butcher's knife. He glanced in Xander's direction ever so briefly and then lunged at Alya.

Alya parried the blow and expertly met each one of his successive attacks, and though she appeared a match in both speed and strength, the illusion was broken by the increasingly apparent sluggishness that reverberated through her defensive form. On the back foot and with all attention fixated on the aggressive onslaught, she barely glimpsed the opportunistic lunge from a nearby soldier. She cut down the gutter rat with a single slash, but in doing so, she exposed her left flank to the original attacker. This was all the masked warrior needed, and he drove his blade past her shield and through her armour into her ribs. She let out the smallest of gasps and turned to face him, the numbness of the intrusion not yet having betrayed her fate.

His eyes. So dark. The shadows behind the mask. Her shock for an eternity of a breath turned to painful awareness as fear for her daughter and the loneliness of death enveloped her. The warmth of her life flowed down her side, and her energy faltered.

She pulled back from the blade and held up her sabre, but weakness overcame her. The masked assailant knew the outcome. He fell back and bade his soldiers to finish the job. The attackers swarmed and quickly cut her down, and the ferocious bloodlust that seemed so powerful moments ago slowly faded into nothingness. Without mercy and without respect, she was dragged into the street, head and body limp, and the sabre taken undeservedly as a trophy.

Xander stared into the wet, blood-marked courtyard, her heart pierced and her world violated. The sickening grief in the pit of her stomach was outmatched only by the destructive rage she felt boil from within, a rage held in check by her knowledge of the sacrifice her mother had just made.

CHAPTER 4

Septembrix 16, 476; the wilderness, fifteen kilometres south of Borealis, Borlencia—Xander's legs were weak and her stomach painfully empty. She was one of a thousand tired, filthy refugees traversing that stretch of farmland south of Borealis, fleeing the embers of the crumbled city and the gangs of masked marauders combing the wilderness for survivors and soldiers.

Despite the dust on her clothes and in her hair, Xander's cheeks shone bare, cleaned by the stream of tears that had yet to stop. It was an image mirrored all around her in the faces of the other frightened refugees, with one glaring difference. In her vicinity, she could see no other child so blatantly alone. Every miserable, dirty youngling had a relative, a friend, or a guardian by their side—a living, breathing piece of home to accompany them as they trudged south, tails tucked, lives changed.

As Xander plodded along, feet sore and nose runny, her eyes locked on a girl no older than she. The girl also wore the filth of the road, but she wasn't alone. A man and woman with strikingly similar features held her hands, and even with everything that had happened, the girl carried a sense of peace behind her tears. Her parents, like her, had survived the attack, and together they would now navigate the inevitable hardship that was to come.

It was a tender sight that was suddenly too much for Xander as the weight of her own loss abruptly tore into her heart. She quickly gripped her chest, and desperate for respite, she pinched the skin of her breast until it was raw and the superficial pain was just enough to cover the searing pang of despair.

Her thoughts were stained by the horrific memory of her mother's broken body as it was dragged away into the thick of the conflict. And her senses were completely shredded by the brutal hopelessness and utter loneliness that had followed in the aftermath. It was an unbearable, agonising torture greatly compounded by the unknown fate of her father. It was too much for any one child to bear alone, especially without guidance.

In the days since her escape through the recaptured South Gate, dozens of groups of Borlencian soldiers from the province's northern towns had come and gone, but only some had lingered. The vast majority of those nervous men and women were marching at pace towards the constantly shifting front line, determined to combine with larger forces before trying their luck against the mysterious marauders.

And yet, despite the danger those soldiers marched towards, Xander unabashedly envied them. Her fierce hatred for those that had slain her mother, and likely her father, was dangerously alive, and it had birthed a deep, cold desire for justice. In that moment, however, she was bound by her unquestioning need to survive, and too, the heavy sorrow that now verged on incapacitating her. She knew vengeance wasn't a possibility yet, and because of this, she wanted nothing more than to find a hole to crawl into and cry. Cry until sleep would take her and bring her some semblance of peace from the cruel visions haunting her every waking moment.

But it was a peace she would never truly find again—at least not in any manner she had known before.

CHAPTER 5

Septembrix 28, 476; Borlencian refugee camp, ninety kilometres south of Borealis—Huddled half frozen with a dozen others in a small, shoddy tent without ventilation, Xander pulled her legs to her chest and began to scrape away the filth gathered within the crevices of the trinket she had discovered under Borealis.

Her mind was numb and her grief heavy. She had barely spoken since she had arrived at the civilian-run camp several days prior and felt no real urge to eat or sleep. In the beginning, the adults had thought her a mute and had taken turns force-feeding her with whatever scarce rations were available. And though, with time, she had opened up to speaking the odd word to convey whatever information it was they were looking to retrieve from her, they still struggled to get her to eat willingly.

An involuntary sigh escaped her lips.

A voice interrupted the quiet. "It'll be okay, child."

Xander looked up at the woman that had arrived in the camp several days prior with her husband, though the woman was alone this frigid evening.

"It'll all be okay," the woman repeated, her crooked smile and beady eyes doing little to reassure.

Xander still couldn't pinpoint the uncomfortable feeling that had accompanied the pair on their arrival, and so she ignored the woman's gaze and returned to picking at the trinket with her cracked nail.

"It can't be," said a man outside the tent a moment later, causing all those within to peer to the tattered sheet separating them. "You're sure?"

"One of the soldiers just confirmed it," another responded.

"Then that's all of Borlencia's senior ministers," a third interjected.

"And majority of the common ministers—"

But Xander wasn't listening anymore. She and the others had heard the rumours, and deep down she had suspected the truth, but the man's words were confirmation. Like a shard of glass twisted oh so painfully into her heart. She was on her own, alone in the frigid wilderness, surrounded by other empty shells that had also lost it all when the city had fallen.

She wiped a lone tear with her grubby arm and climbed out of the tent into the sharp cool of the early evening. The ground was soggy from that day's downpour, and light smoke from the unregulated campfires tainted the air.

The three men who'd spoken without care for the harm of their words paid her no heed as she walked past them to the camp's boundary. It was marked by a lone soldier more concerned with the mud stuck to his boot than the security of his charge.

The tranquil woods that stared back from the camp's perimeter wore the reds and yellows and oranges of autumn and carried none of the bustle of Borealis. The usual drunken giggles so commonplace in the city as the sun sought to set and the inhabitants transitioned from work to pleasure had been replaced by the rustle of the breeze against the trees' dying leaves and the calls of the wood pigeons and the owls. It was a frightening void of eerie quiet to those ears unacquainted with nature's peace.

She turned to the lone guard as he stood, his suddenly alert eyes lost in the shadows ahead, and she tensed as he put his hand to his sword's hilt. But the moment was brief, and seconds later he slackened and returned to the dirt wedged stubbornly in his boot.

She, too, relaxed, but as she was about to trudge to the firepit nearest the crowded confines of her assigned tent, a gentle, melodious whisper carried from the woods by the wind caught her attention. She held her breath and cupped her ear in search of more but could find none. She shrugged and had made it all of five metres back into the camp when the barely audible murmurs brushed by her again, causing the fine hairs on her neck to prickle.

"What is it?" the guard asked, spooked by her abrupt stop.

She glanced at the forest, then back to the guard. "Nothing."

"Better be nothing," he muttered as he marked himself superstitiously.

But it wasn't nothing. No, she had heard something, something delightfully soothing and somewhat alien, and now her curiosity cried for her to find the source. Not wanting to raise the alarm, she walked along the bend of the boundary, then disappeared into the forest once she was out of the guard's sight.

The air under the forest's canopy was heavy and a tad warmer than in the open, and the rocks and plants of the undergrowth glistened with dew. She was a dozen metres into the shroud and already her tattered leggings were wet. But she cared not, drawn excitedly towards the ambient whispers that grew with her every step. Through brambles and ditches and the weight of the mud accumulating on her shoddy boots, she sauntered on, recklessly uncaring of the dangers that haunted the now-lawless wilderness of Borlencia's northern reaches.

A hundred metres from the refugee camp, she stopped, her gaze locked ahead on the obscured grove where a shadow danced back and forth whilst singing the soothing melody. Unable to tame her curiosity, Xander crept towards the thicket that lined the grove and peeked through the bushes. She blushed.

A woman dressed in scant robes and with red hair down to her knees twirled and pranced around the grove, calling to the trees and the moon in chants and hums and gestures. Her pale skin appeared translucent under the moonlight, and in the centre of her dance, jutting from the soil, was a thick wooden beam with markings scratched into its surface. The markings emitted a faint silky glow under the moon's light and resembled writing.

Eager for a better look at the scripture, Xander edged forward ever so slightly, until her little nose poked from the leaves. Gibberish immediately came to mind, beautiful gibberish. But like any child with an inquisitive mind, that was not enough to satiate, and thus she began to scour every inch her vantage point would allow her, determined to find familiarity. So zealous was her fixation that it took some seconds for her to realise that the woman had stopped performing and now stared at her with a curious smile.

"Hi there," the woman said softly.

Xander glanced nervously back to the woods.

"I mean you no harm," the woman said. "Come, enter so I may see you."

"So stupid!" Xander lambasted herself internally, caught between lingering and elusion.

"Or go. The choice is yours."

Though Xander felt no malice in the woman's invitation, caution stayed her.

"I heard your song," she said after several moments, still without entering. "From the refugee camp. It's lovely. I couldn't stop myself. I just had to see who was singing."

"And you found me."

"Where are you from? And aren't you cold dancing around like that?"

The woman walked casually to the edge of the grove and pointed in the opposite direction of the refugee camp. "I'm from the village over there. And it's but a mere autumn evening. Too early to be getting worked up about the cold. Plus, the dancing keeps me warm."

Xander relaxed a little. "I like your accent."

"Thank you. And I yours. Tell me, where are you from?"

"Borealis."

"Ah," the woman said sadly, and a look of steadfast concentration stole her features.

"What is that?" Xander asked of the wooden beam, bringing the woman to.

"Full of questions, aren't you? It's the prow of a ship."

"Out here!"

"Yes, out here."

"But how?"

"I don't know. But it's been here all my life, and my mother's, and her mother's. As has the writing," she said, anticipating Xander's next question.

"What does it say?"

"I have no idea."

"Then why dance around it like that?"

"Because every twenty-eighth day, when the moon is at its fullest, on the last night of its journey through the sky, ready to begin its next cycle, the words on that prow glow. And on this day, when I, or any other from the village visits and pays respect, through voice or dance, good things happen. You don't believe me? You're telling me you've never seen or come across something you couldn't explain? Something truly remarkable?"

"I—"

A chorus of panicked screams and shouts pierced through the woods from the direction of the camp, putting them both on edge.

"Oh no!" Xander said fearfully, staring into the dark.

"That's a bit too close," the woman said nervously. She turned and grabbed her jacket from the ground. "Best be on your way, Xander. The spirits may have seen the need to draw you away, but you'll still need to find your own way through the night." She started towards the tree line.

"Wait, where are you—" Xander had begun when her stomach dropped, and a cold shudder took her. "How do you know my name?"

The woman stopped and turned around, pity in her eyes. "Avoid the camps, Xander. They're not safe. And please don't follow me. I can't put my own in danger for your kind." She swiftly disappeared into the woods.

More frantic cries emanated from the camp, pulling Xander's gaze into the dark vacuum of trees between her and the growing chaos. She straightened up, and though instinct begged for her to slip away into the night, the woman's parting words tore at her, leaving her desperate for answers. At a crouch, and clinging to the shadows, she made her way back.

The camp was alive with movement. What few guards there were had been tied up or killed, and the refugees, men and women and children, sobbed and swore and struggled as they were bound in chains by a group in unmarked uniforms. Dozens of the mysterious men combed through the tents, rounding up any that had mistakenly convinced themselves they could avoid detection, and another dozen or so walked through the already chained groups, wiping dirt and soot from the faces of the children.

Xander looked to the side as a handful of men entered the woods in search of stragglers, then she jumped as the bush next to her rustled. Lips clenched, as if her breath would make her presence known, she breathed relief as a pair of playful squirrels came into view. That was all the scare she needed. But before she could peel away and vanish into the forest, a shouted order from the soldiers' leader stopped her.

"They're Borlencian…" Xander stuttered, louder than intended, and turned to the camp in time to see the strange woman—whose insincere words of comfort from earlier in the evening now rang hollow—and her husband approach the leader.

Words were exchanged between the trio, then, despite the noisy happenings of the camp, the leader's next words, cold and uncaring, carried clearly through the air and hit Xander like a stone to the head.

"You'll get a solid price for this lot."

Anger and shock rose through Xander like fiery heat, but the immediate desire to foolishly intervene was fleeting, for what could a half-starved child alone in the wilds do to answer such treachery? The refugees were beyond help. With deep, painful regret, she slunk away from the camp into the shadows, tears in her eyes.

CHAPTER 6

A child's recollection on the dangers of the lattleberry: *"Xander, remember—green over blue, and blue over red. Do you hear me?"*

"Yes," she whispered as she eyed the bush of lattleberries calling her name. They all looked so delicious, but it was the allure of the red ones that really drew her in. She turned to her mother, a quizzical grin on her face and her eyes squinty from the glare of the afternoon sun. "Why not the red ones?"

"Because, Xander, the red ones will fool with your mind, and the green ones won't."

"You mean like Ricard?"

Her mother laughed and knelt beside the girl. "No, not like Ricard. These red ones…many good men have lost their wits because of these. Delicious though they are, they'll take away your reality long before you know what has been taken."

▲ ▲ ▲

Octobrix 11, 476; the wilderness; 110 kilometres southeast of Borealis, Borlencia—Xander stared curiously at the handful of blue and green berries with a single red one lodged in the middle of her grubby palm. Her face was gaunt, and again her stomach grumbled as it gnawed on itself. Slowly she bit into a blue one, and barely had the sweet juices of the lattleberry touched her tongue when euphoria rushed through her. She greedily took another bite, and another, and before she knew it, she had gobbled the whole handful.

"Well, that was a little slice of blissfulness," she said, referencing a saying her mother often used after a delicious meal.

Xander climbed out of the dark, abandoned fox den and breathed in the smoky afternoon air. The surrounding fields had all been scorched, by which side she did not know, but she could still feel the heated soil under her worn shoes. She bent over and picked up a broken branch from the dirt and started along the edge of the razed field. As she plodded along with only a vague idea of which way was south, she tried to whistle. Her father had shown her once before, but she always struggled to put her lips in a cone, and as with every other attempt, she found herself humming rather than whistling. Still, it staved off the boredom and the tedious passage of time, and if she could say so herself, she had decided she wasn't half bad.

And like any busywork at that age, it was also an easy, albeit fleeting, distraction from the anguish that was akin to a knotted twig slowly thrusting back and forth through her innards. Night and day, there was seldom relief from the all-consuming weight of her loss.

As she wandered the gentle lull of the seemingly endless farms and their hedgerows, she dwelled on the absence of companionship and, oddly enough, smiled at the thought. In the weeks since she had escaped the marauders and their vicious army, the solitude of her forced exile had grown on her. The large crowds of the refugee camps, a mesh of civilians and soldiers alike, had quickly demonstrated an incapacity to evade and fend off the packs of horsemen that now scoured the countryside. And the seemingly rampant betrayal of a number of refugee camps by fellow Borlencians had rendered trust scarcer than the rarest of gems. Even with Anemoi's combined armies fighting the skirmishers and razing fields to starve out the disease of the invaders, the survivors now took solace in group sizes that were easy to scatter and hide among the burnt countryside south of

Borealis's once-mighty walls.

She could only imagine the state of Ricard's vineyards, but the instant pang of loss she felt at his unknown whereabouts abruptly jumped to the berries she had eaten before and the apparent lack of side effects that her mother had warned her of. She giggled at the thought.

Xander had lost count of her steps and was repeating for the third time all the song tunes she knew when she first saw them. She needed more numbers than she knew to count the quantity of soldiers that marched along the broken road that cut across her chosen route. She didn't recognise their insignia or their features, but they didn't bear the menacing masks of the marauders, nor did they speak the guttural language she had come to fear. But then, they didn't speak much, if at all, the apprehension of what probably lay ahead of them a deterrent to all light-heartedness and conversation.

She sat and waited from afar. The afternoon light soon turned to night, and still the soldiers marched in silence and darkness, determined not to betray their presence to those with a keen eye or ear. Her stomach grumbled, deeply and painfully.

"Maybe they have food," she thought. "But why would they give it to me…I could always ask them…unless, maybe…is it really stealing if my life depends on it?" Her eyes perked, and she licked her lips greedily. "What about their scraps? I'm too small for them to care. I can walk with them, and as soon as they drop something, anything, I'll just take it and run."

"I wouldn't do that if I were you."

Xander jumped and peered into the dark. "Who said that?"

"I did, silly."

She still couldn't see the owner of the voice. "And you are?"

"Joyce, but my brothers call me Jo."

"And you wouldn't do what?"

"Follow them, of course. I can see you thinking it, but it's a bad idea."

Xander looked back to the soldiers that still passed her by, determined to make her plan work.

"I know somewhere we can get food," Jo said excitedly.

Xander's entire face brightened, and she glanced back into the shadows as the scrawny girl crawled into view, no older than six or seven. The condition of the girl's dirty face and matted hair was not too different from her own.

"Why wouldn't you follow them?" Xander asked cautiously.

"You won't be the only one to try. You can't see them, but I can. The scavengers, they hide in the bushes. Always ready to fight for the scraps or…kill those that wander too far," she said solemnly and then burst back into a smile. "I know somewhere we can get food. Come, it'll be easy, and there won't be nobody else to take from us."

"Where?"

"Oh, not far from here. Come on, I'll take you."

Xander pondered for the briefest moment, and then she crawled through the bush in pursuit of the promised sustenance.

▲ ▲ ▲

"That looks like a military camp!" Xander said in disbelief. "They have guards and dogs and—"

"And food!"

"I don't know…"

"Come on, it'll be fine. You worry too much," the girl said, and crawled into the undergrowth.

"What in Anemoi?" Xander hesitated, more worried that she'd have to steal than afraid of being caught. The grubby girl, betrayed by the rustle of the bushes, moved quickly, and still Xander fretted in indecision. "I don't have to take much…not enough to hurt them or that they'll notice, just enough to be full. Can it really be called theft if my life depends on it? No, it's necessary." Her stomach rumbled again, its mind made, and she gave chase.

She nearly hurled as a man stood up at the edge of the smelly ravine that snaked its way into the camp and pulled his trousers up over his bare bottom. Content with his completed business, he whistled and hummed his way back to his post.

But for the obscured moon and a few dying fires, the camp was dark and eerily quiet.

"I wonder why they have no guards at the ravine," she whispered, but Jo didn't respond, her eyes fixated on the prize ahead.

"Do you see it?"

"What?"

"The tent."

"How do you know that's the one?"

"I can see the smells." Jo's eyes gleamed.

"Are you serious?"

The grubby girl nodded.

"And back there?" Xander said.

Jo nodded again in disgust.

"That's amazing! Crazy, but amazing."

"Come on!" she whispered, and pounced to the nearest shadow with Xander in tow.

They quickly fell into a game of cat and mouse as they danced and skipped through the darkness towards the prize. No more than two tents away, the spicy aroma of a soldier's dinner abruptly penetrated Xander's nose and overwhelmed the stench of the ravine that still clung to her nostrils. She stared dreamily at the embers and the weary-looking man, longing for a bite of whatever it was that he ate.

"Not that way, silly," Jo giggled, and pulled Xander back towards the prize.

They lay on the trodden ground in the shadow of the tent nearest the one Jo led them towards, ready to make the last hop. And though giddiness had taken hold at how close they were, Xander's excitement quickly died as she remembered this was only half the journey.

"How far to the next tent? Ten metres?" she whispered.

Jo appeared to count the distance on both hands and then shrugged.

The ground was marked with the footprints of men and horses and made for a messy affair. Already half the distance, Xander felt her breath catch in her throat as two guards, deep in conversation and, for the moment, oblivious to their presence, rounded the corner of the destination tent with their dog. She couldn't make out what they said, and though they didn't look like the marauders, she doubted they would respond kindly to the prospective thieves. Fear enveloped her.

Her eyes flickered back, and she grimaced at the distance they had made from the ravine, not to mention the guards in between. She caught a glimpse of Jo's grin out of the corner of her eye, and the girl nodded in the direction of their supposedly bountiful target. Initially confused, Xander flinched. Jo still edged forward, intent to continue their game, and if it wasn't for the fear of capture, she would have reached over and wrung the girl's neck herself. Instead, Xander subtly inched backwards, but she had made it only a short distance when the dog's ears twitched and its back became rigid, forcing them both to freeze.

The men hadn't noticed and continued, unaware, until a loud growl emanated from the beast and stole their attention. The shorter of the two stepped forward and stood less than a metre from Jo's face. He scanned the horizon as the two girls held their breath but dropped his guard when the dog relaxed. Both girls breathed a sigh of relief, the mischievous grin rightly gone from the little one's face. Eventually the men continued away from the tent with the dog in tow.

Once they were around the corner and out of sight, the girls clambered the rest of the way. Carefully they put their ears to the cloth. Content the tent was empty, they entered and slumped into a heap on the floor, smitten with nervous laughter at the close call.

"Silly girl," Xander scolded Jo light-heartedly.

"You're the silly."

Xander shook her head and stood up to see their reward. The beautiful, rich scent of the baked bread drew her in like a moth to light, and she nearly crumbled. Within moments Jo had already devoured half a loaf and looked ready to finish the job.

"You'll make yourself sick," Xander scolded lightly.

"I'll be fine," she responded with a mouthful.

"Come on, grab as much as you can, and let's get out of here."

Xander grabbed a sack and threw in several loaves with a bundle of vegetables, and Jo greedily followed suit. They lugged the heavy sacks through the door and into the dark, and they had made it a couple of metres when Xander accidentally kicked an unseen cockerel asleep in the muck, causing it to scream in fright. More cockerels across the site quickly joined the chorus, and moments later the camp awoke in alarm.

Men scrambled out of their tents with swords and short knives in hand, but instead of lighting torches, shouting orders, or bearing armour, they threw dirt on the already dying embers and made silently for the shadows. Some prepped horses whilst others gathered valuables, and only a couple made an attempt to locate the cause of the cockerels' fright.

"They're not soldiers!" Xander gasped.

"Why would I take us into a camp full of soldiers, silly?"

"Then who are they?"

"Smugglers."

Xander's stomach dropped. "We need to get out of here—now!"

"Relax, silly."

"No, you don't understand. The smugglers, they're worse—much worse," she snapped back, and grabbed the girl's arm.

A shout came from behind. "Hey!"

"Run!" Xander screamed, and they dropped the bags that weighed them down.

They darted and wove through the maze of tents, the majority of the camp still unaware of the intruders, but the man that gave chase quickly gained on them, and only metres from the ravine, he grabbed Jo.

The scrawny girl turned and swung at the burly man, but he easily brushed aside the threat and pushed her off balance into the mud. Xander lunged towards him and tried for his groin with her foot, but he again brushed aside the threat. He laughed at the attempt, though it was not a wicked laugh.

"Hey, no harm meant," he said softly, and backed off with his arms held up. On the shorter side, his tanned skin carried the dirt of the road, and his dark eyes and hair proudly wore their fatigue. To Xander, nothing in the man's demeanour suggested deceit, but that wasn't enough to allay her caution.

Another half a dozen men appeared and slowly approached the man and the two girls, with their hands also held high to show no malicious intent.

Xander backed up slowly and beckoned to Jo with a flick of her head. The ravine was only twenty metres away. Close enough to make an escape, even if the thought of climbing through the filth made her cringe.

"We mean you no harm, child." The man spoke again. "You look hungry…we have food."

Xander looked at Jo, who still lay in the dirt. "Come on, we can make it." The man tilted his head, confused.

"Come on, Jo, we can make it," Xander repeated.

"How do you know my name?" the man responded quizzically.

"I'm not talking to you…come on, Jo!" But the girl refused to budge. "Jo, what are you doing? Why aren't you moving?" she repeated, agitated.

"Child, who are you speaking to, if not me?"

"I…I…who are you?"

Confusion and delirium took her, and desperate for escape, she ran and leapt into the filth and prickly shrubs of the ravine. But she had made it only a short distance from the camp when fatigue and lack of air brought her to a crawl and then a mere shuffle. She was drained. Her head slumped onto her hands, and suddenly, sleep was all that occupied her thoughts.

CHAPTER 7

Octobrix 23, 476; road to Etlinga, Borlencia—Xander ran her spoon through the steamy broth in front of her and parted the carrots and dumplings for the umpteenth time. Despite the warm aroma invading her nostrils and the sparse rations over the past couple of days, hunger was elusive, stayed by the nerves gnawing painfully at her stomach.

She looked up and took in the bustling tavern filled with townsfolk eager to wet their lips and fill their bellies after a long day. None carried the physical and emotional fatigue of their northern cousins, and most laughed and bantered as if the destruction of Borealis in the north was a grim reality that could not reach them. It was a struggle not to resent their fortune.

The bench she sat on shook with a thud, and she turned to see Joseph staring back at her, his smile wide and his eyes bright.

"Good news," he said.

"You found her?" she asked nervously.

"Turns out we had some luck. Hadn't realised, but both Etlinga and Nhata lie within the same county lines. Bit embarrassed I didn't know this, given Etlinga's my hometown and is the last stop before Nhata. Anyway, means my friend in the mayor's office was able to pull up the last county census for Nhata without issue. It's a couple of years old, but your aunt

Evia's name's on there."

Xander nodded and looked back down to her bowl.

"It'll be fine, Xander," he said softly.

"What if she says no?"

"She won't."

"And what if she doesn't like me?"

"What's not to like!"

She lifted her gaze, and buoyed by Joseph's warmth, a small smile slowly crept onto her face.

"That's better!" he said. "Come on, finish your supper and we'll see to getting some sleep before tomorrow. With an early start, we should be in Etlinga by the evening, and we can spend the night with my family. Then onto Nhata Bay the next day."

"And you'll show me your warehouse?"

"Wouldn't be able to refrain, even if my life depended on it!"

Excitement took her. On their lengthy journey south, Joseph had had much opportunity to entertain Xander with his many tales of dangerous trades, close calls, strange acquaintances, and rare artefacts, both within Anemoi and beyond. His life as a smuggler and trader in fine goods had fascinated her so much that the promise of seeing his warehouse of relics was one of the few thoughts that had kept her lingering nerves and sadness at bay.

With Joseph's treasures and her aunt Evia both on the near horizon, she knew sleep wouldn't come easy that night.

CHAPTER 8

Novembrix 30, 476; Nhata Bay, Borlencia—The cold stung as it tore through a crack in the window's seam, and despite the multiple candles dotting the walls and on the table, the bare room was gloomily dark.

Sitting quietly on the edge of her bed, Xander tightened her scarf around her neck in an attempt to block the chill and then sat on her hands for warmth. The bitter cold of the lakeshore's autumn was nothing like the cool dry of Borealis's, and she could already taste the faintest hints of a cough worming its way into her chest.

Sadness hung heavily over her, and she wished to be anywhere but the dark, empty house that had become the reminder of her new life, devoid of warmth and closeness. She gripped the sheet under her legs and clenched her teeth as another bout of tears threatened to spill. She thought she was done for the day, exhausted to the point of numbness, but the waves of unrelenting hurt were mostly random. Sometimes invoked by her dreams, but most often spurred by simple, unwanted recollection.

She looked to the window as more excited murmurs sounded from outside, and she immediately welcomed the interruption. Joyous calls of children playing tag were interrupted by the unintelligent gossip of accompanying adults, and like the multiple groups before them, the ensemble was headed in the direction of the woods. She frowned as the fade of their voices into the distance and the dying glow of their torches refracting eerily through her window compounded her sense of loneliness. She longed to follow. To witness the fuss before it was over. And yet, she couldn't, bound to the room until her aunt returned.

The aunt that was wholly unaccustomed to the company of a child. The aunt that had somehow seemed unable to shake the shock and intrigue of what had unexpectedly appeared on her doorstep.

Xander couldn't tell if her aunt Evia searched for every reason to shirk the newfound responsibility, or if her aunt truly was always this busy in her old age. A flush of anger rose through her at the unfairness of the situation. She wouldn't be held hostage by her aunt's indifference. Spurred into rebellion, she angrily pulled on her overcoat and hurried through the unlit house into the biting cold outside, then started for the cemetery hidden within the forest.

The town was a quaint fishing settlement wedged between the west shore of Lake Anemoi and the plains and woodlands to the west. Many dozens of thatched homes were nestled onto the shallow slope that overlooked the lake's placid water, and though Nhata lacked the bustle or diversity of a larger town, it was renowned locally for its incredible food markets and made-up festivals. "Any excuse for a drink," Evia would say.

On this frigid night, however, the empty cottages lining the street were spookily dark and completely void of the cosy warmth of their usual selves. Xander could only imagine that the spirits forever tied to such old buildings stared at her with envious eyes as she wandered freely, her broken shackles discarded. A thought that, when coupled with the haunting figures of the leafless trees watching from the line of gardens and the woods on the horizon, had her inadvertently glancing around to make sure she wasn't being followed.

Spirits not unlike the one presumed to have led Xander into Joseph's camp all those weeks ago. The girl that nobody else could see or hear—Jo.

It wasn't until several days after the incursion that Xander learned it wasn't Jo that Joseph had grabbed as the pair tried to escape—it was she. She still couldn't explain what had happened and had put it down to the lattleberries. The natural conclusion drawn by the traders, however, was that Jo was not of the living.

Though Xander's familiarity with the town of Nhata was limited, the whispers of a group of stragglers walking northwestwardly through a farmstead into the woods was her guide, for tonight had been the only night on the tip of every villager's tongue since she had arrived in Nhata.

It was the annual celebration of the county's delivery from the hands of a violent outlaw and his gang some two centuries prior, whereby towns all throughout the area lit huge bonfires and subsequently tossed effigies of the man and his thugs into the flames. The spectacle was a reenactment of the gang's horrific demise, a demise that was supposedly deserved after a reign of brutality against those that had little to nothing. Or so she had heard from one of the farmers. It was a night that had become a fitting culmination to a month otherwise dedicated to the dead and the wisps they tended to leave behind to scare and torment the living.

As the chorus of songs and chatter grew, accompanied by the fiery orange of the town's giant bonfire invading the nighttime slumber of the woodland, she found her excitement building. Through the tree line she could see children chasing around in ghoulish masks and adults, donned in white robes, huddled around smaller firepits, all contained within the giant grove that was Nhata's cemetery. In the air lingered the heavy scents of tobacco, wine, and scorched meats.

She found herself smiling, lifted by the warming smells and the nearing company of so many. As she was about to enter into the space, she stopped and peered at the tree overlooking the entrance. On one of the many branches sat a boy draped in a tattered cloak and wearing a turnip sack for a mask. His glare was piercing, and it put her on edge.

"Who are you that seeks entry onto these hallowed grounds?" he asked in a deliberately deepened voice.

"Xander. And you are?"

"I'm asking the questions. And where are you from, Xander? I don't recognise you."

She hesitated, saddened by the name she would have to speak. "Borealis."

There was silence, and she could sense the boy's pity even through the grim mask.

His voice lightened as he spoke again. "Where's your mask?"

"I don't have one," she responded.

"Well, that won't do," he said, and jumped from the tree to the hard ground. He wasn't much taller than her and looked a tad silly in the cloak that was clearly too big for him. "Here, I always carry a spare."

"Do I need it?" she asked, taking the damp turnip sack from him.

"Can't enter the cemetery without it, not this month anyhow. If you do, the ghosts will get you."

"In that case…" she said, and pulled it over her head. Dirt still clung to the inside, and the rich, earthy smell was wholly unavoidable. "What's your name?"

"Hemish. Come on, follow me. I want to show you something."

Though the bonfire was cordoned off to one side of the grove, away from the unkept tombstones of the town's ancestors, Xander could still feel the warmth of the blaze as Hemish led her through the maze of people to the other side of the cemetery. Some of the more intoxicated adults already struggled to stand, and despite the full plates and mouths, there was still an abundance of meat on the spits.

Out of the rowdy throng and suddenly able to see more than a wall of white cloth, Xander spotted the boy's intended destination.

"It's a temple," she said as they pulled up to the stone building adorned with stained-glass windows and an antiquated spire.

"That it is! Come on, let's go inside."

Hemish pushed open the heavy door and bounded inside excitedly.

Wooden benches lined both sides of a narrow aisle, and a small altar stood at the front. The place was lit by small torches on the walls.

"Smells like oak," Xander remarked as she followed him in. "Oak and—"

"Damp?"

"Yes!"

"Mum says it's the pews," he said, the brown colour of his eyes now visible through the mask. "Old as time itself. And the damp is because the mayor never sees the need to have the bloody place cleaned. Not that anybody uses it. You see that?" He pointed to a stairway at the rear of the temple leading to the next floor up. "My grandad used to tell me that one night, when he was keeping watch of the cemetery as a kid—"

"Keeping watch?"

"Making sure none of the newly buried are still alive. They've all got bells tied to their toes, you see, but little good it does if there's no one there to hear them ringing. So the town elders would always have him or one of the other kids keep watch at night."

"Scary!"

"That it is. Anyway, one night, when he was minding his business, he thought he saw a man walking on the grass through the cemetery. He called after the man, but the man didn't stop. Just continued walking and entered into here. My granddad, the brave soul, entered in after him. At first he couldn't see him, but then he saw him climbing those stairs."

"And what's up there?"

"The priest's office. But this wasn't the priest, at least according to my granddad. Again he called after him, but nothing. At this point, he figured the man was just hard of hearing. So he chased up the stairs after him and entered into the room…"

"And?"

"Nobody in there. Just four brick walls and a window too small to climb through. Place was empty."

"A spirit then."

"Must've been."

A chill traversed her spine, and she suddenly desired to be out of there.

"Wait," Hemish said before she could turn around. He removed his mask to reveal freckled cheeks, lightly tanned skin, and a mop of sandy hair. "How old are you?"

"Nine."

He smiled happily. "Great! You'll be in my class then."

"What?"

"At school. I'm eleven, but they keep us in the same room until we're sixteen. You are going to go to school, right?"

Truth was, she didn't know. Evia hadn't mentioned it, but in what world would her aunt say no to an education?

Xander nodded. "I think so."

"I'll teach you everything you need to know. About the teachers. The cretins to avoid."

"Cretins?"

"The ones that'll make—"

Loud cheers emanated from outside, drawing their attention.

"About time!" Hemish said. "Quick, or we'll miss it."

They rushed out into the cemetery in time to see a burly man in a black mask throw the first of the effigies into the fire. The villagers howled like wolves as thick smoke rose into the air, then roared as the burly man brought up the next to be chucked in.

The pair pulled as close to the fire as the heat would let them, and with every cheer of the crowd, Xander could feel her heart thump with excitement.

"It was a cruel death." A woman spoke from beside them after the second effigy had been thrown in and the crowd's fanatic cries had subdued marginally.

Xander shrunk, recognising the speaker, and the pair turned to see Evia standing beside them, staring into the fire. Petite in stature and with a youthfulness that belied her many years and long white hair, her forlorn expression and the emotion behind her words were chilling.

"Aunt Evia—" Xander began.

"The men were labelled thieves and miscreants," she continued, her grey eyes and fair skin illuminated by the flames. "And they were. But the truth was far more complicated. Should they have been tried? Of course. But burnt alive without a trial at the hands of the mob? No. Those that stand accused deserve the opportunity to defend themselves. And these men were not granted such rights."

"You speak as if you knew them!" Hemish said, somewhat mockingly.

Expecting a rebuke, Xander relaxed as Evia's expression lightened.

"Where's your mother, Hemish?" Evia asked.

His lips tightened. "Around."

Evia chuckled. "Don't worry, I won't tell her. Just be good to my niece and make sure she's home before too late."

"Where are you going?" Xander asked as Evia turned to leave.

"It's been quite the day for me, and you're in good hands. I'll see you in the morning."

"But you only just got here," she said sadly, wishing to know more of the mysterious woman.

"My dear, I…okay then, a little while, then I must rest these eyes of mine."

Xander beamed, and Evia returned the smile. Then, despite the festive raucousness that made them all hard of hearing, Evia regaled both Xander and Hemish with tales about the gang. Their bad deeds, and their good. Their respect for the vulnerable, and the misinformation campaign launched against them by the authorities. There was more to the story than most knew. And Xander found herself captivated by the woman who spoke as if she had borne witness herself.

CHAPTER 9

Aprix 3, 477; Nhata Bay, Borlencia—Xander held her breath and pulled in close behind the moss-covered wall that separated the schoolyard from the farms and, behind them, the spill of the rich forest that easily withstood the humble sprawl of the town.

And though the flowery scent of spring tickled her nose and the delightful harmony of the region's many songbirds beckoned her to join in and celebrate the jubilant thaw of winter, she was sworn to unmoving silence, for she could hear her three tormentors bickering on the other side of the wall. To make herself as small as possible, she wrapped her green jacket tightly around her chest and stuffed her schoolbag between her legs.

"Bet you she ain't left," Nicholas, the boy with curly ginger hair and who was a foot taller than Xander, snarled.

"Ain't taking that bet," a thicker boy, whose name she didn't know, said. "The runt's probably done a fast one and found herself a hidin' spot or something."

"Or gone into the forest," the third, and shortest of the bunch, cackled. "Mum says the little weirdo's always rummaging the woods on her own."

"Ha! Wouldn't expect any less from her and that miserable aunt of hers," Nicholas muttered. "Never mind. The runt clearly knows what's in for her again. Come on, let's get back before Mr Porky finds us—"

"What are you lot doing back there?" an angry voice sounded from one of the school's many windows.

Xander didn't need to peek to know the source. Mr Porky, as the kids referred to him, was a stout man with a vile temper and an appearance completely befitting of the name, with his peculiar nose and large, distended belly.

"Get back inside before I cane ya!" the man shouted.

She could hear the boys swearing under their breath as they made for the building and didn't doubt that they'd likely receive the beating, regardless of their obedience. Of course, so would she, given she'd missed the last class. Her fate was sealed. "So what does it matter?" she thought.

As soon as the door was slammed shut and the yard was quiet, she pushed away from the damp wall and disappeared onto the nearest street leading into the town. Being careful not to veer too far from the garden hedges or the quieter roads in case she needed to make herself scarce, she made her way to Hemish's home. His mother's bungalow was a quaint affair in need of basic repairs. Still, it was cosy, and Xander rather enjoyed visiting.

Crouched at the end of the garden path, she looked around for any onlookers. Comfortable there were none, she crept to Hemish's window and rapped on it. Two moments later his head popped out.

"You trying to wake the monster?" he asked, slightly annoyed.

"Your mum's not here," she retorted cheekily.

"And how do you know that?"

"How do you not? It's lunchtime. Course she's gone!"

"Still, you shouldn't be here. She'll kill you and then me if she sees you."

"Relax. Why weren't you in school today?"

"Sick. And you? It's not four o'clock yet."

"Bored. Come on, let's check out Dogner's farm."

"Are you mad?"

"Are you? It's a beautiful day. Why waste it locked up?"

He glanced behind him into the dank room filled with the odour of sickness, then to the clear skies and the soon-to-be-flowering plants at the end of his mother's garden.

"Alright then! Give me two minutes. And Xander, if I get in trouble—"

"You won't."

"Says you," he muttered as he turned to change into something more suitable.

The town was alive with farmers, merchants, and fishermen, more so than usual, so to avoid detection, the duo snuck to the nearest fields to the west and then began the trek to the farms south of the town.

It was still too early to spot the sprouts of the spring wheat and barley, and the muddy fields were nothing like the massive rolling landscapes of tall wheat Xander loved to explore to the south of Borealis during the summer months. Nonetheless, she basked in the tranquillity afforded by the rabbits scurrying between the bushes and the various species of bird toying with the multiple scarecrows on that fine spring afternoon.

"Why Dogner's farm?" Hemish asked after nearly slipping on a mound of muck.

"Heard he's got a new litter of pigs."

"Is that so! Well, would've rather headed over to the tanner."

"And get caught!"

"Some risks are worth it. The man has apparently brought in elk hide to sell, and—" He coughed into his hand. "I've never seen elk hide. Didn't even know the creatures existed until my mother mentioned it."

"Gruesome."

"What do you think your clothes are made of?"

She ran her finger over her jacket. "Not hide."

"Still from an animal."

"It's not wool. It's from a plant. Not sure which one, though."

"Either way—"

He flew face first into the dirt as Xander pushed him to the ground.

She slumped beside him and dragged him to the nearest hedgerow.

"Have you—" he had begun when Xander put her finger to his mouth.

"It's my aunt," she whispered cautiously.

His confused gaze followed Xander's into the next field along. There Evia stood, not twenty metres away from them, with a basket in one hand and her ear seemingly to the wind. The pair could just make out the stern look of concentration written on her face.

"What's she doing?" Hemish asked.

As if in response, Evia took something from the basket and tossed it to the ground. Moments later a small rabbit emerged cautiously from the hedgerow, grabbed whatever had been thrown, and then disappeared back into hiding. At that, Evia continued her stroll towards the town.

"What's she doing out here?" Hemish said as they stared after her.

"There's a mushroom patch in the woods to the west. I think she was gathering some for dinner."

"Fair enough. Bit too close for my liking."

"Let's get a bit closer to the woods then. We'll be safer."

"Right!"

They veered west to the tree line across a dozen acres of farmland, and once comfortable with the cover afforded by the wooded giants and their shadows, they turned southward towards Dogner's farm. Along the edges of fields brimming with cattle and horses and freshly sown crop. Over narrow creeks and overgrown paths. It was a noticeable affair, despite their greatest efforts to hush each other, that might have landed them in trouble if not for the fact that the farmers and the foragers and the lumberjacks were not tending their steads on that particular day.

"Been awfully quiet, don't you think?" Hemish said as they emerged from the pen holding Dogner's litter of piglets in the afternoon sun.

"Aren't you glad? Gave us plenty of time to see the little things. They're so cute."

"That they are. But still slightly odd."

"What are you two doing here?" A gruff voice sounded from behind them.

It was one of Dogner's farmhands. A middle-aged man with a thick neck and unusually large hands. He was "good farming stock," as Dogner had once remarked.

"Came to see the litter!" Xander said excitedly, ignoring Hemish's muttered curse words.

"Cute, aren't they?" the man said cheerfully.

"Exactly what we said."

"And where is Dogner?" Hemish asked cautiously, wary that the farmhand might give them up.

"In the town with the rest of the workers. Surprised you're not down there with them, given what's going on."

"What's going on?"

"Go see for yourselves. And don't worry, Hemish."

"What's there to worry about?" he asked without betraying his uneasiness.

The man grinned cheekily. "I won't tell your mum you were up here on a school day. Just make sure to bring me some of that bread she makes next time you're visiting."

"Always a price with you."

"Always. Now hurry along."

The commotion along the main street was audible before they had even caught sight of the throngs of villagers lined along its route. Cheers and emotional cries rang from the crowd that was a dozen deep for most of the road's length. Determined to know the magnet that had drawn in even those that couldn't afford to miss a day of labour, the pair squeezed through the wedge of bodies to the front.

"Soldiers!" Hemish said as the hundreds of uniformed men and women stood to attention while their captain spoke with the mayor and his entourage.

"What are they doing here?" Xander asked.

"How should I know?"

"Enlisting," a nosy man interjected.

"Enlisting who?"

"Veterans. Anybody that can fight. Arrived a couple hours back and will be gone before the hour's up. They're marching north to take on the masked bastards. Troops from all over Anemoi are gathering, seeing if they can push 'em back to the city. Mayor of Crowton and a couple of the other big towns are leading the Borlencian regiments."

Xander felt the joy of the day immediately dissipate, replaced by the same numbness that plagued her sleep. She peered to the nearest row of troops. Most carried the weight of the mission in their tired eyes, but there were a select few that didn't, their impartiality to death enough to stem any bother at what was to come. She let out a shallow sigh, but it was enough to garner Hemish's attention.

"I'll take you home," he said softly.

A woman in the crowd suddenly wailed as her husband pulled from her grip and walked towards the captain. Xander recognised the couple from a little antique store Joseph sometimes took her to. To see their usual bubbly selves torn by the man's unmalicious attempt at relationship sabotage was enough for a day. She nodded to Hemish, and they withdrew into an empty street and walked home in silence, the rowdy noise of the main street never far from earshot.

▲ ▲ ▲

Xander turned over in her bed, again unable to find a comfortable position despite the sleep-conducive coolness of the sheets against her skin. Her thoughts darted this way and that without any real cohesion, stirred into chaos by the flashbacks that had become synonymous with sleep. The memory of her mother as she lay dying at the base of the altar, her bloodied expression helpless and fearful. The imagined scene of her father's last moments with his soldiers as they fought gallantly to protect the city from the scourge. Then Lawrence, her brother, who surely must have drowned or burned with Anemoi's northern fleet, destroyed half a world away by the same vermin that clearly had no regard for borders.

"Enough," she thought, and shifted onto her back in search of distraction. On the oak beams overhead, a spider, barely visible through the dark, crawled between two of the thick supports, and she shuddered at the thought of it losing its footing and toppling down onto her face, or worse, into her mouth. Lips curled up in disgust, as if the crawly had already committed the deed, she shook her head of the unpleasant picture and tried to focus on something more pleasant.

She conjured an image of her aunt who, despite her seemingly perpetual absence, had grown on Xander, though Xander wouldn't have called it love. Companionship, perhaps. Maybe adoration. Adoration for the woman's gentle smile and caring demeanour, especially in the company of Joseph.

The gentle patter of raindrops on the roof drew her attention to the window, and caught in the tranquil stupor so often induced when one was sheltered from the elements in the cosy confines of their own home, her mind soon drifted back to her brother.

Even before Borealis fell, it had been some time since she had seen him, and still she could clearly recall his dark hair and flecked green eyes; his tall, muscular build; and the cheeky grin that was a near-permanent expression of his.

A warm smile of recollection crept onto her face at a conversation between him and their father the day before he left the city with the fleet. The last conversation between the two that she could remember, except for when they all had seen him off the next day.

"My new first mate's a jackass," Lawrence had said, his indignation evident in his sharp features.

"And has the jackass got the ear of the captain?" Carolus had responded.

"That's putting it lightly."

"Well, knowing you, and I'd like to think I know you pretty well, keep your lips sealed. Don't make an enemy of the first mate if it's going to cause you grief down the road."

She remembered Lawrence shifting awkwardly as he cleared his throat, and Carolus shaking his head, barely able to contain his urge to laugh.

"Too late?" their father had asked, fully aware of the answer to come.

"Something like that," Lawrence had said.

"In that case, it'll be a good lesson for you. No better teacher than a horrid couple of years on the water, where a hot meal and good bed are hard to come by, and you've got your superior breathing down your neck."

Though Xander was usually saddened by her memories, she chuckled at this particular one and then, altogether weary of trying to force sleep, got out of bed and entered the hall. Her aunt's door was closed, which meant Evia must have arrived home in the fleeting hour Xander had managed sleep. Careful not to creak the floorboards, Xander crept downstairs into the living room.

The furniture was old, even by Evia's standard. The wooden chairs, veiled by thin cushions, did little to follow the natural contours of the body and would have been more at home in one of the museums in Borealis, pre-destruction. Still, she lit the candle on the worn table in the centre of the room, grabbed the book perched on the corner, and then sat back on the least uncomfortable chair of the set.

It was a lengthy, dreary book on the countries in the north, and though much of the language was too advanced for Xander's level, there was just one page that brought her back night after night. A nocturnal ritual for when sleep reached that frustrating stage of elusiveness, and one that her aunt regularly disapproved of.

There was no picture on this page, or map. And like every other hefty vault of knowledge on the history or facts of nations they had found, there was just the one, almost pointless paragraph on the people they had come to suspect for the attack on Borealis. A name she had heard in passing just once before, though she couldn't quite recall when and where: the Cresedi.

"Thought to have come into existence through conquest in the early first century, the empire is governed by three concurrent emperors. Despite its vast reach and wealth, much of the empire's ruling families, customs, and complex laws remain shrouded in secrecy. The empire's armies are best known for engaging in international conflict whilst wearing masks designed to invoke fear in their enemies."

CHAPTER 10

Januarix 15, 476; Borealis, Borlencia; nine months before the fall of Borealis—The small restaurant was teeming with all varieties of people and was warmed by a large brick oven in the centre of the crowded room. A popular spot on any given day, this evening was especially busy with families queuing outside and servers racing this way and that.

Xander dipped her bread into the last of the mashed white beans drenched in olive oil and took another clumsy bite. She was so focused on the barely contained mouthful that it took her several moments to realise her parents and brother looked on with amused grins, and that several onlookers from the next table over also watched in amazement at just how much food she could fit into one gulp.

"What?" she asked when comfortable she wouldn't choke on what was left.

Alya chuckled. "Hungry?"

"Always!"

Carolus called over the server. "Another of those, please. Some would liken my daughter to a bottomless pit."

"Yes, Senior Minister," the man said, and swiftly disappeared.

Carolus winced at the formality.

"What do you expect him to call you?" Alya queried softly. "They all know you, and they respect you."

"Most of them, anyway," Lawrence said before jabbing his fork into the steaming meat on his plate.

"Why do some people not respect you?" Xander asked.

Carolus looked at her, eager to teach but wary of her innocence. "No elected official is without fault. And none secure one hundred percent of the vote in any election—"

"Unless they cheat," Xander said with a full mouth.

"Unless they cheat."

"But your father didn't cheat," Alya added.

"No, I didn't," he said.

"You didn't cheat, and they still don't respect you?" Xander asked as she looked upon her soup with greedy eyes. "That's not fair."

"In some instances, respect has to be earned," he said. "And to be blunt, for some, well, they struggle to show kindness when they're not in agreement."

"Yep, a lack of kindness that has absolutely nothing to do with the fact that our grandfather isn't from Anemoi," Lawrence said sarcastically. "Granted, I've no idea why a dirt-poor fisherman from the north would cause issue."

Carolus's expression hardened.

"Don't worry." Xander spoke, sensing her father's growing irritation. "I already know."

"You already know what?"

"That our grandpapa's home makes people unhappy."

Carolus's features softened under his daughter's smile. "It's not his home itself that makes people unhappy. It's because he's not from Anemoi, which to some people means I'm not one of them."

"Xander," Alya said curiously. "Has someone said something to you about your father?"

"One of my teachers," she answered.

"What did he say?"

She shrugged and hefted a large potato from her soup. "Nothing bad. He just thinks all our ministers should have both parents from Anemoi. That's all. He still likes you."

Alya sat back in frustration, her eyes boring worriedly into Carolus's. "The laws don't prohibit candidates with foreign parentage, and you were elected fairly."

"It comes down to perception," Carolus responded. "And trust."

"But why's it becoming an issue now when this isn't even your first term? Not to mention you've been the garrison commander for years. I could swear it wasn't more than a few months ago that the people could find no fault."

"She's got a point," Lawrence said. "And what about that one senior minister? The one missing a hand. Isn't his father an ex-Buto pirate? Never hear his name come up in conversation."

"It's the army of slippery tongues," a man's voice interjected.

"Ricard!" Xander screamed excitedly, startling a nearby server. She jumped up and hugged him.

"Hey, kiddo! What a delight!" He put her down, and she returned to her seat.

"Ricard, pull up a chair," Alya said warmly, buoyed by the stocky man's presence.

"Please," Carolus insisted.

Ricard opened his mouth to protest, but the sight of his favourite people melted any resistance. He nodded his acceptance and joined them.

"Just a coincidence you happen upon us here?" Carolus asked as he poured Ricard a cup of wine.

"You know it isn't. But I think our business can wait. Wouldn't want to spoil a moment."

"What did you mean by slippery tongues?" Xander asked, eager to know.

"Maybe a conversation for another time, kiddo. I'm sure there's lighter—"

"You started it. Now you have to tell us."

Lawrence chuckled. "Bet you're regretting your choice of words."

"You could say that," Ricard said, looking awkwardly to Carolus and Alya for guidance.

Carolus shrugged his shoulders. "She'll have to learn these things sooner or later, and she'll not let go of it now."

"Nope!" Xander said, lifting her chin proudly.

"In that case, let's get straight to the point," Ricard began. "Some of your father's policies threaten the power of some of the wealthier families. To counter, they've hired an army of slippery tongues to drag his name through the muck. His father's origin appears to be fair game."

"But that's definitely not fair!"

"That's politics," Lawrence said. "Politics and greed."

Ricard looked at Carolus. "There's always going to be a minority that has issue with your parentage. It's just a few more than usual. Nothing to worry about," he said, patting his friend reassuringly on the back. "Anyway, now that that's out the way. How about we take that trip to my vineyard this weekend? The new patio's put in. And we can take the hunting wolves to help track the game in the local woods."

"Sounds pleasant," Alya said.

Xander giggled. "Those aren't hunting wolves. They're hounds."

"Is that so!" Ricard said. "You've got me there. So what do you say? This weekend sound alright?"

Carolus took in his friend's cheerful demeanour, and after a moment's thought, clasped his arm. "This weekend."

CHAPTER 11

Julyx 3, 479; Nhata Bay, Borlencia—As was usual for a breezeless summer afternoon in Nhata, the sun was hot and the air unbearably stuffy. And though the town still moved with the townsfolk running their errands or seeking their vices, the energy of the bustle had been sapped by the heat-induced lethargy so prevalent in Julyx. Despite the affliction, however, Xander, Hemish, and Evia still found themselves eager to brave the discomfort and entertain Joseph on his brief visit.

"What's that for?" Xander asked as they watched the owner of one of the town's many taverns climb a ladder and hang a green flag above the entrance. In the three years since the fall of Borealis, she had sprouted a good measure, though she still carried the chubby cheeks of childhood.

"It's for the Ranclet," Hemish said excitedly. Taller than Xander, Hemish had a scrawny build and a tendency to slouch, which made him appear almost equal in height.

"The Ranclet?"

"Three years and you've still not heard of the Ranclet?" Joseph said, surprised.

She shook her head.

"Well, fancy that," he said. "Never could've imagined it'd take that long for you to hear of it. Not in this town. Clearly these two aren't keeping you abreast of Nhata's traditions."

"Hey," Evia scolded playfully. "In our defence, none of us thought it'd be held this time around with the war in the north."

"Or after what happened last time," Hemish added.

Joseph shielded his eyes against the sun as he examined the owner of the next shop over hanging a yellow flag. "Don't think you could stop it if you tried. Every town in the county goes zealous for this."

"So what is it?" Xander asked with growing impatience.

"It's a weeklong competition held every four years in Augustx. Five events over three days. There are events for stamina, strength, grit…" He scratched his chin, trying to remember the other feats.

"Sounds like fun."

"You'd have to be a loon to participate," Hemish scoffed. "Men have gone mad from getting stuck underground. Two broke their legs last time. And what about that guy that nearly drowned?"

"I heard he did," Joseph said.

Evia chuckled. "No, he was quite alright. But good to hear the rumours worked their usual charm."

"Still sounds like it could be fun," Xander said.

"If you don't mind the risk of death!" Hemish said. "There's a reason only adult men compete. It's too dangerous."

"Oh!" she said with disappointment. "I hadn't realised it was only open to men."

"It's not only open to men. There's just no woman or child mad enough to try it."

"Weren't there those two boys that competed?" Joseph queried. "If memory serves me correctly, didn't they complete it?"

"Two out of how many?" Hemish said. "I stand by my words. You have to be mad or a brute to try it."

"Now Hemish," Evia began. "I think that's a bit unfair—"

"Evia!" a woman interrupted. Her hair was matted with sweat, and her cheeks were red from exertion. "It's Tomasz. His cough's gotten worse. We need you."

"That damn boy. I told him to stop with the pipe."

"He did."

"Too little, too late."

"And Evia, the convulsions have returned."

She nodded, her worry evident. "Joseph, we could use an extra hand, if you have the time."

"For you, Evia, I've got all the time," he responded, and the three of them rushed down the street, leaving Xander and Hemish on their own.

"Your aunt gets more business than the village doctor," Hemish said once they were gone.

"She doesn't charge her patients," Xander replied.

"Makes you wonder how she actually makes a living—ouch!"

There was a noisy splatter as something hit Hemish in the back of the head. He put his hand to the area of the impact and withdrew it.

"What is that?" Xander asked of the gooey substance.

"Egg," he said, looking up into the sky.

Another hit him in the chest with a crunch, and they looked to where the egg had been thrown from.

"It's Nicholas!" Hemish spat angrily.

The boy stood by a corner shop with his two minions. One of them carried a basket, presumably full of eggs.

Without taking his eyes off the miscreants, Hemish wiped his hand on his trousers. "What a waste of an—" He ducked the egg thrown at his head by the shortest bully and then attempted to catch one thrown by Nicholas. It broke in his hand and cut his palm. "Time to run—"

Xander caught the egg about to hit him square in the face, then threw it back and hit Nicholas on the forehead.

"Definitely time to run!" Hemish urged as Nicholas's face scrunched into a fuming glare.

The pair darted down a quiet side street with uneven cobbles and slipped into a narrow alley where the stench of stale beer clung to a moss-covered bench, and bottles and food scraps littered the ground. They crouched behind an uncovered bin and watched as the trio ran past.

"That was close," Hemish managed, his chest heaving.

"You're bleeding," Xander said, lifting his hand.

"That lot will never give it a rest."

"Why do they pick on us so much?"

"Don't think they're quite the brightest. Always thieving and wrecking."

They tensed as the shortest of the bullies peered around the corner.

"They're in—" the bully had begun when Xander grabbed a discarded bottle and lobbed it at him.

The bully ducked out of the way of the projectile, but in his distraction, he didn't see Xander racing at him. She got within reach and punched him in the chest, causing him to keel over in a fit of splutters.

"Hurry!" she called back to Hemish.

They darted back onto the main street and started for Evia's cottage. Though the street was teeming with townsfolk, it wasn't difficult to navigate the tired pedestrians. Still, they had only made it half the distance when they spotted Nicholas a dozen metres behind them. As they were about to turn onto a minor street, Hemish gasped and then collapsed to the ground with shards of egg tangled in his hair.

Xander turned around, ready to defend her friend. Nicholas had a small gash on his forehead where the egg had made impact, and by his side was the thickest of the trio. Despite the comparative sizes of the bullies, and the fact that they outnumbered her two to one, she wasn't afraid.

"You'll not get near him!" she shouted threateningly.

Nicholas smirked and then lunged at her but was knocked from the side onto the road with a thud.

"What the—" the other had begun when he realised just who had thrown his leader to the ground. "Dogner, I'm sorry. We didn't—"

The thicker bully turned and ran, leaving his compatriot. The rest of them looked up at Dogner. A big chap easily in his sixth decade, he had white skin perpetually tinged red by the sun, and the odour of raw meat followed him around like a stray dog begging for scraps. He had more kids than hairs on his head and almost always sported a big smile under that big red nose of his. In this moment, however, his hardened expression was frightening.

"Expected better from you, lad," Dogner said to Nicholas. "I'll not be needing your help around the farm on the weekends no more."

"Dogner, please!" Nicholas said with alarm. "My father will beat me, he will. Please! You can't do this. We need the money."

"Sorry, lad. You should've thought about that before you picked on these two."

"And what about my family? My father's your friend too."

"And how disappointed he'll be when I tell him what you've been up to."

Nicholas stood up. His cheeks crimson red with fury. "You'll regret this. Especially the both of you!"

Hemish was still on the ground, though he had managed to sit up. "Can't get worse than this, can it?" he quipped, showing his bloodied hand.

Nicholas stormed off without another word, his back and shoulders rigid.

"I'm sure that'll not be the last of him," Hemish remarked.

"I'll have a word with his father," Dogner said. "The man's not too unreasonable. Maybe we'll see eye to eye. Come on, let's get you cleaned up."

"I could do with a drink," Hemish said as he stood up.

"Is that so, lad? Bit on the young side, don't you think?"

"Depends who you ask."

"Aye, 'tis true."

"Where did you come from anyway?" Hemish said as they started walking towards Evia's cottage.

"Just running an errand in the area and saw you two could do with a hand."

"Your timing was a bit off, wouldn't you say?"

Dogner chuckled. "Perhaps I should've left it a bit longer?"

"No, no, that's alright. Thanks."

"And you," Dogner said, looking at Xander. "Got quite the fight in you."

She shrugged but didn't smile. Her hands were still shaking from the encounter, and she felt exhausted, both mentally and physically, her mind having already raced through a dozen dark scenarios since the incident.

CHAPTER 12

Julyx 14, 479; Nhata Bay, Borlencia—"Xander, listen!" the skinny man at the front of the room scolded petulantly, frustrated by the continued disobedience from those he sought to teach. But in his hysteria to exert control, his odd-shaped spectacles slumped to the end of his pointy nose and magnified his awkwardly furious glare, invoking a sudden round of amused giggles from the classroom. Hemish was particularly mocking in his laugh. "Quiet, before I whip the lot of you!" the teacher bellowed with little effect, and only when the rascals had fallen silent through sheer exhaustion from laughing did his gaze fall back on Xander.

"Sorry," she whispered guiltily under the silent onslaught.

"What do you think your aunt would say if I informed her of your poor behaviour?"

"She'd tell me to cane the little whelp," Mr Porky said menacingly from the doorway.

The larger man's emergence instantly tempered the students' underlying desire for mischief, and most took to staring at their desks or risk the ire of his cane.

"Now, what was I just talking about?" the skinny teacher said, emboldened. "See what happens when you don't listen—"

"The Houses of Parliament. Each province has twelve elected ministers, made up of four senior ministers and eight common ministers," Xander began quietly. "And also dozens of locally elected councilmen, depending on the size of the province, and then there's also the non-elected civil servants…"

"So you were listening." The teacher smiled, both proudly and in exasperation.

Xander stifled an internal chuckle. She had become particularly adept at scouting the last couple of words before any scolding, and from this she was usually able to infer the topic of conversation and then recall her teachings from both Evia and the tutors before her.

"And what are the functions of the senior ministers?"

"The senior ministers from each province make up Anemoi's Senior Council. The senior ministers are the most senior representatives of their provinces, and when in Special Council, they become the de facto leaders of Anemoi with the ability to mobilise the army and navy and propose constitutional changes. They can also vote through legislation without a quorum of the Upper House, though this is rare and doesn't mean they won't still seek advice from the common ministers to show respect for protocol."

"And the Upper House?"

"The Upper House consists of both the senior ministers and the common ministers and is responsible for passing all legislation affecting the whole of Anemoi."

"Good, Xander. Not bad for a little squirt." He smiled. "And remember, though the Senior Council can vote through legislation without a quorum of the Upper House, this doesn't include constitutional changes. The proposition of constitutional changes by the Senior Council does still require a quorum of the Upper House." He looked at her for a moment and then grinned connivingly. "Now, tell me about the Lower House…"

"The Lower House passes all local legislation, and each province has its own. It consists of a province's senior ministers, common ministers, and the councilmen, though the Lower House can discuss a province's minor matters without all members present."

"Very good, Xander. Very good. How funny that you can recite facts about the Lower House when I haven't even gotten around to talking about it."

She blushed.

"Nothing to be ashamed of. It shows initiative and curiosity. I'm sure the rest of you could learn from Xander's example."

"If you'd give us half a chance, you might be surprised," Hemish said light-heartedly.

"Sure, you and all the other little whelps are geniuses just waiting to shine."

"Easy when your father was one of the snivelling rats," Nicholas muttered to a reaction of gasps and laughs.

Without a word, Mr Porky rushed to Nicholas's desk and yanked him to the front of the class. Then, for all to see, he belted him ten times until his skin was swollen and broken.

"You'll think twice next time, I'm sure," the big man said, and shoved him back to his desk.

"Ouch," Hemish whispered into Xander's ear as the red-faced boy took his seat at the back of the class. "Bet he blames you for that."

Her stomach tightened. She didn't doubt it. Already she could feel Nicholas's angry gaze piercing into the back of her head.

"Now, what of the much-coveted prime minister chair?" the teacher continued, uncaring of the harm just caused. "Anybody?"

The next hour was torturous. Xander barely acknowledged the ramblings of the teacher as he rabbited on about Anemoi and its political structure. She was solely focused on the trouble to come, for it wasn't just the two of them that had caught a glimpse of Nicholas's growing fury. Every couple of minutes, someone would glance back at him and then at her, excitement or worry painted on their cheeks.

"As soon as that bell rings," Hemish whispered.

"I feel like I'm going to throw up," she muttered.

"What was that?" Mr Porky questioned from the doorway.

"Nothing, sir."

He stared at her with disdain, the same that usually preceded his undeserved beatings, and then walked over to the teacher's desk and grabbed the brass handbell that sat on the corner. "You'll do the honour today, I think," he said to her.

Hemish cursed under his breath.

Mr Porky looked at him threateningly. "Something you want to add?"

"It's just us and two other classrooms, sir," he responded. "Does she really need to do the rounds? Can't we just tell them the day's over?"

"And break tradition? What do you think I am, a heathen? Now get up here, girl, before I cane you."

She trudged over to the man and took the handbell. She glanced at her ginger-haired tormentor and quickly shied away from his scowl. A thought struck, and she walked to her desk and grabbed her bag.

"Without the bag," Mr Porky said.

She held her tongue as she dropped it to the ground, then left the room. Hemish was right—it was a pointless task, but what could she do? Tradition was tradition, and each day a different child was picked at random. Unfortunately for her, today was her turn. Eager to get it over with, she practically ran her five circuits of the building whilst ringing the handbell for all to hear. The school day was over, and so was any chance of her escaping Nicholas's wrath unbothered.

All the teachers had already left for home by the time she returned to the school entrance, and almost all the students stood in the schoolyard, waiting for her to return the handbell and come back outside. By the entrance were Nicholas and his two henchmen, their expressions mischievous. Between them they held Hemish and her bag.

"We'll be seeing you in a minute," Nicholas said.

"Just run!" Hemish blurted, and the shortest of the trio slapped him in the back of the head.

Nicholas grinned. "Don't worry, we won't hurt him. Just don't be running off now."

Fists clenched and brow rigid, Xander entered the classroom and placed the handbell back on the teacher's desk. She looked through the window into the empty street beside the school. An easy escape, but what about Hemish? She thought back to the cruel pranks the trio had pulled on both of them and the times they had caught Hemish on his own and beaten him. Any urge to run instantly dissipated. With an air of defiance, she walked back outside and squared up to Nicholas, her nose an inch from his.

"Let him go," she said. "And give me my bag."

"Why would I do that?" Nicholas retorted.

She backed away, repulsed by his smelly breath. "I don't want to fight you."

"Take after your father, I see."

"My father?"

"The idiot couldn't even find it in him to protect his people."

Xander's fists balled as a surge of anger rushed through her, but her desire to do damage to the boy was swiftly held in check by an idea. An exhilarating idea. She released her clenched hands.

"I don't want to fight you," she repeated.

"And if I give you no choice?" he said threateningly.

"You'd fight a girl?" Hemish blurted, eager to distract, though his words earned him another slap on the head.

"The rules changed when she drew blood. She's brought it on herself."

"Still a bit weaselly, wouldn't you say?"

"Watch yourself, Hemish. You know where this path leads."

"Just trying to enlighten our audience on what it takes to stoop to—"

Nicholas turned around and punched Hemish in the face.

"Hey!" Xander seethed angrily, again on the verge of losing her control.

Nicholas turned back to her. "I think you do want to fight. Maybe if

I hit him here—"

"The Ranclet," she interjected calmly.

"What of it?"

"You and me. Best of the five races. We both have to complete them all. Winner gets their way."

There were gasps from the shocked students, but it was intrigue that took Nicholas.

"Winner gets their way?" he repeated.

"Piss off, Nicholas!" Hemish swore. He ducked the swipe aimed at his head and ripped himself free of the trio to join Xander by her side. The shortest bully reached out, but Nicholas stayed his hand. "You can't do it, Xander. You can't beat him. He—"

Nicholas stepped forward, causing both of them to step back. "What do you want?" he said to Xander.

"You'll leave Hemish alone. And me," she responded.

"Sure."

"Xander." Hemish spoke. "He—"

"And you?" she asked Nicholas, ignoring her friend's plea.

"If I place in front of you," Nicholas said. "I want that jacket you're always wearing in the winter. The green one."

"Oh! Good one!" the shortest bully said elatedly, his embarrassment at being winded by a girl still evident.

"Yeah! That'll teach the runt," the thicker miscreant agreed.

Xander's stomach dropped, and her chest tightened. "That's my mother's jacket."

"I know." Nicholas smirked.

"But why? It means nothing to you. I don't get it."

"Call it justice."

"Justice for what? The egg? Because Dogner fired you? All that was your own fault."

His face hardened. "It's justice for my uncle. He was a soldier in your father's garrison and was in the city when it was attacked. He died because your father couldn't do his damn job and keep the city safe."

Her anger subsided. "I'm sorry for your loss," she said sadly, much to everybody's surprise. "I accept your prize."

"This is a bad idea," Hemish said.

"No, it's not," Nicholas said, and chucked Xander's bag in the bush.

Without looking back, he disappeared into the town with his two fellow ruffians and the rest of the students immediately behind them.

Hemish sighed as he bent down to collect Xander's bag. He turned to her, concern in his eyes. "Remember when I told you there'd only been two children that ever attempted the Ranclet and completed it?"

Her eyes widened.

"It was Nicholas and his brother," he said. "They're the only two since the competition began."

Dread reared its way up her, souring the odd blend of sadness and excitement she had felt previously.

"But in truth," he continued, "it's not even him you have to worry about. People die in this competition. There's a reason why children our age won't do it."

"And if it means he'll leave us alone?"

"But at what cost?"

She bit her cheek. Despite the fear of losing her mother's jacket, her eagerness still lingered. "I think it's the right decision."

"It's your jacket," he said, shrugging his shoulders. "And how do you intend on convincing Evia?"

Her face dropped, causing him to chuckle despite his worry.

"You know," he said as they began walking into the town. "I really thought you were going to hit him. What made you choose the greater of two evils?"

"Something my father once told me."

"And what was that?"

"Violence isn't always the answer."

"So you chose the Ranclet over the school bully?"

He began laughing, and soon enough she joined in, both unable to stop until the struggle for breath became too much.

▲ ▲ ▲

Evia was sitting alone on Nhata's pebbled lakeshore with a flower in her hand when Xander found her. She was watching the fishermen reel their lines under the stuffy evening sun, and an air of melancholy hung over her.

"If it's what you want, then yes, you have my blessing," Evia said after Xander mentioned her desire to compete in the Ranclet. "What?"

"I don't know," Xander said, suddenly unsure of herself. "I really thought you'd say no."

Evia chuckled. "Who am I to stand in the way of your path? Just know, it's a dangerous competition. Hardened men come in from all over the county and beyond to compete. It'll not be easy."

Xander's gaze locked on one particular woman whose net had caught on the lake bottom. "I understand." She felt a tinge of guilt at not revealing what exactly was at stake.

"Okay, then. It's settled. But we'll need a little help."

"Help?"

"You didn't think I'd let you do it unprepared, did you? You've got five weeks. We'll need to work on your endurance and strength. And maybe a little self-defence."

"Self-defence? Am I missing something?"

"Can't be too careful, dear child. Come, follow me."

Together they trudged along Nhata's main street to Dogner's shop. The big man was alone inside, tenderising a slab of meat thicker than a grown man's leg.

"Well, that's a dangerous endeavour," he grunted as he whacked the meat with his hefty pulveriser.

"Hence why she could use some help," Evia said.

"What kind of self-defence are we talking?"

"As much as you can teach."

He put the hammer down and grinned. "She'll need more than a month to learn all that's in here," he said, tapping his head.

"We can continue her training for as long as it takes."

"Now I'm definitely confused." Xander spoke. "The competition will be over in a month. Why do I need to continue after that?"

"Your father thought to train you, did he not?"

"Yes, but—"

"Then let's fulfil his wish. For the competition. For life's hurdles. It doesn't matter. Why limit yourself to your books?"

"But then why Dogner? Sorry, I don't mean to be disrespectful. It's just that, well, you're a farmer. In Borealis, the head of the barracks helped to train me and the other ministers' children. He was a soldier."

"Tell me, lass, do all soldiers soldier until the day they die?" he said light-heartedly. "Or do they get a wee break before time takes them?"

"You were a soldier?"

"Aye, and not just any soldier," he said proudly. "The ex-marine general of Anemoi's raiding fleet. And let me tell you, it's not the city folk that make the best troops. It's the miners and the farmers and the builders. The ones used to a hard day's labour. Mind you, been a bit of a while since I held a tool of the trade. Nonetheless, I'm happy to oblige and help with your training."

"Great," Evia said gleefully. "She'll start tomorrow."

"Tomorrow?" Xander asked, surprised. "I've got school."

Dogner chuckled. "Not in the morning and the evening, you don't."

The next four weeks were gruelling and unlike anything Xander had ever experienced. Every morning before sunrise, Dogner would knock on her door and begin the morning exercises. The routine always began with a long run through the farms, usually those fields with a gradient or vast stretches of uneven ground in which to punish the calves, followed by rigorous strength training. Whether it was sacks of grain or bales of hay, the process usually entailed carrying the weight between the various barns and fields. It was a strength-training regimen much adored by the farmers who benefited from Xander's unpaid labour.

After a heavy breakfast and a tedious day of learning, Dogner would then greet Xander at the school's entrance with a bag of snacks. Enough to energise, never enough to put her to sleep. From there they would begin the evening class. Wrestling and the use of knives, to Xander's confusion, though Dogner promised they'd move on to more advanced weaponry when she was ready.

Like clockwork, every day brought with it a new ache or bruise. But Xander could feel herself getting stronger, faster, and fitter. And much to Dogner's surprise, she was proving herself to be more resilient than anything he could have imagined from a girl of her age. Whether she would stack up against the men in the Ranclet, he didn't know, but with time he could certainly see her faring well in any sport or labourers' job that would accept her.

And still, even with such resilience, he knew the need for rest. In week five, the long runs were reduced to shorter stints. The strength training to minor sessions every other day. And the wrestling and knife play to much gentler daily exercises.

She was ready.

CHAPTER 13

Augustx 13, 479; Nhata Bay, Borlencia; five days before the Ranclet—"I thought Nhata was meant to be muggy this time of year?" Xander said to Dogner as he examined the inside of a hollow log.

"Meant to be," he called without looking up.

They were scouring the woodland floor for goodies and were some two kilometres north of the town where the trees and undergrowth reigned unchecked. Mushrooms and herbs and berries were all fair game to the two eager foragers, and already the two baskets they carried were heavy with edible treasures. It was a joyous hunt marred only by the sweltering heat and the obvious lack of movement and noise from the woodland critters too lethargic to venture out.

She craned her head up as she took in the forest's canopy shuffling ever so slightly under the harsh afternoon sun. Even with nature's umbrella overhead, she could feel her skin burning, and coupled with the aridity of the air, her lips were cracked, and her lungs and nose tickled with irritation.

"Then why's it so dry?" she asked, and took a swig of water.

He stood up straight and waved for her to follow as he continued down the winding dirt path that stretched into the woods. "Happens every once in a while. Nothing much we can do about it. Just got to let nature run its course."

"Half the gardens on our street have died. Not Evia's though. It's the only one that seems to be the same. Hemish thinks it magic, but I'm certain it's the fact that she keeps asking me to fetch water from the lake."

Dogner chuckled. "Can only add to your training. Look at that. Bet you there's a couple mushrooms in there," he said, pointing to a small den formed from the roots of a thick oak. "So what did your aunt get you?" he asked as he bent down for a closer look.

"A book."

"Another book!" he bellowed light-heartedly. He stood up empty-hand-ed. "Haven't you got enough?"

"It's…different."

"How so?"

"It's a fantasy novel."

"Giving up on the history books then, I see."

"No. I didn't ask for it."

"Maybe she thought it time for a change. Come on, let's carry on," he said, and they continued walking.

"I guess."

"Well, I think it's a very thoughtful present for a girl of—how old did you say you're turning today?"

"Twelve."

"Twelve! Not long before you'll be moving out into a place of your own."

"I think I've got a while before that happens."

"We'll see."

"Dogner!" came a call from a short way away.

The pair turned to see a man in the distance.

"Who is it?" Dogner asked.

Xander leaned forward. "I don't know. He's carrying something."

"Dogner!" the man called again, and started to jog towards them, though the item he carried made his gait clumsy.

"Farland, what a fantastic surprise." Dogner roared in delight as the man drew near.

"Your eyes need checking, old man," his friend retorted as they locked arms.

The man was as large as Dogner, and he carried a lumberjack's saw.

"You're the same age, last time I checked," Dogner said. "So what brings you this far south? You're some way from home."

"Beech. A friend said he spotted some down here a couple weeks back. Yet to see any, though."

"Beech? Ha! Can't recall the last time I spotted beech around these parts. Practically logged to extinction. Maybe his eyes were mistaken."

"Maybe," Farland said disappointedly.

"Anyway, what were you going to do when you found some? Carry it back yourself?"

He laughed. "I'm camped a short distance from here. Got several of the younger loggers with me."

"Good thing too. Otherwise, you'd be putting that back of yours out."

"Can't argue that. And you? This one of your daughters?"

"This one? No, she's Evia's niece. Farland, meet Xander."

"Evia's niece. You don't say. Pleasure to meet you, Xander."

"Likewise," she responded.

Farland peered down to the baskets. "He's got you combing the woods for food in this heat? Hope he's paying you!"

"That's an option?"

"Hey, you!" Dogner prodded the man cheerfully. "No need to give the lass ideas."

Farland chortled. "My apologies. Never the harm meant. So what's the latest in Nhata? Evia's doing fine, I imagine?"

"Evia's fine. And life's continuing like it has the past century. Uninterrupted."

"Figures. Same back home. Half of Anemoi could disappear, and I doubt we'd see any change unless it hit us directly. Ridiculous when you think on it."

"Aye, agree with you there. And what's the news from the north?"

Xander's ears livened and her face hardened, though neither man noticed.

"Nothing's changed," Farland said sternly. "Since the bulk of the marauders' army withdrew behind Borealis's walls, it's been quiet for the most part. There's some movement to and from the desert, and sometimes the odd skirmish between our troops and theirs when caught in the open, but nothing major to report. Heard some talk of the provinces relaunching the attacks, but reckon they'll struggle to get the numbers to take those walls now that they've been rebuilt."

"They're going to get away with it," Xander muttered, her expression a blend of anger and sadness.

"Hard to tell," Dogner said, scratching his nose. "Too many unknowns."

"Isn't that the truth," Farland said. "The marauders have nothing to gain by occupying that city so far from home. And I think we've all gathered that home's a way away for them, given we'd not heard of them before now. But that means they're either just looking to sack the city and withdraw once the pillage is over, or they're going to use Borealis as a staging ground to take the rest of Anemoi. Whatever the case, Parliament better figure it out and commit now, or I can see this getting much worse."

Dogner glanced at Xander, aware the prospect was a frightening one.

"My apologies," Farland said, understanding Dogner's look.

"It's okay." She spoke, pleased they had included her in a conversation most tended to avoid around children.

Several calls came from behind Farland, and they turned to see Farland's fellow lumberjacks waving him over. One of the loggers subsequently pointed to a nearby tree and made a cutting motion.

"Looks like they found one!" Farland said excitedly. "Care to join?"

"And see you and the lads at work?" Dogner said with similar enthusiasm. "Of course!"

The three of them left the path and started for the group busily readying themselves to bring down their find. But as the team brought the giant hacksaw to the tree's bark, Xander abruptly stopped and peered into the forest from whence they had come.

"What is it?" Dogner asked as he and Farland also stopped.

"I—I thought I heard a voice," she responded confusedly.

"What did it say?" Farland asked cautiously.

"I'm not sure. But it wasn't happy."

The two men shot each other worried glances and immediately began calling to the group to stop. There was a brief moment of confusion amidst the lumberjacks, but they quickly got the warning and halted their work.

"Why are they stopping?" Xander said.

"Self-preservation, that's why," Farland remarked.

"Aye, that was no coincidence," Dogner added.

Farland lifted his arm and pointed into the distance. "That's all the confirmation I need."

"It's a deer," Xander said, her eyes bright with joy.

The muscular stag, with its crown of antlers and bronzed skin that almost seemed to sparkle under the sunrays, stood majestically amidst the trees as it looked directly at them. An eerie feeling took them all under its onslaught, and several of the men marked themselves superstitiously.

"I think we're done here," Farland said. "Plenty of trees back home that'll do." He turned back to his colleagues. "Pack up! We'll camp the night and head home on the morrow." He looked back to Dogner and Xander. "And let's hope we last the night."

"It's a warning, not a bad omen," Dogner said. "Just be sure to keep your hands to yourselves tomorrow, and I'm sure you'll be fine."

Farland nodded his understanding, then locked hands with Dogner. "I'll be seeing you around, old man. And you, little one," he said to Xander.

He turned around and marched to his men, and within a minute, they were off on their way, headed back towards their camp. Once the men were out of sight, the stag turned and cantered off into the forest.

"You really think that was a warning?" Xander asked as the pair stepped back onto the path.

"You tell me—you're the one that heard it."

"I don't know what I heard. It could've been the wind."

"What wind?" he said, holding his hand to the still air.

Baffled, she shrugged and pulled up beside him as he began along the path towards home.

"The forests don't always work the same as our world," he said. "You could've heard nothing, but sometimes you've just got to listen to your gut and go with it. And I think it's safe to say, in this instance, all of us felt a tad uneasy. Anyway, nothing to worry about. There are a couple hours till dark, and we'll have you back long before then. Oh! And that reminds me."

He reached into his pocket and pulled out a small wooden coin.

"What is it?" she asked.

"It's your gift. What? You thought I didn't get you anything?"

She jumped and hugged him.

"You're welcome," he managed through her grip.

She dropped back to the ground and examined it. "There's no writing, just a picture of a—"

"Shoe. Figured you could do with a new pair before your events."

They both peered down to the ones she wore and swiftly descended into laughter. Whilst they had been perfectly fine for use some five weeks prior, the rigorous training had worn the soles thin and completely damaged the toe area on the right one. So much so that her big toe now poked through.

"Anyway," he said once they had caught their breath. "Take it to the shoemaker, and he'll fit you for a new pair."

"Thank you, Dogner."

"It's alright, lass. Just be sure not to tell your aunt. Not that she'd mind me gifting you them, but I wouldn't want her to feel bad about not noticing the disrepair herself."

"Don't worry, I won't."

"Good lass."

CHAPTER 14

Augustx 16, 479; Nhata Bay, Borlencia; two days before the Ranclet—It was midmorning, and already the heat of summer had infiltrated the usually cool interior of Evia's cottage.

Xander was strewn on her bed with her new novel in hand. Despite the light gown she wore, she was uncomfortably hot, and although the air was still much drier than was typical, this hadn't stopped an army of sweat beads from forming between her skin and the bedsheets. A horribly cringey feeling she detested. She huffed in frustration. Her desire to finish the book was at growing odds with her need to seek out more bearable pastures.

She was again about to try and reread the page she had glossed over twice in her flustered daze when the trinket she had found under the City Temple of Borealis fell from its shelf onto the bed. She picked it up and ran her finger over the metallic skin that drew her gaze every time she strolled past it. Its origin was still a mystery, though this wasn't for a lack of trying to unravel it. Whether in the town's perpetually frigid library or the many antique shops she had frequented with Evia and Joseph, she was constantly trying to find something. It was an obsession not too dissimilar to her need to learn more on the Cresedi.

Spurred by the thought, her mind jumped to the refreshingly cool confines of the library's walls, and an idea sprung to mind. Excitedly, she slipped into her summer clothes and left the house.

The large stone building, with its tattered collection of books and picturesque spire, was in the centre of town and a fifteen-minute walk from home. Under less extreme temperatures, it was ordinarily a pleasant stroll through Nhata's quaint streets. Of course, today was anything but pleasant, and her clothes were damp by the time she arrived.

Unlike some of the older, poorly lit buildings in Nhata, the library was illuminated by tall windows and carried none of the stuffiness one would expect from a structure without decent ventilation.

"Xander." A short woman with rosy cheeks and round glasses greeted her. "It's been some time since I've seen you in here. I was starting to worry you'd lost interest like all the other little ones."

"Sorry. I'm always so tired when I'm done training."

"No need to apologise. Do tell, though, what are you training for?"

"The Ranclet."

The librarian giggled. "I see the heat's got to you, then. What could've possessed you to put your name down for that?"

Xander shrugged.

"Well, never mind," the woman said. "I take it you're here to escape the warmth? Your friend had the same idea. What's his name? Hemel."

"Hemish?"

"Yes, that's it. He's downstairs in the basement. Pretty sure he's just sleeping down there, mind you. Wait, would you do me a favour and take this down with you?" She passed Xander a tray of books. "Mind your back. Wouldn't want you to put it out before your race."

Unbothered by the weight of the cargo, Xander crossed the empty room and descended the narrow flight of stairs into the basement. The temperature was wonderfully frosty compared to outside and provided her with instant relief. She placed the tray on the table nearest the entrance and walked to the end of the candlelit room. As the librarian had suspected, Hemish was fast asleep on one of several thick wooden tables.

Not wanting to waste a perfectly good opportunity, she crept right up to him until she was inches from his face, then lightly grabbed his throat and growled like a dog. He sat upright in fright and let out a little squeal. She burst into laughter.

"Curse you, Xander!" he muttered. "I was having the best kind of dream, and you just had to spoil it."

"Oh yeah! What was it about?"

"Mind your business," he said playfully, and hopped off the table to the ground. "So what brings you down here? Come to catch a nap also?"

"You come to nap or to get away from your mother?"

"Both! And you?"

"Thought I could get away from the heat."

"And you're telling me you're not here for the, you know, history books you've read five dozen times already?"

She blushed. "No. Really, I'm not!"

"Guess we'll see how long you can resist." He put his hand into his bag and pulled out a handful of sweets. "Which one do you want? I've got those red sour ones you like and also some of the spicy mint jellies."

"You know how they make the jellies, right? They—"

He abruptly covered his ears. "I don't want to know. I'll not let you ruin these ones for me also."

Grinning, she took several of the red sour candies from his hand and put three of them in her mouth.

"These ones are strong, right?" he said as her face scrunched up.

"Could've told me that before I ate three!" she gasped, her eyes watery.

"Nope. This is more fun."

"Rascal."

She climbed onto the nearest table and sat with her back against the cold brick wall.

"How's the training coming along?" he asked as he jumped up and sat beside her.

"It's a rest day today. Dogner said it's important to give the body a chance to catch up. So we're not doing as much."

"You think you've done enough to beat the cretin?"

"I don't know. Maybe."

"What happened to all that confidence? I'm sure it'll be fine."

"Says the one that told me not to do it."

"I've been known to be wrong. Not often, but it does happen."

She laughed. "You're so—"

The table collapsed with a loud thump, causing them to sprawl on the ground.

"Oh no!" Hemish said with alarm as they scrambled up. "She's going to kill us."

They went quiet and listened out for the librarian's footsteps. Nothing.

He knelt down and tried to heft it up. "You going to help? What?"

He followed her gaze to a little drawer that had come loose. She bent over and opened it to reveal a worn parchment inside.

"What does it say?" he asked as she read it. "Well?"

Confused, she looked up and handed it to him.

"The handwriting's not exactly something to brag about," he scoffed.

"Just read it."

"Who's Marcus?"

"I don't know."

"And this is your Evia? The paper looks like it's a hundred years old."

She took it back from him and read it out loud:

"My dearest Evia. Time cannot erode that which cannot be eroded. Marcus."

"What an odd thing to say," Hemish said before popping another sweet into his mouth. "You should ask her about it. I don't know too many Evias around these parts. None, in fact."

"What have you done?" the librarian interrupted crossly. "I hope you'll be paying for that, the two of you. These tables are as old as this town and were a donation. They're priceless."

"Then how can you expect us to know how much they cost?" Hemish retorted smugly.

"Laugh now, but wait till I tell your mother, Hemel."

He held his tongue and looked to the floor.

"We're sorry." Xander spoke up. "We'll help you fix it. We really didn't mean to break it."

The librarian was about to rebuke them, but her soft spot for the girl held her in check. "I'm sure it was just an accident. If you can, ask your farmer friend, Dogner, if he can help." At that, she turned and left the room.

"That was close," Hemish muttered, relieved.

"You don't think she'll tell your mother?"

His face dropped. "I'm sure I'll know before the day's up. So you going to ask your aunt about that note?"

"How can I not?"

Though she was in no hurry, for she had no idea where her aunt was and had little desire to brave the uncomfortable temperature so soon. Sheltered in the basement, they spent most of the day laughing and sleeping and reading, emerging only when the librarian forced them out into the dying bustle of the town. The short walk home was more tolerable at that hour, and Xander arrived home to see the windows alive with candlelight.

"I trust your day went well?" Evia said as Xander entered.

Her aunt was tending a small pot on the stove, the unwanted warmth of which had already spread through much of the cottage's ground floor.

"I was in the library with Hemish."

"Ah! Exactly what any parent or guardian should hope to hear," she responded without looking up. "Though I imagine you've likely read most of the books in there that aren't too mundane."

"Evia?"

"Yes, dear."

"I found this. I think it might be yours."

Evia turned around, and Xander handed her the note. A sad smile crept onto Evia's face as she read it.

"Where did you find this?" she asked.

"It was in a drawer in one of the tables at the library."

Irritation took her. "All this time they were in one of those tables! I thought I'd never see this again. A good deed comes to haunt."

"Who's Marcus?"

"An old friend."

Xander waited for Evia to say something more, but her aunt turned back to the stove without a word. And though Xander couldn't see Evia's face, she suspected her aunt to be crying. A suspicion confirmed when Evia laid the table with bloodshot eyes.

"I'm sorry," Xander said after several awkward minutes of silence.

"For what?"

"For making you sad."

"Sad? You didn't make me sad, dear child. Quite the opposite, in fact."

"But you were crying."

"Yes, I was. I want to cry even now. But not because of you. I remember when Marcus gave me this note many, many years ago. It was the last time I saw him. And yes, it was a terribly sad day. But you bringing this back to me after what feels like an eternity, well, it gives me indescribable joy. Thank you, Xander. I mean it. Thank you."

"He must've been special."

"He was. But alas, not all things can or will endure forever."

"Who was he to you?"

There was hesitation in Evia's expression. "A colleague turned friend." She spoke carefully.

Xander knew there was more to it, and she desperately wanted to ask, but something told her Evia would divulge soon enough. So she left it, and they returned to eating quietly with the odd comment on the weather and school and life in general. A subdued evening quite unlike the surrealness of Xander's earlier find.

CHAPTER 15

Augustx 19, 479; Nhata Bay, Borlencia—Xander winced as she stretched her right arm. It was still tight from the tree climb the evening before, whereby each contestant had had to scale the tallest tree in Nhata's woods and retrieve one of the rare bluebells atop its crown. Beautifully vibrant flowers with a four-year growth cycle, and the reason for the competition's frequency. The tree climb was traditionally the first challenge in the series, and unlike the other challenges, it never changed, even when nature's gusts were rampant. And fortunately for them, the winds had been timid at best.

She relaxed her right arm and began to stretch the left. She stood at the northernmost edge of Nhata with Hemish, Evia, and Dogner by her side. There was a large throng of noisy people crowded around the four dozen contestants. She was the only girl, and one of only three challengers not an adult. She looked to Nicholas. He was laughing with his brother and seemed unbothered by the next event. Both of them had beaten Xander in the climb, and though Xander hadn't placed last, or fallen like several of the other competitors had, she still felt dismay at the prospect of him besting her again.

"Xander, concentrate!" Hemish interrupted her thoughts.

"I'm concentrating," she lied.

"Been some time since they've done this one," Dogner said sternly. "You'll not be the only one that has no idea where you're going. The exit changes every time they organise it. Just keep an eye out for the markers. They'll be infrequent, but if you come across one, you'll know you're on the right track. Main worry is whether you'll be able to handle the feeling of being trapped. It's a mind game, you see."

"It is a long time to be crouched underground," Evia said worriedly.

"And one of the lads was telling me they've made it extra difficult this year. Cornered off some of the easier routes, forcing the contestants to take the narrower tunnels. It'll be more convoluted than anything we've seen."

Though this added to Evia and Hemish's angst, Xander had ample experience scouring the tunnels underneath the City Temple and Parliament Palace in Borealis, so the thought of navigating the drainage channels and old mining shafts beneath tiny Nhata seemed somewhat thrilling.

She looked at Nicholas again and caught his scowl. She could feel his dislike for her oozing from him. Dislike that she now knew wasn't simply the result of her friendship with Hemish, but one born out of misplaced blame.

A call for the contestants to ready themselves rang out from the crowd, drawing her attention. Along with the men twice her size and the two brothers, she walked up to the start line. Ahead of them was the dark entrance to the labyrinth of tunnels etched into the slope of Nhata's foundations. It was an entrance too small for more than one man, though this mattered not, for they would be called up one at a time in the order they had placed the day before, with thirty-second intervals between each.

Cheers abounded as the first name was called, then the second and the third. By the time the announcer got to Xander, however, most of the crowd had already left for the designated exit, where they would drink and eat until the contestants emerged from the shadows. But this didn't stop Xander's supporters from hooting raucously as she approached the tunnel.

The dank, cool air hit her as soon as she entered and was a refreshing welcome from the irritably dry outdoors. The first tunnel, which was high enough to stand, was sparsely lit by the entrance behind her, allowing her to race through into the next. Slightly lower, the next was illuminated by a narrow drain leading to the street above, and again she made quick work of it. The next two weren't as forgiving, however. They were almost pitch black and required her to feel her way forward. Still, the excitement of crawling into the unknown was bountiful, and it only grew as she sped through them into the next series of tunnels that were just high enough for her to crouch.

From the onset she could hear murmurs and footsteps ahead of her, but it took a full fifteen minutes before she caught up to the next contestant. She couldn't see him, but she could hear his heavy breaths as she crawled forward.

"Who's that?" the frightened man said, startled by her approach.

She didn't recognise him. "It's Xander," she responded.

"Oh! The little girl. Ha! Guess it was inevitable."

"Why are you waiting?"

"Why do you think?"

"I don't know. I can't see, and you're in the way."

She heard shuffling from in front of her.

"Come see," the man said.

She crept forward until she could feel his warmth.

"See how small that is?" he said with a quiver.

She reached forward and ran her hand around the rim of the next tunnel. It was narrow enough to fit snugly around a grown man's chest and shoulders.

"Wait!" he said in a panic as she began to crawl into it. "You can't leave me."

She hesitated. "Follow me. I'll go slow enough for you to touch my feet."

"Heck no! I ain't going down there."

"Then I'm sorry," she said bluntly, determined not to lose her mother's jacket.

His pleas followed her as she descended into the space that had her on her belly and elbows. It was at a downward gradient, and it stretched a good fifty metres. And whilst she may have thought twice about traversing it under normal circumstances, up to this point, there had been no other passages than the ones she had followed, meaning every other contender in front of her had already passed through this one safely.

The tight squeeze became the norm as she negotiated uncomfortable squeeze after uncomfortable squeeze. And though no two tunnels were the same, she swiftly came to prefer the natural ones. Despite their often-difficult gradients and bumpy unlit surfaces, the earthy scents they carried were absolutely delicious when compared to the stench of sewage many of the man-made corridors offered.

Thirty minutes from the man too frightened to continue, she happened across her first fork. Five minutes later, her second fork. Fifteen minutes after that, a three-way split with her first marker and a sour odour to accompany. It was an odour that irritated the nose and clung to each of the three tunnels at her disposal. Eager to escape it, she climbed into the darkest of the three where the initial intensity seemed less, but it wasn't long before it became apparent that she had chosen wrong. Holding her nose to protect from the burn, she clambered forward awkwardly. But even more disgusting was the slime that carpeted the tunnel and stuck to her hands and knees. On the verge of gagging, she practically threw herself into the illuminated chamber at the end of the seemingly eternal tunnel, where a drain to the world above helped keep the pong at bay.

Keen to rid herself of the slime that was stuck to her hands and knees, she rubbed them roughly against the brick wall of the chamber. Somewhat cleaner, she pushed ahead into the abyss, each time taking the route that instinct seemed to suggest, though in truth she had no real concept of which direction she was headed in. Even Dogner's advice to imagine herself going in the direction of the exit—as if she were above ground—had proven completely useless within the first few minutes. By all indications, chance was her guide.

In one particularly close-fitting corridor, a full two hours after she had entered the maze, twenty minutes after she had passed her fourth fear-stricken competitor, and five minutes since her sixth fork and last marker, she was forced to a stop in a crumbling mining shaft. She came face-to-face with a barely visible man, and when she was unable to pass him, he informed her it was a dead end. Desperately hoping no one else would enter behind her, she began the crawl backwards. An awkward manoeuvre that put her on edge for the first time since she had entered the maze.

"That was a bit cosy around the chest, wasn't it?" the man remarked when they reached the dimly lit room with the fork. It was hardly large enough for them both to fit. His features were not too different from those of the desert people she had met in Borealis, and he had a deep scar stretching from his eye to his mouth. She figured him to be in his forties. "Been a while since I was down here, but reckon that's the one I was looking for," he said, pointing to the opening next to the one from which they had just emerged. Several voices echoed into the space. "Looks like someone's catching us up."

He casually turned and entered the opening. Keen to track someone who was comfortable with their whereabouts, she entered in after him. Despite the man's size, he navigated the confinement with ease. Silent but for the grunts of exertion, they pushed forward at pace and had passed at least half a dozen stranded men overcome by terror before the man hesitated and then stopped.

The corridor in which they had stopped was so constricting, Xander couldn't quite get her elbows under her or fully raise her head. The light was nonexistent, and breathing was difficult. Muffled sounds came from in front, but she couldn't make out anything. Suddenly the man tried to edge backwards, but as she tried to follow suit, she was stayed by a hand behind her.

She tried again. But still the person behind her wouldn't move. An uneasy feeling immediately wormed its way into her stomach. An aggressive feeling that compounded as two minutes dragged into five. And then five into twenty. Unable to shift and find reprieve for her increasingly sore elbows and neck, and unable to take a breath sufficient enough to satiate her lungs, a frightening dread was taking hold. Whispering and conniving against her internal implorations for calm. Eagerly encouraging her to writhe free and scream for help. It was a feeling absolutely unlike anything that had gripped her before, and it was rapidly dissolving whatever peace was once synonymous with her courting the dark, intricate catacombs under Borealis. Just as her last semblance of sanity readied to depart, the man in front began moving forward.

Her relief was overwhelming as she clambered after him. Twelve metres later, she tumbled into a sizeable chamber. It was illuminated by a drain overhead, and a hefty pile of broken bricks on the opposite end of the room seemed to partially block the only other way out. Inside the chamber, seven others waited, including Nicholas's brother. All were filthy. All carried a look of unease.

"The roof caved," one of the men said as Xander stood. He was topless and had an obscene tattoo on his chest. A marker was on the wall to his back. "We were trying to see if we could clear some of the debris when the end of the tunnel you just came from also collapsed."

Xander inadvertently peered back to the damaged tunnel from where she had come, and anger took her as she saw Nicholas's dirtied face emerging.

"Why didn't you let me out?" she asked furiously.

"Huh?" he said with a confused expression, dusting himself off. "Had no idea it was you in front of me. Couldn't see a thing."

"You did! You knew it was me, and you stopped me from getting out," she said, squaring up to him.

"Not the time, you two," the man with the tattoo said. He looked to Nicholas and the man that was emerging from behind Nicholas. "How many behind you?"

"No idea," Nicholas responded.

"One of you best go back and warn the others to hold off until we clear this rubble."

Nicholas didn't budge and instead just stared at the man that had appeared behind him.

"Alright, guess that'll be me," the man behind Nicholas said, irritated at the lack of respect from the teenager. He entered back into the damaged tunnel.

"The fall catch anyone?" the man with the scar asked worriedly.

"Couldn't tell ya," the man with the tattoo responded. "But we might have to accept we're not getting out this way." He pointed to a small hole in the pile of debris on the opposite end of the room. "It's the tunnel. But unless you can break your bones and squeeze through, it's not much use as is. We were trying—where you going, little girl?"

Xander ignored the question and approached the pile. The hole was uneven and slightly narrower than her shoulders, but she could just make out the room on the other side of it. She looked back to her onlookers, then to Nicholas, whose expression hovered between scowl and sneer. She still reeled internally from the fact that she had verged on sheer panic mere moments ago, but her determination to best the boy was fierce.

She turned back to the hole, made herself as narrow as she could, and then pushed her way into it.

"It's unstable!" one of the men called alarmedly.

But she disregarded the warning and continued to pull herself through, wincing as she scratched her arms and legs and body against the rough surface. The stretch of corridor was only ten metres, but on two occasions, she had to move rubble and dirt to create enough girth for her to fit through. Dust still hung heavy in the air, irritating her throat and eyes.

"I'm through!" she called back when in the next chamber.

Elated cheers greeted her, though she was pretty sure she could feel Nicholas's rage seeping through the debris.

The next series of tunnels was an easy feat, for the chatter and music of the congregation eager to crown a winner acted as a whispering guide as to which route to pursue. Glee took her as she exited the labyrinth into the open. Buoyed by raucous applause, and shielding her eyes from the painful light, she jogged clumsily to the finish line where Dogner, Hemish, and Evia rushed to hug her.

"You're first!" Hemish said joyfully.

"Who would've thought!" Dogner said, his relief evident. "And only a couple nicks and bruises, I see. Come on, tell us, how many poor souls did you leave in your wake that had gone mad?"

"Dogner," Evia scolded lightly.

"Oh, right!" Xander said, recalling the men left behind.

She walked up to one of the organisers who was drunkenly courting two pretty young women.

"One of the tunnels collapsed," Xander said worriedly. "The others can't get through. They're about ten minutes from the end. You need to send help."

The man shrugged. "It happens. We'll send someone in if they're not out within the hour." And at that, he turned back to his conversation, keen to entertain his admirers.

"They'll be fine," Evia said, having overheard. "Now let's get you fed and cleaned before the next event. Wouldn't want you getting an infection from all the filth down there."

▲ ▲ ▲

Xander peered around at the other twenty-three contestants that had also made it out of the tunnels within the allotted time. Unlike the morning event, it was just them and the race organisers positioned on Nhata's beach under the dying light of the evening sky. The rowdy audience was instead perched on the slopes of the torchlit town, looking down over the lake with drinks and food clasped greedily in their hands. Despite the encroaching dark, the dry heat hadn't subsided, and there wasn't a single person in sight that didn't long to cool off and wet their mouth.

Most of the contenders were still covered in filth, having not had an opportunity to wash after the last event, and all of them were knackered. Both Nicholas and his brother were there, as were the other men that had been stuck in the chamber. It had taken them a little while, but they had eventually cleared enough of the debris to squeeze through the damaged tunnel that had gifted Xander her lead.

"Gather round!" a race organiser bellowed.

Xander edged closer along with the others.

"It's been a while since we've done this one," the man shouted. "And I doubt there's one in the lot of ya that knows what to expect."

A mix of excited and concerned murmurs did the rounds, for despite Nhata's location on the water, not everybody knew how to swim, especially some of those from farther inland. And given where they currently stood, it didn't take someone in the know to figure out what was going to be expected of them. Still, Xander had heard that the swimming events were exceedingly rare for this reason alone.

"When the flag drops," the man continued, "you'll race out to the buoy—"

More grumblings abounded as they all looked out to the buoy some seventy metres from the beach.

"Hush! Okay, good. You'll race out to the buoy, and you'll dive—"

"Oh! Come on!" the man with the obscene tattoo yelled angrily. "You trying to drown us? What are you playing at?"

"My good man, if you'll please let me finish."

The man with the tattoo shook his head, his expression one of defeat.

The organiser cleared his throat. "You'll dive and grab a pebble. And we'll know if you've cheated. We've painted them pink. Anyway, with pebble in hand, you'll then race back to the shore and cross that line."

They turned around and took in the finish line at the top of the pebble beach where the stones were sharpest.

"You're having a laugh, you are!" another man yelled. "You're sick in the head."

"You're free to forfeit," the organiser said smugly. "Now find your marks!"

"Can you swim, little one?" the man with the scarred face asked Xander as he took the spot beside her. Scars riddled his bare upper body.

She nodded.

"Good," he responded. "Hold back and let this lot go first."

"But—"

"Trust me. It'll be like watching the lambs slaughter themselves."

"Okay."

"Friend of yours?"

She followed the man's gaze to Nicholas. Several places down, Nicholas was staring at Xander with his usual scorn. She looked away and focused on the water ahead.

"Guess that answers that," the man said.

"Ready!" the race organiser shouted, bringing the chatter to an abrupt stop. "Go!"

Instinctively, Xander was about to run as the majority of the group sprinted forward, but she quickly held herself in check as the scarred man had advised and settled for a gentle jog behind the pack. The decision proved sensible.

The mass of bodies in the shallows was more akin to a melee than anything resembling a finely synchronised school of fish. Those that couldn't swim were flaying their limbs wildly in all directions with some hope of finding traction, and those that could swim were kicking and pulling with brutal force in the hopes of catching the competition off guard.

Happy to avoid the scramble, Xander and the man entered the lake a few metres down. The water was warm, albeit refreshing, and both swiftly found their stride. Past the throng that hadn't fully dissipated, they were now behind approximately half the contestants.

The big man's comparative size saw him pull ahead of Xander initially, though she managed to keep pace once in his wake. Together they swam through the ache of their already fatigued limbs, braving the odd man eager to yank them back as they passed.

Sixty metres along, with the buoy in sight, Xander risked a glance ahead to see men rising from the lake bed with pink stones in their hands or empty-handed. Excitement took her, though as the pair approached the marker and the man dived down without any hesitation, Xander found herself unable to replicate the transition without first catching her breath.

She paused for a brief moment, then readied herself to make the dive. About to go under, Nicholas emerged from the depths a metre away with a pink pebble between his fingers.

"Good luck, runt!" he hissed between heaves, and pushed past her.

She abruptly dove into the water that had been obscured by the disturbed sediment on the lake floor. Two metres down, the big man with the scar brushed past her. Five metres down and she could feel the pressure on her ears and sinus. Six metres down and her hand hit the relatively cool floor. She grabbed a barely visible pink pebble and pushed off the lake bed, breaching the surface with a deep gasp for air.

She spotted Nicholas's mop of red hair some fifteen metres ahead. Frantic to catch him, she drove forward desperately, putting her all into her strokes with no thought to the exhaustion that would surely follow. To Nicholas's complete shock, and her own, she caught up to him as he sought to stand in the shallows.

Through the chaotic chop of the ruffled water, Xander reached down with her foot and gripped the coarse sediment between her toes. She pushed herself upright and began to wade after him, her legs wobbly and her lungs screaming for reprieve. She was a full metre behind him when she emerged fully from the lake water onto the uneven beach. Lugging one heavy leg after the other, she began her chase to the finish line some twenty metres ahead at the top of the incline.

Fifteen metres from the finish, where the rocks had begun their transition into sharp malicious toads determined to invoke agony, she reached level with Nicholas and could hear the roar of the crowd from the town above. Ten metres away and she was edging slightly ahead. Five metres away, an involuntary smile found her. She was going to do it. She was going to beat him. And then pain. The sharp, mocking pain of a jagged rock finding her knee as she collided with the ground, tripped by an unseen divot.

That was all the delay Nicholas needed. He stumbled past her as she tried to right herself, and he threw himself over the line, uncaring of the pain that awaited his reckless lunge. Greeted by the boy's gloating grin, Xander felt only numbness as she crossed the line.

"Nearly beat him," the man with the scar said, but Xander ignored the well-intentioned comment and headed straight for the stairs that led up to the main street.

"It's customary to wait until everybody finishes," Evia said as Xander reached the top.

Her aunt stood alone.

"I'm going to lose my mother's jacket," Xander whimpered, verging on tears.

"To the boy?"

"Yes," Xander said guiltily.

"A bet too far, perhaps?" Evia said, surprised by the revelation.

"I know. But I just want him to leave us alone. I thought I could beat him. That it'd all be okay for us after this."

Pity stole Evia's features. "You can still win."

"He's already won two events. He only needs one more."

"Then best put the doubt from your mind and get some rest for tomorrow. Give yourself a fresh chance. I know, easier said than done."

"Xander!" Hemish interrupted.

The pair looked up to see Hemish and Dogner, and somebody hidden behind them.

"Look who I found," the boy said excitedly, stepping to the side.

"Joseph," Xander murmured, her spirits lifting.

▲ ▲ ▲

Joseph's arrival had coincided with dinner, and though Evia had insisted they hover at the beach until the last of the contestants crossed the line or accepted defeat, it wasn't long before the five of them soon scuttled back to her cottage, where a cold fish broth awaited them. Armed with sliced bread, apple juice, and spoons, they chatted away in a joyous stupor as they tended the deliciously refreshing meal.

"What is it?" Xander asked after nearly choking on a mouthful too ambitious even for the likes of her.

"An aulos," Joseph said, passing her the wooden wind instrument. "No idea if it plays anymore, but I was able to get it for a cheap shilling in Zyphyr. I think it's maybe five hundred years old."

"Five hundred!" Hemish blurted.

"I'd say so, yeah. Look at the engravings. They depict one of the old western kingdoms, and the design itself is characteristic of that age."

"Who do you reckon the owner was?" Dogner asked curiously.

"Soldier, maybe. Doubt we'll ever know."

"It's been some time since I've seen one of those," Evia said. "May I?"

Evia took the instrument from Xander and began to examine it, testing its weight and running her fingers over its markings. And then she put it to her lips.

"I don't know if—" Joseph had begun when Evia blew into it.

A deep, mellow sound escaped the end.

"That was beautiful," Xander said, her eyes filling with awe.

Evia smiled and again blew into it, but this time she didn't stop. A calm ambience befell the room as she played a soothing song characterised by long notes and smooth transitions. It sounded almost ancient, as if from a time before theirs, and on several occasions, Xander felt her skin tighten in a spasm of goosebumps, entranced by the tune. So relaxing was the melody that by the time Evia blew her last note, they all struggled to keep their eyes open.

"Full of surprises, aren't you?" Dogner said softly.

"Like I said, it's been a while," Evia said, handing the instrument back to Joseph. "I'm sure I was a bit rusty."

"Rusty!" Joseph said in disbelief. "Doubt there's a soul in town that would agree after hearing that."

Xander yawned exhaustedly. "Enough to make me want to sleep, but in the best of ways."

Dogner chuckled. "A compliment if ever there was one."

"And a cue, I do believe," Evia said. "Finish up and get some sleep. All of you. We've got a long day tomorrow."

Xander stood up without any of the nerves that had plagued her in the aftermath of the swim, and she stretched long and hard. She was knackered, more so than usual, and in need of a good nap. "Thank you," she said to Evia, grateful to have heard a song with the power to quell her mind just as she craved it most.

"It was my pleasure."

▲ ▲ ▲

Despite the wholesome lullaby, Xander struggled for sleep, and after several hours of tossing and turning, she awoke with a start. The room was still dark with the night, and it took several groggy moments for her to realise she was no longer in dream world. Damp blanketed her sheets and pillow, and her head throbbed.

Thirsty, she reached for the glass of water on her nightstand and took a sip, but abruptly recoiled. Her throat was painfully swollen. Worried at the prospect, she clambered out of bed and knocked on Evia's door.

"Xander," Evia said, bleary-eyed. "What's wrong?"

"I think I'm sick."

Evia instinctively put her hand to Xander's forehead. "Feels like a temperature. Get into bed, and I'll be right back."

Xander did as her aunt said and crawled back under the covers. Several minutes later, Evia appeared with a candle and a small toolbox filled with her medical equipment.

"Open your mouth," she instructed Xander, and she positioned the light for a better view. "Well, that's not something you see every day."

"What is it?"

"I think you might have inhaled something you shouldn't have. Tell me, do you recall any odd smells from the tunnels this morning?"

"Lots. I was climbing through sewers and mine shafts."

"Of course. Then any that stand out from the stench of excrement?"

She blushed. "I don't think—wait, there was one. It was sour. And it burned my nostrils."

"Was the tunnel dark? I mean, really dark. So dark that nothing could possibly grow in there?"

"Yes."

"And the floor covered in a thin, sticky substance?"

"Yes!"

"Well then, I'd guess that you've accidentally inhaled parsley weed."

"Parsley?"

"Parsley weed. Parsley's drunk cousin. And known for making you feel like you've got a nasty cold and a hangover."

"Oh no! What about the race?"

"What about it?"

"How can I win feeling like this?"

Evia got up and left the room and returned with a glass filled with purple liquid. She handed it to Xander. "Drink this."

"But I can't swallow."

"Trust me."

Scared of the pain that would surely follow, Xander reluctantly swallowed a very small drop. Her face immediately brightened. "It's like cold water on a burn!"

"Less talk and more drinking."

The girl nodded and swiftly finished the soothing liquid. "My throat already feels better. But my head still hurts a bit."

"The medicine helps to dull the symptoms, but you'll still feel like you've gone several rounds with a bottle of wine. At least you might be able to get some sleep. We can check how you're feeling in the morning and take it from there."

"It's like I'm not meant to keep that jacket," Xander said glumly as she pulled the covers to her chin.

"Ah, yes! Someone or something is conspiring against you with the sole purpose of depriving you of your mother's jacket," Evia retorted light-heartedly.

"Don't be mean."

"I'll stop being mean when you stop being silly. Now sleep."

CHAPTER 16

Augustx 20, 479; Nhata Bay, Borlencia—Xander fell to her knees and dropped the heavy sack onto the hard ground. Her lungs burned from the dry heat, and her eyes stung from the streams of sweat she was unable to keep at bay. And whilst Evia's concoction had helped to subdue some of the parsley weed's more severe effects, she was struggling to keep up. Of course, she was luckier than the two other contestants who had been forced to quit after their interactions with the vile plant.

Exhausted, she looked down the steep slope she had just climbed. It was the last hill of the fourth event, and she was only halfway up it. She was in the middle of the pack and nearly spent, and now several of the men were gaining on her. And much to her fright, Nicholas, who had stormed ahead at the start, was nowhere to be seen.

She cursed as she stumbled to her feet. Her every urge screamed for her to sit back down and rest, but she couldn't. Not with her mother's jacket at stake. She took a deep breath, reached down, and picked up the sack that had been filled to weigh the same as she. A feat that had had the entire town cheering in awe at the start line some two kilometres back.

"Come on!" she seethed, blowing droplets of sweat into the air as she did. With what little energy she had, she forced herself forward until it almost felt like she was stumbling up the hill. Metres from the top, she glanced to the side as a much larger man pushed past her. It was the man with the scar. He murmured encouragement under his breath but didn't stop. Part of her was elated to see him, but her growing panic and fatigue still reigned dominant.

Completely drained, she rounded onto the flat a metre or so behind the man. Gaze locked on his broad shoulders as she pounded forward, she used his bulk as her windbreak just like Dogner had taught her. And though she couldn't see the finish line from behind him, the cheers of those waiting ahead lured her onwards until she saw the marked line cross under her feet.

She gasped and collapsed to the ground, her lungs heaving and her arms and legs barely able to keep her on all fours. Despite the ecstatic cries of a crowd mesmerised by a girl as young as her completing such a gruelling challenge, she felt none of their joy. From the corner of her eye, she could see Nicholas perched on his sack, looking at her with a chuffed, albeit tired, grin. He had beaten her again. Anger suddenly rushed through her, and she slammed her fists into the ground, fighting every impulse to approach him.

"It's okay, Xander," Evia's soft voice interrupted.

"There's nothing I can do now," she responded, her lips trembling.

Dogner emerged from beside Evia and helped Xander up. "If you place first in the next event, you may beat him yet," he said.

"He's right." Joseph spoke. Hemish was by his side. "You can beat him on points. But he'll need to come near to last."

"Not going to happen." Nicholas's conceited voice pierced their circle.

They turned around to see the boy stood with his brother. Both sported arrogant smiles.

"Push off!" Hemish growled.

"And miss the runt crying?" Nicholas taunted.

"Give it a rest, boy," Dogner said menacingly.

"Or what?" Nicholas retorted, but he quickly backed down from his threat as Dogner's irritation became clear. "Three events out of five. That's how many I've beaten you at. We never agreed to points. I'll be waiting for that jacket at the end of the next event. Don't forget it, runt." He wandered off with his brother.

"Cretin," Hemish said angrily.

"You've done well, little girl." It was the man with the scarred face. His brown skin was burnt and his cheeks sunken from dehydration. "Nearly collapsed myself, so to see you cross that line was quite the sight. You should be proud." He put his hand to his back and winced.

"You okay, lad?" Dogner asked.

"Think I've torn something."

"Let me have a look," Evia said.

The man waved his hand dismissively. "No, that's alright. A good lie down and a drink will fix it. Good luck, little girl," he said, and began to descend the hill.

"Wait, where are you going?" Xander asked. "The next race starts from here."

He turned around. "I'm done. It's been fun, but not worth breaking my body over."

"There's one race left. You're nearly there."

He smiled, buoyed by her grit, and then walked up to her and held out his hand. "The name's Santos."

She shook it. "Xander."

"You're a man of Nasdir?" Joseph spoke up.

"I am," Santos responded.

"But you speak like a Borlencian."

"Born in Nasdir. Raised in Crowton."

"Who would've thought."

"Who would've thought. Anyway, you have my blessings, Xander. And if you're ever in Crowton, just ask around for me. Not too many of my kind south of Borealis. That goes for all of you. Can never have too many friends."

"You'll not wait to see the winner?" Xander asked.

"I'm sure I'll hear about it before long. The Ranclet's famous, even as far north as Crowton."

At that, he turned away and headed back down the hill.

"He was so close," Joseph said, puzzled. "One more event and he would've completed it."

"The pain's far worse than he was letting on," Evia said as she peered after the man. "I wish he would've let me treat him. He'll be in for a rough ride back home."

"Look at how he carries himself," Dogner said. "The man's a soldier. I'm sure he's experienced worse."

"You can tell that just from how he carries himself?" Hemish queried, surprised.

"Absolutely—"

Dogner paused as the crowd suddenly erupted into cheers. Three men were running clumsily towards the line, each eager to beat the other. Metres from the end, one of them tripped and took the other down, allowing the third to cross ahead of them. As the last of the three crossed, one of the organisers waved his hand and signalled to the other directors to begin preparations for the next race.

"What about the others?" Hemish said.

"Likely quit," Dogner said, peering down the empty hill.

"Wow, that leaves only nine contenders still standing," Joseph observed. "Tell me, Xander, what if Nicholas doesn't complete the last race?"

"Ever heard the saying, 'grasping for logs'?" Hemish jibed.

"I have, but that doesn't answer my question."

"Then she wins, of course. And it's why she needs to complete it. But it won't happen."

He stroked his chin. "Was just a thought."

"With that in mind," Evia said, "let's get you some water and a light snack, Xander. And how's the head?"

Xander grumbled in pain.

"I was worried about that," Evia frowned.

It was early afternoon when Xander and the other contestants readied themselves along the same line they had crossed with their sacks in the earlier race. In the short time between events, the air had grown even more arid, hindering the ability of the contenders and onlookers to take full breaths, whilst a thick haze had crept across the sky, spurred by a strengthening breeze originating from the woods. Despite the reprieve from the sunrays, many coughed and sneezed as a result of the fine dust kicked up from the dried soil underfoot, and plenty worried about the implications for the racers.

Xander looked to her side and took in the boy standing beside her. Nicholas's ginger hair was matted, and his pasty cheeks were tired and dirty. He caught her staring.

"What?" he practically spat through that perpetual sneer of his.

She didn't say anything and just looked ahead.

"Thought so, runt," he hissed. "Not sure why you're even continuing. Might as well quit. I've got you beat. Ain't a chance I'm dropping out of this one. Too easy."

And to her own gloom, she agreed. A ten-kilometre race around the town. Even if he walked half of it, the chances of him not completing it were almost none. She sighed and looked around at the other competitors. Besides Nicholas and his brother, she didn't know any of them. They were an assortment of ages, and for the most part, they all seemed fit and strong. Doubt reared into her at even placing. She turned around and peered at Evia and the others.

"You can do it, Xander!" Hemish yelled suddenly, causing some of those nearby to flinch.

Her four supporters then cheered and were soon joined by swathes of the crowd who came to understand the target of the encouragement.

Xander inadvertently smiled, buoyed by the hail.

"It'll not help you," Nicholas muttered.

"Shut up," she retorted.

One of the organisers walked up to face the crowd and put his finger to his lip. It took a little while, but the rowdy crowd soon fell quiet.

"Contestants!" the organiser yelled. "Ten kilometres around the town. Follow the markers. Ready yourselves!"

Xander tensed and peered ahead to the pair of white birches standing guard over the path that would lead them into the woods and around the town and farms. She could feel Nicholas get into a crouch, eager to spring forward, for the path was narrow and would provide few opportunities for overtaking.

The organiser cupped his hands over his mouth. "Three! Two! One!"

Xander jumped into a sprint and garnered a head start on the older, less nimble challengers, though she lagged behind Nicholas, his brother, and a man in his twenties as they entered the woods. The hard ground was unforgiving on the feet, despite her new shoes, and the path on the other side of the birch guardians was marred by overgrown nettles and crooked roots peeking from the dirt. A tricky combination that kept her attention locked on the ground ahead.

But as the minutes dragged on and she passed the one-kilometre marker, she could feel the ache in her head compounding and her chest tightening. Evia's concoction was not enough to stem the effects of the parsley weed when coupled with the rigorous exertion of the run. Slowly but surely, she was losing speed, and Nicholas's silhouette was shrinking.

Distracted by the affliction and struggling to keep up, she didn't notice a thickset man gaining on her. As she rounded a bend and hopped over a fallen branch, she felt an arm grip her shoulder and shove her.

She tumbled into the bush with a crash and smacked her hand. Sheering pain shot through her finger, causing her to curse through gritted teeth. Still strewn in the dirt, two other sets of footsteps thudded past her uncaringly, and another one could be heard coming up the path. Unwilling to risk a glance at the damage to her finger, she climbed to her feet and rejoined the route.

But the pain was immense and worked only to amplify the gritty headache that had already taken hold. Akin to a nasty cocktail, anger surged through her like fuel at the unfairness of the situation, and it wasn't long before she was at war with both body and mind. Her willingness to fight on had been compromised.

Emerging onto a short but steep incline, her will gave out, and she came to a stop. "What's the point?" she thought. The jacket was lost, whether she finished or not. She balled her fists and screamed with furious frustration until the last of her impetus had been spent. Shoulders slumped, she started back towards the town, but had made it all of five metres when a lone lightning bolt shrieked through the sky and hit the forest a couple of hundred metres behind her in the direction she had been headed before resigning.

Curiosity immediately got the better of her, and she began towards the area of impact, though at no real speed. Ten metres along and a thin man in his mid-forties passed her, his pace slow but sure. Fifty metres along and the last of her competition, a heavy, muscular man with a long beard brushed past, leaving his sweaty stench to linger. It was then that Xander spotted a thin wisp of smoke rising to the sky like a winding grey pillar from where the bolt had hit.

"Fire," she blurted alarmedly, and was about to run and warn the town when a desperate cry for help caught her ear, stopping her still.

Another call abounded. It had come from the impact zone. Still on the path, she forced herself into a run towards the yells. Within metres of the source, she deviated into the bush and breached into a small grassy opening, where she could see clouds of smoke hurtling through the undergrowth as if blown from a pipe.

"Hello!" she called just as a brief gap opened in the wall of smoke, revealing for the first time the flames of a wildfire greedily consuming the arid forest around her.

"Help!"

A hand bristled from the long grass.

She rushed over and gasped, "It's you!"

Nicholas pointed to his leg, his brow and mouth creased with agony.

"It's broken," she uttered. "How?"

"Never mind, runt," he managed. "Just get me out of here."

She reached down, about to grab his hand, and then stopped. She straightened and stared at him with a cold, unforgiving expression, a look that was made all the more sinister by her sudden indifference to the deadly smoke creeping towards them. "If I continue the race and beat you, you'll not get my jacket."

His eyes widened in alarm. "Xander!" he spluttered.

She turned away from him and looked to the path that was on the verge of being cut off by the encroaching flames.

"Please!" Nicholas pleaded frantically. "I'll die if you don't help me. Please! Forget the jacket. It's yours. Please, you've—" A nearby tree with a rotten core collapsed into the undergrowth, knocking red-hot embers into the air.

She looked at him with the same frightening coldness. "Swear on it."

"I swear on it!"

Xander's relief was nearly too much, and she had to force herself to maintain the rigidly uncaring expression that had underpinned her ploy. For whilst she disliked the boy, she didn't wish to see him dead.

With a strength that surprised him, she knelt down, picked him up, and slung him over her shoulder, her physical and emotional injuries somewhat numbed by her fierce urgency to get to safety. It was an astonishing recovery that also had her in shock.

Unburdened by his weight or her own affliction, she rushed through the opening with the boy on her shoulder and jumped onto the path. Already the fire had spread through much of the surrounding forest, but the path remained intact for as far as she could see. Eager to beat its onslaught, she shuffled towards the town until there was a good two hundred metres between them and the lethal flames. Careful not to hit Nicholas's leg, she put him down and then helped him to stand whilst supporting his shoulder. Fear still stained his expression at the fact that she had been willing to leave him for dead.

"We can walk from here," she said emotionlessly.

He nodded, and together they clambered on. Though the fire moved quickly, they were able to keep some distance ahead of the flames but not the smoke, which rapidly dispersed through much of the forest in the direction of the town.

Some three hundred metres from the farm where they had started the race, Nicholas hacked violently into his hand. "We're not going to make it," he gasped, struggling to breathe.

Betraying her act, Xander shot him the same worried look, and though the thought to just leave him ever-so-lightly touched her mind, deep down she knew she couldn't live out her earlier threat. "We'll make it," she muttered, and urged him forward at a faster pace, unbothered by the pain it caused him.

But as they neared the farmland surrounding the town, and with a hundred metres of smoky forest path still left to conquer, they both collapsed to the ground in a fit of coughs. Their lungs had been singed, and a confusing haziness had taken hold.

Xander glanced back and spotted the faint flicker of orange and red through the heavy cloud of smoke that had enveloped them. Still she knew it was not the fire itself that would kill them, but the poisonous gas they inhaled with every breath. She looked down to Nicholas and squirmed. He was unconscious. Again the thought to just leave him and save herself crossed her mind, but she brushed it away.

An idea arose, and she clumsily pulled his shirt off and ripped it in two. She quickly wrapped the first piece over his mouth and the second over her own. Then, summoning whatever energy she could, she stood up, grabbed his arms, and began to drag him down the untamed path. Each metre brought with it a new scratch or violent cough, and on one occasion, Nicholas's bad leg caught on a root, requiring her to yank it free. And though the need to survive fuelled her relentlessness, it wasn't long before she was completely unable to open her irritated eyes, leaving her blind to navigate the route.

Metres from the white birch guardians, and oblivious to the open fields that offered reprieve, she fell to the ground in a bout of coughs. On all fours, she turned around and slumped over Nicholas, as if their entwinement could somehow protect them both from the poison entering their lungs or the wildfire racing towards them.

Struggling to stay awake and unable to muster the energy to even crawl, she opened her mouth and cried for help. A barely audible croak was all that escaped her chapped lips, and still she swore she could hear a voice calmly and clearly respond, "Speak, Xander."

She tried to open an eye but instantly flinched at the discomfort caused. Again she called out, and again the voice responded with the same words, as if the owner crouched beside her. She reached around frantically but could feel nothing other than Nicholas's prone body and the crumbly dirt path. It was an impossibility, she thought. A figment of her delirium. Their predicament wasn't even known to the town.

And before she knew it, the roar of the wildfire was upon them. She lay her head hopelessly on Nicholas's chest and again called out. But this time there was no verbal response. Her response came in the form of a pair of hands gripping her and Nicholas and then dragging them from the grasps of the hungry fire into the open air of the field.

CHAPTER 17

Septembrix 16, 479; Nhata Bay, Borlencia—Xander held in the cough that threatened to spill into a bout and looked to the teacher as he continued his uninteresting conversation on the importance of doing one's homework. Even though her eyes had rediscovered their clarity and her body its strength, her bound finger still throbbed painfully every now and then, and right now was one of those moments.

She reached into her bag and withdrew one of Evia's candies. Designed to numb the pain of broken bones, the effect was always instantaneous. About to pop it into her mouth, she caught Mr Porky staring at her from the door. But what usually would have spurred a reprimand or look of disapproval simply garnered her a slight nod of the head. Permission granted, she tossed the chewy candy into her mouth and, too lazy to bite down, swallowed it whole.

The throb in her finger disappeared, and even her lungs seemed to loosen. She breathed in relief and then glanced to the back of the classroom. Nicholas was there, his leg in plaster and his uncovered limbs still carrying the scabs of their survival. He looked at her, and though he didn't scowl or mutter a curse, he didn't smile. He simply ignored her and turned his head back to the teacher. A consequence of her victory that caused her no discomfort.

She had earned his and the town's silent respect and had retained her jacket in the process.

She glanced at Hemish, with his ruffled sandy hair and unblemished cheeks. He caught her looking, and a joyful simper stretched across his face. He had spent countless days by her side during her recovery and had made sure to deliver her homework daily without fail, much to her annoyance. The thought warmed her.

In the minutes before Xander and Nicholas had been pulled out, the town had been made aware of the wildfire. Not by those still lingering at the start line, however, but by Evia. From the bottom of the hill, she, too, had spotted the lightning bolt strike the forest, and her intimate knowledge of the hazards of arid woods had pushed her to immediately raise the alarm.

Still, it had taken two days for the wildfire to be tamed, and though Nhata itself had been saved from the brunt, some of the settlements submerged within the woods hadn't been so lucky. Men and women from all the surrounding towns had marched and ridden to the devastated areas in a bid to control the flames and protect their brethren's homes, but alas, it was nature's shower that had eventually quelled the lethal flames.

Much of the nearby forest had been scorched, and even now, thin wisps of smoke still climbed into the sky. To many, the scene resembled the fields of the underworld, where they presumed those who had lived a life of poor deeds were destined to spend their afterlife eating and drinking dust, forever unable to find the comforts of the living. A silly notion to Xander, but one she had been taught to respect nonetheless.

Though Xander and Evia insisted the lone lightning bolt had been the cause, rumours had circulated that maybe one of the contestants had started the fire. The townsmen, in their fervour, eventually laid the blame on the man that had thrown Xander into the bush and, as it had turned out, broken Nicholas's leg as he stopped to tie his shoelace. It was an accusation so heinous that the man had been left little choice but to leave the town and county under the cover of darkness, never to return.

Sitting back in a slouch, Xander unconsciously sighed a peaceful sigh. Whether it was Evia's medicine or the certainty that she had vanquished her schoolyard foe, she didn't know, but she felt some semblance of peace as the teacher droned on about his point of irrelevance. She still didn't know who had spoken to her as she slumped on Nicholas's chest. The general consensus was that it had been her own mind trying in vain to keep her awake, but despite the contrarian evidence, she was unconvinced.

CHAPTER 18

Marx 11, 476; Ricard's vineyard; ten kilometres south of Borealis, Borlencia; six months before the fall of Borealis—Xander knelt down and stroked the hunting hound she had taken a liking to, with its shaggy brown-and-white coat and its crooked tail, broken on some previous excursion. In its excitement it licked her mouth, and she immediately recoiled with a laugh.

"Careful," Ricard said as he prepped his horse. "No telling where that mouth's been."

"It's okay," Xander said, standing up.

"I was talking to the dog," he said with a grin.

"Hey!"

She stifled an aggressive yawn and then stretched as she took in the small field of bare vines overlooked by the rear patio of Ricard's weekend villa. Though the hour was early and the morning frost still lingered, both she and Ricard wore light gear in preparation for the day's ride. And she could barely contain her excitement for the day ahead. An opportunity to hunt, or at least witness a hunt that entailed more than a meagre rabbit or squirrel.

Voices emanated from the villa, and she turned to see Carolus, Alya, and Lawrence exiting onto the rear patio with mulled wine in their hands.

"You sure you don't want to join?" Carolus asked Alya. His guilt at leaving her alone was evident.

"And miss out on a day of quiet with just me and my book? I'd have to be mad."

"Not every day we're in the sticks."

"Not every day I'm without responsibility," she chimed. "Plus I've got the sounds of nature to keep me company."

"Can't hear much of anything at the moment," Lawrence said. "I think even the critters are sleeping in."

"Be that as it may, I'm decided. So Ricard, where are you taking my world today?"

Ricard clasped the final strap on his horse's saddle and turned to them excitedly. "There's a small pond a couple of kilometres from here. It's at the end of a dry ravine with scree slopes on either side. Sometimes if you catch the critters off guard, they spook and trap themselves on the wrong side."

"That doesn't sound fair," Xander uttered suddenly.

"And chasing them through the woods until they tire out is?" Lawrence said, eyebrow raised.

She puffed her chest defiantly. "At least they have a chance."

"She's right." Carolus spoke up. "Not that we're doing this for sport, but any way we can give them a fighting chance, Ricard?" Carolus turned and winked at Xander. She beamed happily in response.

Ricard scratched his silvery beard as he peered into the distance. "There's some dense woodland to the east of here. Can usually find a buck or two scouring it. We should get moving, though. Will take us a solid ninety to get there."

"Goat or deer?" Lawrence asked.

"Both."

Carolus glanced at Xander. His original reluctance to bring her was still obvious to the rest of them, but there was no doubt that he was also excited for what she would learn. "Okay, but anything too big to handle, and we turn back."

The big man looked at him as if insulted by the suggestion that he'd had any involvement in the decision to take the girl. "Of course!"

Horses and hounds ready, the four of them departed the villa and skirted along the edges of vineyards and villas belonging to some of Borealis's wealthiest families, most vastly larger than Ricard's quaint affair. Thirty minutes along, they deviated into the nearby forest that was riddled with pines and bristly shrubs. For though Borealis's northern boundary bordered the Ignis Desert, and thus was no stranger to the harsh elements often bestowed by such a hostile environment, the land immediately south of the city's wall was teeming with woods and arable land. A blessing courtesy of the river born from the Mountains of Ouran to the east.

Like a winding root, the hefty body of water descended from the snow-capped mountaintops and meandered westerly through the otherwise arid plains situated to the east of Borealis. Piercing the heart of the city, the river then joined with the North Bantou Sea, or as the locals liked to call the immense sea, Borealis's western wall. The river was a natural barrier to the slow, sandy creep of the Ignis Desert and a lifeline to the fertile grounds to the south.

Amidst the trees imbued by the cool morning breeze, they rode uninterrupted for an hour, jesting and storytelling, until an oddity stopped Ricard still.

"What is it?" Xander asked of the face-like marking etched into the tree in front of them. It was a rectangle with two circles carved into the upper half and what looked like a horseshoe carved into its centre.

"A warning," Ricard muttered warily. "Well, a shrine, but can't say any good usually comes from their sightings."

"Anything to worry about?" Carolus asked cautiously.

Ricard glanced around before looking to Carolus. "It's probably fine. Could've been here for months. No way to tell."

"The hounds don't seem too bothered," Lawrence said, and they peered to the pack of six lounging lazily on a bed of pine needles, their leads slack.

"What's it a shrine for?" Xander asked.

"Shepherds." Lawrence brought his horse close to the tree and pointed to the shape in the centre.

"It's a horseshoe."

"No, it's a rod. Pretty formidable weapon when the owner knows how to use it."

"Keen eye," Ricard remarked. "They cross through these woods into the pastures to the north and south of here. The grass isn't great, but it does the job. Anyhow, some of the nuttier shepherds carve these into the trees to ward off the nasty spirits that supposedly lurk in the woods and pick off their flocks."

"They think it's the spirits that eat their sheep?" Xander said, shocked.

"They think the spirits inhabit the woodland critters and make them do it. It's a silly superstition, but like I said, these ones aren't quite right in the head. Anyway, the bastards have been known to lash out at folks like us after a heavy loss, incorrectly assuming the spirits have taken ahold of our minds."

Xander was about to say something, but not quite able to grasp the apparent lunacy, she went quiet.

Carolus cleared his throat whilst subtly readying his hunting spear, a weapon Xander still wished they had allowed her to also carry. "Then let us hope the spirits have been behaving." At that, he nudged his mount into a trot, and the others swiftly joined him along the path, leaving the peculiar marking to itself.

As Ricard had promised, the forest was much thicker as they neared their intended destination. Brambles littered the undergrowth and bare rock the ground underneath. And though the morning had dragged on, the breeze still carried its late-winter chill. They were no longer on the trodden path, instead cautiously stalking a narrow strip of stone unhindered by the vegetation.

"Droppings," Ricard said excitedly, just as one of the hounds perked up and approached round droplets of excrement strewn across the rock in front of him.

Suddenly the other hounds also came to. Their backs were rigid and their tails alert. Well trained, they didn't bark.

"They're onto something," Ricard said quietly as he, Carolus, and Lawrence readied their spears.

Again Xander felt excluded without a tool of the gruesome trade. Granted, it would have been an unwieldy instrument in her petite hands. And then, as children so often do when deprived of opportunity, she began to imagine herself carrying a bow and arrow, fearsome like the famed archers known for turning a battle with their shot alone. She smiled at the thought but abruptly peered into the undergrowth ahead, where a rustle sounded.

The hounds, clearly eager to be let loose, quietly tugged on their leads. But just as Carolus was about to climb off his horse and untie them, Ricard motioned for him to stay still.

Effortlessly, the big silvery man positioned his spear on his shoulder and, within a breath, launched it two dozen metres into the bush from whence the sound had come. The spear landed with a thud and the briefest of squeals before whatever had been hit slumped to the ground in silence.

"Take the right," Ricard called to Carolus. "And careful. Might not be dead."

Carolus nodded in acknowledgement, though having done this many dozens of times throughout his life, he needed no instruction. He pulled up to the right of the bush, and Ricard took the left. Slowly, with spears lowered, they edged forward on their mounts. Both siblings tensed as the two men drew near, but to Xander's unacquainted eyes in particular, the tension was unbearable. Suddenly aware that she had been holding her breath, she forced herself to loosen her grip on the reins and breathe out.

Ricard roared, startling the lot of them, though it wasn't a bellow of fear or anger but one of joyous celebration. He dismounted and bade them to come forward as he parted the bush. Xander visibly cringed. It was a muscular male goat with impressive horns, and the spear had torn right into its chest.

"Poor thing," she whispered as Ricard hopped to the ground for a closer look.

"Has to be three hundred pounds," Ricard marvelled.

"It'll last you a week then, I'd guess," Lawrence jibed.

"Be nice," he retorted as he drew his knife and cut the critter's throat. "Will be a pain getting it back, but we've got plenty of light left."

It took them a good forty minutes to build a gurney sturdy enough to hold the buck's weight. Though dragged by two of the mounts, every now and then, they had to shift it or assist in hefting it around obstacles or up awkward slopes. A pain, as Ricard had said, but not one that could consume an entire day. To Alya's surprise, they were back at the villa by midday.

"Quite the size, isn't it?" she remarked to Ricard as Lawrence, Xander, and Carolus headed to the stables to clean and feed the mounts and hounds.

"Certainly is," Ricard said proudly, unable to take his gaze from the win.

"And I assume you'll be doing the honours of skinning it and preparing the meat?"

He peered up at her with the same insulted expression he had shown Carolus earlier. "Tell me, woman, have I done something to displease you and your husband? First the child. Now the goat. Why in Anemoi wouldn't I prepare the bloody thing? I'm not going to let it rot here, and I'm certainly not going to let my guest do it, if that's what you're insinuating. Now take that bottom of yours into the pantry and fetch me a wine." He winked at her as she humorously feigned disbelief.

Ricard opted to smoke the majority of the meat to ensure it would keep, but for that afternoon, he selected five tender cuts to be thrown on the grill. Protected from the cold by an outdoor firepit and copious amounts of spiked wine and warmed cider, the group spent the afternoon reminiscing as they stared over Ricard's vineyard.

And though Xander enjoyed the banter and the stories and the deep conversations on current affairs, she couldn't shake the feeling of guilt she had for the buck's abrupt end. A guilt that was amplified when she took a bite of the meat after it was served up. Of course, Xander's preoccupation hadn't gone unnoticed, and just as the sun sought to set and Ricard stumbled inside to retrieve more firewood, Alya put her hand to Xander's right arm.

"Are you okay?" Alya asked softly.

Xander nodded.

"I don't believe you," Alya said, pulling Xander in close.

"I feel bad," she finally managed.

"For the goat?"

Lawrence and Carolus stopped their conversation and looked to the pair.

"Yes," she responded quietly. "It didn't harm us, and we still killed it."

"To eat, not for fun," Lawrence said.

"I know." She shrugged. "I still feel bad."

"You've hunted rabbit before. What's the difference between the two?" he asked curiously.

"I guess I feel bad for the rabbits as well."

"You know, you don't have to eat meat," Alya said. "There are plenty of people that don't. But sometimes you'll find it's all you can get that'll keep you strong."

Xander sighed. "I don't think I'll stop. But I still feel guilty."

"I know the feeling," Lawrence said, glancing at Carolus. "The same thing happened to me after my first hunt."

"Is that so?" Carolus asked, surprised.

"Yep. Fortunately, the guilt lessens with time—"

A loud crash emanated from the patio, causing them to jump out of their seats. It was Ricard. In his drunken state, he had fallen down the patio steps and dropped a bin of chopped firewood onto the ground.

Lawrence chuckled. "Always the entrance!"

"Absolutely!" Ricard said, standing up. "So you going to help me?"

"Me?"

"No, your father. Of course you."

Lawrence stood up and began to help the large man gather the logs whilst Carolus pulled up close to Xander's other side.

"It was a clean kill," Carolus said. "The buck was lucky to see a quick end, and for that we should be grateful."

Xander took a sip of her cider and forced a smile. "I am grateful. And I know sometimes we need to do certain things even if we don't want to. Things that need to be done. I just…"

"You're just still coming to terms with it, that's all," Alya said.

Carolus pulled Xander in close and hugged her. "Every day brings with it a new slate, and often with that slate, a lesson that'll teach you something about yourself. Something that'll stick with you for all your years, even if you don't act on it. Today was one of those days for you, Xander."

CHAPTER 19

Julyx 9, 480; Talum, Borlencia—Perched on the front bench of Joseph's cart, Xander leant back in search of as much comfort as her thin cushion could provide, and she soon lost herself in the rolling landscape of green-and-yellow grasses that was, every so often, choked up by a scorched field or abandoned farmstead, the still-lonely remnants of the battle tactics that had befallen the region several years prior.

To her side, Hemish lounged in a lethargic coma of his own, and behind them, Evia and Joseph chatted away. And though the pair's conversation was for the most part unintelligible, the sound of Evia's voice on that particular day irked Xander.

A shallow sigh escaped her lips and caught Hemish's attention, but being a tad brighter than the usual scrawny village boy, he knew better than to ask.

Determined not to let her distaste for her aunt's unusual chores taint the day, Xander wished the thought from her mind and instead focused on the soothing charm of Joseph's voice and the excited howls of a group of riders kicking up yellow dust on the next field along.

But as the kilometres dragged on, a cocktail of boredom and uncomfortable afternoon heat soon wreaked havoc on her ability to remain awake, and it was Hemish's rude interruption that roused her from the stupor. Initially disorientated, she felt her threatening expression quickly dissipate as she followed his pointed finger towards the yellow dust clouds that hovered above the colourful town ahead.

▲ ▲ ▲

"Phew!" Hemish muttered in disgust and waved his hand in front of his face. "Was that the horse or the owner?"

"Whatever it was, it nearly made me keel," Xander retorted, brushing the dust from her hair.

Joseph had just bitten into a chunk of chewy meat skewered on a stick when a group of dusty townsmen barged through the four of them and knocked it to the ground of the crowded street, a melting pot of riders, hagglers, tourists, horses, cattle, dung, and rubbish.

"Talum's a lot filthier than I remember," he said, amused by the mishap.

"Don't recall there being so many drunks either," Evia added, unimpressed by the rider thrown off his horse whilst reaching for another's jug of wine.

"I wonder…has the essence of dung always been a key feature of this horse festival that you two so greatly hyped up?" Hemish laughed.

Evia chuckled. "Careful, you. I'm tempted to say that standards have dropped since the last festival several years back."

Xander looked towards the cattle ring at the end of the street, where a swell of people crowded the fence. "Well, hopefully the entertainment lives up to expectations," she said with excited anticipation, the chorus of cheers a charmer for the hairs on her neck.

▲ ▲ ▲

The rider expertly dodged the lobbed spear as he turned his horse. His features were sharp and tanned, and he bore a thick scar on his cheek. He drew his sabre and charged the assailant, flicking rocks and sand into the rowdy spectators. He swiped viciously at his young opponent's pale neck but was kept in check by the opposing sabre. A flurry of successive swipes and parries hastily followed, until one particularly aggressive swing knocked the sabre clean from the young man's hand.

Defenceless, the young one cowered as the man with the scar paused and a menacing grin crept across his face. Surprise took the young man as his scarred opponent simply relaxed and nodded, content with the outcome of the spar. "Thank you!" he muttered harshly and led his horse from the ring.

"Wow, that was intense!" Hemish said over the rumble of the crowd. "I thought the pale one was done for, never mind the rules."

Xander ignored his observation. Preoccupied by the ferocity of the fight and the distant memory of loss it had invoked, she turned away to glimpse her aunt's inquisitive stare, concern etched in the woman's eyes.

"Are you okay, Xander?"

"I think so. Just a bit unwell all of a sudden."

"Oh dear. Let me take a look," she said softly, and put her hand on the girl's shoulder.

"No, I'm fine. I just need a bit of space. The press of the crowd is a bit much," she said, and pulled away from her aunt's touch. "I'll be over there for a few minutes." She pointed to the nearest side street.

"I'll come with," Hemish offered quickly.

"No, it's okay. I just need a moment."

Xander slumped against the stone wall of the nearest townhouse. The street was quiet but for a couple of beggars harassing a group of tourists and the muffled cheers from farther down the street.

A couple of riders strode past with their horses on the reins and stopped in front of a white building with large black gates and a green door to the side. A scruffy rider strolled out and ushered them through the gates. He returned to his stoop, only to walk out again and shove one of the tourists who had ventured too close.

In a moment of hilarity, the tourist spewed profanity at the man and then sprinted down the street with the scruffy rider narrowly behind. In need of distraction, she made for the now-unguarded door.

The heat of the branding fire in the entrance hall prickled her skin, and the smell of animal waste hung heavy in the air. To the left, she spotted the inside of the black gates, and it looked like the hall ahead contained a network of paddocks and aisles. As she drifted through the maze of dimly lit enclosures, stone and straw underfoot, she could hear muffled laughter, cruel and feverish in nature, accompanied every so often by a whimper. Careful in her step so as not to spook the horses and cattle, she drifted towards the sound.

Deep inside, she spotted shadows dancing against the wall at the end of one of the aisles. She counted four or five in total.

"What you doing?" Hemish whispered, making her jump.

"Damn, Hemish! Keep your voice down," she retorted, irritated more so by the fact that he had sneaked up on her undiscovered than by the fright.

"I reckon we should leave this place before your aunt skins us both," he cautioned, and grabbed her arm.

A loud cry emanated from ahead, followed by more hysterical laughter and cheers.

"Let go!" she whispered, and started along the paddock wall and out of his grip.

They had neared the corner where the shadows danced when another pain-filled cry tingled their blood.

"We have to do something," she said.

Indecision clearly tore at Hemish for the briefest of moments before he nodded in agreement. "Let's open the stable gates and create a distraction."

She returned the cheeky smile. Hidden by the shadows, they made their way through the different aisles and opened the paddock doors as they went, all the time wary not to disturb the animals.

"Now what?"

"Now we create chaos," he said mischievously. "Wait here."

Gone for a moment, Hemish reappeared from the entrance hall with an orange branding iron.

"That's just as cruel," she protested softly.

"Don't worry. I'm not going to harm the animals. Head over to the black gates. When I give the signal, open them." He vanished back into the maze of paddocks.

"Wait, what's the signal?" she called quietly after him, but he was out of earshot.

About to pursue, she stopped and shuddered at the wicked sensation boring into the back of her skull. She turned slowly towards the entrance hall, and her vision locked on the scruffy rider, who stared at her. An imagined pleasure seeped from him, and the lick of his lips told all.

"I'm gonna enjoy this," he choked, the struggle to contain himself obvious in his awkward approach.

She edged back, her expression one of shock and disgust at the act to be committed. "Back off!" she stammered, but her revulsion worked only to amplify his lust and feed his desire to control and hold dominion over her.

Several times her size, he attempted to backhand her, but her speed left him dumb and clumsy. Again he tried to hit her, and again she ducked.

"You're a little irritation, aren't you?" He scowled. The stench of his breath lingered in the air. He started for her again but stopped as commotion emanated from the maze, and surprise and confusion quickly stole across his face. "You little bastard. What've you done?" he spat, and stumbled past her to investigate.

The sudden onslaught of hooves from the end of the aisle very nearly trampled the rider as he jumped to the side. Xander turned and sprinted through the entrance hall towards the gates, and only seconds ahead of the charge, she used all her weight to push the gates open and throw herself out of harm's way. With an unimpeded exit, the stampede reverberated with renewed vigour, and a chorus of curses soon ensued as the other men gave chase into the street.

She turned back to the rider, but he had vanished. She hurriedly unhooked a branding iron from the firepit and proceeded into the maze, searching each aisle and set of paddocks in search of Hemish or the ruffian. At the corner where the men's shadows had danced against the wall, she spotted Hemish's lone figure strewn across the ground, his face pale and his arm bruised.

"Hemish!" she whispered from afar, still wary of the evil threat that lurked.

No response.

She approached him cautiously and tugged his shirt. "Hemish!"

"Ouch!" he muttered. He clutched his arm and tried to rise. "Well, as fun as that was, I think it's time to get out of here."

"Hold on. I need to make sure whoever it was got out okay. Wait here."

"As if I'm going anywhere with you," he quipped in agony.

Xander edged forward with the branding iron still in hand and glimpsed around the corner. The yellow eyes that stared back were wrought with fear, and a profound sadness swiftly overcame her at what she saw. She approached slowly so as not to startle the poor creature, but her attempt to walk gently was met with the horrid noise of her boots on the fragments of mangled antlers and blood strewn across the floor.

"That there's a bronze deer," a voice muttered from behind as she rested her hand on the young stag's neck. The antlers on the frightened deer's right side had been clumsily sawn off.

Both of them stiffened at the sound of the rider's voice, and she turned to face him with hatred and fierceness etched in her expression. He held Hemish's limp body by the arm, and he still wore the same wicked grin as before.

"Usually, we just gut them and sell their fur for a hefty price. They're incredibly rare, you see. But it's even rarer to catch one so young, and a stag at that. No, this one we want to break. Could make a nice pet for some aristocrat." He sneered menacingly. "And now it's your turn!"

He threw Hemish to the floor and started towards her with a club in hand. But he had barely raised his weapon when Xander swung the branding iron and knocked him flat to the ground with a crack to the head that would make a seasoned warrior cringe. He quivered as he desperately tried to right himself, his body suddenly unresponsive.

"Help me! Please, I beg you, I didn't mean to," he spluttered pathetically at the unexpected change in fortune.

She stepped up to the lump as blood pooled on the stone floor. She felt no pity for this man, only a desire to remove the scourge from existence, this cretin who knew only brutality and wickedness. Silently and without emotion, she raised the iron.

"Xander!" Evia bellowed.

She looked up to see her aunt and Joseph, watching in stunned disbelief.

"He must not get away with this," she cried, and readied the iron.

"He won't. He's already passing. He hasn't long left," Evia responded.

The rider began to struggle for air. Evia walked towards the man, placed her hand over his face, and whispered something under her breath. His head lolled and his eyes closed, the heave of his chest now only a shallow murmur.

She turned to the constrained stag, oblivious to the shock of the others, and the same profound sadness took her expression. "Aes, my dear, what have these monsters done to you?" She rested her hand on his neck, released the chains with another whisper, and smiled as he struggled to his feet. "Come, let us leave this wretched den."

CHAPTER 20

Xander cringed as Hemish began his third humorous recount of his inability to dodge a pregnant mare back in the stable, and she subtly sought out a seat on the other side of the moving cart from which to admire the passing horizon and avoid the sight of his bruised arm and face.

And still, the boy's chuckle and the tread of Aes's laboured steps as he trotted behind the vehicle gratingly pierced the silent company of the unusually bright moon and stars clustered above the plains and the nearing forest. She sighed, burdened by the guilt searing through her every vein like fiery acid. Desperately wishing the journey to be over, it was some relief when Evia spoke.

"Stop the cart, Joseph, and wait here with Hemish. We'll only be a moment."

She beckoned the girl and stag to follow, and Joseph simply nodded without protest, aware Evia was more than she had previously let on. They glided through the crisp moonlit ambience of the undergrowth, and Xander stared after the woman who radiated tranquillity. It was a combination at odds with what she knew of her aunt, and one that aroused both mesmerisation and confusion at the strange turn of events. It was a strangeness compounded by Aes's awkward gait and the joyous hum and whispers that seemed to follow his bronzed glow through the forest.

She looked at his mangled head and squirmed. She felt anger for the man she had killed, but even worse was the guilt she felt for taking his life.

"Be at peace, my child. You feel guilt for an action that was deserved," Evia said softly from ahead. "Do not destroy yourself over vanquished evil."

"What right did I have to take his life?" the girl responded quietly.

"Your right was born out of necessity."

"But…I wanted to end it. I wanted to see him pass!" She trembled. "The same way I want to end the men who killed my parents and burned Borealis, the same men who murdered thousands of innocents and have still not answered for their crimes," she cried as her mind jumped to the memories of her childhood, long ago warped into a mesh of darkness and torment.

Evia embraced Xander and spoke with measured softness. "You will find that your drive to mend the unjustness of this world will grow as you witness all the horror there is to witness. This is inevitable. But I ask you now, do not let this drive become rage, for it will consume you and all you love."

As they stood intertwined, Evia's heartbeat thumped hard against her own. Xander had known love once, but the concept seemed foreign and unwelcome, and yet for the first time in a long time, she felt it. She felt it for the woman who held her, and though she did not know if it was Evia's unique abilities or the serenity of the forest, she felt a weak semblance of peace that she desperately wanted to remain. Aes, who watched from afar, sensed the girl's struggle and instinctively wandered over and placed his muzzle on Xander's shoulder.

Though Xander could have happily remained clasped between the two, she gently pulled away and looked into Evia's eyes. "How did you do that in the stable?"

"I would say a story for another time," Evia responded. "But perhaps now is as good a time as any, given the forest in which we stand."

"The forest?"

"A forest without reserve, that might teach a lesson or two. Listen, Xander. What do you hear?"

"What do you mean?"

"What do you hear?"

"The breeze. You breathing. Aes breathing."

"And?"

"…nothing."

"Don't think, just listen."

Xander's face scrunched with frustration, and she closed her eyes. "I hear…" Her expression brightened with excitement. "Voices. Some whisper. Some sing. The same I heard earlier as we were walking. There must be a village nearby."

"No village."

"Then what?"

"Look around you. What do you see?"

Xander lifted a confused eyebrow.

"Well?" Evia asked.

"Trees, plants, fireflies. Lots of fireflies."

"So?"

"That's not possible!"

"Who else would it be?"

"So I've finally gone mad?"

Evia laughed. "No, you haven't. But the trees and the plants and the forest critters surely would if they couldn't talk to one another, rooted for so long as they are."

"And what are they saying?"

"They're happy to see Aes. They were worried for him."

The thought jogged a memory, and Xander's mouth slowly opened in shock as a dot was joined and then another and another.

"What?" Evia asked curiously. "Ah, this isn't a first."

Excitement began to course through Xander. "It's not. It's not the first time I've heard whispers in the woods that I had to try and explain away. But how are they able to talk? How am I able to hear them?"

"Humans aren't the only ones capable of communicating with one another. Whether we like to think it possible or not, all the animals and plants and trees can speak and sing and jest. They can even mourn. And you don't have to be a sky-whisperer to hear their song—someone that can hear and communicate with others without a spoken word."

Xander immediately thought back to the woman outside the refugee camp that had known her name without her providing it. She had initially put it down to not remembering she had told the woman, but now she figured otherwise.

"It takes an opened mind for us humans to understand that we are not the only ones capable of communication," Evia said. "And it takes an opened mind to understand that not all is as it seems in this world."

She held out her hand and faced her palm upwards. Xander gasped as a cluster of leaves lifted from the dirt and drifted into the space between them.

"How are you doing that?"

"I'm manipulating the energy that binds our reality."

"You can see the energy?"

"I can feel it."

Xander instinctively waved her hand under the cluster of leaves.

Evia laughed and then let the cluster collapse to the dirt. "The abilities are…odd. You can't just pick them up. In almost every recorded instance, the person was born with either or both. Though it is uncommon for someone to be both a sky-whisperer and an energy manipulator."

"What causes the abilities?"

"We don't know exactly. But think of it as an exceedingly, exceedingly rare anomaly—or spark—in our anatomy that arises at random and can, on very rare occasions, be passed from parent to child. If a person has the spark and becomes aware of it, they can train their abilities to become stronger and more efficient, but most won't get further than being able to shift a pair of dice or hear the odd random thought."

"So how do I know if I've got the spark?"

Pity stole Evia's features. "Having an opened mind, as you've clearly demonstrated, isn't enough on its own. And sadly, I've not seen or felt anything to suggest you can or will ever have the ability to manipulate energy, nor toy with another's mind. Your mind just doesn't flare like that of someone with the spark."

Glumness took the girl.

"But who's to say! And even so, it doesn't make you any less extraordinary," Evia continued warmly. "Take solace in the knowledge that you've only just begun to understand and explore a world most will never have the fortune to glimpse."

"Seems unfair."

"I know, but—"

"Seems unfair that you can hear my thoughts, but I can't hear yours."

"Ah! Well, interestingly, I can't actually hear yours. Not that I've pried!"

"Really?"

"Really. I can feel your wanted and unwanted emotions as they come and go, but not your thoughts. Just because a person is a sky-whisperer doesn't automatically mean they can speak into everybody's mind or hear everybody's thoughts. Granted, it's rare—well, very rare—that I've come across somebody I can't glimpse. You just happen to be one of those unique individuals."

"I guess that's kind of special."

"It is."

"Still not fair."

"No, I guess not."

Xander was quiet as they continued on, and though her guilt had subsided, she felt both glee and dismay at the discovery of a world she might never truly be able to dive into. Weighed down by the thought, she quickly lost count of the minutes that passed after that, and it wasn't until she felt a gentle gust of wind part her hair that she knew they were near to wherever her aunt was leading them. Then, from the forest edge, she took in the dark-green grass of the vast meadow that swayed in the cool breeze, the hum of the thick forest enclosure that was hypnotic, and the shallow pool of water that rippled in the moonlight. Tranquillity enveloped her, and moments later, her mouth dropped in awe at the bronze glow that emerged from the depth of the tree line on the opposite side.

"They're beautiful!" Xander said as the herd of bronze deer cantered to the water's edge and swallowed Aes in an emotional reunion. The largest of the herd looked similar in appearance to the one she had seen with Dogner and the lumberjacks, just north of Nhata.

"And very rare."

"Because of the hunters?"

"To an extent, yes, but much of their home has been cut down over the centuries to make room for farmland and settlements. These forests are some of the last in the valley that can support a herd of their size. For how long, though, I don't know. Look, Aes approaches."

The stag walked to the pair and softly nudged them both with his nose.

"You're very welcome!" Xander said before he turned and hobbled back into the forest with his herd.

"Cheer up! You'll see him again."

"I hope so."

"You will. Now, let us head back to the cart before Hemish becomes the death of Joseph."

CHAPTER 21

Aprix 4, 483; Nhata Bay, Borlencia—"Xander!"
She sat up at the interruption, her eyes bleary and her mouth dry from the slumber. Though her groggy mind was still stuck somewhere between dream world and reality, only her aunt's kitchen could produce such a wonderful array of aromas, and she felt an involuntary smile creep across her face at the goodies that awaited her downstairs.

"Xander!" her aunt bellowed again. "Get that derrière out of bed and come help with breakfast."

"I'm up!"

Snug in her nightgown, she swung her feet from under the duvet and into the cold morning air, and she had very nearly crawled back into the warmth of her bed when the delicious aromas continued their onslaught.

At the age of fifteen, Xander was already taller than most Borlencian women, and she carried a lean, athletic build, courtesy of Dogner's training regime. Somewhat belatedly for a town attuned to hard labour, however, the soft cheeks of her childhood had only recently begun their transition into the sharp, angular features that would define her adulthood.

Careful not to step on the mess of books and maps that littered the floor, she exhaled deeply and took in the trinket on the wall that she had discovered all those years ago in Borealis, a morning ritual if ever there was one. And whilst her free time still tended towards the research of its origins, more often than not, she found herself absorbed in the discovery of Anemoi's history and its government as well as her collection of relics accumulated over the years.

"Can you fetch some eggs from the pantry?" Evia asked as she reached the kitchen.

The pantry was always stuffed with an overwhelming assortment of tasty edibles, but today there were no eggs, and she suspected Evia already knew. "I guess we're overdue collecting them. I'll head into town and pick some up."

Wrapped up in her green jacket to protect against the chill, Xander observed the families tending to their gardens over the morning frost and producing delicious breakfasts through their crooked kitchen windows as she wandered the path to the market. Not a shy face in sight, the villagers greeted her with smiles and waves.

"Xander! So nice to see you on this fine chilly morning," Hemish called from behind. "Off on another reckless adventure, are we?"

"How wonderful to see you too! And I'm surprised your mother let you out without an escort."

"Ah, game of straws to see who had to go buy the eggs. I lost!"

"Ha! You and me both. Come on, let's get this over with. I'm starting to get a chill."

He grinned at her, his eyes mischievous, then burst into a sprint towards the market in the hopes of besting her in a race, but she was too quick, and his lead was swiftly overtaken as she pounded by and left him staring at her backside for the remainder of the distance.

"Xander!" Dogner beckoned from behind a stall decorated with an assortment of local and foreign meats as they clambered through the crowd of shoppers from near and far. "What can I do for the two of you?" he asked cheerfully.

"Eggs, Dogner. We need eggs," Hemish responded.

"Eggs, aye, well I have plenty of those today." He looked at Xander and reached his gigantic hands over two boxes of them. "I was down at Etlinga Village yesterday, and I bumped into Joseph. Says he has some new trinkets if you want to head down one of these days. Said he'll save the best for you."

She beamed. "Sounds great, doesn't it, Hemish?"

"Yeah, huh, what? You know I can't just get up and leave. I have chores and other things that need my attention," he responded hesitantly.

"Things? By 'things,' do you mean you're too afraid to ask permission from your mother?" she retorted, and she and Dogner keeled over with laughter.

He sighed in defeat. "Okay, I'll try. I have only you to thank for her transformation into an impossibly overbearing mother. You know, she still threatens to kill me for Talum. So with that in mind, be sure to call the village constable if you don't hear back by lunch."

"You'll be fine. My aunt can fix you right up if there's any mishap."

Hemish straightened his back awkwardly, his grin gone. "I think that'll be quite all right. Best leave your aunt and her foul-tasting remedies out of this. Death actually sounds rather fitting, now that you mention it," he said with a straight face to their laughter.

⚞ ⚞ ⚞

"Wait, so the book says Borealis isn't called the Rose of Anemoi for the reason we've all been taught since birth?" Hemish asked sceptically. He jumped from a fallen tree, nearly twisting his ankle.

"The book says that whilst Borealis is called the Rose of Anemoi because people see it as the capital of Anemoi and because of the city's contribution in the Revolutionary Wars, it was actually given the name because of the desert rose that grows in the mountains nearby," Xander explained excitedly, still bloated and uncomfortable from the feast her aunt had prepared for breakfast.

"Ah!" He leapt over a shallow puddle and nearly slipped into the mud on the other side. "Sounds odd!"

"The city's emblem is a desert rose, so maybe there's some truth to it."

"I guess. So you ever seen one?"

"What?"

"A desert rose?"

"No, just on the emblem and in some historical books. My father and I used to search for them, but it's been years since anybody's seen one."

"Overharvesting?"

"Huh?"

"You know, when people get a tad greedy and pick too much of something. Happened in Nhata as well. There used to be this beautiful yellow flower, a bit like a dandelion, that grew around the forest edge. Anyway, some out-of-towners got a bit greedy, picked all there was to pick, and spoiled it for the rest of us," he said, irritated.

"Ha! Putantis used to say something similar. Might be the case with the desert rose. He did tell me that the last time anybody saw it was during the Revolutionary Wars."

"Long bloody time, that." He laughed.

They walked in silence for several moments, the sounds of the forest and the breach of the sun through the canopy shadows euphoric to the senses.

"You think you'll ever go back to Borealis?" he asked hesitantly.

"I don't know. If we ever get back to the city, then maybe," she said solemnly, though in truth she knew the chance for retribution would be enough for her to risk the army that stood behind its walls. "You think your mother will ever let you move out?" she retorted cheekily, to his dismay.

▲ ▲ ▲

Xander adored the enchantment of Etlinga, the village that snuggled into the forest. The crooked rooftops and chimneys. The stone bridges that arched over the glistening stream interwoven with the cottages. The ambience of the trees that swallowed the perimeter. And, more than anything, the magical combination of the moonlight and fireflies during the nights.

"I see a lot has changed since we were last here," Hemish said sarcastically of the overly friendly inhabitants.

She chuckled.

Despite the wisps of white smoke that breathed through the chimney, Xander's gentle rap on Joseph's door fell on deaf ears. Nobody was home. "I don't see his pony either. We can ask the villagers."

Back at the garden fence, the front door creaked open, and a small red face peered from behind it.

"Look, it's Joseph Jr.—or is it Joseph Jr. Jr.? Either way, not so odd a name, given the creativity of these village folk," Hemish said with a foolish grin.

"Joseph! Is your father home? What about your mother? Is it just you and your brother at home?"

Hesitant at first, the boy quietly responded, "Mother's in the next town, and Father's gone to the watermill to crush grains…but he left before dawn. He should be back by now."

"How do we get to the mill? We'll go look for him." She smiled, both as reassurance for the boy and the predicament she had just created for Hemish.

"Xander?" Hemish whispered, pulling her to the side. "I'm not sure this is such a good idea. We don't know where the mill is, and I'm sure Joseph will be back sooner or later. Let's just wait here with the boys."

"Come on, it'll be fun. Plus I have yet to see the inside of a watermill."

Her dangerous green eyes broke his resolve. "Okay, let's get a move on before it gets too late to head back. Otherwise, I hold you fully responsible for my disappearance," he said with a mixture of amusement and genuine concern.

▲ ▲ ▲

"We left Etlinga an hour ago and still no field," Hemish muttered in frustration.

Only a short distance from the village, the woods were already much thicker and darker than either of them had thought possible, and except for some hoofprints, the path they trod was covered in bramble and weeds.

Then, as if on cue, they spotted an opening in the darkness of the undergrowth. It took a moment for their eyes to adjust—a throughway into a sunlit meadow. The meadow was boxed in on all sides, and the mill stood on the other side of a river seemingly born out of the bramble, reachable only by a lone stone bridge.

"Well, that's creepy," he blurted out at the ominous stone building staring back at them.

The mill's steep roof was weathered and tattered, its windows obscured. But what unsettled them most was the torn binding of Joseph's pony strewn in the grass.

"This isn't good." Xander spoke worriedly.

"I think we should leave this place. This doesn't feel right," Hemish whispered, and edged away from the building's chilly shadow.

"We should at least look inside, make sure he isn't hurt. You heard the boy. It's not like Joseph to be gone so long. Come on!" she said sternly, and opened the door.

He cursed under his breath.

The room was cold and dark, the light of day scarce but for a single ray peeking through the attic window. The wooden gears of the mill dominated much of the room, and crushed grains lay in the corner closest to the door.

"Look!" Hemish pointed to a wooden trapdoor at the farthest corner. "Footprints in the dust."

"This is comforting," he said, lifting a broken piece of what looked like an unusually thick broom handle.

Xander tried to shift the trapdoor open. "It won't budge."

Hemish also tried, but no luck. "Look, I really think we should go back to the village and try for help," he said sheepishly, aware of Xander's growing irritation at his reluctance to remain.

"Leave if you want! I'm staying till I figure it out."

He nodded, content to remain quiet until she gave up.

She crouched and eyed the moving gears. Joseph wouldn't have left the grains, she concluded, and the pony's binder wasn't undone—it was torn. Something must have spooked her. She glanced at a stationary wooden gear that protruded from the wall, hinged out of place.

"How odd!" she whispered. "Help me with this."

They moved the gear back into place, and it caught one of the moving gears. Noisily the trapdoor opened, but barely had a moment passed before it closed and the gear unhinged.

"He must've tried to keep it open," Hemish said, eying the splintered wood.

"Let's find something sturdier."

Minutes later, Hemish reentered with a thick branch. Xander put the gear back into place, and he lodged the thick branch between the opened trapdoor and the floor.

"Again, I think the word for this is 'creepy,'" he whispered nervously as they peered through the trapdoor, down a vertical shaft the length of two fully grown men, and into a dimly lit room.

In spite of Hemish's silent protest, Xander stepped onto the metal ladder knocked into the length of the shaft and descended into the room below. Carved out by natural light from the adjoining tunnel, it reeked of mouldy air and earth.

"I found the other end of the wooden handle," she called, and picked up half of a lumberjack's axe. "Not surprised it broke," she observed of the wooden handle that was manky and rotten where it had snapped.

Provoked by an unsettling sensation that gripped them both, she readied the axe head. Huddled together, they continued down a seemingly infinite number of identical corridors and rooms, all illuminated by narrow open-air shafts connected to the surface and all breached by tree roots that protruded through the mossy walls and ceilings.

"What is that?" Hemish said in disgust as they entered another corridor, and he desperately tried to cover his face from the putrid, acidic stench that stung their nostrils.

"Nothing good," Xander choked, and she, too, plugged her face, the desire to gag at the vileness overwhelming.

Ahead of them was the only door in the complex they had happened across. She twisted the door latch, cold against her skin, and nudged it open. The room was far larger than the previous ones and was illuminated by a large circular opening in the centre of the ceiling, the forest above marginally visible. Water dripped profusely into an equally large pit of soil directly underneath.

"I don't see him," Hemish whispered.

"Look!" She pointed at the soil, some cloth barely visible underneath. "Is that him?"

"Get behind me," he said, and stepped protectively in front of her.

Together they edged forward, eyes intent on the horizon. Crouching low, he reached out to the muddied cloth, but just as he tugged it, the soil shifted, and a thick vine burst out of the softness and knocked him into Xander, the force enough to take them both down. They scrambled to their feet and backed up to the wall, the wooded snake kept at bay by the axe alone.

"What in Anemoi is that?" Hemish muttered in shock.

Drawn to the harshness of his voice, the vine whipped at him again, but Xander swiftly deflected the blow with the wedge of the axe, the force enough to numb her hand.

"It's so fast!" she said quietly.

Patterned in a web of pale-red-and-green stripes, it swayed from side to side, its attention completely focused on the intrusion. They tensed as the rest of the creature clumsily clambered out of the pit.

"Well, that isn't something you see every day," he whispered.

Frighteningly similar to a spider, the thick vine was carried by a dozen roots more akin to long, slimy tentacles, and it wore a crown of straggly branches that were just as chilling as the body itself.

"Pass the axe," Hemish said quietly, reaching his hand out. "I'll distract it while you pull Joseph out."

She raised an eyebrow.

"What?" he said.

"Was wondering where your manhood had gone." She carefully passed him the weapon.

He ran and called to the creature as he banged the axe against the wall. The vine turned towards him and spat a series of sharp projectiles, one of which he took in the neck, felling him.

Xander stopped and stood motionless, the drum of her heart and the draw of her breath rapid. But the creature remained stationary, listening intently for her whereabouts.

"Over here!" Hemish managed.

The creature turned and darted towards the interruption, with Xander close behind. It viciously threw the boy against the wall, but that provided all the distraction she needed. She picked up the axe and landed it deep into the base of the vine, the screech of the creature primeval. It whipped towards her, but she agilely rolled to the side and swung again at the first infliction. Again and again, she swung until her arms burned and the cries of the creature had long fallen silent in a tangled mess of white liquid splayed across the moss-covered floor.

Exhausted and weak, she turned wearily to the low grumble emanating from the pit.

"Joseph!" She crawled over as he attempted to pull himself out, and she tugged him the rest of the way. "What just happened?" She breathed heavily.

"Xander, I kid you not when I say I have absolutely no clue. First time I've seen any of this. The trapdoor, the tunnels, that bloody thing," he responded groggily, hunched on all fours and dazed with confusion. They looked to Hemish as he groaned. "Guess we should help the boy."

"The creature shot him with something, then threw him pretty hard against the wall."

They turned Hemish gently onto his back, and he winced in pain. Joseph retrieved the black dart from Hemish's neck and placed it next to one he held in his hand. "Same thing that caught me."

"You kept it?"

"How else am I meant to identify it? Anyway, I wouldn't worry too much about it. I think it's just a sedative…but that—that might be a problem," he said worriedly about the blood on Hemish's skull. "We need to take him to your aunt. She'll be able to mend him."

But on their way out, Xander found herself suddenly entranced by the pit in the middle of the room. Something she was not meant to leave behind beckoned her still. Then she glimpsed it. Obscured and partially hidden, the dirty rag blended in with the soil of the pit.

"Xander! We don't have time for this," Joseph called, but her curious mind was suddenly oblivious to the urgency of the situation.

She approached the pit and carefully withdrew the dank cloth. Her eyes widened, and her mouth dropped at the worn leather gauntlets that fell to the ground, the broadleaf of her family's legacy etched into the material and an ancient parchment inside revealed.

▲ ▲ ▲

Xander wiped the tears from her eyes and stifled another involuntary sob. Slumped in the stairwell of Evia's cottage, she was absolutely spent.

The race to get Hemish back to Nhata had been brutal in every sense.

It had taken her and Joseph an hour to simply get the boy back to the surface, and then another two to get him back to Etlinga. Bruised and knackered, the pair had cried for help as soon as they were within earshot of the settlement. And though the villagers' eager hearts had seen the three of them on the road in minutes, with a borrowed cart and Etlinga's only nurse to accompany, nightfall was the group's unwitting partner as they breached Nhata's perimeter.

A distressingly slow journey, defined by the curious whispers of the forest and Hemish's grunts as he drifted in and out of sleep. But as infuriating as the maddeningly sluggish pace was to Xander, the nurse's evident worry, revealed every time the woman turned from the boy's line of sight, was much, much worse.

Now collapsed on the stairwell in a pitiful heap, Xander was sandwiched between the stern conversation emanating from the study, where Evia, the nurse, and Nhata's doctor worked on Hemish, and the sound of Joseph doing his best to stop the boy's mother from barging down the door and "rescuing" her son.

Guilt overwhelmed Xander. The kind that burns one's innards, permitting one to do all in one's power to rectify a wrong. Hemish's mother would see to it that he never set foot in the sun again. Xander knew that much. She knew it was why he'd had little desire to venture beyond Etlinga that morning. And yet she, his friend, had forced him to brave his mother's unreasonable wrath. She sighed. Any warmth she had felt from before they had come across that cursed watermill was vanquished, as was that tiniest glimmer of excitement she had felt from rescuing Joseph and unearthing the gauntlets.

It had taken six hours for them to stop the bleeding. And though Evia was confident of the prognosis, none of them slept easy once comfortable they could let slip their guard. For the next week, Hemish slept in Xander's bed, and both Evia and the nurse took turns sleeping beside him. Despite Xander's silent protests, Evia had allowed Hemish's mother to take her own room. The living room had been set up for the rest of them, Xander included.

And though Hemish's recovery was surprisingly speedy, as evidenced by his quips come day five, his mother's rage had not diminished. Xander was given little opportunity to see Hemish alone, and as soon as the boy was able to walk unassisted, he was whisked off back home.

Weeks passed with Xander unable to see him or get a word out of his mother as to his well-being. And it was only when Evia sat her down in the living room with a solemn expression that realisation dawned.

"Where's she sending him?" Xander asked before Evia could say anything.

Her aunt looked taken aback.

Xander shrugged, her feelings numb from all the crying. "His mother's been threatening it for a long time. I kind of thought he was joking, but it's pretty clear now that he wasn't."

Evia frowned. "I'm sorry, Xander. I truly am."

"So, where? I'm guessing far enough away that I won't be able to find him. Ah! Let me guess, she told you not to tell me?"

"No. That's not it."

"Then where?"

"Can I trust you won't try and find him?"

"I'm a fifteen-year-old girl. What do you expect me to do? Use the five shillings under my pillow to charter a cart or boat or horse to go find him?"

Evia paused for a moment and then spoke: "You're a resourceful girl, Xander. I don't doubt you'll find out some way or another, so it's my hope that you don't act on what I'm about to tell you. He's gone to the province of Notencia to join his uncle."

"To do what?" she said irritably.

"The family business."

"Figures," she said, looking to the ground.

"Xander—"

Xander stood up and walked out of the room, determined to flee before the tears could start again. As she passed the study door, she glimpsed the gauntlet and unrolled parchment strewn across her aunt's table. On several occasions, to distract from her guilt, she had sat down in an attempt to figure out what exactly both were, but she had never gotten further than stroking the broadleaf carved into the gauntlet or running her finger over the blank, discoloured paper that had left her confused as to its purpose when she first opened it.

"And this time would be no different," she thought, and made for her bed.

CHAPTER 22

Marx 27, 476; Borealis, Borlencia; five months before the fall of Borealis—Xander woke with a start, beckoned by her full bladder. She managed to open one of her eyes, but the second was sealed shut by the light gunk that sometimes crusted over in the night. Through her one gem, she could glean that the moon was still at full mast, its soft glow reflecting from the neighbour's pale-yellow walls into her bedroom.

She crawled from the warmth of her duvet and started for the door, careful not to stub a toe on the army of toys littered across the floor. Not wanting to wake the house, she gently opened the door, but rather than be greeted by a lifeless hall, she was met by the warm flicker of candlelight coming from her parents' bedroom. A closer approach revealed soft chatter. Hidden in the hallway, she crouched by their door and began to eavesdrop.

"Seems a bit far-fetched, don't you think?" Carolus said. "Hard to imagine she's capable of that."

"You don't think there's some truth to it?" Alya asked.

"That she's the reason the bodies of young, mutilated girls have been appearing all over Zyphyr? You really think a senior minister would risk everything for a cruel obsession?"

"She has the power. The resources. Why not? If anybody could get away with it, she could. I know it's why you insist we keep it from—"

"Alya—"

"You're clouded by the fact that she's your relation."

"Relation?" Xander whispered in confusion, though swiftly put it to the back of her mind as the pair continued talking.

"Alya, it's a rumour at this point. A rumour started by two exhausted maids likely over her demanding attitude. I know the woman, and she *can* be a lot. What better way to get revenge on her than start a rumour that'll ruin her reputation?"

"And what about the accident? It was horrific. We all heard as much. But you can't tell me it's a coincidence that it happens to one of the maids so soon after—"

"I did not take you for a gossip. Unless you've got evidence to the contrary—"

Xander let slip the cough she had been trying to hold captive, and seconds later Carolus appeared at the door.

"Bit late, don't you think?" he asked.

"I was going to the bathroom," Xander retorted.

He grinned. "Which is in the other direction."

"And then I saw you were both awake, so I thought I would come say hi," she lied.

"Well?"

"Hi!" she said, and swiftly turned around and scurried to the bathroom, though she could feel her father's gaze following her until she closed the door.

CHAPTER 23

Augustx 10, 484; Nhata Bay, Borlencia—A chill traversed Evia's spine as the cold bit through her cloak. The absence of cloud cover had allowed the moonlight to escape the night sky and illuminate the forest floor below, but the absence of the clouds had also allowed the heat of the ground to escape into the atmosphere above. She blew into her hands in search of reprieve and studied the road again for his whereabouts. It was unlike him to be late, and a hint of worry began to take hold.

She glanced towards a rustle in the bushes. "Trust you to sneak up on me," she said to the shadow that emerged from the thicket.

"I had to be sure."

"What, that I wasn't followed? Or that I'm me?" She laughed.

"Both," Joseph said, and stepped onto the moonlit trail.

"She's asleep, and I am me. At least I was the last time I checked."

"Good to know. Unlike Xander, isn't it? Thought she only sleeps in, never at night?"

"And you? Were you followed?"

"I want to say no, but I can't be sure. It's not good, Evia. The rumours are true about Carolus's sister. Erzse has taken near absolute authority in Zyphyr and the province of Zylencia and has dispatched the garrison up and down the lakeshore north of here…Borlencia is quickly coming under siege. Her soldiers have blocked off roads and settlements and have enforced curfews in some of the larger towns. It's just a matter of time before they reach Nhata," he said solemnly.

"So she's taken advantage of Borealis's occupation and used the lapse in oversight to consolidate power in her province and now ours."

"The Borlencians should've rebuilt their parliament as soon as Borealis fell, but the idiots were too damn concerned with which town would host, and they never got around to actually electing the damn officials. Now with the other two provinces in turmoil, Zyphyr has been presented an opportunity to expand the settlements directly under its control. Erzse and her cronies need resources and people to support their aspirations—"

"And what better way than to commandeer that which isn't secured? How long have we got?"

"A week, maybe two. Some of the settlements just north of here have shown their teeth, so Erzse's armies are in the process of subduing the resistance."

She sighed again and looked up to the stars. "Does Erzse know Xander lives?"

He looked at her long and hard. "She can't stay here, Evia. You said it yourself all those years ago. Your trick to make visitors forgetful of the girl's identity as soon as they leave the area is effective because of Nhata's low foot traffic. How can it be enough once that army reaches our borders and you're dealing with hundreds of soldiers? Even if you ignore the fact that Erzse may not find out that Xander lives by word of mouth, the woman has strange…tastes. Xander would be safer if she remained out of that witch's reach."

"Do you have to use that word?" Evia balked.

"Well, I can't really think of another way to describe your abilities other than to refer to the old fairy tales. Anyway, there are good witches and bad witches in those old stories. You're the former, I think."

They both peered into the shadows as the wind whistled through the leaves of the forest and caused the undergrowth to dance with its rhythm.

"Where will you take her?" he asked.

"You mean where will we follow her? I cannot do this alone, Joseph. Look at me. I've seen more summers than the oldest of great oaks. No, she'll need the help of us all before this is over."

He looked at her pensively, his eyes betraying his protest.

"She cannot run, Joseph."

"You expect her to fight," he muttered in disbelief.

"I expect her to follow her heart, and I know her heart won't let her run from injustice."

"She doesn't need to know the truth."

"No, she doesn't, but if what we have heard is true, then this cruelty and lust for power will engulf the whole of Anemoi. There will be nowhere left to run. She and everybody else must stand up to this attack on the sovereignty of Anemoi. It is the only way, and I will not bestow the privilege of inaction on Xander just because she is my niece—granted, a few generations removed."

Joseph fell silent as he took in the woman's words.

"And you will join?" she asked.

"I will, or at least I would like to…"

"Your family?"

"Yes, my family."

"We can't do this without you, Joseph. You of all people. We need you. She needs you."

Joseph stood rigid and bowed his head. "Give this to her for me," he said, and passed her an envelope. "I will be back before the end of the week, and then I'll take the both of you and my family away from here until we can figure out the next step. If I'm not back in five days, head south without me. I'll find you."

"Where are you going?"

"I have one more errand to run before we leave," he said, and swiftly disappeared into the darkness.

Evia watched after him, her concern for his revelation not insignificant. She sighed. Part of her wanted to leave with Xander that night. Find safety until they could regroup and strategise. But they couldn't depart without *it*, not if they wanted a fighting chance. And unfortunately for them, *it* wouldn't be ready until the last breath.

"It's going to be a rough couple of nights."

CHAPTER 24

Augustx 13, 484; Nhata Bay, Borlencia—Xander tightened the scarf across her face in a bid to protect from the unusually cold spray of the choppy lake. But for the colourful moored skips and the foamy runoff of the rapidly rising surf, the pebbled bay below was deserted and dreary.

She slung the heavy wicker basket filled with fish over her broad shoulder and started along the stone path to the candlelit village snuggled into the hillside, the slope's gradient and the weight of the catch tough on the calves all the while. In the distance, trees and grasses bent, and the faint wisps of the chimneys fluttered under the gusts of the approaching storm. Along the muddy street of the village, the last of the shopkeepers closed up shop, ready to head home to light their hearths and feed their families.

"Working late, I see," Dogner said tiredly, the relative heat of his shop providing some relief from the chill outside. "Ah, good catch! I'll give you the usual price for the fish. Oh! And I have a little something for you and your aunt for tonight," he said excitedly, and placed a bag filled with salted meats onto the counter.

"You shouldn't," she responded quietly, hesitant to accept the offer. The flicker of the candlelight accentuated the sharpness of her maturing features and beckoned the shadow of her long yet lean frame to dance awkwardly on the wall behind. She was now as tall as her mother, and every bit as captivating.

"And why shouldn't I, Xander?" the burly farmer asked bluntly.

"It's just that…"

"Look, Xander, you're still moping about your friend, I understand, but this is a big day for you. And as an individual who has cared for you since you arrived in this village all scrawny and snot-nosed, I think it's my obligation to give you a gift. Also, if you don't mind me saying, I don't think you eat quite enough for someone that gives the men a run for their money in their tough-man competitions. And now that that's sorted…" He smiled cheerfully as he handed her the meats and a worn coin purse. "Give your aunt my best, and I'll see you in the morning."

A big grin spread across his face, and he waved her out.

In the dim cottage, she wiped her nose of the cold and threw her overalls onto the kitchen table, the heat of the hearth sufficient.

"Evia!"

"In here!" Evia called from the study. "That smells delicious," she said of the wrapped meats Xander held up.

Evia looked old and tired, and dread suddenly lurked in Xander's stomach, but she quickly brushed it away.

"I received this from the postman today," Evia said, and handed Xander the brown package that lay on the desk.

"Who's it from?"

"Joseph. For your birthday. Not every day you turn seventeen."

Xander forced a smile.

"Well, go on then. Open it."

She opened the slim package and pulled out a coin. It was rounded but with a hole in the centre. She had never seen one quite like it. The colour worn and the numerical unit and scripture etched into the bronze foreign to her eyes, she glanced curiously at her aunt. "Any idea where it's from?"

Evia handed her the note that had accompanied the package, and the girl read it aloud:

Xander, I hope this package finds you in good health. I'm sorry that I can't be there to watch your ascension into adulthood, but I would like to gift you this coin. It was the currency used in an ancient kingdom from afar. Whilst the scripture is admirable, the history is one of corruption and greed. Contrary to what one might think, the hole in the coin is not symbolic, but the result of depreciation. Depreciation of its worth through the dilution of its substance. The lesson: You cannot create value without hard work. Love, Joseph.

She chortled. "Slightly morbid message." Her expression filled with anticipation.

"I'm sorry. Nothing from Hemish. But if it makes any difference, I did hear that he's doing well down in the city of Notos working for his uncle's business. The Notencian capital is now arguably the beating heart of Anemoi's commerce with Borealis gone, and quite the place to master the ins and outs of international trade. He'll learn a lot down there."

Xander's heart hurt. She longed to see her friend; the absence of his laughter still weighed heavily on her well-being, and the anger she felt towards his mother for her unreasonable reaction was still raw. She glanced down at the table, where the parchment she'd found in the gauntlets was rolled out.

"Had a go at deciphering the nonexistent scribbles?"

"Ha! No, dear, that's for you to do," Evia said as she stood up wearily. "Xander, I hope you don't mind if I give you your gift tomorrow. I feel a tad light-headed all of a sudden and think it best I head to bed. Perhaps save me some of those meats for the morning," she managed weakly, and disappeared upstairs.

Xander extinguished the orange glow of the oil lamp that was on its last breath and followed her aunt upstairs. The hypnotic patter of raindrops against the window and the rumble of thunder deep on the horizon filled her room. She glanced at the heavy wooden frame of her aunt's room and felt a pang of worry. Putting it to the back of her mind, she climbed into bed, the sheets soft against her skin and her feet light after the day's work.

▲ ▲ ▲

Despite the tendency of Xander's dream world to mercilessly haunt her, it did, on very rare occasions, bless her with warm recollections that could surely make even the coldest of hearts beam like a toddler.

Xander dragged the point of the stick across the dirt, her eyes intently looking ahead and silently weighing its properties. It wasn't heavy or intimidating, but it had reach and felt robust, and the little nub where a flower may have one day sprouted provided ample grip for its intended purpose.

"Ready to eat mud?" The beastly teen scowled from across the abandoned lot in one of Borealis's quieter residential neighbourhoods bordering the palace.

"Are you?"

"Don't give me that, you wretched mutt. If it weren't for your whore of a grandmother, your father would be no better than a street beggar and you along with him," he spat.

Anger flared within, and it took considerable strength to keep her vision clear and her senses calm. How she longed to rush at the pudgy bully and teach him a lesson, but what would Father say? No, it wouldn't do. She had to remain guarded.

"Is that all you have to say?" she responded casually.

His nostrils flared and his cheeks reddened as his friends chuckled at the blatant retort.

"No, it isn't, you damned mutt. What about that farm rat you call a mother?" Her heart thumped. "How quick she scurried into Borealis's elite, as if she were a true upper-class somebody who couldn't be scorned at every moment behind her vile, fur-covered back. As if she weren't some low-life scum born out of wedlock into a grotty countryside gutter."

His friends burst into tears of laughter, an assortment of sheltered, pampered cretins, the children of wealthy merchants and politicians in all their pomp and inbreeding, and how she both despised and envied their unmixed heritage.

Her breath caught in her throat, and she glimpsed the first vestiges of stars and blackness that came with the blackouts. The hysterics of his cronies only added to the pain of his words.

"I, I—"

"You're a mutt! You always have been, and you always will be. Now piss off before I have you put down," he sneered.

He had her.

In her blind fury, she rushed at the boy several years her senior and swiped this way and that with the stick. But having learned from his first dismal encounter with Xander's rage, he knew to keep his distance, and she was unable to land a blow on his horrid face. Soon, through petulant frustration, she slowed to a halt and eyed him in time for some semblance of control to return.

"The mutt run out of breath?" he taunted.

She didn't respond this time. She just stared at him, her hate and anger evident. He wavered slightly at the onslaught. Then she grinned.

"Something funny?" he said angrily.

"Come on, give her a whack. Get it over with," one of the cretins egged.

"Yeah, it's boring now. She's all wasted. Finish the mutt off and let's go," another chimed in.

"All right! I'll put her down," he hissed, and started towards her, but before he could step, she lifted the stick and launched the point at him like a javelin, knocking him solidly in the cheek.

His agonised cry fuelled her impetus, and she threw herself at his larger body, knocking him to the dust of the ground, and she was quick to rain her fists down on his unprotected face. One of the others ran over and grabbed her hair whilst another booted her in the side, but it didn't faze her. She threw another and another, for each blow was therapy for her wounded pride, and that pride was far from healed. Again one of them tried to drag her off, but she shoved him away and reached for a rock.

"Xander!" Carolus thundered.

She shrivelled at the sight of the city's commander, as did the others, and swiftly removed herself from the fallen teen.

"I—"

"Will leave, immediately!"

She hurried away from the lot and waited in the nearby street whilst Carolus repaired the damaged egos.

"But he started it," she protested when he approached.

"Xander…what did I tell you?"

"Never raise my fists in anger."

"And what did you do?"

"I raised them in anger, but it wasn't my fault. You should have heard what he said about you and Mama. He was awful to me."

He crouched to her level. "The words hurt, I'm sure. But think to yourself, what was to be gained from hurting him? From reacting to his taunts?"

"Justice!"

"And then what?"

"I…I don't know!"

"Violence isn't always the answer, especially against a child who doesn't know any better. Think before you raise your fists. Violence is a last resort, and even then, you mustn't let it consume you."

"I tried. I really did. I tried to be calm, to not let the blackness take me, but it's so hard." She began to sob.

He pulled her close. "I understand. I do. But you must try to control it and use it, and you'll find it makes you stronger and faster than you ever knew possible. Both in mind and presence."

"Like you?"

"If you keep up with your education and your training." He smiled softly. They stood and started towards home.

"It did feel good."

"What did?"

"Hurting him."

"Xander…"

"I know, I know," she said cheekily. "I took him down pretty good, though. You should have seen."

His expression softened, goaded by her smile, though his voice lost none of its sternness. "I did."

"You saw it?"

"Most of it…maybe next time you won't throw your weapon away so carelessly."

She stared at him in silence and took his hand, and as they wandered through the busy street, she longed to see more than the blurred apparition that her mind conjured.

"I miss you!" she said after several moments.

"How so? I'm here with you, and soon your mother shall be too."

She didn't respond. The longer the sleepy memories flowed and the more she tried to stretch them out and control them, the harder they would become to maintain, try as she might.

"I love you!"

She jerked up as the window shook violently, the thunderclap frighteningly close, and stared in shock at the storm that engulfed the village. The tranquillity of the lake disturbed beyond all memory, the crash of the waves level with the cottages midway up the slope.

"Xander!" Evia cried from her room as the wind tore at the thatched roof.

She scrambled to her aunt's room, but the door wouldn't budge. Effortlessly she kicked it open and was greeted by the spray of the rain coming through the torn roof. Sprawled on the floor by the bed, her face pale and eyes sunken, Evia muttered something in her delirium.

Xander was quick to lift her frail form into her own room and place her on the bed. Enveloped with worry, she slumped to her knees and held the woman close through the shattering turmoil of the storm till she, too, fell into slumber.

CHAPTER 25

Augustx 15, 484; Nhata Bay, Borlencia—Since the storm had torn through the village two days prior, the lake had returned to a state of tranquillity more usual for Nhata that time of year. Birds chirped from the woods, humidity hung heavy in the air, and the water exuded calmness. Across the village, on the rooftops, and in the streets and gardens, the villagers sang and pranced and chatted joyously, determined to embrace the rebuild of their battered homes.

And yet no such joy touched Xander. Her mind stubbornly dwelt on the physician's diagnosis of Evia's deteriorated health, and even with the poor woman regaining some semblance of consciousness some hours earlier, the girl felt only dread and sadness for the outlook.

"I think I've got enough," she said tiredly, ready to deliver Dogner's skiff as it tilted under the weight of the objects retrieved from the water, a mixture of family keepsakes and scrap materials to be returned to the village.

"Well, hello there, darling," a cruel voice came from behind. She turned to a skiff full of idiots presumably from the next village along. "Looks like you lot had a bit of a tough time with that storm," cooed the repulsive individual, his bulbous eyes boring into hers, unwavering and suspicious in their approach. The man's build was wiry to the point of being hunched, and his twisted sneer betrayed a life of cruel deeds.

Anger flared at the interruption, her emotions heightened and volatile. "What do you want?"

"Oh! You know. Looking to take advantage of the village's misfortune and in turn collect ourselves a bit of fortune," he chuckled.

The burly guy to his side snickered menacingly at the poor play on words. "Will that be all?"

"That'll be all," he muttered with viciousness in his tone, clearly taken aback by the brazen dismissal.

Xander cautiously picked up the oar and pulled herself through the water, all the time wary of the miscreants behind her, and whilst they did not pursue, they made no attempt to relax their gaze. She looked around, and except for a couple of children playing on the pebbled beach, she was alone on the water.

"Definitely best we head home," she whispered. She had made only a short distance when the skiff shuddered to a stop and nearly toppled her. "What in Anemoi?"

She peeked over the side, careful not to disrupt the balancing act, and frowned at the discarded net snagged on the skiff. Undeterred by the jeers and laughter of the miscreants, she reached over to the snag and had partially grasped the net when it tugged the boat from beneath and flung her headfirst into the chilly water.

Frantic to climb into the boat and carelessly unaware the skiff had shifted, she smacked her head on the boat's underside and swiftly fell into a dreamlike fogginess as the dull impact resonated through her skull. She was motionless beneath the surface and strangely content to let the cool sensation of serenity course through her veins in a watery world away from reality; it took a flicker of white light from the shallow lake bed to arouse her stupor. Intrigued, she let herself sink towards the source, and through the murky water, she glimpsed the narrow hole in the rock from which the light came.

Curiosity beckoned her to examine further, but she was on her last breath and in need of air, so she planted her feet on the smooth stones of the lake bed and thrust herself towards the surface. Halfway up, however, a horrifying realisation soon took hold—the effort of her ascent was being opposed by an equally strong, invisible force. Suspended in watery limbo, and no longer able to quell the growing heaves of her chest or keep at bay the stars bombarding her vision, she slumped motionless as consciousness swiftly abandoned her.

▲ ▲ ▲

The cold, jagged ground on which she awoke had numbed her body and left her trembling with a chill. The cave was small and dimly lit, and in the wall, there was a narrow shaft from which the white glow emanated. She stood warily and reached to her forehead.

"Ouch!" She recoiled at the gash that stung to touch. "And that must be how I came in," she said of the narrow pool of water behind her, and though fear tugged at her urge to leave back through it, her curiosity pushed her towards the shaft.

Narrow and eerily long, the glow beckoned from the other side of the shaft, and bit by bit, she dragged herself along the tunnel, her knees and elbows bearing the brunt of the scrapes and cuts. She entered the next chamber with welcomed relief, and immediately the strange pool at the end of the room took her eye as the white glow of the water transitioned into a deep violet, then a brazen blue, then a luscious forest green. Through the coolness of the cave and the irregular drip of the damp that was so hypnotic in its echo, she edged towards the spectrum of colours that lured her.

But her tranquillity was abruptly shattered by a thunderous crash from behind, and she swirled in shock to see the shaft collapse in on itself. Frantically she ran to the entrance and tried to shift the large boulder that obstructed the hole, tugging and pushing until her hands and back ached, and then she dropped to her backside, her eyes wide in horror at the implication. Exhausted, she turned to the pool, hopeful for an exit.

"It's been an age, special one," a man's voice said from the shadows of the cave, much to her alarm.

She stared into the darkness, cautious of the sinister presence that lurked, then scanned the floor for any hint of a weapon.

"But you're different. You've changed. Yes, the same, but different."

"Who are you?"

"But I have not changed. No, I am the same. It then goes without saying that I've been here for more than an age. How many ages, I do not know, but certainly beyond reason," he said in forlorn realisation. "But now, special one, you can relieve me of this role I so loathe and free me from this damp, eternal underworld."

"Role? What role? Who are you?"

"Protector of the key, of course. Tell me this, special one, because your life and my liberation is tied to your answer."

She squirmed at the threat.

"What is one light made of many?"

"I—I don't know," she stuttered.

The darkness grew.

"Yes, you are different. So quick to admit defeat."

Again the darkness grew.

"Wait, wait!" she shouted frantically. "What is one light made of many?" Her mind scrolled for an answer. "Light itself," she whispered, epiphany claiming her expression.

"Light itself is what?"

"Light itself is made of many. Putantis, my teacher, once explained to me that when the sunlight hits the water in the sky, it bends and slows, and as it slows, it becomes many. The variation in speed of the light within creates a spectrum of colours, or what we know as a—"

"Rainbow."

"Yes! The slowest light, violet, on one side, and the fastest light, red, on the other. Light is made of many lights."

"Well done! In the pool you'll find the key that so eagerly drew you here. Be sure to take the fastest route."

The alluring light of the pool intensified, but her wariness and curiosity stayed her. She turned to the darkness that inhabited the cave. "Who are you?"

"I'm an old acquaintance tasked with guardianship of the key, and I've lived in this cave for near to an eternity, or so it feels, waiting and longing for you to make an appearance when the time called. And here you are, or so I think."

"And what did you mean when you said I've changed?"

"The energy that dwells in us is eternal. Our bodies are not. Now please, I must ask you to leave. I can suddenly bear no more of your presence. How it taunts me so."

She glimpsed a silhouette that seemed human in its outline but withered and fishlike in its details. She shuddered and turned to the pool, reluctant to remain longer.

The pool was wide enough for one grown man and three men deep in its initial drop, and every time it changed colour, the bend at the base of the drop would veer off in a different direction, the length and destination of what lay beyond always out of sight.

"What am I doing?" she said quizzically, confounded by the sudden drive of curiosity that outweighed her sensibilities. "But it's not like I have a choice. Red the fastest and violet the slowest…here goes!"

She dove into the cold water as soon as it turned red and pulled herself to the bottom of the drop and around the bend into a long, horizontal tunnel. The light intensified with every metre, but so did the squeeze of the increasingly narrow space, and soon the dreadful sensation of claustrophobia weighed heavily on the calmness she felt before.

Still she continued onward, and only when the air in her lungs was half depleted did she find herself captivated by the tiny, fantastically bright object on the floor of the tunnel. Eyes wide, she peered into the red glow of the ring that had beckoned her. Greedily she reached for it, but her awe of the treasure quickly turned to shock at the sealed tunnel ahead.

No way forward and unable to turn, she frantically pushed herself backwards through the tight space, teeth gritted in constant battle against the urge to breathe. But no matter how much she squirmed and wriggled her way through the rocky hole, her feet couldn't find the original bend. Panic abruptly overwhelmed as delirium infiltrated. Frantically desperate for oxygen, she instinctively raised her head, piercing through the imaginary rocky roof of the tunnel and into the cool breeze of the lake.

▲ ▲ ▲

Confused and shaken, Xander creased her eyes against the dim afternoon sun, and her skin tingled against the crisp air of evening.

"No skiff…" she huffed wearily, and struggled to shore through the ache of her lungs and limbs.

As soon as the pebbles were underfoot, she clambered up the beach and collapsed against a moored skiff. The gentle ripples of the lake and the rustle of the trees soon soothed her exhausted mind of the terrifying suffocation of the cave, and in her stupor, her thoughts drifted to the den under the mill that chose to reveal itself and the cave in the lake and the ring it gifted.

"How beautiful it is," she whispered, mesmerised by the blood-red circle in the palm of her hand and equally intrigued by the unrecognisable gold engravings etched into the material. She slid it onto her finger and smiled. "Right at home…and still, how foolish I was to have gone down there."

She stood weakly and took in the lake and the shore, but still no skiff.

"Dogner's not going to be—"

A scream emanated from the street, and she sluggishly staggered up the hill to the village. The main street teemed with mayhem, and soldiers blocked the road north. Families scurried south and west, desperate to flee the apparent threat, but others were not so lucky, having already been rounded up and chained.

Instinctively she ran to Dogner's shop just around the corner and burst in, much to his alarm.

"Xander!" he shouted. "Where in Anemoi have you been? Thought those vermin from Zyphyr got the best of you."

"Zyphyr? Why are they rounding up civilians?"

"No idea, but I'm not waiting around to find out," he said, and picked up a sack. "They've already got half the town cornered. Get your aunt and meet me on the road south. Quick! Before they block the other half."

"Your kids?"

"At the house. Be careful, okay—"

A soldier clubbed Dogner on the side of the head as they exited the shop, but the soldier was in turn floored by Xander's fist to his nose, her prior weakness suddenly gone. Two other soldiers were quick to circle her with batons, but back on his feet and with only his cheek bloodied, Dogner invited them his way.

The first swung at his head, but he nimbly dodged the baton and threw the man into the wall of his shop by the face. The second rushed him from behind but was dispatched in a crumpled heap by Xander's elbow to the temple. She turned to the road, ready to proceed, and saw only a flash of the starry abyss, the unseen crack to her head like a whip inside her skull.

CHAPTER 26

"Xander?"

She tried to come around, to force herself out of dreariness, but her mind wasn't ready and pulled her back into slumber.

"Xander, how you doing, child?" The same voice pierced the grogginess.

She half opened her eye to see Joseph beside the bed, his expression warm and affectionate.

"That was a nasty knock to the back of your head, and definitely the worst of the two," he said, observing the smaller gash on her forehead. "But you'll live." He chuckled. "Good to see you're keeping well in my absence."

She smiled weakly, then tried to speak, but her mouth was dry. He handed her a cup of water, and she took a deep gulp.

"Is Dogner okay?" she managed.

"He's fine, although they're not taking any chances. Have half a dozen watching him," Joseph laughed. He took in her quizzical look. "Would seem that after that one knocked you out, he went a bit berserk and took out a few more or so. Lost count. Clearly they're not wanting to take any risks with him."

"But why did they attack him in the first place?" she asked angrily.

"They're subduing anybody that could be a threat."

She pressed her palm against her head as a sharp pang resonated through her skull.

"Are you okay?"

She nodded and looked around the unfamiliar room. "Where am I?"

"You're at the inn. The soldiers refused to let you stay with your aunt. Something about being a troublemaker."

"I need to make sure she's okay," she said, and tried to get up.

"Ah, not such a good idea. Give me a little time to work my charm with your captors, then we'll get you to your aunt."

"The soldiers are from Zyphyr, Joseph. What's that about? They're soldiers of Anemoi."

He looked at her curiously and then threw her a coin.

"An Anemoi shilling," she said, perplexed.

He threw her another.

"Also an Anemoi shilling," she repeated.

"What do they tell you?"

She examined the coins in her hands, attentive to the composition and weight. "The second one weighs less, and the gold and copper alloy hasn't got that rosy tinge I so adore. No, it's much darker. It's been diluted!"

"Exactly." He smiled proudly. "Zyphyr has been diluting the Anemoi shillings. Creating something from nothing."

"But why?"

"Look around you. At the soldiers and the group of mercenaries accompanying them. Now replicate this all across West Anemoi. A standing army is dear. An occupying army is dearer."

"It's not just Nhata?" she asked, surprised.

"Most of the lakeshore north of here. And pretty much all of central and western Borlencia, from what I've gathered."

Xander's mind darted to the vile miscreants on the boat.

"And the courts? What about Parliament? They would allow disregard for the laws?"

"I don't think much power remains with the people these days…" He paused and then sighed. "Would seem that a cruel woman by the name of Erzse has wiggled herself into a position of nearly absolute authority in Zyphyr."

Her memory twitched at the mention of the name, though she couldn't place where she had heard it.

Joseph looked at her, apprehension in his expression. "But that's a story for another day. Best you get some sleep, and then maybe they'll let you see your aunt in a couple of days."

"Is your family okay?" she asked as he walked out.

"Same as here, I imagine. When I'm sure your aunt can manage, I'll sneak out and make sure they're okay."

CHAPTER 27

Augustx 16, 484; Nhata Bay, Borlencia—Xander placed the fresh juice on the bedside table. Evia's features had regained some of the colour and plumpness they had been devoid of in the aftermath of the storm, but the fatigue was still evident.

"I see you got your gift."

Xander followed her eyes to the ring. "How do you…"

"My dear, who do you think opened the cave? Wasn't easy parting the water overhead and then moving the block of earth my younger self placed there decades ago to conceal the cave and the treasure inside—a gift fitting for a newly minted seventeen-year-old, I'd say." She took a sip of the juice and her face scrunched up at the foul-tasting liquid.

"Taste of your own medicine."

Evia laughed. "Was bound to happen sooner or later."

"So you revealed the cave. That explains the storm and you being on your deathbed." Suddenly, a curious thought arose in her. "And what of the shaft in the mill? Was that you?"

"That I did not reveal intentionally, and it was by pure chance that you happened upon it when you did. That creature was placed there to protect something incredibly valuable, and somehow, as young as you were, you defeated it. Now will you be so kind as to run and grab the parchment you found down there?"

Xander entered the study, and her mouth dropped in amazement at the parchment. The landmarks of Anemoi were as sharp and clear as if they'd been recently drawn. The lake, Nhata, Borealis, even Etlinga and Talum. Everything was revealed in black ink.

"Who would have thought this was a map?" she said excitedly as she laid the parchment across Evia's bed. "How's this possible?"

"The ring. It's a key to the map, at least the type of map you see before you."

Xander squinted at the markings and frowned. "It's incomplete. There's a village missing, the one to the south of Etlinga."

"And you know this village how?"

"I've seen it on another map."

"But you've not been to that village?"

"You know I haven't been that far south of Etlinga."

"And there lies your reason. This is no ordinary map. It interacts with the mind of whoever wears the ring, or any of the other items imbued with the same quality, and the ring itself learns from the accumulated memories and experiences of those that have worn it. If you or one of the previous bearers of this particular ring haven't been to a town or walked a particular road or explored a city's streets, well, then the markings won't appear on the map, almost as if they never existed. And the same goes for any of those other very special items that, too, can access these brilliant inventions, each item with its own very different purpose."

"But isn't a map meant to help you find places you haven't been to?"

"An ordinary map, yes, but that's not the purpose of this map. This map is designed to help you find objects—objects tied to the item that unlocks the map."

"What objects?"

"We'll get to that. Do me a favour and visualise the houses and paths of Nhata."

Xander dreamt up the images of Nhata's quaint cottages, kept farms, and rustic boundaries, and her eyes lit up as the map altered.

"What do you see?"

"Nhata! I see Dogner's shop, the market, the streets, even our home and garden path," she said giddily.

"With just a thought, you can change what the map shows, from the detailed intricacies of the most complex maze to a bird's-eye view of the whole of Anemoi. Truly a remarkable invention."

"And what if a place has changed?"

"A detriment all maps are surely vulnerable to. Especially ones built so long ago. And yet in this particular case, the objects will still reveal themselves. Now tell me what you know about the Rose of Anemoi."

"The desert rose. It grows in the mountains near Borealis. Not seen since the Revolutionary Wars. The city's named after it," she said confidently.

"Close, but no crumpet. Remind me, did I ever teach you Curioul's Rhyme?"

Xander shook her head.

"Forgive me the oversight. It was careless of me to have excluded it from your education, given its relevance. It goes as follows:

The bloomed thorn comes
As sharp in touch
As in first light.
Come to bold hero
Our dear old dear
And fell this plight
Rose of Ani Moi."

"Ani Moi?"

"An old pronunciation, before your time."

"And you say it isn't a flower?"

"The Rose of Anemoi refers to a very old metallic symbol. A symbol used to unite the people of Anemoi during the Revolutionary Wars. Rumour is—and I say rumour because it was never actually documented—the symbol either greatly amplifies the unique abilities of the bearer, or if they're without the spark, bestows them with the abilities—granted, those abilities would not be quite as powerful as the former. After the wars, and to avoid abuse through corruption, its creator, along with the bearer who wielded it, shattered the symbol into six shards and hid them. It was merely by chance that the city of Borealis adopted the unofficial name and that the desert rose perished about the same time the Revolutionary Wars concluded."

"And this map will take me to them?" she asked as she looked at the now-legible markings.

"Yes. Xander, your mother's familial line is a long line of bearers. As a safeguard against abuse, it was ensured that only your bloodline could complete and use this symbol, the Rose of Anemoi."

"Wait, but the Rose is ancient. That must mean there are thousands of others that can wield it also?"

"Tell me, how many are in your extended family on your mother's side? Besides me, that is."

"I—hmm. I can't name one. But that doesn't mean anything. Nobody can be expected to name everyone in their family tree going back that far."

"You're right; it's quite the task, but I'll help you. Other than you and your brother, there have only been five other recorded instances of siblings in your mother's bloodline, and as far as we've been able to determine, those siblings didn't have offspring."

"That seems really, really far-fetched."

"It's not."

"But that means at any one time there's almost always been just the grandparent—if they lived—the parent, and the child?"

"Yes."

"But how's that possible?"

"You'd have to ask the man that created the Rose and made your blood the key to its power."

"So it was deliberate?"

"I think that's a safe assumption."

"Okay, then why?"

"Think."

She pondered. "Fewer chances for corruption? Or maybe to remove the threats if corrupted?"

"Both."

Weighed by the revelation, Xander peered at the map and focused on the markers she figured to be the shards. "I only see five…and one of them is in Nhata," she said quietly, and removed from the wall the long-forgotten piece of metal she had found in Borealis.

"And that is how I knew it may be time. For the first to reveal itself to you, a bearer, without prompt or investigation. It could only be a matter of time before the others would seek discovery."

"But why?"

"I assume a threat has arisen, one unlike any witnessed since the Revolutionary Wars."

"The fall of Borealis and now Zyphyr's soldiers," she murmured. "So where's the sixth?"

"It's not in this realm, and the gate to said realm has been hidden. You need to get the key to that realm for the location to be revealed to you. And unfortunately for us, the key is in your mother's sabre."

Xander's fists tightened as stored emotion simmered under the surface; she brushed aside the alluring thought of inflicting her vengeance using the Rose. "The sabre was taken years ago by those savages."

"You'll have to find it. I don't think we have much other choice."

"You mean, *I* don't have much choice?"

"No, sadly you don't. My guess is that the path Zyphyr has taken will lead to all-out war with the rest of Anemoi. It's imperative we prevent that, however possible."

Xander's gaze suddenly lit up. "I know where I've heard that name."

"Whose name?"

"Erzse, the woman that's behind all of this. She was a minister when my parents still lived. There was tension between her and my father. I remember now."

Evia remained stern in her expression. "What else do you remember?"

"Not much. Just that my father didn't agree with some of her policies." Xander could sense Evia's unease. "There's more, isn't there?"

"There is." She paused. "Erzse is your father's sister, Xander. She's your aunt."

"I—I don't understand. Don't you think he would've told me that? Or you? Why wouldn't you tell me that?"

"I can't speak for your parents—"

"But you can speak for yourself."

"It's…complicated."

"Evia."

Evia stared into Xander's eyes for a brief moment of uncertainty and then nodded her head. "Well, I think it's fair to say you're old enough to handle your own affairs now, which means it's only right I bring you up to speed on all matters."

"Thank you."

"I warn you. The background is a tad grim in places."

"I can handle it."

"I'm sure. It wasn't long after Borealis's fall, before the dust could even settle, that rumours began to circulate of a politician in the west searching for the children of Borealis's senior ministers with a promise of reward for all those who could assist. The premise being the children's safety. As you'd expect, soon enough, soldiers, mercenaries, smugglers, and miscreants alike began to frequent the different refugee camps looking for you and the others. All sounds reasonable at a first glance, doesn't it?"

"I think so, yes."

"Well, first glances can be deceiving. The first child picked up by Erzse's hounds, a young boy separated from his older brothers, was found dead in a ditch the next morning right outside the refugee camp from which he had been discovered. Then there were two sisters, both of whom were handed to Erzse's men and later rescued by soldiers of Anemoi from a slaver to the north. It quickly became apparent that none of you were safe. Not even you, her niece."

"But you can't be sure?"

"No, but it's a risk a man like Joseph could never take. By some luck, or perhaps because no one knew what you looked like, you were always out of Erzse's grasp, and again by another stroke of luck, you thought to enter Joseph's camp. Although he knew you not, he and a number of others had already agreed to hide you and the other children if ever they were to come across any of you. They were a minority within a minority, and the odds truly defy belief that they'd be the ones to find you!"

"Am I still in danger?"

"You mean, does she still look for you?"

"Yes."

"It's hard to tell. Her hounds never came this far south, and last I heard they had given up the search. That doesn't mean your whereabouts wouldn't garner her interest. Don't worry; you were never in any danger. I cast a little mind trick, as Joseph would call it, some time ago that makes visitors forgetful of your name and identity as soon as they leave the area. And to our benefit and your own safety, when it became apparent to us you weren't aware of who Erzse was or what her relationship was to you, we decided to keep it quiet rather than burden an already burdened child."

"You mean, risk me talking?"

"To put it politely, yes. Playing with the mind can be tricky. Your name and identity are one thing, but who's to say someone's mind doesn't cling to the little snippet that Erzse has a niece in Nhata? As circumstances would have it, your father's relationship to the woman is not widely known, and certainly not in Nhata, so rather than let it be common knowledge to Nhata's regulars, we simply avoided the topic altogether. And Carolus was still well respected down here, so the very small handful that had heard of the bounties were in no rush to give up his daughter to some politician in Zylencia."

"Do you know why she searched for us?"

"I don't. Maybe for political reasons, but then what's the benefit of getting rid of children who can't legally inherit power?"

"Maybe she knows about the Rose."

"It's not impossible, though I shudder to think about it. Regardless, she's not to be trusted."

"Good thing you told me then," Xander said cheekily. "I still feel like it's something you should've told me sooner. And my parents."

"I don't know why your parents didn't divulge this information, but I do apologise for my part. Please understand, though, that we withheld this information for your own good."

"No more secrets, okay?"

"I'll try my best."

"That's not good enough."

Evia chortled. "I'm an old woman. My memory comes to me in drabs. When something of importance arises, I will try my utmost to inform you. Sound fair?"

Xander nodded, and there was an awkward silence for several moments before she felt the urge to break the quiet. "What about you? Where do you fit into all this?"

"It was actually an ancestor of mine who created the Rose, and for some time now, several others and I have worked to protect it. You had the pleasure of meeting one of my acquaintances under the lake."

"That was a friend of yours?"

Evia hesitated as her brow creased with sadness. "You asked me some time ago about a man called Marcus. Well, that was him. A friend, a colleague…a companion. It was just him and me versus the world for some time. How I miss those days."

Xander was unsure what to make of the revelation. "What's he doing down there?"

"The cave shields from time and is one of only a handful in the region. My poor Marcus was on his last breath, injured in a battle to protect the ring you wear. Not wanting his death to be in vain, and with scarce little time to suss out a more practical location, he offered to secure the ring down there until the bearer came calling."

"But he—he was—"

Evia raised her hand, cutting Xander off. "I'm fully aware of the effects a time capsule can have on the body and mind in so inhospitable an environment. You needn't ruin his memory for me. The man was always so cheerful. And handsome. Oh! And how he enjoyed theatrics. A fine energy manipulator too."

"I'm sorry. I really am."

"It's quite alright."

"Evia," she said, eager to know. "Was an energy manipulator involved in the fall of Borealis?"

"I don't know. There are many out there that I do not know or cannot sense and who have undesirable intentions. As is possible with Erzse, some may know of the Rose, so again, don't be so quick to trust on your journey."

"And what of you? It makes no sense that I should be doing this alone, given the seriousness of the situation. I'm hardly an adult. Why not let me wait until you have your strength back?"

"Truth is, Xander, it shouldn't be you doing this. It should be your mother. She knew what could be asked of her in a circumstance like this. She had years of training behind her, and she carried the sabre that could locate the last shard. But alas, your life came first, and so she sacrificed herself in that courtyard to protect you. As was her right and duty."

Xander nodded, saddened by the recollection.

Evia continued. "In the event of her death, your brother would've been the next logical choice. At seventeen, you're still a smidgen too young. And you're not a soldier, not yet anyway. But life has a funny way of throwing us into the thick of it." She reached her hand to Xander's cheek. "Trust me when I say this: I don't want you to do this on your own, but opening that cave has left me with barely any life. In the interest of time, you can't wait for me. Head to the Great Forest south of here, and find the Great Tree. There you'll find the next shard."

"I can't leave you, Evia. I just can't."

"I'll be fine. Joseph will look after me," she said, motioning to him in the doorway.

Xander turned to him, her concern clear.

"She'll be fine," he repeated reassuringly, though she doubted the surety in his eyes.

▲ ▲ ▲

"I gave her the supplies she needed and pointed her in the right direction…" Joseph fretted.

"Do I need to convince you also?" Evia asked.

"You don't want her to run, you want her to fight…we were meant to be with her on the road, and now she strays off on her own. She's young and inexperienced—"

"And scavenged the fields of desolate Borealis, broke the nose of a soldier of Anemoi, and slayed a fully grown swamp vine before she had even come of age. Do you know how hard those critters are to kill?"

"Can safely say that I've had the displeasure."

"She can handle herself—Dogner's made sure of that. And anyway, from what you've told me, by setting her on the road south, we've pushed her away from this new danger you speak of."

"The movement on the walls?"

"It's been years, Joseph, years with barely the flicker of a shadow and with the only reason to assume their continued presence being the disappearance of whomever ventured too close or the caravans to and from the desert. But now, out of the blue, the glow of torches and the movement of men on Borealis's walls. It cannot be coincidence, the stir of that cursed city just as Erzse begins her campaign. No, I've lived through too many 'coincidences' to think this is so."

"You fear they'll relaunch their attack on Anemoi?"

"The only reason that army from the shadows didn't capture and consolidate beyond Borealis was because it met its match against the combined might of the other provinces, with neither side strong enough to achieve outright victory. And now, as we speak, Erzse demonstrates the cracks in our collective resolve by launching a campaign against her own. She will do to us that which they couldn't do with seventy-five thousand men. She will tear open a wound too grave to allow us the strength to stand and repel invasion. This is why Xander must get the shards. It's clear now that this is an existential threat, and Erzse may be only the first in a line of challenges that come our way."

"Forgive me for digging this up *again*, but wouldn't it make more sense for us to travel with the girl? Surely with everything at stake, working together would improve our chance of success and, you know, allow us to keep an eye on her…"

"There's something else. It was a niggle at first, but what I've been shown is clear now. She's not meant to head into that forest with us."

"No?"

"No. Certain events, if we are with her, might not come to pass."

"All that from a niggle?"

"Never underestimate a niggle, especially if it morphs into a full-blown vision just as you're eating breakfast."

"Who showed it to you?"

"Someone I thought had died many, many centuries ago."

"Wait! What? And you trust them?"

"I do."

He grimaced. "This doesn't sit easy with me, Evia. We should be with her, like originally planned. Not following some voice in your head!" He exhaled long and hard as his shoulders slumped. "I'm sorry. That was too much."

She rested her worn hand on the man who cared for the girl as if he were her father. "Our place in all this will come, my friend. We just have yet to figure out how."

CHAPTER 28

Augustx 22, 484; 105 kilometres south of Nhata Bay, Borlencia—Xander slipped and planted her face in the wet mud of the street, startling two stray cats who were courting, but she was quick to right herself and continue on with the stolen bag of bread in hand, leaving the cats to resume their flirting.

"I see the filth!" a man shouted, the torchlight of her pursuers not far behind.

"Help!" she called to a group of townsmen midway up the next street. Though initially ready to assist, their recognition of the group that gave chase rendered them uninterested, and they callously returned to their conversation.

"Unbelievable!" she muttered and darted into one of the many small gardens that bordered the street.

Hidden in the shadows, the brutes continued down the street unaware, their line of sight broken by the townsmen. She used the momentary reprieve to hop over the town's boundary fence and into the woods.

For two hours she crept cautiously through the undergrowth until the illuminated specks of the town's buildings no longer stained the night, the barks of chained dogs were silent and the chatter of drunkards no longer carried on the lips of even the strongest gusts. Spent and struggling to focus through the ravages of fatigue and hunger, she found herself a small patch of dirt unbothered by rock or roots, and she lay down.

In stark contrast to the cold floor of the woods, the deliciously scented bag of bread was warm against her head and worked to melt the tension in her neck. She yawned as she took in the canopy and the heavens. Even with the rush of adrenaline, her exhaustion was plentiful, so much so that she had managed only one hefty bite of the prize before slipping into slumber.

She was only several days south of Nhata, and the forward ripples of Zyphyr's forces had already caught up. Unable to match the pace of the mounted patrols or the keen sight of their scouts, she had resigned herself to navigating the woods rather than the roads, but the pace was slow and the route cumbersome, and having already depleted the planned supplies Joseph had provided, she had been left little choice but to detour into the town.

"The undergrowth's broken here," a man whispered.

Startled, Xander rolled onto her front and grabbed the bag, ready to dart.

"Not good," she whispered, the three shadows apparent even in the dark undergrowth.

Quietly she stuffed the bag into a dank grotto, hoping to mask the stubborn scent of the bread and then crawled in after it. Barely had she climbed in when a man's silhouette appeared through the moonlit bushes. Scrawny in build and more akin to a sneak or cutthroat rather than any kind of soldier, he paced in his mud-caked boots only inches away from her refuge. He was one of the men from the town. She gripped the dagger thieved from his friend and held her breath in nervous anticipation, prepared to put it through his groin if he so much as suspected.

"Way too close!" she gasped after he and the group had vanished into the darkness of the woods.

Out of sight and earshot, she slowly raised to a crouch with the knife in hand and crawled through the woods away from the town, careful not to disrupt the shrubs and give up her trail.

CHAPTER 29

Augustx 29, 484; 217 kilometres south of Nhata Bay, Borlencia—"They guard the crossing?" she said, perplexed by the guards standing in and around a small wooden shed situated on the only river ford across the rough waters of the River Went and also the only entrance into the Great Forest from the west shore of the lake.

Content to wait until nightfall, she slumped against a moss-covered tree and relished the dampness of the woods and river that were so fresh against her skin. The gentle serenade of the river birds and the ripple of the current lulled her nerves, and as she basked, she took another bite of the purple weed she had scavenged several days prior. Known to stave off hunger and fatigue, the stimulant brought energy to her gaunt and dirty frame and provided an elixir for her weary mind.

Her thoughts drifted to what her aunt had told her: "The keeper of the Great Tree is both a fool and a trickster. Be wary of him, but know, without his blessing, you won't have an easy time retrieving the shard."

"Always the challenge," Xander murmured, and then looked up as a group of riders appeared at the ford and dismounted to set up shop. "More guards! Even with the darkness, someone is bound to see me. But if I don't do this soon, I'll be too weak. No, it has to be tonight, when they sleep."

▲ ▲ ▲

The faded flicker of the brazier gleamed through the blanket of morning haze, and except for a lone guard sitting outside the shed, the men all lay and groaned on the ground, the consumption of the previous evening excessive even for them.

Suddenly, much to her excitement, the lone guard stood and shook off the stiffness in his body. He peered over to the horses tied up on the road and then started towards the river's edge, behind the shed and out of view of the contingent of drunks, the need to relieve himself etched in his awkward movements.

She crept across the muddy road to within a metre of him, the pungent stink of his urine and the grunts of his relief carrying in the air. About to bring the butt of her knife down on the back of his head, she darted her eyes up to the commotion on the far side of the river.

The trees and their branches, partly concealed by the heavy mist, swayed and shook with a vigour unlikely caused by any playful forest creatures she knew. The alarm rang from the ford, and the soldier clumsily pulled up his trousers and sprinted to the beckon, unaware Xander was standing behind him. Curious to observe the stir of the forest that was so eerie in its crescendo, she jogged cautiously to the corner of the shed.

The guards shuffled into a neat line across the edge of the ford and locked their shields whilst the riders formed a second line immediately behind with only swords in hand, their shields and mounts unreachable in a timely manner. All sense of intoxication had evaporated with the un-known disturbance.

The crunch of the branches and the rustle of the leaves died down so only the flow of the river filled the air, and an obscured line of tall, oddly shaped figures formed on the opposite side of the ford. Moments passed without any hint of movement, and then, all at once, the eerie line stepped onto the ford, the thud of the many strange footsteps muffled by the murky river. The men visibly tensed, their expressions wary of the unknown that approached.

Cries of horror escaped their lips as the first of the silhouettes emerged from the mist. Their figures broad and their arms long and wicked looking, the dozen wooded creatures resembled twisted, evil-looking oaks, and dwarfing even the tallest of the men, they brandished heavy wooden clubs that only added to their menace.

The creatures were agile despite their bulky frames, and the heavy swings of their clubs were brutally effective against the guards' short swords. Slowly but surely the men fell back under the onslaught. The guard on the flank closest to the shed ducked and dodged one of the creatures, but a jab to the shield knocked him into the man behind, throwing him off balance. Not fast enough to recover, the guard's skull was shattered by a single blow from the creature. His sword slipped from his grip and landed beside Xander just as he slumped to the ground, and she furtively picked it up.

The rider directly behind the guard stumbled back, his mouth agape in disbelief at the power of the blow. Without a shield and with the rest of the line broken, he succumbed to the futility of holding his ground and sluggishly turned to flee. But the creature was fast, very fast, and speedily knocked him to the ground and stomped on his back, crushing his spine.

The assailant then turned to Xander and instantly swung the massive weapon at her head, but she nimbly scuttled past and dived into the icy torrent, leaving the club to smash through the shed. At the opposite bank, a short distance from where the ford connected to the forest's edge, she threw her kit into the tree line and pulled herself up using the weeds that poked through the muddy film of the slope. From the trees, she risked a glance back into the mist and squirmed at the proximity of the creature that had just given up the chase.

CHAPTER 30

The forest on this side of the river was wilder than the one outside Etlinga and far more colourful and ancient, but strangely the rogue undergrowth was kept at bay from the fringe of the neat forest paths. The whispers of the trees were also a tad different to that which she had grown used to around Nhata, almost as if they spoke a familial language with a degree of overlap.

She threw a wary glance behind to the expanse of the trees. It had been hours since she had emerged from the bitterly cold river and last seen the wooded creatures, and still she gripped the guard's sword cautiously.

Confronted with another fork in the path, she crouched over and frowned. "This is getting a bit ridiculous. Anybody around here I can ask for directions?" The air ahead buzzed. She looked up at the green-and-red songbird hovering level with her eyes. "Well, not really what I had in mind, but still a pleasant surprise."

Its beak pointed and long, it flew into the bramble and beckoned from a ray of sunlight that had breached the canopy a short distance from the path. Curious, she followed through the bush and into a quaint meadow carpeted in thick moss.

"Another pleasant surprise." She spoke softly.

The bird danced ahead and dived into a trickle of a stream, emerging with a tiny frog in its mouth.

"Okay, not as pleasant as you seem." She cringed.

Unashamedly, she took several messy gulps of the crystal water and threw herself onto the natural bedding of the meadow. She was comfortable even with her bony behind, and the weight off her legs was beyond delightful. Content with the cover afforded by the bushes, she shuffled around in the bag and pulled out the map, along with a regular modern map used for referencing. Despite a tear in the bag, the map was dry and undamaged, but the same could not be said for the regular map, which was now a tattered mess on the ground.

"The forest this side of the river has hardly any detail…the only landmark of note is the Great Tree and the shard beside it, but they're almost on the other side of the map compared to the river."

She let it drop to the side and gently shuddered at the tingle sent down her neck as an ant navigated the dirt-caked pores and stout hairs on her thin arm. Her new friend hovered overhead.

"And how can I help you?" she asked cheerfully.

In response, it darted over to a hollow, rotten log and back. She shifted onto her knees for a better viewpoint and stifled a hungry smile. The mere appearance of the puffball mushroom sheltered in the log was delicious to the senses and not too dissimilar to the ones she and Hemish used to pick outside Nhata. The texture of the bounty's creamy skin was soft against her fingertips as she peeled it from the inside. She tore off a small piece in offering to the songbird and then watched as it grabbed the piece and flew into the canopy.

"Guess you're as hungry as I am…well, maybe not quite," she said, and finished off the goodie. She yawned a long yawn, arms and back outstretched. "I hadn't realised how tired I am. A little nap never hurt anyone," she said tiredly, and lowered herself onto the padded ground. "Wake me in a few," she slurred to the bird, and then closed her eyes.

▲ ▲ ▲

To some in those parts, the local puffball mushroom was a magical sphere of deliciousness much desired for its hallucinogenic properties.

"Hey, Xander, what do you think of this one?"

"Which one?"

"The ginger one," Hemish said with a smile.

"It's kind of cute. Not sure why you're looking, though. Not like your mother will approve."

"You know, Xander, sometimes these jokes of yours that are usually at my expense, well, I can't say I always like them," he said with a straight face, his voice strange and distant.

"Okay, I was—"

"Just joking, I know, but maybe you should try a bit of seriousness once in a while." He turned back to the box of kittens.

Her cheeks burned, but worse was the pang of guilt that suddenly burned inside.

"I'll take these two," Hemish said to the bald man selling the litter from his lawn.

The man held up three fingers, and Hemish obliged. He turned around with a ginger kitten in one hand, a grey kitten in the other, and a childlike airiness etched across his face that made her uncomfortable.

"I'm sorry," she said as they plodded along the garden path.

"For what?"

The kittens squirmed roughly within his grip as he turned to her. "Not like you've done anything wrong. Just being your good old self, really, aren't you?"

"I—I don't understand why you're being like this."

"What am I being?" He stopped abruptly in the path.

The kittens' cries stifled as his grip tightened.

"You're hurting them, Hemish."

He glared at her unflinchingly, all hint of ease gone. "You care for these kittens?"

"Yes, and so do you, so maybe take it a little—"

"Easy! You want me to take it easy on them? Like this, perhaps?"

He lifted his hand and let the grey one drop to the ground.

"How could you!"

"What's wrong? Not funny?"

She knelt down, and as she was about to pick up the injured animal, he hovered his foot over its helpless form.

"Don't you dare!" she growled and rushed him, but before she could push him over, he had stomped on the animal.

In the subsequent struggle, he backhanded her to the ground and booted her in the head, causing pain to sear through her neck and back.

"You brought this on yourself, you damned witch. You and your filthy aunt," he spewed venomously.

"Hemish, please!" she spluttered as he raised the ginger one in both hands.

"Your fault, filthy witch," he screamed, and wrung the little thing, its pathetic cries permanently silenced.

"You filthy, filthy witch," he spat again, and then threw the limp body onto the ground in front of her and turned his back to her.

"Hemish!" she cried, but still he kept his back to her and walked away.

"Hemish!" she screamed as she sat up and out of dream world. Her mind shaken and her back and head sore, it was only the frantic calls of the little songbird in the distance that roused her realisation. She was no longer in the sleepy enclosure but strewn on the cold, hard ground of some grassy expanse nestled within the woods. In its centre stood a craggy column of rock taller than anything she had seen, even taller than the great pillars of the City Temple in Borealis.

Panic suddenly ensued, and she instinctively grabbed for her shoulders, fearful she may have left the sack and the map in the grove. She sighed in relief. Though she no longer carried the crude weapon, her bag and its contents were intact and firmly wrapped around her.

Her little friend danced between the trunks of the tree line at the edge of the expanse, its whistles fearful and distraught. But it was the faint screams seemingly from the sky that made Xander's hairs stand on end and her back tingle.

She turned to the craggy column of rock, and upon closer inspection, she could just make out a grassy mound on the top from where the cries of distress emanated. Though she couldn't see the source, she assumed it to be an animal that had gotten stuck.

She did a full circle of the column, which was no wider than a large shed. "And how in Anemoi did you get up there? Maybe I can get you down," she began, then hesitated. "No, that's insane—I can't risk it." As she turned to leave, another distressed cry pierced into her resolve, and she quickly turned around and grabbed one of the divots in the rock.

The little bird cried again from the tree line, but out of fright or simply a desire to accompany, Xander didn't know. Not wanting to waste any more time, she yanked herself up a metre. The bird fluttered and whistled in indecision, then bravely rushed towards her and the outcrop of rock, all the while hugging the ground.

The first twenty metres of the climb were easy, even with her tired, malnourished body, but the higher she climbed, the smaller and farther apart the cracks in the rock face became, and even with the guidance of her little friend, every slight gust reverberated through her gut.

"I need to rest. I—I'm not sure I can do this…" She breathed heavily as she clung to the rock. She dared a glance down, and a precarious dizziness shot through her at the height of the drop. "Okay, I shan't be doing that again." She forced her eyes up and towards the rock face that was suddenly the bane of her existence.

The bird perched itself on her shoulder and whistled encouragingly into her ear, and though she had no idea what was said, she took light from it.

"You know, my little friend, I haven't even thought ahead to how I'm going to get down," she said nervously, and forced her shaky leg to the next crack in the wall.

At this height, her fingers had long ago numbed, and her sweaty back felt every sliver of cool air as it brushed past. Her only impetus remained the crescendo of cries from atop the bizarre column that jutted from the middle of nowhere.

Against her previous advice, she glimpsed away from the rock, and this time her breath caught in her throat at what she beheld. They had climbed higher than the tallest trees of the nearest tracks of forest and now had a magnificent view of the canopy stretched across the horizon.

"It's so—"

Movement overhead caught her eye, and she looked up just as a great slab of goo splashed into her face and mouth.

"Yuck! What was that?"

Another slab of slime dropped from above, and she edged out of the way. The cries from above suddenly sounded less frightful and more menacing, and this time several shards of an object flew down the rock face.

"I think we're nearly there," she panted, and practically jumped the last few metres, her desire to be off the rock face at one with her burning curiosity.

As she pulled herself onto the grassy mound planted at the top, her friend crawled onto her neck, and her eyes widened at the huge nest in front of them. "Now I know why you didn't want to come."

The structure was massive, and the branches and shrubs more akin to tree trunks than what she had seen built by smaller birds. Movement flickered through a gap in the nest. Eager to spy her beckoner, she crept towards the gap and flinched back in horror whilst her friend darted back over the rock face's edge.

More desperate screams erupted from within. Though her instinct begged for her to jump in, caution whispered for her to stay clear of the danger that lurked behind the crude wall. She couldn't risk it. Slowly she began to back away, but as she did, the distant hum of the forest, both reassuring and heartfelt, suddenly begged for her to intervene. At least, that's what it sounded like to her unfamiliar ears. She hesitated until the beckon grew into a pleading howl, its message unmistakable.

Decided in her conviction to help, she swiftly clambered up the wall of the nest and into the pit of egg shards and mangled bodies. The creature that stared back, its eyes bloodshot and beak cruel, was different in all aspects to the fallen chicks that littered the bottom of the nest. Only one egg remained intact, with the rest destroyed, along with their inhabitants. Her eyes fell on a single broken egg with a slight discolouration to it.

"You're like a cuckoo, aren't you? I've never seen one so big…or so vile looking."

It screeched menacingly, and its eye flickered to the last intact egg. She crouched and grabbed a loose piece of splintered wood.

"I bet you can't help it. You're just doing what feels right, but I can't let you do it."

Even as an infant, the chick was nearly her height, though its movements were clumsy and uncoordinated. Slowly it began to circle her, its eyes unwavering in their stare. It screeched suddenly, causing her to collapse to her knees in a fit of agonising spasms. While she was immobilised by the pain, the chick tore into her calf with its hooked beak, and she screamed through clenched teeth.

The chick relished the pain it had just inflicted, but as it went for her again, the little songbird dive-bombed from above and fluttered and screeched enough to draw its juvenile attention. With the animal momentarily distracted, Xander struggled to her feet, grabbed the splintered wood, and dove towards it with the sharp object jutted forward.

The animal howled in pain at the impact, but the wood didn't pierce and instead dropped, broken and useless, into the residue of death in the trough of the nest. In its fury, the chick lunged and threw her into the wall, the impact enough to collapse her onto all fours. Squawking triumphantly at the deed and goaded by her defenceless form, the chick readied itself for one last lunge, and with its beak raised carelessly high in preparation for the final blow, it rushed her.

But it was in that final moment as it closed the gap that Xander felt a smooth, metallic edge under her worn fingers, and she instinctively grabbed the long, slender blade that had found her hand and thrust it into the animal's chest without friction or impediment.

It took but a few heartbeats before the creature realised its fate and slowly slumped to the ground in a heap.

Her mouth agape, she observed the weapon she held. It was unlike any sword or dagger she had seen, and though it shone gold, it lacked the fragile properties of the metal. The curve was slight and the handle a perfect continuation of the blade. But most surprising was the weight.

"How incredible. It's as light as a—"

She was thrown back into the muck, along with her little friend, by a gust from above and felt the nest thud as something gigantic landed in the pit. In the mayhem of her tumble, she clung to the sword and attempted to glimpse the new threat, but before she could right herself, the creature's piercing wail brought her to her knees and made her vomit.

"Not again!" she screamed in fright of the predator that stood over her.

With stars in her eyes and her stomach turned upside down, she looked up and froze. It was a giant eagle, and its dangerous eyes were focused on her and the blade she held. The eagle abruptly stopped its wail and turned to the dead cuckoo and the strewn carcasses of her young, its expression forlorn and distraught. With swift aggression, the great bird grabbed the felled vermin that had devastated her young and lobbed its carcass out of the nest and down the crag of rock.

"You're the mother," Xander said softly from her knees as pity stole her fear, though she still dared not move for dread of unwarranted retribution.

The eagle returned its gaze to Xander and the blade she held, the blade born from its own feathers, and then unexpectedly dipped its head. A subtle appreciation for saving the last of its young, the remaining egg a beacon of hope among the remnants of the slaughter.

The beast approached her and lowered itself to the ground at her feet, an apparent invitation to climb aboard.

"I think I may just climb down the way I came," she said nervously, and pointed to the side of the rock, but the eagle's insisting gaze did not waver. "Or perhaps I just come with…"

▲ ▲ ▲

She gaped in awe at the horizon as the eagle glided southward over the stretch of grassy expanse and into the sky above a seemingly never-ending canopy of trees donned in orange, yellow, purple, blue, and all sorts of colours not usually found in the green forests of western Anemoi.

Initially unable to keep up, the songbird had since taken refuge in the shelter of her pocket and now seemed quite content to remain for the duration of the flight. Xander instinctively patted her jacket's pocket and giggled at the head that popped out.

"You know, little guy, you saved me back there. What's your name?"

The songbird whistled enthusiastically in response.

"Well, that's a mouthful. I think I'll just call you Oscine after the ancient bird deity of wine and mischief, if that's okay."

The songbird chirped cheerfully.

A vibrantly colourful tree on the distant horizon that so easily dwarfed all others packed into the landscape soon captivated their attention, and Xander found herself holding her breath in wonder.

"Are we going there?" she called to the eagle, but much to her disappointment, the bird chose that moment to dive towards the ground into a small enclosure similar to the one where she had consumed the puffball.

She slid from the eagle to the grass below and abruptly clutched her calf at the moment of contact.

"I forgot about that," she muttered through clenched teeth.

Her little friend chirped nonchalantly from her pocket.

"Well, at least you're comfortable."

She looked up to the eagle, but before she could utter her appreciation, the huge beast had launched back into the air and out of sight.

"A bird of even fewer words than you. You know, if it weren't for the crazy colours this side of the forest, you'd think we never left the first enclosure where we met. Anyway, at least we know where the Great Tree on the map is. And over there, that's a path, and I think I saw a house not far from here."

Thunder groaned and drops of water started to pelt down.

"Just our luck. Come on!" she said, and hobbled into the forest.

Though the canopy of the colourful forest deflected the brunt of the storm, the persistence of the downpour, coupled with the sparseness of the trees immediately around the path, quickly left them both drenched and longing for shelter. But determined to find the house, she trod on through the wet and let her thoughts drift to Hemish and the dream.

"It was so unlike him but so real. I know he would never do that, but still…and still I wonder if he could ever forgive me. Perhaps he has forgiven me, forgiven me for—"

She fell to her knees and vomited violently as a sharp, fiery pain shot through her leg and spine and into her head. Terrified and struggling for breath, she had barely unwound the makeshift bandage to reveal green discolouration on the wound when dizziness took her and collapsed her into a convulsing heap.

"Oscine!" she cried.

Alarmed, the songbird scrambled out of her pocket and flew frantically down the path and into the shroud of the rain, leaving her strewn alone in the mud. Her every attempt to relax her body was an attempt in vain, with each spasm worse than the last, and it wasn't long before she began to wish for a slumber that wouldn't come. And it was much to her relief that

Oscine finally reappeared with a cloaked figure.

The energy depletion of the ensuing days wreaked havoc on her body, and though the convulsions eventually subsided, her inability to maintain sleep meshed fiction with reality and left her hallucinating figures from her past and yearning for futures that could not be.

The strangest of all was the cloaked figure who had rescued her. He hadn't left her side since he found her. His face. His voice. So familiar, yet from another time. She couldn't pinpoint it, nor could she decide if he was real or not. What did he call her again? Oh yeah. "Kiddo."

CHAPTER 31

Aprix 26, 476; Borealis, Borlencia; four months before the fall of Borealis—"And why did the end of the Revolutionary Wars coincide with the start of our calendar?" Putantis asked.

Xander twiddled her fingers as she tried to recall what he had told her several weeks prior when her mind had already drifted from fatigue. It was just the two of them sitting on the floor of the minister's office. A warm glow emanated from the afternoon sun outside, and the room was as cosy as ever, much to Xander's delight.

"Come on, Xander, you know this," he said, eyes intent on the girl.

She bit her lip, hesitant to divulge the wrong answer. "Our calendar started the same year Anemoi became Anemoi."

He smiled, pleased she had remembered. "Yes. The end of the war was a pivotal moment in Anemoi's history, because it's when we transitioned into modern Anemoi from what?"

"A kingdom."

"Of sorts, yes. It marked the end of the tyrant sitting on Zyphyr's long-dismantled throne, and the birth of Anemoi's current political structure, with all the warring city-states unified under a single banner and system. Now for a tricky one—what age are we in?"

Xander's mouth screwed up into a pensive pout as she counted her fingers. "The fifth."

"Yes! That's correct. And when did the first end?"

She grinded her teeth and peered up to the ceiling as if she might spot the answer scribbled onto the peeling paint. "The year one hundred ten."

"One hundred eleven."

"That nearly counts!"

"*Nearly* being the key word. But here's an opportunity to redeem yourself. Why did the first age end?"

"That's not fair. You didn't tell me why."

"Did I not? I could've sworn I did. Very well! Then let me ask you this—have you heard of the Upheaval?"

She had heard the word before. Where? She couldn't recall. But what it meant? She had no clue. A tad annoyed that she didn't know the answer, she looked at him and shrugged.

"Like the start of every new age since Anemoi's founding, one hundred eleven marked an event of significant political reform," he began. "An event significant enough to drastically change the political landscape of Anemoi and propel us into the second age."

"And that event was the Upheaval?"

"Correct. The Upheaval is how we refer to the civil conflict that led to religion being banned from Anemoi's politics, permanently."

"But why—"

The pair turned to the door as a man poked his head through.

"Permission?" the man grunted.

"Yes, yes," Putantis responded.

The man stepped in. He was covered in the muck of the road and had swollen black circles under his eyes.

"How can I help you, my good man?" Putantis asked.

"Commander Carolus needs you."

Xander perked up at the mention of her father's military rank.

"Lower House? Upper House? My ear? What's the reason?" Putantis questioned eagerly as he stood up.

The messenger glanced at Xander, who was still sitting on the floor, and then back at Putantis.

"It's okay," Putantis said. "She's the man's daughter."

"It concerns the fleet," he responded after a moment's hesitation.

Xander could immediately feel Putantis's nerves tighten, despite his attempt to keep his face straight.

"Very well," Putantis said with forced calmness. "Would you please see to it that Xander makes it back to her mother's office?"

The man shuffled uncomfortably. "Commander Alya?"

"Yes. That okay?"

"Yes, sir."

"Great," Putantis said as he helped the girl up. "You will give Alya my best, won't you?" he said softly to Xander.

She wanted to ask what had jarred him, to see if he was alright, but thought better of it with the messenger in earshot. "For you, Putantis, any day."

"Good girl. Now let's all get a move on before our respective beckoners begin to worry."

At that, the trio left the cosy warmth of the room into the palace halls.

CHAPTER 32

Septembrix 3, 484; the Great Forest—"Your strength will come back with time, kiddo." Ricard smiled. "For now, it's more important that we rid your body of the poison."

He cut up another of his plants and threw it into a glass of water. Her pale face scrunched up.

"Not sure if I'd rather the poison or your drinks."

He laughed boisterously and handed her the drink. Still built like an ox, Ricard had softened a bit around the midsection, and it wasn't difficult to see why.

"I never realised you were such a good cook," she said greedily, and took another bite of his stew. "I also never realised a stew without meat could taste so good. Or that you, of all people, could forgo the stuff completely, now that I think about it!"

"Ha, trust me, it wears on you after a while. You end up craving cheeses, marmalades, and candies just to fill the void. Basically, anything that isn't good for you. Maybe you realised." He laughed, and pinched an inch from his gut.

"You know, all that time on the road with no cooked meals, and no shelter…this feels like paradise if ever there was one. What a shame it took me nearly dying to find comfort similar to that of my aunt's home."

"And you're lucky I found you. The world works differently down here. Not much that can't kill you or at least give you a good hiding, and I don't think you would've lasted much longer with that wound." He looked at her wistfully. "I thought you were dead…we all did."

"We?"

"Other survivors who were friendly with your mom and pop. We searched for you, but after we abandoned Borealis, and as more and more time went by…well, we gave up hope…and yet here you are."

"What happened to my father, Ricard?" she asked abruptly.

He hesitated. "That's a story for another time, kiddo. Soon enough I'll show you around and introduce you to some of the neighbours. Maybe they can help with this adventure of yours. And drink your medicine. You won't get very far if that sickness returns."

Oscine jumped onto the burly man's shoulder, and together they left the cosy room.

"Something tells me they've met before," Xander said, and took another laboured sip of the bitter concoction.

CHAPTER 33

Septembrix 4, 484; the Great Forest—Xander peered across the wooden table at the husband-and-wife duo no larger than her hand, who looked oddly in place within the cosy confines of Ricard's quaint forest cottage. She was still somewhat bemused by the fact that people so tiny could exist, and she found it difficult not to stare at the pair as they ate their meals using miniature bowls and utensils.

"So where is it you want to go?" Haro, the little man, asked Xander. His dark hair and angular face never deviated far from one of starkness and was quite the opposite to the red hair and soft features of his bride, who seemed unable to take her eyes off Xander.

"The Great Tree." Ricard spoke up.

"No, no, no, it's too dangerous!" the wife said alarmedly. "Tell her it's too dangerous, Ricard."

"He told me," Xander said whilst Ricard worked on a mouthful of stew. "Though he didn't tell me why. Just that maybe you could help."

"Oh! I don't like this."

"Leila, let's take a breath," Ricard said calmly.

"It's too dangerous, Ricard."

"Because of the Lizard King?" Xander asked curiously.

The two little ones shot Ricard a wary glance.

"Partly, yes," Ricard said. "Though I can't say I recall mentioning him to you."

"I heard the three of you speaking about him yesterday," Xander said. "Something about the last time you saw him, Ricard, he seemed a half-foot shorter than what you remembered, though still a touch taller than yourself."

"You were eavesdropping?" Haro said, lifting an eyebrow.

"Hardly eavesdropping if you're speaking with the bedroom door open."

Ricard laughed. "In our defence, kiddo, we thought you were passed out."

"Well, who is he?" Xander asked.

"He's the King of the Great Tree. But—"

"*Was*," Haro corrected.

"Right. He *was* the King of the Great Tree. And then—"

"The war began," Leila blurted.

"Right. Then the war began," Ricard said. "And shortly after it began, he—"

"Was deposed by the Dragon King," Haro butted in.

"Who's telling this story, you two?" Ricard raised his voice.

"We are!"

"Perhaps you should just let me tell it, so the girl has some semblance of what we're actually discussing."

"Okay, okay." Leila leered at the rise she'd gotten out of the big man.

"He was deposed by the Dragon King and had the Great Tree taken from him. That's not to say he and his soldiers haven't taken it back on the odd occasion, but never for very long. Like a hot apple, they're always passing it to one another. For the most part, though, the Dragon King holds it."

"The Dragon King?" Xander said with an amused grin. "Where do they come up with these names?"

The others didn't laugh.

"Well, I guess it does sound a bit worse," she added.

"It is!" Leila yelped.

Ricard looked at the little woman in all seriousness, and she raised her hands in invitation for him to continue.

"It is and it isn't, kiddo. The Dragon King isn't actually a dragon per se. He…or *it* is a dragonfly."

"A dragonfly?" Xander blurted, spooked by the thought of a giant flying insect roaming the woods.

"Yep. And I would also question how much stronger the Dragon King is compared to the Lizard King. But that's not the issue."

"It's the Dragon King's army of minions." Haro spoke up.

"*Army* of minions?" Xander said, again frightened by the implication.

"Yes. The bug has more supporters than the Lizard King, and sadly this is where the power lies. And unfortunately, the bug army has a taste for forest critters and humans. You'll not make it very far."

"Nope, nope, nope." Leila shook her head. "Like we said, too dangerous!"

"Sounds like it's the Dragon King I need to watch out for, not the other one," Xander said with a shudder. "Maybe the Lizard King can help me?"

Haro laughed. "What do you think he's been trying to do since he was dethroned?"

"Get that tree back," Leila said matter-of-factly.

"Which means we have something in common," Xander responded.

Leila looked at Ricard as if asking his permission.

He retorted, "Not as if I could stop you."

"What aren't you telling me?" Xander asked, intrigued by the exchange.

"There's history," Ricard said bluntly.

"What do you mean?"

"He means history between the Lizard King and your father," Leila said.

"He knew my father?" Xander said, surprised and eager for more.

"They were business partners and had a bit of a falling-out," Ricard said.

"A bit?" Haro scoffed.

"What happened?" Xander asked.

Ricard waved his hand dismissively. "Just a matter of not seeing eye to eye on a couple of issues. Nothing important."

"Or perhaps we just tell her the truth," Leila said sternly. "It's not your burden to bear, Ricard. Just as it isn't hers."

"Now you have to tell me," Xander said, leaning forward.

"Your father and a young Ricard—"

"Back when he was a few pounds lighter," Haro chirped.

Ricard ignored the insult and took a swig of his drink.

"Yes, you could say that," Leila said. "They came to these woods when they weren't much older than you. If you think Ricard is a rascal now, you should've seen him back then. All sorts of mischief and youthful arrogance followed that pair. They were like brothers."

Xander smiled as she glanced at Ricard. "Sounds like them. Why were they here?"

"They were adventurers and mercenaries."

"Mercenary?" Ricard said, scrunching his face distastefully. "Such a cold word, don't you think?"

"You sold your skill in a fight for money, no? Then, yes, mercenary. Anyway, back then there was much adventure to be had, and they certainly didn't waste the opportunity. They made a name for themselves, helping to resolve local grievances and find missing artefacts. And with that name came gold and more requests. Soon the Lizard King got wind of their exploits, and he invited them to the Great Tree. This was back when the king still had his throne. At first he had several easy jobs for them—"

"Easy! Says who? Right, right! Keeping quiet now. Please continue."

"It was his way of getting to know them. Once they had earned his trust, he let on to the real reason they were there. War was coming."

"The Dragon King?" Xander asked.

"The Dragon King and its invasion of bugs from the southwest. Settlement by settlement, the bugs were displacing the forest critters. The Lizard King and his warriors were strong, but they didn't have the numbers."

"And how did my father and Ricard fit into this?"

"They became two of the Lizard King's most trusted warriors. They helped him win a number of fights. For a short while, it seemed that with their help, we might actually win." She sighed, and a forlorn expression took her and the others.

"What happened?"

"The bugs retaliated, kiddo," Ricard said ashamedly. "They killed thousands of forest critters. All innocents."

"The Lizard King grew desperate," Leila continued. "As did we all. Then one day a chance presented itself. A chance to catch the Dragon King and—"

"Kill it," Ricard interjected, his expression stern, his eyes distant. "It was an ambush. Carolus, myself, and the king's senior captain were leading the charge. Even this one was there," he said, pointing to Haro.

"But the Dragon King knew you were coming?" Xander queried.

"No. The Dragon King didn't know. It was perfectly executed. Even with our inferior numbers, we slaughtered half of that army. And whilst our soldiers continued the slaughter, Carolus and I backed the Dragon King into a corner with what was left of its personal guard. We launched into them and started to kill indiscriminately." He hesitated.

"What?"

"They all looked alike. We couldn't easily distinguish between them. When Carolus cut into and dismembered one that was only slightly smaller than the others, the Dragon King screamed. A horrible, agonising scream that haunts me still. Without knowing it, Carolus had just killed the Dragon King's child."

Xander's stomach knotted, and goosebumps tightened her skin.

Ricard continued, "As any father would, the Dragon King lost all restraint and recklessly threw itself at Carolus. Carolus, the brilliant soldier that he is, kept his composure and brought the king to its knees. The king's life was in Carolus's hands."

"He could've killed it." Haro spoke. "He could've ended it all."

"He let the king live?" Xander said, both astonished and proud.

"Carolus couldn't bring himself to kill the king," Leila said. "He let the bug get away. And in doing so, brought a plague down on the Great Forest. The Dragon King and its minions have not been kind to the rest of us since then."

"Why the reluctance to tell me?" Xander asked, confused. "My father killed the Dragon King's child, and then the Lizard King was dethroned and his people slaughtered because of his inaction. How could I not need to know this?"

"You shouldn't have to bear the grudge against your father," Ricard said.

"And neither should you," Leila said, placing her tiny hand on Ricard's.

"But obviously you think it's a problem," Xander said angrily.

"The Lizard King won't kill you," Haro said. "Nor will any forest critter that isn't a bug. It just means there's no guarantee he will help."

Xander rubbed her temples like an exhausted parent might. "If he won't help me, what else can I do to get to that tree?"

"Turn back," Haro said nonchalantly.

"I can't."

"Without the Lizard King, your chance of success is laughable. The Dragon King will kill you on sight, and only a group of armed forest critters with knowledge of the tree could prevent it. Why would the Lizard King risk it? Why would you risk it? What's in that tree that's so important?"

"Something that can help her protect her home," Ricard interjected. "She needs to get to the tree to find something that could save her people."

"Ah!" Haro said with a more sympathetic tone.

Xander's shoulders slumped. "Then I'm stuck."

"Maybe not," Ricard said, pondering. "You're Carolus's daughter, which is a problem, but it could also be a blessing. The Lizard King is a firm believer in inherited power, whether true or not. He won't have forgotten Carolus's deeds, and if you're even half as resourceful as your father, you'll be useful. Maybe he can be convinced."

"And who'll convince him?" Haro said. "You?"

"Yes. He still owes me a debt for my service that he conveniently forgot to pay after the whole debacle. If he's not forgotten, I can call it in."

Xander's face brightened at the unexpected offer.

"Something funny, Haro?" Ricard asked sternly as the little man chortled.

"You mean other than the fact you've seen better days?" Haro taunted. "Tell me, when was the last time you held that mighty axe of yours?"

"Or walked farther than your next meal?" Leila chimed in.

Ricard's cheeks shone red. "Ignore these two, kiddo. They have just as much say in this as they take up space," he bellowed to their disapproval. "Anyway, it's just a conversation."

Haro drummed his fingers against the table, his expression pensive. "What the girl has to offer, the king will have to decide."

"She's resourceful," Leila said. "She found her way down here alone. And so young."

"Like old times, perhaps the king can be convinced of her use."

"Yes, it could work."

"But to let the oaf here ruin your only chance would pain me always. The heck with it! I, too, will come with you." Haro stood mightily.

Excitement took Xander. "You know him then?"

"Who?"

"The Lizard King?"

"Not on a first-name basis, no."

"But he'll listen to you?"

"We've yet to find out."

"Then how will you help?"

"With my knowledge of the forest and with my sword!"

Xander stifled an involuntary smirk, not wanting to be rude.

"Something funny?"

She shook her head. "Nope."

"Well, little girl? Spit it out."

"Your sword?"

"As I said, my sword."

"But it must be no longer than a toothpick. What could you possibly use it for?"

Haro's cheeks reddened as Ricard erupted into laughter at the jibe. Leila jumped over and hugged her husband mockingly.

"We will need his sword, kiddo," Ricard managed after he finally stopped laughing.

"Not to mention I know the forest critters and that tree better than Ricard here," Haro said seriously. "Though he likes to think otherwise."

"I still don't understand—" Xander began.

"So dinner tonight?" Leila interrupted cheerfully.

"Not tonight. Xander still isn't recovered. Let's give it a couple more days and then re-evaluate," Ricard said.

"A couple more days for you to shape up," Leila said, and prodded the big man's bulging stomach.

"I think he'll need longer than that," Haro added.

"Not sure who's talking," Ricard retorted, and they all burst into laughter.

CHAPTER 34

Septembrix 6, 484; the Great Forest—"Here, I made this for your blade," Ricard said, and pulled a grey scabbard from beneath a cloth.

He threw it to Xander, and she marvelled at it.

"It straps across your back. I made it from a local material. Like your sword, it's light as a feather but strong as steel. It's so strong, in fact, you could use it as a weapon itself," he said, clearly proud of his work.

"I love it. Thank you!"

"And if you'll let us, Haro and I would be honoured to train you to use it."

"I already—"

"I know. Your aunt's friend back home has been teaching you weaponry, but it doesn't hurt to keep up the training with new teachers. Would be impossible not to learn something new, especially with a tool you've not used before. Anyway, given the road ahead of you, we wouldn't want you getting rusty, would we?"

She smiled warmly. "I guess not. Thank you."

"Oh! And that's not all. I sewed up your mother's jacket. It was looking a bit worn."

"I didn't take you for a handmaiden."

"Hey, none of that. It's just as important for a man to know his way around a needle and thread as it is a woman," he said, and threw her the mended jacket.

She pulled it on and sheathed the sword over it. He looked on in awe.

"You look every bit your mother, kiddo."

She blushed, and it took all her energy to hold back her tears.

"She was both an explorer and a warrior," he said. "Though it was before your time, Alya joined Carolus and me on some of our adventures…I mostly kept them out of trouble, but boy, did we have fun."

"I'd like to hear about it sometime."

"I bet you would, and you will, but not today. Today we go for dinner with the two little ones."

"I've been meaning to ask about that."

"About what?" he responded, pulling from his pocket a short wooden stick wrapped in a worn parchment.

"About dinner at their house."

He eyed her sword. "That really is a nice blade. It'll take good care of you. It's also very rare, legendary almost, that a human should be gifted one. You'll look after it, won't you?"

"Of course!"

"Good girl."

"And you're avoiding my question."

"Am I?" He looked at the blade again and then shrugged. "Fancy a sweet?"

"Ricard!"

"Well?" he asked, holding one out in his palm.

"Before dinner?"

"Before dinner," he laughed, and threw it to her. "Try to savour the taste and see how long you can go without chewing it," he said as both their faces scrunched up at the sourness.

He grabbed his huge battle-axe and slung his bag over his shoulder, then muttered the nonsensical words scribbled on the parchment.

"Wait for it!"

"For what?"

"Bop!" he called, and knocked her in the head with the wooden stick.

"Ouch! Why in Anemoi—"

Stars bombarded her peripheral vision, but all that seemed to change was the sensitivity of her tongue and the amusement on Ricard's face.

"Why did you do that?" she asked, rubbing her head.

"Look around you."

She looked to her side and flinched. The dinner table towered over them. It was huge.

"How—how's this possible? What's happened to us?"

"The world works differently down here."

"But we're tiny!"

"How else did you think we were going to find the Lizard King or enter the tree? Size is everything down here, and only if we're really small, like mice, can we access the inner reaches of the forest."

"But I saw the Great Tree from atop the eagle. We could've reached it."

"Sorry, kiddo, wasn't possible. Even the eagle knew that. That's why you were dropped off near my place."

He swung his battle-axe and flexed his muscles, and then he eyed her blade again.

"Good to see your blade followed suit. Was worried for a second there."

"I don't understand. The stick did all this?"

"That was the Rite of Small Passage written on the parchment. The language is local to the Great Forest, and the Rite itself is a closely guarded secret that only works if you're within the forest's borders. Once you read it, the native trees in earshot use their energy to manipulate the matter in your body, making you very small."

"So why did you hit me?"

"Added effect."

"And the sweet?"

"I like the taste."

A loud thump emanated from behind her, and she turned abruptly to face it.

"Oscine, you're—you're huge!" The bird acknowledged with a loud chirp. "And Oscine?"

"Is already small. Well, he was," Haro called as he strode over.

At this size, he looked formidable with his sword by his side and his shield on his back. Leila walked beside him, and she, too, looked more normal than cute, though she was dressed more appropriately for an excursion than for dinner.

"Are you coming with us, Leila?"

"Yes, yes, I am."

"We decided it's in our combined interest if she, too, comes along," Ricard said, though it was clear he was unconvinced.

"To make certain you lot stay out of trouble," she said. Haro shook his head, also not keen on the idea. "So let's not forget dinner. Come on, we've prepared quite the spread."

"We?"

"Haro helped…somewhat."

"Cutting firewood is considered help these days?" Ricard joked as they made their way to the couple's cottage nestled in the roots of an orange-leafed oak.

CHAPTER 35

Septembrix 7, 484; the Great Forest—Xander looked up curiously at the giant weed towering over the narrow path. "We really couldn't have entered this part of the forest without reading the Rite?" she asked nobody in particular.

"Nope," Ricard said. "Interestingly, though, once you've entered into these parts, you don't need to keep reciting the Rite. Being small kind of becomes your new normal."

"And if we'd stayed in your cottage? How long before the effect would've worn off?"

"A day, maybe two. Depends on the person and their conviction."

"You know what doesn't make sense to me, though? I don't get how we can shrink to this size and not weigh the same."

"She has much to learn, Ricard," Haro said. "Good thing she has us to guide her."

They looked at each other and erupted into laughter.

"Don't take any notice of those two," Leila said.

"Yes, yes, don't worry. With time you'll have that moment of clarity," Haro jibed at Xander.

A gigantic fly buzzed overhead, causing Xander to crouch. "It's hard to believe we're still in Anemoi sometimes."

Haro looked at her and then the others, feigning shock.

"What?" she asked. "You don't consider this Anemoi?"

"Depends who you ask," Ricard responded. "Back in Borealis, the administrators and your friend Putantis would have lumped this forest in with the rest of the boundaries. Of course, to be a part of Anemoi would be to suggest the provinces have dominion here."

"But they have none!" Haro said.

"Nope, nope, nope," Leila added.

"And then you've got the forest critters, like these two, who would proudly state—"

"How can they have jurisdiction if they can't enter?" Haro said.

"Makes sense. Might also explain the soldiers at the entrance to the forest and why they wouldn't enter," Xander said.

"Soldiers?"

"Soldiers at the river ford. They're gone now, though—creatures from the forest made sure of that. Didn't leave much to the imagination, if I must be honest."

Haro looked at Ricard and then back to Xander. "What kind of creatures?"

"Trees, I think. Not bound by roots and not as tall or as thick, but certainly nastier."

"Looks like the Lizard King's replacement isn't making waste of the resources left to him," Ricard observed.

"But to send them across the river..." Leila said, shocked.

"Is he trying to start another war?" Haro frowned.

"Another?" Xander said inquisitively.

Haro stopped in his tracks. "Seriously, Ricard, this isn't funny anymore. Do they not teach children history where you're from?"

"Where I come from isn't Borealis," Ricard said. "And if we are referring to Borealis, well, there've been a few developments since its destruction and all. You may have heard about it. It's a different world now."

They started walking again, and Leila took Xander's hand in hers. "A long time ago—"

"And she means a long, long time ago," Ricard interjected.

"There were some pretty nasty battles between the forest critters and the old kingdoms of what is now western Anemoi."

"But, well…" Xander glanced at Haro, not wanting to cause another insult. "How? Humans can't enter the forest unless they're small, and if the battles happened outside the forest, well, what chance would the forest critters have?"

"Back then there were different restrictions in place. Humans could enter with no problem. There was no need for men to adjust their size."

"And like every other domain, the kings desired this forest for their own and had no problem resorting to force to take what was not theirs," Ricard said.

"Who struck first?" Xander asked.

"The forest critters and their allies, and you're right. They struggled to hold their own because their size worked against them."

Haro abruptly swung his sword and cut an overgrown weed that poked through the path.

"Well, size wasn't an issue for *all* the forest critters and their allies, I might add," Ricard continued. "First off, not all forest critters were always so small like these two here, and even those that were, well, they had their uses."

"We're good for sneaking." Haro winked.

"And medicines," Leila added as she patted her bag.

"And thus, they make fine thieves and assassins," Ricard said, to their embarrassment.

"And then you've got forest critters like the Lizard King and his kind, the Lizard People, that were once big and could also match the humans in combat," Leila said. "And those brutish trees you saw, they're the Guardians of the forest. They protect the forest and everything in it, including the forest critters. Quite the monsters, really."

"You know, back home we always referred to the animals living in the woods as forest critters," Xander said. "It's only in the fairy tales that they could also take the form of little people, like yourselves. When I saw you both for the first time, I thought I had fallen back asleep. Makes me think that our fairy tales were based on the Great Forest."

"I wouldn't be surprised."

"Though in those stories, the forest critters that weren't animals were never big or extraordinary looking. They just looked like little people. And yet it seems different down here."

"It is. Some are bigger, some smaller, some hairier, and some fairer. Forest critters, both the animals and the little people, can come in all shapes and sizes."

"So next silly question: What do the Lizard People look like?"

Leila giggled. "Not lizards, if that's what you're thinking. The Lizard King and his kind don't look too different to us or even you."

"So human?"

"Um, I don't think they'd take too kindly to being called human, so best keep that to yourself."

"And the Dragon King?"

"The bugs!" Haro scoffed. "They'd like to call themselves forest critters, but I beg to differ."

"Some would say they're loosely related, but the general consensus is that they're not true forest critters," Ricard added.

"Right," Xander began, "but what I'm asking is, are they of the smaller variety or the bigger variety when not bound by the forest's size restriction?"

"The larger variety. A metre taller than me when I found you several days ago."

She shuddered. "That's what I thought."

Haro chortled. "And a gruesome thought at that, isn't it?"

"It is," Ricard said. "But don't forget, they're still residents of these woods, even if a plague."

"Sadly."

Leila cleared her throat. "And to continue with the story. Together the trees and the forest critters fought to repel the humans."

"And still that was not enough," Haro said.

"No, it wasn't. Their numbers were too few, and with time they were forced deeper into the forest with each assault until—"

"She came!" Haro stopped in his tracks again and opened his arms to the forest around. "We're still here because of Bronte, our heroine. And you, you're small because of her."

"Bronte changed the law of the inner reaches of the forest with her energy, meaning the humans could only enter as minnows," Leila said.

"Stalemate. Out there, we are small, and our numbers count for nothing. In here, you are small, and your numbers count for nothing."

"Some even refer to it as Bronte's Law," Ricard remarked.

They started down the path again, and Xander frowned at the grey clouds overhead.

"But why would those creatures attack the soldiers?"

"You'll have to ask the new lord of the forest," Ricard said mockingly.

"You don't think the Dragon King would start another war, do you? I mean, with the restrictions in place, how would it be possible?"

"I don't know, kiddo. Just these two thinking aloud."

Xander looked up and abruptly dove into the mud as a giant raindrop splashed to the ground where she stood.

"Quite harmless. Just a little—" A second drop knocked Ricard to the ground, and he grinned through the mud caked on his face.

"That one was a little larger than we're used to," Haro said, and led them through the bombardment towards the shelter of a limp toadstool.

"Must be getting old," Ricard wheezed. He bent over and stretched his back. "Used to find those almost therapeutic back in the day."

"You mean a long, long time ago."

"So it seems."

A loud thump came from atop the toadstool, and a sheet of water slid from the sides.

"Oscine?" Ricard asked.

The toadstool shook as the bird splashed to the ground with a large grub shoved in its beak.

"Lunch, anyone?" Ricard joked as the bird slurped the slippery meal.

Xander screwed up her face. "Ugh, maybe not."

"I'm with the child on this one." Haro grimaced.

"Perhaps you're right," Ricard said.

"Nonsense. I'll prepare something whilst we wait for the weather to pass," Leila said, and started to empty her bag of its treats.

"So, Haro, how much farther to your old stomping grounds?" Ricard asked with a cheeky grin.

Haro looked nervously at Leila, but she seemed not to hear. "Another two hours, weather permitting."

"Stomping grounds?" Xander asked curiously, and again Haro shot his wife a nervous glance.

"You'll see." Leila spoke without looking up. "I'm sure it'll leave a mark like it did on these two." She grinned, to her husband's discomfort.

CHAPTER 36

"What are they?"

"I'd be damned if I knew," Ricard said.

"They're so…so…"

"Grotesque?"

"Eye-watering, perhaps?" Haro added.

Even Oscine looked revolted by what he saw.

"Are they some hybrid of animal and little people?" Xander inquired.

"Big word, that. I'm surprised you managed it," Haro joked.

"Be kind," Leila said. "They're like us, albeit a bit rougher looking than your average little person."

"They do have Haro's look, only they're uglier and a tad hairier," Xander said mischievously.

"Hey, I resent that comment!" he said with a straight face before laughing.

"Well, kiddo, welcome to Boletus. Home of the uglier, hairier versions of Haro. And a centre of trade in this part of the forest."

"Trade of what?"

"Mushrooms, of course," they all said in unison with cheeky smiles.

The town was far from quaint and more akin to the makeshift refugee camps that had sprung up after the fall of Borealis—an unpleasant mix of squalor and miscreants and a hive of the various forest critters going about their business.

"I thought mushrooms were supposed to quiet your mind," Xander said as they made their way down a street buzzing with all sorts of strange and noisy individuals.

"Much to learn," Haro commented.

"The consumption and variety of mind-altering mushrooms wasn't really on the curriculum at school."

"Poor girl."

As they rounded onto a side street, a sly smile of recognition crept across Ricard's face.

"And you call me the animal," Haro hooted.

"Let me guess. Good memories?" Xander said.

"Something like that. Long time ago, of course, but quite the event nonetheless."

"Up to no good, I imagine," Leila said.

Ricard laughed unashamedly.

"What would my father say if he knew?" Xander said cheerily.

"Who do you think instigated it?" Ricard replied.

"You were here with him?" she asked, interested.

"One of our many adventures, kiddo. Come on, we're here," he said, and pointed to one of the more respectable establishments on the street.

About to enter, he turned to Oscine.

"Best you wait out here…wouldn't want you breaking anything. The owner's very particular about his possessions."

The bird frowned, or at least appeared to.

"I think I'll stay out here and keep the bird out of trouble," Leila said.

"Don't wander too far…" Haro said.

The inside of the shop was in stark contrast to the disorder of the streets. Dozens of neat cabinets and shelves lined the walls, and every conceivable space was packed with jars and vials, large and small, filled with all sorts of ingredients.

"Good idea leaving Oscine outside," Xander commented.

"Without a doubt," Haro added.

They continued towards the end of the elongated store, where one of the hairy forest critters stood and observed as they approached.

"It's been a long time, Ricard," he said.

"You remember me after all these years, Nudus! I'm shocked."

"How could I forget? Come to pay your old debts?"

"Hey, those were settled fair and square."

Nudus stared at him and then took in the other two. "Haro."

"Nudus," Haro responded.

"And this must be Carolus's daughter," Nudus said.

They stared in astonishment.

He smirked. "The stink. And that same mischievous grin and desire to cause trouble. Maybe you should've left her outside with that raptor of yours, and no, I'm not referring to Mrs. Haro but the clumsy songbird that stumbles down this beautiful town's streets. Good idea leaving it outside, by the way."

"You can tell she's Carolus's daughter just by the smell?" Ricard had spoken up before Haro could interject.

"That, and I can't imagine you ever finding another human to reproduce with, Ricard, and she's certainly too young and pretty to be your wife or lover."

They all burst into laughter at the crude remark, and even Haro's glare softened at the jibe.

"Anyway, what can I do for you?"

"We need directions," Ricard said.

"To where?"

"The Lizard King."

Nudus eyed Ricard for a moment. "It'll cost you."

"I didn't expect any less from you."

"Good. So you know this won't be easy…or fun."

"Really, you'd take the fun out of it?"

▲ ▲ ▲

"You weren't kidding. You really took the fun out of it," Ricard said as they observed the assortment of forest critters congregated at the base of a huge birch tree, all sitting and standing in excited anticipation of the deals to be struck between the various merchants and their potential clients. On the birch was the source of the crowd's excitement. Hundreds of mantises of all colours and sizes, jumping and climbing. Some with riders, others without.

"Indeed," Haro acknowledged.

They looked to Xander as she and the others climbed the slope towards their position.

"I wonder, does she ride like her father?" Nudus said.

Ricard's eyes widened. "Absolutely not!"

"You want to find the Lizard King, yes?"

"And it's too dangerous. There are too many critters happy to flaunt the rules and kill the competition. I'll not allow it. It'll have to be me or Haro."

"You're too heavy, and I wouldn't trust Haro to make it a tenth of a metre. It must be the girl, and when she wins—"

"You mean, if she finishes…"

"When she finishes—and wins—I'll have my price, and you, you'll have the Lizard King. It's the only way."

"What good does the glory of winning the Moonlight Festival do for you, you cretin?"

"The price I'll be able to fetch for Sol will make it worth my while. Not to mention, the wager I'll inevitably place in the girl's favour. You'll not find the king without me. You know it's the truth."

Ricard scratched his chin. "I don't like this."

"Neither me," Haro said.

232

"Like what?" Xander said from behind with Leila and Oscine beside her.

Ricard groaned and looked at her. "Well, kiddo, hope you're not squeamish."

"It's kind of like a horse," Xander said excitedly.

"I would've preferred a horse for you," Ricard said.

"Not me. This looks far more fun. Plus, I can't remember the last time I rode a horse."

The others looked at her with curiosity, then back to the gigantic birch with its army of carnivorous insects.

"Kiddo, we'll have this conversation again after it's tried to eat you. Then you can tell me how much fun you're having."

"She's more like her father than you know," Leila said softly.

Nudus whistled loudly, and a huge red-and-yellow mantis jumped from the tree overhead to the ground in front of them.

"What's its name?" Xander asked.

"Her name is Sol," Nudus responded.

"And you ride her?"

"Me? Of course not. I'm too big and, like these two logs here, have no dexterity." Haro and Ricard rolled their eyes at the comment. "No, I rent her out to would-be racers for a price."

"Has she ever won?"

"A couple of times, but now she's old and irritable. Still, I get paid, and that's what matters. Well, are you going to give her a try?"

"How do I get on?" Xander asked, and approached the towering bug.

"Climb that flower over there, and jump onto her where the neck meets the back. She'll do the rest."

"I don't like this," Ricard said nervously as Xander climbed to the top of the stem.

"Have faith, old man."

"Don't mean to offend, you filthy critter, but I struggle to trust you, even at the best of times."

"You don't have to trust me. You only need to trust her, and Ricard, you vile man, she'll amaze you more than you know."

"And how could you possibly know that?"

"Instinct."

Ricard glanced at Nudus and then at Xander as she jumped gracefully from the plant onto the insect. He smiled softly.

The vibrations of the insect's heartbeat felt strange but therapeutic on Xander's behind, but in search of a comfortable position, she was abruptly thrown into the dirt by the insect, which proceeded to stare at her menacingly from above with its large orange eyes.

Ricard looked away. "This is not going to end well."

"Use your legs," Haro called.

"I thought you couldn't ride," Xander called back.

"I can't, but most would call it common sense."

"Always the charmer," Leila said.

Xander climbed the flower again and looked down at the mantis below, its eyes still locked on her.

"Okay, Sol, ready for another try?" she whispered, and stepped off the flower, only to land in the dirt as the insect moved to the side.

Nudus chuckled. "I told you she can be irritable."

"And yet you still find others willing to rent her?" Ricard asked curiously.

"Largely desperate people, quite like yourselves. Those that have nothing to lose or that need a way out."

"We have everything to lose!"

"Hence why my price is that she wins. Come on, Sol, play nice," he called out.

Xander took a deep breath and jumped. She landed with a thud, and immediately the mantis bolted forward and leapt into the air, but she held. Evidently irritated by her continued presence, the mantis skidded to the left, leapt onto the birch, and bolted up the side using its powerful legs for grip.

Xander dared a glance down and quickly tightened her hold on the mantis's neck. Far below, the others appeared like little figurines amongst a forest of flowers and shrubs and grasses, and for a second, Xander felt like she was back to her normal size.

Near the top, and dangerously high for her liking, the mantis jumped and glided to the nearest branch with little regard for her safety. And yet, excitement began to course through her, and she found she was actually enjoying the ride.

"Let's see what else you can do," she said through gritted teeth.

She applied pressure against the mantis's neck using her left leg, and the insect turned sharply to the right and jumped to the nearest branch.

"You responded! Wait, wait, hold on!" she bellowed as the mantis continued towards the end of the branch with none other in sight.

"How do I stop this thing?"

She applied more pressure on the mantis's neck, but this time the insect ignored her command and pushed ahead faster and more aggressively, then leapt off the end of the branch into the air with nothing between them and the ground.

Below, the others squirmed in panic, and Oscine jumped into the air, ready to intercept, all while Xander clung to the mantis's rough, hairy neck for dear life. The only one that exuded calmness was Nudus, and it took but a few moments for them to understand why. This mantis had wings, an oddity even amongst the oddities of the Great Forest.

"What a terrifying creature," Haro said in awe.

"Yes, she's a fine specimen, even if a bit seasoned."

With the wind in her hair and her demise no longer in sight, Xander slowly released her clenched arms from the mantis's neck, using only her legs to grip, and she daringly stretched her hands to the sides.

"This is amazing!"

Even the mantis seemed to enjoy the moment and once again showed response from the pressure in her legs. Determined to really see what Sol was capable of, Xander urged on the insect, and they chased through the air and trees and along the ground between shrubs and flowers and houses. It was only when fatigue had begun to take her legs that she directed the mantis back to the others.

"Fascinating!" Nudus exclaimed.

"How so?" Ricard responded suspiciously.

"Can't remember the last time somebody managed to ride her without being eaten or falling to their death." Leila placed her hand on Ricard's shoulder to calm his response. "I usually take payment up front, and Sol likes to play with her food, hence toying with the girl."

Haro quickly put his hand on Ricard's other shoulder as the man continued to stare at Nudus in disbelief.

"Calm yourself, Ricard," Nudus said reassuringly. "She's fine. I have my rider, and you have your means to pay. The race is in eleven days, so she has ample time to practise."

"Well, let's hope that damned insect doesn't have a change of heart before then. Just make sure you feed it, Nudus," Ricard said threateningly.

CHAPTER 37

Septembrix 10, 484; Boletus, the Great Forest—Xander pulled the tattered sheet off herself and sat on the side of the bed. Leila still slept undisturbed on the other side, and the plain room was dimly illuminated by the early morning sun.

She exhaled, frustrated. Though she knew she was without choice, every day they lingered in the same spot compounded her worry for her aunt and Nhata. Of course her hometown was already overrun, and she guessed most of Borlencia must have also been occupied by that point. Still, it was a concern she couldn't shake.

Deciding on a morning walk, she got up and grabbed her shoes, but just as she readied to leave, a faint melody being hummed caught her ear, instantly calming her nerves. Then it stopped as quickly as it had started. She peered out the window. Nobody in sight. She had heard it before, though she couldn't pinpoint when or where. She shrugged and exited Nudus's dilapidated cottage onto the filthy street.

She rubbed her tired eyes and squinted down the empty road. The absence of movement was a peculiarity in the grotty town usually teeming with forest critters and their business. It was early morning, however, and the cool air, mixed with the festivities of the previous night, had made sure there were few early wanderers willing to dare the hour.

As she made her way down the untended road with no destination in mind, her thoughts drifted to the strange song. Even in that briefest of moments, it had soothed her nerves, and with every step, her nagging desire to know its origins grew.

Attention adrift, she turned a corner and bumped into a forest critter busy fixing a latch on their shop window. The critter, a hairy woman sporting stained overalls and who was very similar in appearance to Nudus, fell to the ground with a thump.

"Ow!" she yelped.

"I'm so sorry!" Xander said, and helped her to stand.

"It's alright! It's alright," the woman said, though the wince in her expression and her elevated foot signalled otherwise. "Could you?" She pointed to her store entrance.

"Of course!"

Xander helped the woman to the door and stepped inside with her. Similar to Nudus's shop, potions lined the cabinets and tables, but there was also an array of bookshelves crammed with ancient volumes and a dozen pies lined up behind the store counter. A bitter chocolatey scent hung heavily in the air, and at the back of the store were several tables and chairs illuminated by mellow candlelight.

"It's so cosy in here," Xander remarked as she helped the woman to one of the seats.

"A home away from home, I like to think. Of course, that's nonsense when you consider I sleep in the back, but it's still my little slice of pie. Speaking of pie, would you like a slice?"

"Oh! I couldn't," Xander lied, all too aware of the hunger pangs punishing her for skipping breakfast. "I would hate to impose."

"Impose! It's the least you can do after you nearly broke my foot," the woman retorted light-heartedly. "Go on, you'll find two plates in that cabinet over there and a pie behind the counter."

Xander obliged and walked up to the counter.

"There are too many to choose from."

"And they're all delicious!"

"Which should I bring?"

"Any that take your fancy."

Xander unconsciously licked her lips and grabbed a thin one covered in what looked like cherries.

"Good choice," the woman said as Xander sat down with the pie and eating apparatus. "Gladis is the name."

"Xander."

"Oh! I know who you are," Gladis said, serving herself and Xander slices. "You're Carolus's daughter."

"The whole town seems to know that."

"It's the—"

"Scent."

Gladis chuckled. "The scent. We all carry it, though it's a pungent extension on most humans. But like your father, yours is more akin to a light chocolate with the subtlest of hazelnut sprinklings."

"Nudus doesn't seem to think so."

"What does that miscreant know? Trust me, yours is delightful."

"Thank you, I think," Xander said, and took a bite of the pie. Her gaze immediately lit up, and she found herself finishing the rest of the slice in a matter of seconds. It took her all to not lick the crumbs.

Without a word, Gladis put another slice onto Xander's plate and then, with a bit of discomfort, stood up.

"What do you need?" Xander asked, about to stand.

"It's alright. Finish your pie. I'll be back in a minute."

Gladis hobbled into a back room and re-emerged with a silver pot and two mugs.

"What is it?" Xander queried, her nostrils unable to get enough of the delicious whiff dispersing through the shop.

"Wait until you try it," Gladis said, and handed Xander a mug filled with a rich brown liquid. "Don't let the steam fool you. It's not hot. It's at the perfect touch of warmth and ready to be enjoyed in all its wonderful…"

Xander took a sip and smiled. "Bitterness. But not too bitter to make me want to squirm."

Gladis beamed warmly. "Exactly." Her eyes fell on the broadleaf carved into Xander's gauntlet. "That's quite the design."

"My family's insignia on my mother's side," she responded proudly.

"A family respectful of nature's beauty, I see. So, Xander, with the pleasantries out of the way, what brings you here?"

"Where?"

"To Boletus. What else would I be referring to? I assume you didn't come just to befriend Nudus and feast upon our fine fare."

Xander sensed no deceit in the woman, just curiosity. "I need to find the Lizard King."

"Well, you won't find him in Boletus."

"Nudus says he'll take me to him."

"If you do what? Ride that mantis of his?"

"Yes."

"No surprises there."

"He's the only one we've asked that said he would help."

"And he's probably right. You're an outsider. Only a friend or a critter looking for something in return would make you privy to the king's whereabouts."

"Do you know where the king is?" Xander asked, though she knew a positive response was unlikely.

Gladis took Xander's hand, her expression warm and nonthreatening. "I do, Xander. And even though you and I have been acquainted all of a few minutes, I do like you. But I'll not tell you, for it's not my place."

"I understand," Xander said, still somewhat hurt by the expected rejection.

"Did your friends ever tell you that your father was acquainted with the king?"

"Yes."

"So you know it's quite the ask. For us to divulge. For the king to help."

"I know."

"But worth a try!" Gladis reached into her overalls and withdrew a small pouch. She handed it to Xander.

"What is it?"

"Open it."

"Seeds?"

"Seeds. Seeing as you've made walking a bit difficult for me, could you do me a favour?"

"Of course!"

"I have a little garden plot a small distance north of town. Nothing grand, just enough to grow my ingredients. A thirty-minute journey on that mantis I've seen you riding. You can't miss it. Walk to the end, and you'll see six mason jars filled with compost. The halfway point is marked by a small well. When you find the jars, can you please plant these for me in the five unplanted ones? An inch deep should suffice."

"That's it?"

"Almost. The sixth jar that's already planted, please be sure to bring it back for me."

"My pleasure."

"Thank you, Xander."

Xander pulled Sol to a stop. She had already passed dozens of little plots nestled into the woods, but it was pretty clear this one was Gladis's, given the wooden sign that read her name. She jumped from the mantis and watched as the insect buried itself playfully in the dirt. She chuckled. She had already figured out that Nudus's horror stories about Sol were his way of winding Ricard up, though she wasn't sure if Ricard had caught on yet.

The garden sat at the base of a gigantic oak, and it was overgrown with all sorts of colourful and exotic flowers, some towering overhead and others small enough to fit in her palm. Sunrays peeked from between the branches of the canopy to reveal thick layers of dust and pollen in the air. Instinctively Xander pulled out her handkerchief and covered her nose.

The plot was surprisingly long, and it took her a full five minutes of walking to reach the stone well.

"Nothing grand," she said aloud, amused by Gladis's modesty, and continued on.

Past the halfway mark, the plants and flowers were wilder. Some seemed to turn as she walked past, as if watching her, and others carried pungent scents so strong they tickled her nose even through the protection of the cloth.

At the rear there was a stone bench and a number of small statues of various types of forest critters. She peered around for the mason jars and then spotted them on a small wooden table. They were large, larger than she had expected, and the sixth had a long, bare stalk with a single green bud on the top. "How does she expect me to carry this back?" Xander thought.

One by one, she inserted the seeds an inch deep. Fifteen seeds in total, three per jar. And then with a grunt, she picked up the sixth and started back towards the entrance. But as she did, the same melody from that morning brushed her ear, but much clearer and louder. She turned around, looking this way and that, but could see nobody else nearby. Stranger was the fact that she couldn't quite pinpoint from which direction it was coming. As she was about to put the jar down and do a circuit of the garden in search of the voice's owner, it stopped. But for the creak of the trees and chirps of the birds, there was only quiet.

She lingered for several more minutes, wondering if the song would return, but it didn't. Disappointed, she lugged the heavy jar back to the entrance and climbed awkwardly onto Sol. The journey back took a bit longer than the outbound leg due to the fact that she had to keep repositioning herself and the jar. By the time she reached Boletus, the town had returned to its usual raucous state.

Xander entered Gladis's store, but nobody was there. She placed the jar on the floor by the counter, and as she stood up, she spotted a note.

Xander, I had to run (or I should say, hobble) out. Please help yourself to a piece of pie and the sack of mushrooms on the counter. They dull pain and loosen muscles. Perfect for your adventure. Gladis.

A tad upset she couldn't say thank you, Xander left with the gift in hand.

▲ ▲ ▲

"There you are," Leila said as Xander entered Nudus's home. She was busy stoking the fireplace with a crooked poker, though why she needed the heat on such a pleasant morning, Xander didn't know. "Where've you been?"

Xander slumped on the worn sofa opposite. "I was exploring."

"No practise today?"

"I just took Sol out. Where are the others?"

"Where do you think? Should've known we'd lose the pair to the pubs."

"Leila."

"Yes."

"Never mind."

"What?"

"It'll sound crazy."

"Try me."

"Have you heard someone singing recently?"

"It's Boletus. I hear lots of people singing. Singing from the mushrooms. From the beer. From the joys of a successful trade or from despair. What are they singing?"

"Well, maybe it's more like a hum. A soothing hum, but as if it could be from the forest itself."

Leila turned around and looked at her. "And that would surprise you in these woods?"

"I guess not."

"Has anybody else heard this song?"

"I don't know. I heard it this morning a couple of times. Even in the bedroom whilst you slept. And it sounded familiar, as if I'd heard it before, though I'm not sure from when or where."

Curiosity took Leila's expression. "Maybe next time you hear it, seek it out."

"You're telling me to follow some strange noise in the forest? Bit careless, don't you think?"

"Coming from the girl that sneaked off this morning without telling anybody?"

"But you're not worried it could be dangerous?"

"Not in the slightest," Leila said warmly, and returned to tending the fire.

CHAPTER 38

Septembrix 11, 484; Boletus, the Great Forest—A rap came from the bedroom door, and Xander stirred groggily, the same hum from the previous day swiftly slipping from consciousness. The wonderful scents of grilled tomatoes, bread, and mushroom oil hung heavily in the air. She rubbed her eyes and looked up.

"Leila," she croaked. "It's so early."

"It's noon."

"Noon!" Xander jerked out of bed. "I overslept."

"Too much on your mind, I'm sure."

"Must be it," she lied, knowing the real reason was that she had ventured back to Gladis's garden in search of the song that had returned during the night.

"Ah well! It's a blessing for me. Means you can help me with some errands, seeing as the other two hurried off before I could ask and Nudus is tending that business of his."

With breakfast out of the way, Xander and Leila entered the town. The sun was uncomfortably toasty and the mucky roads smelly. Still they braved the odours and the crowds and wandered the streets, gathering the items Leila wanted for her medicine sack and dinner.

"What does it do?" Xander asked of a dried orange leaf dangling by a string from the roof of a street stall seemingly identical to every other one they had stopped at.

"It prevents foot rot," Leila responded, retrieving the leaf.

"And rot of the nether regions," said the stall owner, a squat forest critter with a bulbous forehead and long dangly arms. "Planning something nefarious?" His vile grin repulsed Xander, and she was glad when they finally continued on.

"Did that song come back to you?" Leila spoke as they rounded onto another street.

"Yes."

"But not enough to seek it out?"

Xander was still a bit puzzled by Leila's suggestion, given most people would caution against chasing spirits for fear of the spirit's intention. "I tried."

"Hence the late start? Thought that might've been the case. Guess you're more curious than sensible. Probably why I like you so. Down here," she said, and they turned onto Gladis's street. "So where did it take you?"

Xander pointed to Gladis's store. "To the garden of that shop's owner."

"And when you got there?"

"It carried on for some time, though eventually it stopped. But as soon as I got home last night, it started again. And much louder this time. Wouldn't leave me even when I closed my eyes."

"Amazing! It does sound like the forest speaks to you. I wonder what it seeks to tell you."

Xander shrugged.

"Xander!"

The pair turned to see Gladis standing in front of her store, waving them over. Her foot was in a splint, and she was leaning on a cane.

"Oh no! How bad is it?" Xander asked worriedly as they approached.

"Broken, says the druid," Gladis responded. "But don't you worry. And Leila, how great to see you. Has been some time."

"It has," Leila said.

"Come on in, the both of you."

The three of them walked to the back of Gladis's shop and took a seat.

"Do you see anything different?" Gladis asked Xander once they were comfortable.

Xander looked around, and her expression brightened as her eyes fell on the stalk in the mason jar. "There's a second bud on the stalk."

"There's a second bud," Gladis repeated, her gaze locked on it. After a moment of awkward silence, she turned back to them. "Shopping?"

"Shopping," Leila said.

"Anything I can help you with? Guaranteed friends and family discount."

"Wow! So kind!" Leila blurted. "Xander really must've worked her charm."

"She did! Follow me," Gladis said to Leila, and the two wandered off, leaving Xander alone in the back.

In need of a closer look, Xander walked up to the stalk and brought her face close, examining its every detail. As she was about to touch it, the humming noise returned, coming from all around her, calling for her. She peered to Gladis and Leila as they chatted away, neither of them seemingly aware of it, and opened her mouth to call them over. The humming stopped as abruptly as it had started, but the message was clear. "It wants me to follow it," she thought, resolute in her determination to suss out the source the next time it appeared.

CHAPTER 39

Septembrix 15, 484; three hours north of Boletus, the Great Forest—The long grasses of the enclosure took on a life of their own, and the trees bent and rustled with the wind as the clouds above turned malevolent. Xander stretched her back and bit into one of Gladis's mushrooms in a bid to lessen the tightness in her body. She looked to the mantis slumped in a tired heap near the tree line, in need of a break from the extended journey, and then turned back to what had brought her there.

It was the large pool of crystal water shivering with the breeze that had seemingly been serenading her with its tranquil hum, and that had guided her from Boletus that morning. It was the first time it had continued uninterrupted and with a direction that was actually discernible. And now with her planted at the water's edge, it urged her to swim to the small atoll dotted in the centre and explore its cluster of trees and light, sandy beaches. She peered into the water and then stepped back. Even with its clarity, she could not spot the bottom, and the thought conjured memories of Lake Anemoi and Marcus, the poor man who had been hidden within its depths for an age.

The air creaked behind her. She turned swiftly with her blade in hand and stared curiously at the owner of the bow pointed at her throat.

"And you are?" the slim, pale girl of even height and wild black hair cooed seductively. Her eyes were a mesmerising deep blue, akin to the caverns underneath Lake Anemoi's lake bed, whose shadowy entrances were just visible from the water's surface.

"I might ask the same…"

The girl shot her a wicked grin. "I'm the one with the bow."

"And I'm the one with a dagger aimed at your crotch."

"Wrong gender, I would've thought."

"Nonetheless, who are you?"

"Somebody curious as to how an outsider has found themselves lost in these woods so far—"

"I'm not lost."

"Then I'm curious as to why you have come to this place, and why you're standing at the edge of this pool, no less," she said, and nodded to the abyss that still called Xander's name.

Even if Xander had wanted to, she didn't know how to answer. She didn't know how or why the water had called her, nor could she remember the blur of the forest and the whip of the branches as she rode to get there. All that seemed certain was that every night since she had first heard it, the melodious hum of the water had infiltrated her mind and her sleep, and it had grown with such intensity and clarity that even her dreams echoed the hypnotic lullaby that drew her in. So unbearable had the curiosity become that she had left in the dead of night with nowt but a blade and water flask in hand and without notifying the others. A foolish move, perhaps, in hindsight.

"I was thirsty and happened upon this pool," she lied.

The girl eyed Xander with a hint of suspicion and gently lowered the bow.

"Careful you don't wander too close. Even if it meant one less competitor for me to trash in the race three days from now, I wouldn't want you to ruin your pretty face."

"Wait, how did you know? About the race, that is."

"I'd recognise Nudus's tired-looking critter in a crowd. How long before she took a liking?"

"Third attempt."

"Not bad." The girl whistled sharply, and a young stallion of a mantis emerged from the woods. A striking blend of green and blue, it towered over the now alert Sol. The girl stared at Xander with a piercing blue gaze. "I've had the displeasure of racing his desperate riders in the past, often cretins of the same mould, though they usually don't last longer than a couple of minutes. With that in mind, brave of you to race the Moonlight Festival."

"I'm without choice."

"Of course. Nudus finds utility in exploiting desperation, hence why he helps. And what's in it for the scourge this time?"

"He's placed a wager on me winning. Also said he'll be able to fetch a decent price for Sol." The thought of parting ways with the insect made her sad. "Regardless, we needed his help, and this is his price."

"Not like Nudus to bet on an outright winner or loser like that," the girl said, surprised. "The winnings are too slim. Sounds like he's being the usual trickster." She turned and leapt onto her mantis with ease and then looked back at Xander. "I would ask him for the truth if I were you. Maybe it changes your mind. I don't know what you expect from that thing, but no good ever comes from a deal made with Nudus."

"Who are you?"

"Aika." She grinned seductively. "And you?"

"Xander. And why mustn't I enter the pool?"

The girl had a dangerous glint in her eye. "She called you, didn't she?"

"She?"

"The spirit in the water."

Xander nodded.

"Like I said, don't wander too close. I've decided I like you." Aika winked.

Xander felt her heart thump and her stomach twist ever so slightly as the attractive stranger glided into the thick of the leaves with a born elegance and sense of belonging.

"How very strange," she whispered, the hum of the water suddenly silent and her desire to enter the pool gone.

▲ ▲ ▲

"You're betting against her?" Ricard said, aghast, and slammed his fist against Nudus's dining table.

"It's a win-win for me, Ricard," Nudus retorted. "If she loses—"

"But you're not betting on her losing. You're betting she'll not even complete the damn thing! It means if she dies or gets hurt, you get your money. You never intended for her to even cross that line. What kind of vermin are you?"

Nudus looked to Xander. "It's nothing personal. It's just business."

She shrugged. Though she had been curious as to Nudus's true intentions, she didn't actually care, provided he gave her what she wanted.

"Don't just wave it off, kiddo," Ricard said, annoyed. "What's to stop the rat from plotting against you?"

"Ricard," Nudus said, hands raised up. "Now you sully my name—"

"Sully your name? Sully your name?" the big man practically roared. "I should've known better than to trust you."

"And yet you did. I'm true to my word, Ricard. If she wins, I will give up the king's location."

"If—if she wins!"

"I'm still racing." Xander spoke calmly.

"You'll get yourself killed," Ricard said angrily.

"You know," Haro interjected. "If he's betting against her, it means there's someone betting for her."

"That's not the point, Haro. What's to stop Nudus from interfering in the race?"

"You know the punishment for tampering, Ricard." Nudus spoke sternly. "I'd have to be a fool to do such a thing."

Ricard huffed and peered to Xander. "We never should've let you continue this journey."

"But you did," Xander responded. "You all did. And now I've waited days for this opportunity. I'll not let it be a waste. And if Nudus will get me to the king, I'll stick with it."

"I'm a man of my word," Nudus said.

"The heck you are!" Ricard spat.

Nudus turned to Haro. "Would you please go and get the mayor?"

"The mayor?" Ricard said. "So, what, you're going to have me arrested now?"

"No. I'm going to sign a contract and have the mayor adjudicate. Would that satisfy your worry?"

Ricard opened his mouth, ready to hurl an insult, and then shut it. "It still doesn't stop you from interfering in the race and getting her hurt."

"The bookies would have my life if I did such a thing."

"They certainly would." A voice came from the front door.

They turned to see Gladis standing there with a freshly made pie in one hand and her cane in the other. Xander jogged over and took the pie, then led her in.

"Gladis," Nudus said with the same dislike he had shown her every night since she had started joining them for dinner at Xander's insistence.

"Nudus." She returned the greeting without the hostility.

"And what brings your fine presence here?"

"The girl invited me."

"Of course she did."

Ricard cleared his throat, drawing their attention. "Sorry to interrupt your little catch-up, but back to the issue at hand. We can't know for sure that Nudus won't try to tamper."

"I'm standing right here, Ricard," Nudus said, irritated.

Gladis took a seat and looked at Ricard, her expression mischievous. "Do you know who the major partner is to each and every bookie in Boletus?"

Ricard shrugged his shoulders.

"The mayor." Nudus spoke up, rolling his eyes.

"And who do you think is the mayor's best friend and sister?" Gladis asked.

"Like I told you, Ricard, I'd have to be mad to try such a scheme."

Xander could feel Nudus's intense hatred for Gladis, and something told her he had fallen afoul of the woman in the past.

"So, Gladis," Haro said, pulling up to the pie with greedy eyes. "Will you permit us to serve this delightful surprise, or should we just sit here until we wither into oblivion?"

"Always the dramatics with you," Ricard said, patting his friend on the back, though his demeanour softened as a whiff of the pie caught his nose. "In all seriousness, though, couldn't hurt to start serving it out before it gets cold."

Gladis smiled. "Please do." She turned to Xander. "Have you a moment?"

Xander nodded, and she helped the woman outside into Nudus's unkept garden. They sat on a wooden bench covered in moss.

"Don't worry about Nudus," Gladis said. "He knows the punishment for interfering in the race."

"I'm not worried. I'm actually quite excited and certainly ready to get it over with."

"I'm glad," Gladis said, and pulled a little pouch from her trousers. She handed it to Xander.

"More of those mushrooms?"

"You recall the stalk you brought back for me?"

"How could I forget?" Xander opened the pouch, and her eyes widened. She withdrew a miniature leaf of the same design and shape as the broadleaf that was her family's insignia.

Gladis reached out and took Xander's hand in hers, then turned it until the broadleaf etched into her gauntlet was revealed. "Would seem you have history in the Great Forest beyond that of your father."

"I—how—"

"Not my place to meddle. Just thought perhaps you'd like to know why I asked you to get it for me."

"Yes, of course! But, well, how did it grow so fast?"

"Oh! The miracles of a little love. It's a special plant. And extremely rare. So rare, in fact, that it's the only plant of its kind that I know of in the Great Forest, and those two buds are the first for many, many generations. And trust me, I've looked."

Xander raised her eyebrow. "And you cut it off."

"Yes, I guess I did," Gladis said guiltily. "But for a good cause. The stalk was given to me by my mother. And to my mother by her mother. And so on. I don't know who originally gave it to my family, but the tale we were all told was the same. That one day the stalk would sprout two buds, and when it did, an outsider would appear in the Great Forest looking for something they need. We were all told to give that outsider the smallest of the two leaves and to plant the larger one. And so, I'm here."

"Why not just tell me that before?"

"Well, firstly, you broke my foot, Xander. Couldn't exactly get up and ride to my garden to see if the stalk had budded."

"And every day since when you saw it had?"

"I wasn't convinced until I saw the two buds uncurl."

"So what do I do with it?"

"I don't know. We were never told. My great-great-grandmother, in her senile mutterings, would always talk about a puzzle piece whenever she spotted the stalk or the sketches of the bud that had been handed down to us. But she was the only one. I always thought she was mad, but then maybe she could see something we couldn't. I guess you'll figure it out when the time is right."

"And how do I keep it?"

"It's an evergreen. A bit of water and sunlight every day, and it should last some time."

Xander beamed mischievously. "Seeing as you're meant to help me, does this mean you can tell me where the king is?"

"Absolutely not!" Gladis retorted light-heartedly. "What do you take me for? My only instruction was to give you the leaf, and I've done that."

"Oh, okay. Well, thank you, nonetheless."

She leant over and hugged Gladis, much to the woman's surprise.

"The pie's getting cold, and at this rate it'll be gone," Ricard called into the yard, startling them both. "Haro, the little pig, can hardly keep his hands to himself."

"Talk for yourself," Haro muttered, his mouth full.

CHAPTER 40

Septembrix 18, 484; Boletus, the Great Forest—The moon weaved in and out of the clouds, and the forest danced between a white-and-grey sheen. Xander tied her hair back to stop it from whipping into her face and secured the blade on her back. She looked up as the tree overhead creaked with the ferocity of the wind.

"This isn't good," Haro muttered.

He stood interwound with Leila and Oscine, a cooperative brace against the force of the wind as it scoured the grass of the hill.

"Nudus, will they still let the race go ahead?" Ricard called over the howl.

"They've never stopped it before."

"And in the same breath, you would say you've never seen such dreadful weather during the festival."

Nudus looked at him seriously. "Not in my lifetime."

"Seem odd to you, then?"

"I don't make the rules. They've never called off the race, and I don't suspect tonight will be any different."

Ricard muttered something under his breath and held back his undiminished irritation at Nudus's revelation of what he stood to gain.

He peered at the crowd of gathered strangers and familiars from near and far and in between, and he walked up to Xander and placed his hand on her shoulder. She didn't seem to realise his presence, her eyes intent on Aika limbering up amidst the swarm of forest critters.

"Not too late, kiddo."

She turned from her trance, her expression a mix of steely determination and exhilaration. "I want to race. It feels right. Not just the excitement, I mean, but the need to participate. It's as if I must do it; otherwise, we'll have no chance of finding the Lizard King and getting the shard."

"There's always a way, Xander. If we give it time, we could find another way to locate him and continue to the tree. We don't need Nudus."

"I can't wait any longer, and something tells me if I don't compete, then we lose all chance of getting the shard. I can't explain it. You'll just have to trust me on this."

She turned back to the crowd, and Ricard followed her eyes to Aika.

"Who's that?" he asked.

"Her name's Aika. I don't think she'll be an easy win."

"I would second that sentiment," Nudus observed casually. "Keep an eye out for that bow."

She turned to him, amused by his nonchalant statement of the obvious.

Leila walked over with Haro and Oscine. "Xander, here, I put together a little snack for your ride."

"She'll hardly have time to eat," Haro scoffed.

"Of course, of course, that's why she should eat it now, you old fool," Leila said, and handed it to the girl.

"What is it?" Xander asked.

"Why don't you have a bite and see for yourself?"

Xander took a bite of the crunchy biscuit and immediately felt a warmth traverse her body. Her muscles relaxed, but she felt an unending energy rise from within.

"Wow! Quite the kick, but I feel amazing," she said.

"A little homemade recipe using Gladis's mushrooms."

"Damn, woman. You didn't mash it with the stinkweed, did you?" Haro scowled. "The poor girl will be hallucinating before the end of the race."

"Just a bit. She'll be fine."

A horn blared from the start line, and the crowd reverberated with excitement as the riders took their marks. Xander looked over to Aika as she unslung her bow and flexed her lean shoulders and back. Her hair was also tied in a knot, and as she prepped, she caught Xander's stare and winked at her. Again Xander felt her stomach twist.

She wiped her clammy hands on her jacket and took in the initial stretch of the partially moonlit course, each visible bend or straight illuminated by fireflies and torches. She had walked parts of the course in the morning and felt excitement at the whole slew of tracks, tunnels, and death-defying jumps that would make tonight memorable, if not dangerous.

A forest critter with a flag in hand and a cheerful grin marched to the start line, where all the riders could see, and a hush fell on the crowd in anticipation. Her heart thumped nervously, and she tightened the grip of her legs on Sol's back, much to the creature's annoyance.

"My dearest forest critters, let me be the first to welcome you to this year's race of the Moonlight Festival…"

A loud, raucous roar erupted from the crowd and then quickly dissipated as the official lifted his hand for quiet.

"Are you in for a treat this year with all that we have to offer! A course designed down to the littlest detail with the intention of weeding out the undeserved and championing the deserved."

He nodded to Aika, and again the crowd roared before settling to listen.

"And whilst I'm sure we'll hope for our riders to return unscathed after this brutal marathon of a race, it would be remiss of me to not point out that we will not be without the odd accident, no doubt in small part due to this slimy weather and, more than likely, in large part due to the despicability of this year's competition." He grinned, taking in a few of the more unsavoury riders. "And may the best critter win!"

Cheers and foot stomping rang through the crowds gathered on the ground and in the trees, truly an amazing and noisy spectacle presented by such an odd assortment of forest critters.

"Three…"

The distant roar of the crowd echoed in Xander's mind as the critter raised the flag.

"Two…"

A nervous sweat enveloped her pits and her grip, and her ears thumped with the erratic rhythm of her heartbeat.

"One…"

Time seemed to slow in painful anticipation of that final breath.

"Go!"

▲ ▲ ▲

Xander clumsily wiped at the dirt plastered across her face and scanned the darkness of the bushes for Sol. She was still dazed from the fall, and her shoulder ached from where the unseen projectile had made contact and knocked her off the mantis.

"Who the heck threw it?"

No other riders had been in sight along this lengthy stretch of dark forest, with the nearest barely visible torch a good ten metres ahead.

Her gaze jolted to the side in search of the short-lived flutter of sound that just emanated from the bushes. If not for the creak of the trees and rustle of the leaves under the weight of the heavy winds, the silence would have been eerie. There were no cheers or onlookers where she had been stranded, just the creepy shadows of the forest staring back at her.

"Sol!" she whispered, as if the mantis would somehow hear her barely spoken word. "Sol!" she repeated a bit louder.

The same flutter of sound answered her call but was again quick to disappear, like a bird that had wandered in too close, only to swiftly glide away in fright. Instinctively she reached for the blade tied to her waist. Little good it had done her so far. Reluctant to use such a fine weapon on the other contestants, some of whom carried flimsy spears and swords, she had struggled to maintain her position near the front, and it was only her surprising skill as a rider that had kept her in a race otherwise dominated by tricksters and cronies.

"Where are the other riders?" she said nervously.

Another rustle emanated from behind, but it was different to the sound that had her on edge. She crouched low, ready for what approached, and visibly relaxed as Sol charged through the undergrowth with several riders in tow.

"How did she end up back there?" she said, relieved, and waved down her ride.

Within moments, the pair had lost the two rough-looking miscreants immediately behind them and were well on their way to the next torch.

The moon bulged in the centre of the night sky by the time they had made the halfway point, its white and creamy glow a mesmerising backdrop for the black-and-blue silhouettes of the uppermost branches of the passing forest. By now, Xander's back and legs ached, and she longed for some more of Leila's biscuits, though all that was left were crumbs.

She hadn't seen any other riders since her skirmish with a trio of wrangling critters in one of the marsh pits, or at least she thought it was a marsh, with puddles up to the mantis's knees. So intent were the critters on each other that they hadn't noticed Xander until she was right on their hind, by which point it had taken little effort to remove them from their mantises using a thick branch she had scooped up earlier, a less lethal substitute to her golden blade and one she was actually willing to use.

She tensed. Two riders a small distance ahead weaved in and out of the thicket, both with awesome grace. Given their comparatively slower pace and willingness to swerve recklessly towards each other, she figured them to be adversaries.

Her heart skipped a beat at the sight of Aika's black hair under the light of several torches, and warmth swiftly took her at the knowledge that she had correctly identified the strangely familiar fragrance trailing the two riders.

Aika swiped her bow to the side and fended off the assailant's rotted sword as it lurched towards her body. Quick to counter, the assailant lobbed a small projectile of sorts at her, but she was fast—very fast—and easily ducked out of its path and lashed out with her bow, only to meet empty space as the assailant took a branch in the chest and fell to the ground.

As the assailant tumbled along the track and under Sol's legs, Aika's trailing gaze locked with Xander's, and she smiled a mischievous smile. But before either could acknowledge or tease, Aika was thrown to the ground, and moments later, so was Xander. An invisible whip had stricken them and knocked them onto their backsides a short distance apart.

"What the—" Aika muttered, and tried to right herself.

Xander's chest was tight from the impact, and she struggled for breath for a good few seconds.

"It's a wire!" Aika uttered. "Somebody tied it between the trees."

Xander stood up warily.

"I raced with the lead group until I broke off. Nobody was in front of me," Aika said, and nervously gripped her bow, though Xander noticed she had only two of the permitted seven arrows left in her quiver.

Aika came in close, so close that the heat of her recent exertion warmed the fringe of Xander's sweat-cooled skin, and together they scanned the horizon, weapons ready.

"Where the heck is my mantis?" Aika whispered.

"My mantis has a tendency to continue even after I've fallen off. She'll be back."

"Not mine," Aika whispered cautiously. "He's usually on point. Something's wrong."

"Look, it's the rider you knocked off."

"Dammit, he's a miserable critter. He won't be too disappointed to have me here like this."

"Did you hear that? It's the same sound from before."

"I don't—"

The critter had heard and stopped warily in the middle of the track. Again the sound that had been following Xander carried in the wind, and suddenly Aika's ears perked, and shock took her eyes. She instinctively drew her bow.

"We need to get—"

A spear took the critter in the back, and as he slumped forward onto his knees, Aika shot into the dark, and a gurgled cry emanated from where the arrow struck true. Abruptly Xander shoved her into the dirt and out of the path of another spear veering in from the side. On her knees, Aika speedily landed her last arrow in the owner of the spear.

They bounded into the bushes and off the road, and the flutter of sound quickly gave chase, but as they ran deeper and deeper into the woods with only the light of the moon to guide, the intensity of the flutter and the heckles of their chasers betrayed their odds.

"We can't keep this up," Xander spluttered long after she had lost count of the steps pounded and the huge trees navigated. "We need to—"

A jeer emanated from in front of them, and Xander had only just caught a glimpse of the shadow lurking in the dark when Aika tugged her arm and pulled her to the side and into a bed of wildflowers. Aika nearly stumbled as a thorn from a particularly nasty stem caught her arm, and they had barely made it a dozen steps before a series of taunts rang from in front of them and then behind and to the sides.

"We're surrounded!" Aika muttered through broken breaths, fear etched in her eyes. She drew a curved knife.

"Who are they?" Xander shouted over the growing menace of the heckles and the shadowy owners closing in.

Aika didn't respond and instead desperately scanned the landscape for escape.

"Aika, Aika, Aika!" a horrid, cruel voice tutted from the shadows. The chorus of jeers abruptly died off. "What would your father think if he found you so far from home, and with an outsider, no less?"

"What do you want, Damain?" Aika shouted with a tremble, despite her best attempt to come across as unafraid.

"Your father, of course."

"Leave us alone. You have what you want. We're of little threat anymore."

"Threat? Who said anything about a threat? I'm just looking for a bit of fun."

"At our expense?"

"Your father did worse," the voice spat harshly. "You should've known better than to venture from your father's side. You did this to yourself."

The owner of the voice emerged from the shadows, and Xander shuddered at the insectoid that stared back, a hybrid between man and insect, its four wings lax at its back and its eyes sinister and almost human-looking. A deep scar ran the length of its chest.

"I say this as much to you as I do to Carolus's daughter," it continued softly. Aika turned to Xander with shock. "What, you couldn't tell? That stench on her is not too dissimilar to that of her wretched father."

"You're the—" Xander began.

"The Dragon King, of course, though I met that cretin long before I officially took the title, and not too long before I received this wretched scar from his cursed spear."

"It's because of your father…" Aika looked at Xander without the same softness and mischievousness as before, and Xander felt a twang of pain because of it.

"Aika—"

"It's because of him. All this is because of him." Aika backed away from Xander as if Carolus's deed, or lack of, was her own. "If he had just finished it, finished this monster, so many thousands might still be alive, and instead, this disease…this disease that has crept and poisoned the whole of the forest with its venom."

"She's not wrong. And I must say, in spite of his generosity, I would like to do to him what he did to me," the bug said viciously, and subconsciously scratched at the scar. "A child for a child."

The bug stepped forward whilst loosening its shoulders and arms, and Xander could feel the other hecklers crowd in as one would a wounded animal. She looked to Aika, but the girl responded with uncertainty. She peered past Aika, and her eyes lit up.

Sol broke through the rings of attackers, easily breaking two of the bugs in half, and Xander rushed to climb up as the insectoids hesitated in a state of shock at the intrusion and wariness of the mantis's giant claws.

"Quick, give me your hand!" she yelled to Aika, still cautious of the spears aimed at them.

The girl's reluctance showed, but as Xander was the lesser of two menaces, she effortlessly jumped onto the mantis's back without a glance at the outreached hand, and they raced out of the flowerbed into the dark.

"She won't be able to keep this up for long," Aika said after several moments. "We're too heavy, and she's tired."

The intensity of the flutter grew throughout the sombre silence of the trees and the whisper of the wind but without the heckles of before.

"They're catching us," Aika shouted nervously.

Xander could sense that the girl felt naked and panicked with an empty quiver.

One of Damain's minions dove in from the shadows with an outstretched spear, and Xander viciously and instinctively lashed out with her blade, the ease at which it cut the bug in half almost throwing her off balance. Aika quickly reached over, grabbed the bug's spear, and then drove it into the chest of another attacker that came at them with a small blade.

"There're too many!" Aika said alarmedly. "And do you even know where you're going?"

"I didn't have a chance to check a map before they started chasing us.

Did you?" Xander responded sarcastically. "Come on, you know these forests. Where are we?"

"I don't recognise this stretch…"

And then they heard it, the same melodious serenade that had lured them to their first chance meeting three days before, and oh, how it was beautiful and compelling.

Without prompting, Xander directed Sol towards the origins of the hum and urged the mantis on with greater impetus, though she could feel the poor thing faltering from fatigue and the headwind.

"Come on, Sol," she whispered. "It's not far now. I can feel it. We're nearly there."

Aika knocked a bug into a tree with a long sweep of her borrowed spear and then lobbed it at another in mid-throw.

"We're nearly there," Xander whispered again, the blare of the hum practically deafening.

"I think that's it, straight ahead!" Aika called out excitedly.

Two spears shot out from the bush into the mantis's chest cavity—the first and only two to pierce the insect's hide, but it was enough. Sol crashed to the ground with a startling cry, and the two girls were thrown into the bushes. But there was no time to mourn or search for wounds, and they bolted towards the enclosure through the overgrown shrubs with the bugs on their trail.

Spears flew overhead and to their sides as they breached the grassy enclosure, and they quickly sped towards the depth of the sparkling water through the long grasses swaying under the creamy brilliance of the moon.

With the bugs crowding the edges of the grassy expanse but still not daring any farther, Aika hesitated at the pool's shore. Sensing Aika's fear, Xander grabbed the girl's arm and yanked her into the sharp coolness of the liquid.

CHAPTER 41

The swim was deceptively long, despite the apparent nearness of the islet, and the two girls found themselves struggling on the soft, sandy edge with the water between them and the insectoids hugging the tree line. The breeze chilled the cool moisture on their skin, and they both felt the fatigue from the night's chase begin its onslaught on their sensibilities. And still the hum beckoned them from the cluster of trees.

"We shouldn't be here," Aika muttered, her wet bow held tight, the charm and relaxed demeanour of their first encounter gone.

Xander ignored her concern and started sluggishly towards the cluster.

"What are you doing?"

"We swam all this way. Aren't you curious?"

Aika hesitated. "I've heard the stories. All the forest critters have. And I mean *all*. Even now I can hear the echo of the warnings in my mind, the result of forced repetitions as a child, but that's not what worries me. It's rare to hear her song, and her lure isn't indiscriminate. She chooses her victims. Her beautiful voice tempting, always pulling and calling…I've always resisted."

Xander looked at her in surprise.

"But that night…" Aika continued. "I've never heard it so intense or fierce or difficult to withstand…and then I meet you, drawn in by the same serenade. Daughter of the man that could have stopped Damain from wreaking havoc and prevented so much pain."

"Victims of what?" Xander asked, ignoring the attack on her father.

"I guess nobody really knows for sure. I've never heard of anybody who returns from the islet after making the swim."

"So nobody knows for sure…and you've never been curious to—"

"Tempt fate?"

"Well, I mean, to explore the islet. Find the owner of the voice."

Aika stood quietly for a moment. "Despite the warnings in my head, the fact that there're two of us makes me think maybe we should have a little look. Anyway, look at our options."

They peered back to the tree line, and although the bulk of the bugs had regressed into the forest, a few remained watchful and eager. Their minds made up, the girls pushed their way through the overgrown shrubs and vines of the islet, the soft muck underneath surprisingly warm in the cold of the night, and it wasn't long before they both stopped and stared in amazement.

The small, flat-roofed structure was eerily similar to some of the ancient temples of Borealis, though the grey stones were dingy and moss-covered, and vines poked through the cracks. They both shrank at the scrutiny of the stony entrance that stared back, even the gaze of the moon unable to penetrate the black shroud within.

"Did you know this was here?" Xander whispered.

"I had no idea. I've never heard it described as such."

"It's not that big," Xander said after doing a circuit of the structure. "Maybe we can see without torches."

"Did you not see the blackness of that entrance? Well, outsiders first," Aika said, and invited Xander to lead.

The entrance opened up into a large chamber where bricks layered the ground and roots and vines broke the stones of the ceiling and walls. The air was absent the odour of soil and dampness and carried an atmosphere of magic and familiarity. And the hum, the hum that had beckoned them with all its beauty, echoed throughout the chamber, on top of them and around and close enough to touch, but not so loud as to bring discomfort. They were drawn to the end of the chamber, where the moon shone through a skylight into an elongated pool etched into the floor.

"What is that?" Xander whispered, mesmerised and suddenly forgetful of caution. She began towards the water, and Aika grabbed her arm.

"What are you doing?"

"Well, I'm a bit thirsty, if I must be honest."

"You didn't get your fill when you pulled us into the water?" Aika responded sarcastically.

"No, I didn't, actually."

Xander broke free of the grip and edged slowly towards the water with Aika close behind. On the cusp of the stone pool, with the moonlit water illuminated and the soothing beckon of the hum suddenly distant, they stopped and stared for many moments, unable to comprehend what they saw.

"Who is she?" Xander said quietly.

A pale lady with long, dark hair was lying dreamlike within the liquid, her body wrapped in a green garment, her eyes closed and her features sharp but untouched. She radiated with the glistening of the moonlight.

"I don't know," Aika said. "I don't recognise her garment. It seems old… in fashion, I mean. Antiquated almost."

"Is she alive? She doesn't look rotten."

"No, she looks like she sleeps," Aika said softly, her expression mesmerised. She reached a hand gently towards the water, and Xander grabbed her arm.

"What are you doing?"

"She might be alive."

"That's what I'm afraid of. Maybe you were right. I think we should leave," Xander said, suddenly uncomfortable.

Aika nodded, taking her cue from the tightness of Xander's grip, but as they backed away, the hum grew in intensity, and the water simmered with vibration.

"Oh no! Where's the door?" Aika gasped.

They rushed over, and with one eye trained on the shallow, watery bed, they frantically ran their hands over the wall in search of any crease or hint of the entrance but found none. And as the once-soothing song peaked at a near unbearable level, the hum abruptly stopped.

Aika drew her knife, as did Xander her blade, and they stared through the uncomfortable silence at the glisten of water on the opposite side of the chamber.

"We shouldn't have come," Aika whispered harshly.

"Bit late to worry about that now."

"What should we do?"

"Looks like our only way out is the skylight above the…well, her."

Aika looked unimpressed. "Any other ideas?"

"Well, what choice do we have?"

"Sound familiar?"

"Okay, okay! Suggestions then?"

"What about the other walls? We should check them all," Aika said after a moment.

Wary of the body in the centre of the room and practically hugging the stone walls, they began to scour for any hint of a way out, moving closer and closer to the other end of the chamber as they did.

Then Xander froze, and her ears twitched. She cautiously glanced behind but saw only Aika fidgeting with a stone on the other side of the chamber and, quick to shrug off the disturbance, returned to the motions. Another metre along, and she heard it again, ever so faint. She glanced behind and, gut clenched, followed Aika's shocked eyes to the gentle ripple that cascaded the length of the shallow pool.

Instantly they both scrambled back to the wall where they had originally entered, weapons drawn and eyes fixated on the submerged body.

"Did she just move?" Aika whispered.

"I don't know. It was one ripple."

"In a room with no breeze."

"What in Anemoi is this place?"

"Sanctuary," a voice hummed gently.

They turned this way and that in search of the owner, but none could be found, and still the water remained placid.

"Be at peace, my children."

"Easy for you," Aika blurted.

"Who are you? What did you mean by sanctuary?" Xander stammered.

"Sanctuary from what?" Aika added.

"Why, from the dead."

"That's not comforting!"

"Who are you?" Xander repeated, agitated.

"Should you not know this? It is you, after all, who has entered my abode, not I into yours."

"You brought us here with your song. You invited us."

"And you would listen to all those that would call? A daughter of Anemoi and a bearer of the Rose. One that must lead succumbed to the whims of mediocrity and servitude."

"How do you know who I am?"

Aika looked at Xander, puzzled, aware she had missed something.

"Your energy," the voice said.

Xander had heard this before, and her mind jumped to Marcus under the lake and then to her aunt.

"Are you a witch?" Aika asked cautiously.

"And you, a princess and future queen, so quick to drop all pretence of strength and defiance in the mouth of the unknown. Is it not you who would stand by the bearer in the odds of defeat?"

This time it was Xander's turn to look at Aika.

"Princess? Did I miss something? Who are you?"

"You couldn't put two and two together back there with Damain?" Aika retorted.

It clicked. "Your father's the Lizard King!"

"He is. Will you tell us your name?"

"Bronte."

Aika slumped to her knees in awe, her face whiter than white, and Xander froze with shock.

"Enchantress!" Aika stammered. "But how—how do you still live? The folklore is thousands of years old."

"Who said I still live, child? No, this chamber is my tomb. A realm not quite that of the living or quite that of the dead. A sanctuary from the ravages of time but also from the absence of time."

"The ravages of time?" Xander asked.

"A chamber from which the flow of events of your reality has no passage, but one that is not completely free of said flow, for there must always be a price."

"It's a time chamber. Time flows slower in here."

"It is as you say."

"But why?" Aika said. "Why prolong your life if it means being stuck in this chamber? And why bring us here?"

"My time has come, but yours is yet due. When my energy fails—and it falters even now—the law I created to protect the Great Forest from the brutalities of the outside world will revert, leaving this land to bend and wither before the greed of those whose thirst cannot be satiated. Already I feel the first of the timbers come to a head, and the Guardians of the forest stumble before the axe and the torch of the new armies of Anemoi."

"Erzse," Xander muttered.

Aika panicked. "You must let us out. We need to warn the others. My people are bound by your law, but if your energy fails, we'll become large again. We'll be able to stand up to the armies. We can protect the forest. Give us a chance to prepare!"

"Your father will fall, and you will not witness his demise."

Aika slammed her fist against the wall. "Let us out!"

Silence.

"To heck with this!" Aika started towards the skylight, but as she reached the watery tomb, she was knocked back by an unseen force. "Let us out!"

"If you leave before the day is up, you will perish, along with the Great Forest, and the bearer not much soon after. I will not allow you to leave before then."

"How long is a day?" Xander asked as Aika feuded with the decision.

"When the day is up, forty-two days will have passed in your reality."

"That's six weeks…how much damage can really be done in such a short time, especially if her law still holds?" Xander said to Aika. "When we're free, we'll join your father and fight back."

"And your law, enchantress…it holds as long as you live?" Aika spoke up.

"It will revert long before the day passes, child. I can afford protection to only this chamber up until my last breath…"

"What does that mean?" Aika let out violently. "I choose my own path. I choose to be out there with the others. You must let us out. I would not have come if I had known!"

But the voice did not speak again, nor hum, forever silent as the last vestiges of tired energy flowed from the owner's will. All that remained was enough only to maintain the sanctuary of the chamber, protection for the bearer and the princess. Shielded as the army of Erzse drove inward from the borders of the Great Forest and slaughtered and pillaged the forest critters no longer able to withstand the onslaught, the Great Tree always in the villain's sight.

CHAPTER 42

Forty-two days on the outside was only a day within the enchantress's tomb, and still it was not too short a period of time for two young women forcefully confined together to go without a spoken word. Eager to distract Aika's evident worry and determined to learn more about the girl, Xander broke the sombre silence.

"I'm sorry," she said quietly.

They both sat on the cool stone floor, their backs against the wall.

"For what?" Aika's voice was hoarse from crying.

"For my father."

Aika puffed her cheeks and then sighed. "It's not your fault. It's not really his fault, either, despite what my father says. Compassion in war is dangerous, and your father let it get the better of him. But he did what he thought was right. Sadly, history—"

"Has shown us otherwise."

She nodded. "So, Xander, are you going to tell me what exactly the enchantress was talking about? What does she mean by 'bearer of the Rose'?"

"The same army that the enchantress warned us about is the same that has occupied my home." She eyed Aika, searching for any reason not to trust her, but she found none. "My aunt Evia told me of a weapon that could help us defeat this army and the one that occupied Borealis."

"The army that occupied Borealis," Aika repeated with surprise.

"Yes."

"And this weapon is in the Great Forest?"

"Part of it is. The other parts are scattered all over Anemoi."

"Not very convenient."

"No, but it was done to prevent someone misusing it. It's the same weapon that united Anemoi."

"And if you find it and liberate your home, you by extension liberate the Great Forest."

"Yes, pretty much."

"It sounds like the enchantress spoke the truth, and I trust her with my life," Aika said, her expression more hopeful. "Do you know where in the forest?"

"The Great Tree."

Aika's expression dropped.

"That bad?" Xander asked.

"It's not good. The bugs have controlled it for some time, and I'm sure they'll be guarding it, even with this invasion." She pondered for a moment. "Once we can leave here, we'll need to find my people. If we're to attempt this, they're our best chance of getting into the tree. The part you search for, is it in the section at the bottom of the tree? It must be. It's the only section we've not been able to access; otherwise, I feel we would've found some evidence before now. But then we'd still need to find an entrance. What?"

"I'm not sure where in the tree it is."

Aika raised her eyebrow. "You know, it's a lot to ask my people to risk it all on an uncertainty."

"I have a map that'll show me the way. It'll lead us to it."

"But let me guess. You don't have it on you."

She frowned. "It's with my friend."

"Ricard?"

"You know him?"

"Of him. He's your father's friend. One of the critters told me it was him that spoke to you at the beginning of the race. Though they failed to tell me who you were. The man's got a brutal reputation. I'd bet my bow he still lives."

"If I get the map, will you help me?"

She glanced towards Bronte and then turned back to Xander. "It depends on what the map shows us. But if I do help you and I can get you to the tree, in return you must promise me you'll stop the woman responsible. What was her name? Erzse?"

"Yes, Erzse." Xander paused, unsure of whether to reveal her relationship to the woman who was nothing more than a name.

"What? Too much of an ask?"

"Erzse is my aunt."

Aika's mouth dropped, though not from anger or fear or concern but simply amused surprise. "First your father and now your aunt. Quite the family!"

"I'm sorry."

"Don't be. You're trying to find a weapon to take the woman down. So you'll stop her when the time comes?"

"I will."

"Auntie Erzse. I'll not forget the name." A slight smirk kissed Aika's cheeks. "Which brings me to Nudus. He promised you passage to the tree, didn't he?"

"To your father."

"I told you not to trust him. My father can't stand the thing. Doubt his soldiers would've let you anywhere near with him asking."

"Can't say we had much choice."

"No, I guess you didn't."

There was a brief pause before Xander broke the silence again. "What's it like in the tree?"

Aika smiled, though there was a glimmer of sadness in her eyes. "It's been a while since I've been inside, but it's not a place you easily forget. And trust me when I say this: I've explored every inch it has to offer. At least every inch we've had access to. To start…"

And so, Aika excitedly regaled Xander with tales of her adventures within the tree and the forest at large. Stories about her father and the history of her people. And before they knew it, they had moved on to Xander's life in Borealis before it fell and her upbringing in Nhata. Memories of her aunt Evia, her friends and her adventures. At least, whatever stories could be exchanged before their exhaustion caught up with them, convincing them to lay their heads down for some much-needed rest.

CHAPTER 43

Mayx 5, 476; Borealis, Borlencia; four months before the fall of Borealis—"Again? How do you always get sixes?" Xander called joyfully across the living room.

Lawrence glanced at Alya. His grin was mischievous. Alya chuckled whilst shaking her head and then picked the pair of dice from the carpeted floor. The cosy room was warm, heated by numerous candles, and it smelled of earthy spices and dry wine.

"Well, are you going to show her?" Alya asked, handing the dice back to him.

"If she says please," Lawrence toyed.

"Please," Xander said, and jumped and hugged him.

"Ha! Guess I have to tell you now. Open your hand."

She pulled from the embrace and opened her hands. He dropped the dice into them.

"What do you feel?"

She held the dice close to her face and then moved them around in her palm. She shrugged.

"Come on. You can do better than that," he said.

She moved them around again and then twirled one of them between her finger and thumb. Her eyes lit up. "There's a weight at the bottom."

"There's a weight at the bottom," Lawrence repeated.

"But that's cheating."

"It is." Alya spoke up disapprovingly. "And why he would never dream of using them in such a filthy game."

"Never," he said sincerely. "Wouldn't want to lose my hand. Tempting, though, isn't it?"

The door creaked open, and they turned to see Carolus entering, his trousers and shirt a plain grey, his expression tired. Xander ran up and squeezed his waist in a loving embrace. He smiled tiredly as he stroked her head.

"Everything okay?" Alya asked.

Xander released her hold and took a step back. Carolus glanced at Lawrence, whose demeanour showed none of the same weariness.

"Have you told them?" Carolus asked.

"Haven't found the chance," Lawrence responded.

"Told them what?" Alya asked with growing angst.

"The fleet's being mobilised," Carolus said. "They're shipping off at the end of the week."

"For what reason?" Alya asked, puzzled.

"It's—"

"An expedition," Lawrence interrupted his father. "We're headed north. Some of our allies are having trouble with pirates and a growing number of refugees from some war too far away to concern us. But they've asked for our help. Nothing to worry about."

"But there'll be combat?" Alya asked.

"It's unlikely," Carolus interjected calmly.

"Then why the glum look?"

His gaze didn't waver from Alya, but Xander could tell it was her own presence that held his tongue.

"I can go," Xander said nonchalantly, though she was desperately curious to hear what her father had to say.

"Nonsense," Alya said. "You two carry on. Your father and I will go to the bedroom." She left with Carolus, leaving the siblings alone.

"He's worried for you?" Xander asked Lawrence once the bedroom door was closed.

"He doesn't understand why the entire fleet needs to go. Or why the matter is so pressing."

"Then why's he letting it happen?"

"He may be a senior minister, but his power has limits. He's still got to contend with the other provinces."

"Then who's pushing it?"

"The Zylencians. Some of their communities have strong ties to the city-states in the north."

"The Zylencians? But the fleet is Borlencian."

"Is that what they're teaching you at school? I should have a word with that teacher. No, the fleet doesn't belong to us. It's Anemoi's northern fleet. All the provinces can mobilise it—granted, the Zylencians and Borlencians have more of a say, given that we make up the bulk of the sailors and it's parked in Borealis's port."

"Do you agree?"

"With what? The order?"

She nodded.

"Doesn't matter if I do. I've got my order, so I have to follow."

"Even if you don't agree?"

"Even if I don't agree."

"Seems silly."

"It is a bit, but it's necessary. Our armies and navies would be useless in battle if the soldiers and sailors could just say no."

She frowned.

"What?" he asked.

"Nothing."

"Ah! You're worried. Don't be. Everything will be fine."

"How long will you be gone?"

Lawrence's posture hardened, and he hesitated. "Two years."

Xander visibly shrank at the revelation and had to strain to hold back the tears.

"It'll be over before you know it," he said cheerfully, and he gathered her up in his arms and squeezed her.

CHAPTER 44

Octobrix 30, 484; Boletus, the Great Forest—"It's dark. I've never seen the clouds so thick or violent looking…or purple," Aika observed as they trudged through the forest, which seemed less gigantic and more ordinary since they had left the remnants of the collapsed chamber.

"And the trees seem different. Sad almost."

Aika peered at Xander, surprised by the insightful comment. "They hurt. Their whispers tell of something bad that's happened. Something cruel. I fear what we might find."

Xander came to a stop and put her hand to Aika's arm. "It's Boletus."

They walked up to the town, which was now miniature to them, and crouched over as they carefully trod through its abandoned streets, searching for life. The majority of the buildings showed little damage, including Nudus's home, and they couldn't see any signs of bloodshed.

"The little critters were probably of little concern to the humans," Aika observed.

"Gladis," Xander blurted worriedly as they came upon the woman's trampled store. She lifted the crushed roof off with ease and sighed in relief at the empty abode. "Where do you think they all went?"

"The critters would've gone to my people for protection, I think. Same for your friends."

"How far is your home?"

"I don't know. I've never walked through the woods at this size."

Xander sighed, her heart heavy with the unknown. "I hope they're safe."

"Looks like they got out fine."

"Getting out is not the problem. It's not so easy for Ricard to hide himself like the smaller forest critters."

"As long as he's within the forest's borders, he should still be able to use the Rite. Would only last a couple of days at most, but then he'd only need it when the soldiers are close."

Xander nodded, but it wasn't just his welfare she felt apprehensive about. She fretted over the map and the shard left in his custody, and though it was never confirmed, her gut feeling suspected Erzse was after the shards the same as she was. She unconsciously fondled the ring and felt a glimmer of hope. Erzse couldn't read the map without it, and she certainly couldn't use it even if she had it.

"Do you see that?" Aika whispered cautiously. "Through the bushes, directly ahead."

Xander followed her finger to the flicker of movement in the shadows.

"Let's have a look," she said, and they crawled through the bush until they were within fifteen metres.

"That stench, I recognise it."

"It's a swamp vine, but I've never seen one around here. They usually grow southeast, towards the swamps…outside the boundaries."

"Didn't take it long to find its way inside. Maybe it was put here."

"Would take a sadistic individual to do that. They're real buggers to kill, and they go for anything."

"Yeah, agree with that sentiment. Real buggers."

"You've killed one?"

"The one under the mill."

Aika's eyes widened. "I thought that was an exaggeration."

"What did you think I meant when I told you it was a vine?"

"Not one of those! You really killed it with a broken axe?"

"Wasn't easy, but yeah."

"I'm impressed!"

"Don't be. Like I told you, I nearly lost my friend because of it. Actually I did lose my friend because of it. Haven't seen him since it happened, and I sometimes doubt I'll ever see him again."

"Hemish."

"Yes…so what're we going to do about that thing?"

"Can't leave it here. The smaller critters won't stand a chance."

"And what do you propose? Your bow is useless without arrows, and your knife…well, not sure that'll be enough."

"Agreed. So I'll be the distraction, and you come at it from behind."

"That's quite literally what happened last time, Aika, and it didn't end well."

"You had a rusty axe, and your friend wasn't much more than a boy."

"You're not much older!"

"No, but I'm a hunter, and I've fought before. It'll be fine." She smiled through the dark, her hair and features unsullied even after the minimal sleep and marathon exertion.

Xander subdued her breath as she edged through the bush to get as close as she dared. Something littered the ground around the creature, though she couldn't determine what from where she crouched. A raspy whistle sounded ahead, and Aika darted into the creature's line of sight, drawing in half a dozen spikes that sailed through the air and lodged harmlessly in the trees, the girl too swift in her movements.

That was all the distraction Xander needed, and she leapt through the thick of the bramble and swiped her blade at the exposed back of the creature. The sharp edge of the blade veered clean through the vine's trunk and rendered it decapitated.

"See, wasn't so difficult, was it?" Aika said. She went over to the trees, pulled out the spikes, and placed them in a small pouch. "They'll make a fine poison."

Xander knocked her foot against one of the objects she had seen and then shuddered.

"Can you tell who they are…or were?" Aika said as she walked over.

"Humans, I think…but these two…they're dressed like you," she said, analysing the broken weapons by their sides, a combination of snapped swords and splintered arrows evidently useless against the vine.

Aika made a motion with her hand and then bent over and shuffled through the belongings of her kin to find a nearly empty quiver and a small pouch of rations.

"These'll keep us going," she said, and threw some of the contents to Xander. "Don't feel quite so naked anymore," she said, restocking her quiver. "Still, if we see any more of these creatures, I'd prefer to continue as we just did and save the arrows."

CHAPTER 45

Novembrix 1, 484; the Great Forest—Xander stretched her back and muffled an exhausted yawn from their perch atop the tree. They had encountered many more of the creatures since the first, and there were numerous victims each time. Sometimes forest critters, sometimes humans and bugs—the unselective destruction lethal to all and the hardiness of the beasts not like the vine she had encountered near Nhata.

"I don't think that battered old axe would've saved me against this lot…"

"I wonder who placed them here," Aika said as she stared into the distance.

From their vantage point, they could just make out the Great Tree, though that was not where they were headed. Since leaving the chamber, the pair had only happened across razed or abandoned settlements and the rotting remains of slaughtered critters, bugs, and humans alike. Despite the all-too-gruesome scenes, however, there was hope. Per the whispers of the trees, the vast majority of Aika's people and the other forest critters had evacuated into the depths of the forest, away from the encroaching armies to the north and the bug camps dotted sporadically around the tree. It was a direction Xander and Aika were all too keen to pursue, eager to find their own.

"Seems strange that the humans would do it," Xander commented. "Risk their own, that is."

Aika chuckled. "You speak of them as if you aren't one of them."

"I sometimes struggle to relate. I've seen such cruelty at the hands of men and women, it's hard to believe we can change. After Borealis fell and we were left for dead outside the walls, hunted day and night by the shadow warriors, it didn't take long for the survivors to turn on each other. Hustlers and traders set up shop with the sole purpose of extortion. People fought over food and shelter…and I remember this one couple, early on, no more than a few days after the exodus. They seemed ordinary enough, kind of nice, I guess, and they stayed with us for several days…but there was something about them that at the time I couldn't put my finger on, something that wasn't right. I couldn't explain back then, but now I guess the word would be devious. They pretended to be like the rest of us, and I think they once may have been, but they were quick to sell our location and numbers to the highest bidder, and when the gang attacked, they slaughtered most of the men and enslaved the women and children."

"But you escaped."

"I was on my own, unburdened by family or possessions."

"Perhaps be thankful they didn't sell your people to the shadow warriors."

"I think if that was an option, they may have done. Anyway, who's to say some of those traitorous traders didn't sell the people to the shadow warriors?"

"I didn't realise the aftermath was so cruel. We'd heard about it, of course. We're not so isolated down here as the humans may think, but the stories, the experiences of those on the ground…I just can't imagine it."

"And yet, here we are, reliving it to some degree."

"I guess we never figured the fall of Borealis would affect us down here. We're so far from that city and have, for a long time, been considered insignificant to the humans. Just another 'jurisdiction' of Anemoi, as your people like to say."

"But you're still a part of Anemoi, and if Erzse's intention is dominion over the region, then I can understand her attack on this forest."

"And especially if your hunch is right and she does want that shard."

"If she gets hold of the Rose, then I'm not sure there's anybody that can stop her from taking what she wants. So you see why we need to get it before she does?"

"If it's still in the Great Tree."

"I won't know until I get the—"

A flash of darkness crossed the base of the tree and disappeared into the shadows of the bushes.

"What was that?" Xander said.

"Too fast for me to catch it. Look, over there. I see torchlight."

"Your kind?"

"Unlikely, too easy to be seen. Probably humans—I mean, your people."

Moments later a dozen men crossed the base of the tree, spears and dogs at the ready. The girls squinted, unused to the torchlight that illuminated the forest beneath.

"First humans or critters we've seen alive," Xander murmured. "The entire forest has seemed a graveyard since we left that chamber."

"Who would've thought so much destruction could be wrought in only forty-two days?"

Several loud shouts came from ahead.

"Come on. I think they're after whatever it was that rushed through the bush," Xander said, and they climbed down.

They followed the soldiers for nearly an hour, always no less than fifty metres behind—enough to track, but not enough to stumble across any stragglers.

"They've cornered it," Aika whispered, her eyesight in the dark especially keen. "Quick."

Xander couldn't make out what they had cornered, but whatever it was, it was exceedingly strong, and it easily flung one of the men into a thick tree with a crunch of bone. Another man rushed at it with a spear, but Aika unleashed one of the many arrows she had scavenged in the preceding day into the man's back, and instantly the others turned and came at them. Aika had dispatched another three of the men with her arrows before she and Xander leapt into the fray.

With every swift stroke, Xander's blade cut through the dark in a golden flash, invoking fright in the nearest attackers, the fluidity and strength of her aggressive movements suddenly too much to bear. When combined with the whip and thud of Aika's sporadic arrows and the cruel, almost ghostly cut of Aika's unseen knife as she danced viciously between the men, the two soldiers that remained unscathed could do nowt but turn towards their initial victim in flight, and this was their undoing. Whatever they had cornered made easy work of them.

As the last torch dropped, the shroud took over. Xander cautiously walked up to where it was strewn and lifted it into the air to better see what the soldiers had chased.

"Aes!"

"You know him?"

Xander stepped towards the deer, but he didn't flinch, aware of who had rescued him for a second time. He was much larger than she remembered, even with her own teenage growth, and he seemed to tower over her memory of the larger stags in his herd. The huge deer closed the gap and brought his muzzle to the fold of her neck, his mangled antlers lopsided and not what one would expect of an adult stag.

She turned to Aika.

"This is Aes. He's my friend, though it's been a while. And Aes, this is Aika."

Aika smiled. "Aes. It's been a while."

"You know each other?"

"Aes and his herd used to frequent these parts when I was younger. It's been years, though."

Aika put her hand to his neck and flinched as if burned.

"What's wrong?" Xander asked.

"The pain!"

Xander touched her hand to his neck and jumped as visions of the destruction that had been wrought on the forests and settlements to the west of Lake Anemoi appeared to her. The scenes of slaughter and rampant violence, including the decimation of his own herd and the village of Nhata, shook her very core.

"But…how's this possible?" she whimpered as the images continued to bombard her vision.

And then her stomach clenched, her heart twisted, and a cold sweat took hold as she saw her, frail and bruised and alone.

"Evia…"

"Xander, my dear child, it's so good to hear your voice."

"I—I don't understand. What is all this? What's Aes showing me?"

"Memories. Mine and his. He's allowing me to connect with you—I'll explain later. It seems I may have miscalculated these turns of events, so clouded and swift were they in their approach. And how I've misjudged Erzse's ruthlessness and cunning."

"That was all Erzse's doing?"

"Yes."

"Does the woman have no bounds?" Xander seethed angrily. "She's also laid waste to the Great Forest. There's so much death and destruction. We wanted to stop her, to help the critters, but an ancient woman—"

"Bronte."

"Yes," she said, confused. "But how do you know her?"

Unable to see or hear what Xander could, Aika showed surprise at Xander's words.

"I've known the name for some time," Evia responded. "But it wasn't until recently that I had the opportunity to speak to her. She's been watching us. Gently influencing events. Pushing us to this moment. She's who spoke to you when the forest was in flames during the Ranclet. And it was she that conjured that girl that led you into Joseph's camp all those years ago."

"Jo," Xander uttered, jarred by the memory that had long ago sunk into the recesses of forgotten time.

"And now you being down there without me—there was more to it than my frailty. When the attack was on Nhata's doorstep, she reached out to me and convinced me it was necessary for you to do it alone. She convinced me that she would let no harm come to you, and that you must ride out the storm for there to be any glimmer of hope. Knowing what I know now, I'm glad I let you go."

The dreamy vision blurred.

"Are you okay?" Xander asked.

"I'm safe as can be, given the circumstances."

"And the others? The destruction Aes showed me…"

"I'm sorry. The attack was swift, violent, and without mercy, and when—"

The connection collapsed.

"Evia? Evia?"

But Xander could no longer see or hear her aunt, and as the witnessed images of the slaughter recommenced the throttling of her mind, she slumped to the ground in grief, and it took both Aes and Aika to beckon her back to reality.

It was too much. She slammed her fists into the dirt and screamed, though not a scream of despair or fear, but one born of hatred and anger, a scream enough to send chills down Aika's neck and make Aes's bronze fur shiver with fright. A scream so loud and so menacing that the critters of a tiny nearby village huddled close and slunk deep into their homes through sheer dread of what could have made such a distraught sound.

For a long time, she wouldn't speak, and Aes and Aika slept by her side to keep her warm in mind and body. Eventually Xander put her hand back to Aes's neck and searched for her aunt's face, but she couldn't find it, and she felt a strong pang of guilt at having not asked where the woman was.

Aika laid her hand on Xander's, but about to say something, she hesitated.

"I need to find her," Xander said.

"What about the—"

"It can wait."

"I don't think this is what your aunt intended."

"She's alone. And—I think something bad happened to my friends."

Aika pulled Xander close. "I'm sorry. I understand your need to leave. Did she tell you where she is?"

"No."

"Then how will you find her?"

"I don't know."

Gently Aes nudged his nose into Xander's neck, and a sad smile crossed her cheeks.

"I know it's silly, but I don't know what I'd do if something were to happen to her," Xander said softly. She looked up and caught Aika's confused expression. "What?"

"Um—you're speaking to me?"

"Aes, of course. He just told me…" Shock took her. She pulled away from the stag and peered into his gaze. "I—I can hear you in my head."

Aika's face brightened. "Impossible!"

Xander wiped a tear from her cheek. "He says it's not what my aunt wants, and that I'm being silly to think I can just go up north and find her without a plan. He says I need to get the shard, and then together we can figure out the next step." She shook her head as if in a daze. "Is this really happening, or have I gone mad?"

"Sounds like it's really happening," Aika said excitedly. "And I do think you're mad, just so you know."

Xander's expression grew distant as Aes spoke to her again.

"What did he say?" Aika asked as Xander came to.

"He thought he felt a connection to my mind in the woods the day we first met, but it was gone before he could be certain. He said it's been coming and going since I left Nhata, and it was just strong enough to track us down here. He says that once he's bonded with someone, the connection forms, allowing him to communicate through…did I hear that correctly? How odd! The bonded connection allows us to communicate through the tiny vibrations of our minds, and it allows the communication, regardless if the other is a sky-whisperer or not." She rubbed her forehead as bafflement crept into her eyes.

Aika chuckled. "Can't believe it?"

"That and—" She looked at Aes. "How can I understand you? You're not speaking my language, but I know what you're saying."

Her eyes grew distant as she listened, and then they widened with pleasant surprise.

"Well?" Aika said eagerly. "Don't keep me waiting."

With a warm smile, Xander turned to Aika. "It's the bond. The bond is making all this possible." Aes spoke again into her mind, and she nodded. "He says Evia was using him to communicate with me." She looked at Aes. "So you're also bonded with Evia? You're not—wait—is it just Evia you can speak to without the bond, or are there others? There are others! That must mean you have the spark?"

Aes snorted.

"So you're a sky-whisperer," she said as a wave of goosebumps erupted across her body. "And the sky-whisperers you can speak with—they also don't need to understand your language? Amazing. This is so surreal."

"That's playing it down! I have to tell you, I'm pretty jealous of that connection right now," Aika chimed in, her desire to be privy endearing.

Xander giggled, her burden momentarily forgotten. "Says the girl that can speak to the trees and knows a dozen forest critter languages?"

"Well, when you put it like that," Aika retorted, and playfully pushed Xander into a bush.

CHAPTER 46

Augustx 16, 476; Borealis, Borlencia; one month before the fall of Borealis— Sitting on a long stone bench amongst a dozen others too tired to continue standing, Xander yawned as she took in the rowdy market square south of the river. Noisy and crowded, it was not too different from the dozens of other markets that adorned Borealis's streets, though there was one glaring difference noticeable to even those without keen noses. A difference that would unfailingly hit visitors once they entered the streets two or three blocks from the famed bazaar.

Every stall within the square—and there were hundreds—was tended by a man or woman from near or afar, skilled in the art of perfumery. Their work surfaces, more often than not, were cluttered with messy arrays of glass bottles of varying colours, all carrying musky colognes and sweet perfumes destined for the poor and wealthy alike. A beautiful harmony of scents to the resilient, and a torrid blend of chemical irritation to the sensitive.

For Xander, it was the latter. And coupled with the unpleasantly stuffy afternoon heat, and the boredom of sitting around with no end in sight, she found herself desperately wanting to move on as far from the square as she could manage. Of course, that would require her mother to wrap up her conversation with a brown-skinned woman from the Ignis Desert, which she seemed in no rush to do.

Xander sighed, then trudged over from the stone bench and tugged on Alya's gown. "Can we go? I'm tired, and it's getting late."

Despite Alya's look of disapproval at the interruption, an inquisitive smile took the desert woman.

"This is your daughter?" the woman asked in a heavy accent. Despite the fact that she looked to be in her late thirties, her eyes were clouded, like those of someone who had spent half a century exposed to the fierce glare of the desert sun.

"She is," Alya responded warmly, her immediate irritation gone.

The woman peered at Xander, as if examining her. "Her features are familiar. And her skin—it's darker than yours," she said to Alya. "Her father is Cresedi?"

"I'm not familiar with the Cresedi. My husband's father is from a small town just north of the Ignis Desert, and his mother is from Borealis."

"Ah! Then perhaps I'm not so good a judge of origins. The Cresedi Empire is quite some distance from the desert. I could've sworn—never mind. So would you like two of the rose waters or just the one?"

Alya wrapped up her purchase, and Xander eagerly ushered her mother out of the square onto a busy street. But just as the crowd sought to swallow them, Xander glanced back to see the desert woman staring after them, the look of curiosity steadfast on the woman's features right up until she could be seen no more.

"That was intense," Xander remarked.

"What?"

"The woman."

"She was just making conversation. So where next? I promised you sweets, but you do seem in a hurry to get home—"

Xander's face brightened. "Sweets. You did promise."

"Ha! That woke you up. Okay then, I know a place close to here."

Holding Xander's hand, Alya led them onto an adjacent street that was only slightly less busy than the last. Walking along the uneven tiles at a leisurely pace, Xander scanned the two-story buildings that lined the edge. Some were stores that opened directly onto the road, and others were clearly residences, the majority multifamily, with sturdy doors and shutters to keep the weather and miscreants out at night. And soon enough, much to her delightful relief, the delicious aromas of cooked spices and vegetables were all her nose had to contend with.

Five minutes along, they pulled up to a busy crossroad and came to a stop. Several groups of men and women lined the corners, chatting and dealing away, and a heavy chariot navigated the crossing. The gossip of the merchants and pedestrians was deafening, and the only things that could be heard over it were the chariot driver's curse words as he urged those on foot to get out of the way. Despite the potency of the man's words, however, Alya made no attempt to shield Xander from language that was so commonplace on the tongues of Borealis's inhabitants.

Instead, Alya scratched her head. "I must say, I can't quite recall which road to take."

"That's not like you."

She chuckled. "Isn't it?"

"If in doubt—"

"Ask. Yes—" They stumbled forward as a thickset man knocked through them.

"Road's for walking, not gawking," he grunted back, and turned right at the crossroad.

Alya pulled Xander to the side, out of the way of the traffic. "But maybe not around these parts."

"It's not safe?"

"More unnecessary attention than we would like," she said, taking in a group of young men staring at them from one of the corners. "You know, Xander, maybe we just visit the sweet shop near us. It'll still be open by the time we get back."

Xander wasn't bothered where they got the sweets from, provided that they got them, so she simply nodded her acceptance.

"That's my girl. This way, then," Alya said, and they began forward, around the chariot stalled by a bunch of kids eager to irritate the driver.

The next series of streets was even less busy than the prior ones and almost exclusively residential. Large, colourful houses and sturdy walls lined the roadside, and even the road itself seemed in better condition.

"It's very different from the last one," Xander said of the unworn stones.

"Less traffic and more money."

"More money?"

"Look at the houses. In neighbourhoods like this, either the local politicians will make sure to maintain the street to build favour with those that can help them financially, or the families that do live here will fund it themselves."

"Sounds like more cheating."

"Cheating?"

"They're paying people to vote for them."

"It's called 'buying votes.' And there are all sorts of ways to do it. In the poorer neighbourhoods, the politicians will give out free food or make promises of wealth. In the wealthy neighbourhoods, the price is a bit steeper. This way," she said, and they began down another road with a small temple at the other end. "Sadly, it's the world we live in."

"There must be a way to stop it."

"Your father thinks so."

"He does?"

"He does. He thinks by taking some of the power out of the hands of the politicians and giving it to the scientists and engineers and merchants, we can create a more stable system." Alya looked down at Xander and smiled. "Maybe it's a bit complicated."

"No, I understand."

"Then why the confused look?"

"Well, do the people get to vote for the scientists and those other ones?"

"No. They get the job through merit."

"But then doesn't that mean you take some of the power away from the people?"

A proud expression took Alya, and she stopped them in the middle of the quiet street, some twenty metres short of the temple. "Very observant, Xander. Very observant. It's not a popular push, especially amongst those that stand to lose the most. What?"

Alya followed Xander's pointed finger to one of the temple's thick pillars. Covered in graffiti, there was a clear depiction of Carolus at the bottom, wearing the robe of the desert people and a crown. In his hands were chains wrapped around the necks of the people of Borealis, and behind him were the city's treasures.

Alya's face hardened. "Case in point."

"But—but that doesn't make any sense," Xander stammered angrily. "He's not trying to steal from anybody."

"I guess it depends on whose eyes you're looking at it through."

"Who's that?"

Again Alya followed Xander's finger, this time to a woman drawn on the same pillar a metre above the depiction of Carolus. The woman wore the robes of the Zylencian senior ministers and carried an air of magnificence, evident even through the scribbles. Behind her were dozens of stick men carrying spears and swords, and her eyes were clearly focused on Carolus.

"Who is she?" Xander asked again.

"I don't know," Alya said, though Xander strongly suspected she knew.

"It looks like she comes for—"

Alya tightened her grip on Xander's hand to the point of it being uncomfortable.

"What's wrong?" Xander asked, and then followed Alya's gaze to the temple corner, where a person donned in a hood watched them.

The man's features were concealed, though Xander could just make out the dark skin of his hands. He exuded an unmistakable hostility that both of them could feel.

"I think it's time to get home," Alya said with forced calm.

Xander nodded and they began for home at a brisk stroll. The character did not follow, but even with the temple long behind them, the haunting image of Carolus as the villain and the eerie stare of the cloaked man left Xander feeling ill at ease.

CHAPTER 47

Novembrix 2, 484; the Great Forest—Despite the hour, the afternoon sun struggled to pierce the eerie fog that had blanketed the Great Forest. Consequently, the air was nippy and the visibility hazy. Xander, Aika, and Aes were hidden within a thicket, spooked by an obscured movement some distance ahead where their path crossed through a heavily wooded gully and over a narrow stream.

Aika nodded to Xander, and she returned the gesture. There was no need for them to exchange words, for they knew what had to be done. The vines were too dangerous to leave alive, no matter the risk to themselves, and so they emerged slowly from the bush, determined not to give up their presence until the final moment. As they were about to sneak forward and catch their prey off guard, a most wonderful sound brushed their ears and brought them to a standstill.

"Was that what I think it was?" Aika uttered.

Xander could feel her friend's growing relief as she, too, found herself hoping. And then they beamed.

A mother and child of a similar complexion to Aika's had emerged onto the path with buckets in hand, ready to pull water from the stream. They were the first critters the girls had seen alive since they had left Bronte's chamber, and the first of the Lizard People that Xander had seen besides Aika.

"We should be careful not to frighten them," Xander said quietly.

Aika raised an eyebrow. "We don't scare easily, if that's what you're implying."

"Did I say that?"

"It's what you were thinking, right, Aes?" Aika chuckled and nudged the stag. "Let's take the path—"

She drew her bow and swiftly aimed it at the bush to their right.

"Thought I'd have my knife at your neck before you realised," a voice came from the leafy shroud.

"Not a chance, cousin," Aika retorted. "I was giving you a chance."

"Cousin?" Xander said, confused, as a slim man with sinewy muscle emerged into view.

His features were similar to Aika's, and he was topless, revealing a myriad of fresh scars across his torso and arms.

"Ratin," Aika said softly. She lowered her bow as he stepped onto the path. He was alone. "Good to see you still live."

"And you," he responded.

They clasped arms and then released each other.

"Who are your friends?" he asked.

"This is Xander, and this is Aes."

Ratin tilted his head in acknowledgement, and they responded in kind. He then looked back to Aika and smiled in relief. "Between the vines and the bug alliance, we thought you were dead."

"Bug alliance?"

"Where have you been?" he said, surprised. "The humans and the bugs. They're working together."

"The bugs hate the humans."

"Not these humans. There was some initial tension between the two sides, but with us picking them off and the vines attacking anything that moves, they've become pretty much inseparable. It's been difficult."

"I can tell," she said, taking in his cuts and bruises.

"It means Erzse and Damain have a common goal," Xander remarked tiredly.

"Maybe it *is* the shard she's after," Aika responded.

"I really hope not."

"Erzse?" Ratin queried.

"She's the humans' commander," Aika said.

"Ah! The woman with the permanent scowl?"

"You've seen her?"

"No, but that's how our spies described her. She left the forest some weeks ago, taking a small chunk of soldiers with her. About the time the alliance was assured, if I recall."

Aika shot Xander a worried look. "Then maybe she did get it."

"I won't know until I read the map," Xander responded tiredly, burdened by the thought.

"She was in a hurry, from what I was told." Ratin spoke up. "I don't know if she had this shard you speak of, but it's not unheard of for some commanders to leave their occupying force once they've secured local troops. Usually with the promise of something in return. Not sure what exactly is in it for Damain, but an alliance with the humans would give the bug army the strength it needs to drive us from the Great Forest. It's what Damain's wanted since the wretch could crawl. That and your father's—" He glanced awkwardly at Aika.

"Where is my father?" Aika asked with a lump in her throat.

Xander tensed, knowing Ratin's hesitation had already confirmed Bronte's predication. His shoulders slumped.

"Who did it?" Aika said, barely able to contain the quiver of her lip.

Ratin stared at her sternly, but rather than deflect or try to comfort, he spoke bluntly. "Damain. The bugs caught us in the initial evacuation. They were everywhere. We were trying to cover the civilians when a bug squad came in from above. It was Damain that grabbed your father."

"How did Damain do it?"

He shifted uncomfortably, though Xander didn't blame her friend for asking. "Dropped him," he said.

"Was it quick?"

"Yes."

It was a lie. Xander could tell Ratin had withheld the truth, but it wasn't her place to say. She wondered if Aika had caught on also.

"What will you do?" he asked.

"What do you think?" Aika said coldly.

"I thought as much. The camp's close," he said, and began along the path.

"What about them?" Xander asked of the woman and child.

"They're safe," Ratin called back without turning around.

Xander followed Aika's pointed finger to a group of archers perched across a dozen trees overlooking the gully. Archers who hadn't been visible moments before. It was a sight multiplied many times as they continued along the route to their destination. The camp itself was broken into multiple pods, each with its own security, and long before they reached the first, they could see Aika's people combing the forest floor for loose wood and food.

As they passed the first pod, Xander saw a number of weary critters, small and large and of different kinds, staring at them. And in particular, Aika.

"It's been a while since we've had any survivors arrive," Ratin said, understanding Xander's interest. "They also thought the princess was dead."

"Right! I forgot you're a princess," Xander said as her cheeks reddened.

"The elders will be happy to know she lives. They won't have to perform the ritual now."

"Ritual?"

"Ritual to find and appoint a new leader. Aika's father is the Lizard King. Provided that she can pass a number of tests to prove she's no simpleton, his throne is hers." He looked at Aika and grinned mischievously, keen to lift her mood. "I'm still holding out hope that they'll give it to me instead."

Xander could feel Aika's pain subside somewhat at her cousin's jibe.

Aika returned the grin. "If I don't pass, then you definitely won't."

"We'll see," he said, shoving her lightly. Taking in their position at the second pod, Ratin stopped, as did they. "You're Ricard's friend, no?" he asked Xander.

"I am," she responded with a flutter of excitement.

He pointed to a small hut positioned near the centre of the pod. "Aika and I will wait here for you."

Xander's calm evaporated, and she rushed towards the hut, leaving the pair and Aes on the path. Small fires dotted the site, and the light odour of leafy broth hung in the air. From the outside of the hut, she could hear the bass of Ricard's voice reverberating through the thin walls. She hurriedly opened the door to see him sitting on a mat with Leila, Haro, Gladis, and Nudus perched around him like little mice listening to a forest lion regale them with fairy tales. The big man's eyes widened and his mouth dropped, and the others, too, stared in a daze.

There was shocked silence for the briefest of moments, and then Ricard roared, "I knew it! I damn well knew it!" He jumped up and, nearly treading on the others, stumbled over and bear-hugged the girl. "I knew you lived. I could feel it in my water."

"Ricard," she managed, teary-eyed. She pulled away and grabbed the others in her hand, though Nudus stopped her before she could collect him.

"Xander!" Leila cried, hugging the girl's wrist.

Haro put his hand to his chest. "How very sorry I am that I underestimated you."

"This is the most pleasant of surprises." Gladis beamed. She was no longer wearing her cast.

"Quite the surprise," Nudus remarked, though with less enthusiasm than the others.

"Wait, where's Oscine?" Xander asked worriedly.

"He's fine," Leila responded with a smile. "He's made some new friends amongst the bird community, and now they're carrying out spy missions for General Ratin. He'll be back in a few days."

Ricard shrugged. "Not sure how they can see a damn thing with this fog. So, kiddo, how did you keep in one piece?"

"It's a long story I'll tell later," she said. "Come with me. Aika and Ratin are waiting for me outside. We're going to the main camp. Their princess has returned."

"The princess also lives," Nudus said, again with little interest. "Truly a remarkable day. But I will let you all do the honours, as I have business to attend to." At that, he got up, walked over to a little bed, and dove onto his pillow. "Maybe I can get some sleep without the oaf's snoring."

"Suit yourself," Ricard scoffed. "Come on then, kiddo. Lead the way."

Chatting joyously between them, they followed Ratin to the main pod, where the elders and Aika's extended family rejoiced at her arrival. Tears and laughter were the emergent theme, with much disbelief as both parties brought the other up to speed.

It was confirmed by all that the bugs and the humans had formed an alliance and together had whittled much of the Lizard People's land. But in return, the Lizard People had inflicted heavy losses against the alliance, destroying settlements and plundering supply lines. In the vines, however, both the Lizard People and the alliance had a common enemy. An enemy that had decimated much of the eastern fringes of the forest and had, according to Ratin's intelligence, found its way to the Great Tree.

Aika's anger shone darkly in every one of her people. They had all shared loss and were all determined and ready to rid the forest of the infection. But first there would be a traditional test to determine the princess's fitness.

▲ ▲ ▲

The light pitter-patter of a dozen drums and the quiet whispers and chants of hundreds of forest critters filled the damp, moonlit night. Even the whispers of the trees were prevalent, singing and gossiping joyously, with none of the nervousness that had characterised their conversations in the prior days. There were just two small fires, both for heating dinner.

Sitting cross-legged at the edge of a large circular opening were Xander, Ricard, Haro, Leila, and Aes. Within the circle, a hundred Lizard People sat facing the centre where Aika, Ratin, and seven elders spoke amongst themselves. The nine in the centre were donned in long robes, and they were overlooked by a crooked tree trunk absent its crown. Etched beautifully into its ancient skin were the heads of a dozen types of forest critters, the original races to have faced the soldiers of West Anemoi all those centuries ago.

Xander looked down to the wooden bowl that had just been placed in front of her by two children. Hungry, she eagerly put the bowl to her lips and took a sip of its contents. It was bitter, too bitter. She tried in earnest to not reveal her dislike, but the children giggled at the subtle face she inadvertently pulled. Confident the liquid wouldn't come back up, she put the bowl to the ground, vowing to go the night without food, and then thanked the children.

"It's been two hours," Ricard whispered into Xander's ear as the younglings wandered off.

"What?"

"It's been two hours. I can only sit cross-legged for so long before I start to go numb."

"I went numb long ago," Haro interjected. "You just have to embrace it."

"Embrace it! My legs will drop off before long."

"Always the baby," Leila chided.

"Here," Gladis said, pulling something from her pouch.

"No offence, woman, but have you lost your mind?" Ricard chuckled. "I'm no longer a littl'un. Whatever you give me isn't going to do anything."

"And I beg to disagree."

He peered at the tiny bundle with curiosity and took it between his comparatively gigantic finger and thumb.

"Not even sure I swallowed it," he grumbled after tossing it into his mouth. "You sure—" His eyes suddenly glazed over, and an intoxicated smile spread across his cheeks. "Okay, works the charm."

"Maybe Aika is a simpleton," Haro pondered.

Leila chortled. "Do you really think that?"

"Two hours, and they're still trying to work out if the princess can give an order here or there. What do you think, Xander? You've spent the past month with her. Is she a simpleton?"

"I told you, what was weeks for you was only a couple of days for us."

"So she might be?"

Xander laughed. "No, she's not."

"Well, I think it's a possibility. Which begs the question: Do I really want to join you if she's giving the orders?"

"She's not a simpleton."

"Maybe that's why Nudus didn't join," Leila said with a shrug.

"Exactly!" Haro said. "He knows it's a waste of time."

"Well, have you got somewhere else to be?" Xander asked.

"Seeing as you mention it—"

The drums and the chants stopped. The group looked to the centre, where one of the elders, a frail man with a beard down to his waist, held up his hand in a call for silence.

"A decision has been made," he croaked. "Princess Aika has agreed to take her father's mantle."

Excited gossip and applause erupted.

The man held up his hand again, and the noise quickly subsided. "On the condition," he continued, "that in the event she must leave the forest, Prince Ratin will take on her military duties and we, the elders, her civil duties."

This time, confusion did the rounds.

"What's the problem?" Xander asked, confounded by the disarray.

Gladis spoke. "It's not normal for the king or queen, as will be the case with Aika, to leave the forest. Even less so for them to relinquish control."

"Relinquish control to her cousin and the elders. Still don't see what the issue is."

"The elders are advisors. The Lizard People's oldest and wisest, each with a unique experience or skill. They're not supposed to hold power. And Ratin will have full control over the critter armies."

"Quite the ask for a soldier that's still relatively fresh on that level," Ricard remarked. "Of course, could say the same of Aika."

Haro grunted and turned to Xander. "Makes you wonder. Is the princess planning to leave the forest?"

Xander shrugged. Aika hadn't mentioned leaving the forest. "She didn't say anything."

"Maybe she seeks to join you," Leila said.

"Maybe."

▲ ▲ ▲

Xander and Aika sat on a downed log a short distance from the circle where Aika's people and Xander's friends celebrated in quiet rejoicing.

"I think I'm going to come with you," Aika said.

"Bronte really left a mark, then?"

"It depends on what we find in that tree. But if all the death we've seen since leaving that chamber has spread across the whole of Anemoi, I don't see what choice I have."

"And your people?"

"The elders and Ratin are capable. Probably more capable than me. Have you had a chance to look at the map?"

"Briefly."

"And the shard?"

"It's still there."

Aika breathed relief. "And did you find out how to get to it?"

"Not yet. I'll look at it in the morning. I can bring it to your tent."

"I can't do the morning. We've got a hunt." A fierce expression took her. "Want to join?"

"What are we hunting?"

"Bugs."

CHAPTER 48

Novembrix 3, 484; the Great Forest—Xander rubbed at the dirt dried to her arm. It stank and itched horribly, but Aika had said it was the only thing that would stop the bugs from catching her scent. She pulled her hand from the irritation and clenched her fists, determined to ignore the urge to scratch.

It was early morning and too dark to see clearly, and the air felt muggy, despite the prevailing seasonal cool. They had travelled on foot for two hours to reach this point, through dense vegetation and around the edge of a swamp. Aika, Ratin, Xander, and Ricard, along with fifty soldiers, were dispersed around a poorly guarded camp. Xander could feel the tension in the five soldiers joined to her and Ricard, but none in the big man. He exuded only exhilaration, an oddity amidst her own nerves.

Some distance ahead, partially visible through the thick bushes that concealed their presence, was a lone bug guard, and behind the creature, the bug settlement. Dozens of tents with no discernible layout and an appearance not too dissimilar to what Xander might have expected from a human camp.

"You were expecting burrows or something else equally revolting, weren't you?" Ricard whispered into her ear.

"Yes."

"These are civilised bugs," he jibed.

"They're ready," the squad leader said quietly. He pointed to their right.

"I can't see," Ricard whispered.

"Aika's given the signal." Xander spoke.

"About time," he muttered, and began forward.

He had barely made it a metre when an arrow whistled past his ear and hit the bug sentry in the throat. It was a scene imitated across the camp. With the handful of sentries downed, the party emerged from the bushes into the encampment at a creep.

Slowly and cautiously, the party drifted to the first set of targeted tents, all on the outskirts of the site. An acidic stench clung to the earth, and bone fragments and garbage littered the ground.

Simultaneously each group entered its allotted dwelling with the utmost silence. Xander followed into her group's targeted tent after her squad leader. She nearly hurled. The odour was disgusting, and it took her all to not run back out. There were six bugs dotted around the space, fast asleep. She edged up to one and readied her blade as the others found their marks.

She felt pity as she watched it sleep, its chest gently moving up and down as it snored. Oblivious to her presence. Its face, though not as distinguishable as a human's or an animal's, was still unique. She peered up to Ricard, who showed no emotion as he looked his bug up and down as if it were a straw dummy to be used for practise.

The squad leader gave the signal, and a shallow sigh escaped Xander's lips. As one, the group thrust their knives into the hearts of their sleeping prey. The only sounds were the noises of their blades piercing the shell-like skin of the bugs, and the subsequent gurgles of the victims choking to death.

Methodical. Efficient. They crept to the next set of tents and repeated. Then again. And again. Within fifteen minutes the entire camp had been slaughtered, and 170 bug carcasses had been tossed onto a hastily made firepit in the centre. There had been no casualties, and no bug had stirred in alarm, much to Xander's surprise. The only telltale sign of the gruesome deed was the thick blood plastered on all of them. A horrid reminder that not all deaths were equal.

▲ ▲ ▲

"What's wrong?" Aika asked as Xander took another sip of her broth. They were alone in Aika's tent, which was bare except for a mattress, a couple of hastily made chairs, and a table and cabinet.

Xander looked up, her expression distant. "Nothing."

"You're lying. You've been quiet since the attack."

She rubbed at her tired eyes, keen to break away from Aika's inquisitive gaze. "It felt wrong."

"What? The attack?"

"Killing them whilst they slept."

"We're at war. What the bugs have done to my people, to the forest critters, is far, far worse. They're lucky to have been killed in their sleep. We easily could've cut their limbs from them or burned them alive. Both are tactics they've used against their prisoners of war."

"I've heard. Guess it felt wrong not giving them a chance."

"You would've rather we risked our own to give the bugs a chance?"

"Maybe 'chance' is the wrong word. What?"

"You're definitely Carolus's daughter, and it'll get you killed. Compassion's not a welcome ally in war."

Xander nodded acknowledgement and then returned to the broth. She was hungry from the morning's excursion. They both were, and they quickly scoffed down their rations in silence. Warmed, fed, and in a better place, Aika peered to Xander's sack and spoke.

"Shall we look at the map?"

"Have you got—"

Aika withdrew a book from the cabinet.

Xander chuckled. "Some would think you're a mind reader. Curious, though, where did you get the materials to build a book? Or did it resize after the law reverted?"

"This one was taken from one of the human camps. Ratin's been salvaging wherever possible. Anything to help our people adjust without having to rebuild completely." She opened the book and laid it on the table, then pulled out a pencil. "The paper's too thick to trace, so hopefully you can draw."

"I think I'll manage." Xander took out the map and unrolled it next to the book. Her expression glazed over as she focused her mind on the Great Tree. It appeared on the map, though still only visible to her. She then zoomed in with her mind until she had a bird's-eye view of the tree's interior.

"Where's the shard?"

"It's at the bottom of the tree."

"Then I was right. It's in the section we've not been able to access. Do you see a way down there?"

"I—I don't know. Let me keep looking."

For two hours, Xander combed through the Great Tree via the map, exploring the paths and rooms, searching for a way to that bottom level. She could see every nook and every cranny of a structure far larger and far more complex than even Aika could give justice in her description. At least it felt like every nook and cranny, which did leave her slightly puzzled.

"When in Anemoi did the last bearers have time to explore all this?" she thought to herself, amazed by the fact that some of her predecessors must have passed through each of these spaces for her to be able to see them on the map.

It was two long, tedious hours that saw Ricard come and go with afternoon tea and Ratin visit with the positive results of two other hunting parties that had gone out that same morning. He was still there, slumped on the bed beside Aika, when Xander stirred.

"I think I've found something," she said cautiously.

The cousins' ears perked, and they quickly got up and stood beside her. Xander took the pencil and began to draw on the untouched book.

"It's not exact, and I can't really see how it accesses that bottom level, but it seems to happen through there." She looked at them excitedly, but her face soon dropped. "What's wrong?"

"There's nothing there," Aika responded hopelessly as she took in Xander's sketch.

"What do you mean?"

"We've been there. Both of us. It's just a small patch of grass with a couple of markings etched into the wall. There's nothing there."

"There must be something."

"She's right," Ratin said. "There's nothing there."

"And what about the markings?" Xander asked.

"The tree's covered in markings," Aika answered. "Thousands scratched into the wood on every level. Everybody wanting to leave their signature over hundreds of years. The markings don't mean anything."

Xander puffed her cheeks. "Then what do we do?"

"We can't risk it," Ratin said bluntly. "It's dangerous enough, us following you on a possibility. But we can't risk our soldiers if you don't know with certainty what we're looking for."

Aika sighed. "He's not wrong. Doesn't mean you won't find something, though. Keep looking. In the meantime, we'll keep raiding the alliance's settlements. Kill as many of the bugs and humans as we can until they leave. It's all we can do."

Disappointed by the impasse, Xander simply nodded.

CHAPTER 49

Novembrix 8, 484; the Great Forest—"That's quite the warhorse you have there, kiddo," Ricard said, and entered the grove where Xander sat beside Aes.

She looked at Aes, sensing his same amusement. "Aes is hardly the warhorse type."

"He certainly has the size and daring but none of the weakness in stamina. He would make a fine warhorse."

Aes grunted and she laughed.

"What did he say?"

"It's not what he said. It's what the tiny vibrations of his mind conveyed."

"I know that. I'm still coming to terms with whatever connection it is that you two have," Ricard said with a hint of jealousy.

"So am I."

"Well, what did he say?"

"He said he knows far too many warhorses to ever want to aspire as such. They can be stubborn buggers with all brawn and no brain."

"Surely they can't be that bad."

"No, not all—he says he's known worse."

"So be it. Point is, he will be a useful ally if the time calls for it."

She put her hand to Aes's neck and ran her fingers through his fur.

"The time has already called for it," she said solemnly. "And he has already accepted, even though I didn't ask."

Ricard sat on a fallen trunk and tossed a pebble into the water. "I enjoyed this forest much more when light could actually penetrate this damn miserable fog. How it has changed in such a short time."

"It can't be permanent. The shroud, the vines, the soldiers—sooner or later the circumstance will change. They'll be overcome, and normality will be restored."

"Sorry, kiddo. I wish it were so, but this is the new normal. It would seem that even Bronte's power had limits, and to know that all these years she lived and that it was only her prolonged dying breath, though in itself a testament to her power, that weakly bound the forest's normality…well, it underscores the lack of permanency in everything we know."

"Who's to say that her law can't be re-established, meaning humans and critters can only enter if they're small?"

"I don't doubt you'll find another as powerful as Bronte, but still… look around you at the destruction wrought. No, it can never be the same, but that's not to suggest we can't build a new normal that is agreeable to us survivors."

"My aunt once said that people who are content with their lot—content, not thrilled—are still likely to reject change if there's even the slightest suspicion of short-term hardship, even if it meant the prospect of long-term reward for themselves and others."

"She's not wrong about the stubbornness of our kind. Nobody enjoys disruption. We're creatures of habit, even if we wake every day despising that habit."

They fell quiet, with only the chirps of the bugs to fill the silence.

"You heard or seen any more of your aunt?" he asked after several moments.

"Just that once…and I'd be lying if I said the images don't haunt my every moment. How lucky I must be to have escaped that hardship, and all the same, how callous I must be to not heed their distress."

"You're strong, kiddo, and I sympathise with the situation, but with all that has happened and all that could be, you've made the right choice to continue the path your aunt put you on and strengthen our cause."

"'Patience is like a fine wine. It can't be rushed for fear of simplicity and prematurity in its development, and it can't be left too long for fear of souring and tastelessness. Only when it has been perfectly aged and fully settled will you reap the full bounty of what you have sown.'"

"You're kidding!" he laughed boisterously. "All these years and you still remember."

"Hard not to forget. It's one of my few enjoyable memories. Sitting at your vineyard with my parents and Lawrence, watching the sun set on the walls of Borealis and with all the meats and cheeses one could scoff. Hard to forget a moment like that."

"That it is, but you were a wee lady when I blessed your father with that handy piece of wisdom. Took him a while to stop laughing, if I recall."

"Even a month afterwards, he would recite it after every glass of red."

"Ha! That fool." Ricard laughed. "How I would trade the rest of this lifetime to relive that moment once more."

Again the grove fell silent.

CHAPTER 50

Novembrix 9, 484; the Great Forest—The frigid water stung as Xander dipped her hands into the stream a short distance from her pod. She watched as the blood on her skin slowly unravelled and released into the flow of the translucent, liquid-like paint. A beautifully morbid blend of red and yellow and green, the reminiscence of her victims from that morning's raid, both human and bug. A recurring scene of violence that had become as regular as taking breakfast.

Her mind flashed back to the attack. A gruesome replay of her blade cutting cleanly through a bug's torso after the camp's alarm had been raised and its inhabitants awoken in a fright. She could still see the belated look of horror on its face as it came to realise what had happened. She shuddered at the thought and jerked her hands from the stream.

"Innocence is as rare as the rarest of commodities in war," a voice interrupted, startling her.

"Nudus. Sorry, I didn't know you were there."

He was on the other side of the stream, lounging on a toadstool. "I'm seeking much-needed solitude. I can only take so much of that bickering married couple and Gladis's condescending remarks. Why the woman's chosen to home with us rather than that brother of hers will forever grate me." Xander could sense his intense dislike for Gladis. "Anyway, where was I? Yes. Maybe the children and the already dead can wash their hands of any guilt. But for the rest of us, we're marked."

"You've taken a life since the invasion?" she said, surprised.

"To take a life is just one of the many ways to mark oneself. Sitting idly by and watching your colleagues dirty themselves doesn't absolve the observer of his or her guilt." He sat up awkwardly and hopped off the toadstool onto the ground. "Many can render their guilt thornless by the simple conjuring of a justification. Perhaps you should try it." He started towards the bushes away from the camp.

"Where are you going?"

"There's a small patch of mushrooms a few hundred metres from here that deserves a visit. An easy distance for you, but quite the distance for me. If I leave now, I should be back before nightfall."

"It's dangerous to leave the camp alone."

"Ratin's men are everywhere. And I'm quite the expert at hiding. I'm sure I'll be fine." He disappeared into the shrubs without a look back.

She returned to cleaning her hands, her thoughts dwelling on Nudus's words. Aika had suggested the same. And Ricard. They were at war, a war started by the bugs and the humans. That was their justification. That's why they felt no guilt when sneaking into these camps and killing their unaware foes. It was a justification she, too, could latch onto if she just tried.

Back in the camp, she entered the tent she shared with Ricard and the others. But for several untidy beds, large and miniature, and a small plant pot protecting the leaf Gladis had given her—which had interestingly grown without Bronte's Law intact—it was empty. The map was unfurled on her mattress, staring at her, and her all-too-familiar impatience suddenly reared its head, begging for her to search the parchment for something, anything, that could convince Aika to take her to the Great Tree. But her exhaustion was also persuasive, overwhelmingly so.

She slumped onto her bed beside the map and passed out. It was a restless slumber stained with feelings of guilt from the deaths she had inflicted, a longing to see her friends in Nhata, and also Hemish, the boy whose face she couldn't seem to remember beyond a sad blur. An onslaught of confusing dreams and uncomfortable nightmares she couldn't quite wrest free of—that is, until a panicked voice pierced the fog and woke her.

"Xander, Xander!"

She opened her bleary eyes to see Leila standing over her.

"It's Ricard!" Leila cried. "The humans got him."

Xander jerked up, nearly knocking Leila to the ground. "Where?" she said, and frantically grabbed her blade and kit.

"Nudus said it happened on the path north of the camp."

"Nudus?"

"He was out—"

"Searching for mushrooms."

Haro entered the tent, his sword and shield ready. "The guards won't go out there without Aika or Ratin. They've sent a runner, but I fear they will be too late to help."

Xander stumbled out into the nippy air with Haro and Leila behind her. Nudus was beside one of the fires, his cheek bleeding. Gladis was tending him.

"Nudus, what happened?" Xander asked.

"An ambush. The oaf was at the same mushroom patch when they attacked. They came from nowhere. Five of them. They took him and kicked me into—ouch!"

"Sorry," Gladis said unsympathetically as she dabbed his cheek with a local herb. She looked to Xander. "I know the patch. It would've taken this one some time to get back from there. Ricard and those soldiers will already be long gone."

"I can track them, if you get me out there," Haro said to Xander.

"You're only two," Gladis interjected sternly. "You'd have to be mad."

"Ricard's got a reputation." Nudus spoke. "Can't see them being too kind to him."

Desperation filled Xander, and she turned to the pod's entrance, where a small number of Aika's men were earnestly discussing the breach in the camp's perimeter. She hurried over to them. "If we leave now, we might still have a chance to catch him."

One of the guards looked at her, irritated by the irresponsible suggestion. He was tall and sported a long ponytail. "Not without more soldiers."

"The longer we leave it, the harder it'll be to catch them," she retorted angrily.

"Not my order to give," he said dismissively, and turned back to the other guards.

Xander's temper rose. About to scold the guard and get herself into trouble, she turned to see Aes racing up to the pod. He had heard her panicked thoughts. Without saying anything, she jogged up to him and jumped onto his back.

"Not without me!" Haro called as he ran towards them, drawing the guards' bewildered stares. He leapt shockingly high into the air and clung to Xander's thigh, then scrambled up onto her lap.

"Xander!" Gladis called. "Take the path north for three hundred metres and then two hundred metres northeast along the stream. You'll see an opening to your right. That's your patch."

"Thank you!"

"Onwards!" Haro bellowed.

Aes turned towards the trail and transitioned into a sprint, swiftly leaving behind the pod and the shouted warnings of the guards. He made easy work of the path, but the vegetation to the sides of the stream was thick and unruly, whipping them as they sped along its banks.

"I see the opening!" Xander said, pointing ahead, though closer approach also revealed two dead archers strewn at the entrance.

Aes walked warily over the two bodies and entered the small space, trampling the mushrooms as he did. There was a narrow path on the other side of the grove, leading away from the stream.

"Which direction?" Xander asked.

"Humans didn't do this," Haro uttered suddenly, his eyes pulling away from the dead archers in a panic.

"What—"

The flutter of bug wings sounded from above them.

"Quick!" Haro shouted alarmedly, but as Aes struggled to turn around in the tight space, a net was dropped on them by two bugs hovering overhead.

The two insectoids hurriedly pulled out long handheld darts and abruptly dove downwards. Still tangled in the web, Xander braced as the first lunged towards her. But just as the bug breached the two-metre mark, Haro leapt onto its shoulder and drove his knife into its neck, killing it instantly. He then speedily jumped onto the others, where he repeated the deadly action. The two limp carcasses plummeted to the ground, though Haro seamlessly jumped from the second onto Aes's back before they hit the dirt with a thud.

Cries of rage pierced the forest around them as Xander cut through the net with her blade.

"These are assassins," Haro said, taking in the green substance plastered onto the end of one of the darts. "We must—"

A bug with a long spear emerged from the path at a charge, the deadly spearhead directed at Aes's unprotected rear. Xander pounced to the forest floor and cut cleanly through the weapon, then stabbed the bug in the chest.

"Duck!" Haro bellowed.

Xander instinctively dropped to the ground, leaving the dart launched at her neck to sail harmlessly over her head.

"It's you they want," Haro hissed, and he leapt at the owner of the dart hidden within the trees, driving his sword into the bug's eye. The creature fell limp to the ground, causing Haro to tumble.

Five more bugs emerged from the woods. Two on each of the exits, and one beside Haro. The one next to Haro tried to stomp on him like a rat, but he skipped to the side and jabbed his sword into its foot. The bug howled in pain. Using the distraction, Haro jumped up and stabbed the bug in its stomach, causing it to keel over, at which point he slashed its throat.

The other four bugs remained steadfast, their spears lowered, their eyes locked on Xander and Aes, both of whom now stood back-to-back. Xander carried her blade in one hand and the bug's broken spear in the other.

"What are they waiting for?" Haro said worriedly as he entered back into the space and climbed onto Aes.

They tensed as a chorus of howls sounded from somewhere above the canopy.

"We need to get out of here," she said sternly, gaze unwavering from the threat in front of her. "Aes," she said into his mind. "We must get to the camp before those bugs arrive. The stream is the only way. When I say so, charge at the two blocking the way."

He snorted angrily.

"Ready yourself, Haro," she said aloud. "Now!"

She turned around and threw the broken spear into one of the bugs blocking the route to the stream, and Aes charged at the other. The stag deflected the bug's spear with his antlers and rammed the insectoid into a tree with a sickening crunch.

The other two bugs hadn't wasted any time, however, and were quick to give chase as Xander ran and threw herself onto Aes just as he was gaining speed. She awkwardly sat up as he began down the stream back towards the camp.

"Oh boy," Haro muttered as he peered back.

Xander, too, glanced back. She tensed. Dozens of bugs pursued them, far more than they could handle alone. Fortunately the trio had a sizeable lead, and within moments they could see the camp unobstructed directly ahead.

Even from that distance, Xander could see the guards panic at the sight of the incoming bugs, but they were well trained and quickly unslung their bows and readied their line. Thirty metres from the pod, the first round of arrows was let loose with impressive accuracy. All found their mark, and there were multiple screams as a number of the bugs crashed into the trees and onto the ground.

Another round was suddenly let loose from a handful of archers hidden within the trees, again with frightening accuracy. It was enough. The remaining bugs faltered and immediately dispersed into the woods.

Barely into the pod, Haro jumped from Aes, then stormed over to Nudus and grabbed him by the arm.

"Another game, little man?" he snarled.

"Haro!" Leila scolded. "What's gotten into you?"

Nudus stuttered, "I'm sure—"

"It was a trap," Haro interrupted angrily. "The rat tricked us. The bugs were waiting for us."

Gladis turned to Nudus with an inquisitive expression.

His posture visibly shrunk under her onslaught but then hardened. "This is ridiculous! How dare—"

"Get the girl!" the guard with the ponytail called as Xander climbed down from Aes.

Two of the guards scurried over and grabbed Xander's arms, whilst the rest looked on with indignation.

"What's the meaning of this?" Gladis shouted angrily. "Let her go!"

"She could've gotten us all killed," the guard with the ponytail said coolly. "She can explain herself to the princess."

Aes approached Xander and the two guards, his height and bulk threatening.

"It's okay," Xander said calmly. "I'll explain myself."

Haro shoved Nudus to the floor. "You'll be explaining yourself also!"

▲ ▲ ▲

"It was thoughtless, Aika," Ratin said sternly.

Aika glanced at Xander and then back to her cousin. The three of them were in Aika's tent, along with Haro, Leila, and Nudus. The latter three sat on the bed like children about to be scolded. Gladis had chosen to remain behind, eager to consult her brother in the wake of the accusation against Nudus. The evening was cool, and a single candle lit the space.

"We're lucky nobody else was hurt," he continued.

Aika looked back to Xander, concern etched into her brow. "You should've waited."

"I know," she responded. "But I had to try."

"None of this makes sense," Haro interjected. "The rat here said it was the humans that captured Ricard. We show up, and there's a swarm of bugs waiting for the girl."

"Last time I checked, they're in an alliance," Nudus said bluntly.

"You know for certain they wanted Xander?" Ratin asked Haro.

"Absolutely!"

"Damain looking for vengeance, no doubt." He walked up to Nudus, causing the critter to cower. "Why was Ricard at the patch?"

"Why—why?" Nudus stammered. "How should I know? The oaf's a drunk. Always looking for his next high."

Haro squared up to the critter. "And how did the bugs know Xander would come looking?"

"The two of them are inseparable. Hardly requires a genius to figure that out."

"So you think they were waiting for an opportunity?" Ratin asked. "Kidnap Ricard when he's alone and force the girl out?"

"Your guess is as good as mine."

Worry took Ratin, and he turned to Aika. "If he speaks the truth, it means they've been watching undetected for some time."

"I'm sure they've known we're here for a while," Aika said, absent the same apprehension.

"Still, I think we should move the camp. If they're familiar with the area and our routines, it'll only be a matter of time before they try something else."

Aika nodded. "Give the order, then. We move at first light."

"Wait," Xander said agitatedly. "What about Ricard? If we—"

The tent door opened, and one of Aika's men entered. "We've found the trail. Human tracks. Seven soldiers, maybe eight. Five mounts. And one prisoner being dragged."

"I thought you said five soldiers?" Haro said suspiciously to Nudus.

"I wasn't exactly counting!" the critter spat angrily.

"Distance?" Ratin asked the messenger.

"They're moving slowly in the direction of the Great Tree. Besides the mounts, the rest are on foot. If we leave now, we can catch them and get back before sunrise."

Hope coursed through Xander. "Please, Aika."

The princess thought for a moment and then nodded. "Get fifteen of our best hunters, Ratin. We'll use the stolen horses."

"Have you lost your mind?" he responded. "Fifteen's not enough with the vines and the alliance out there. And what about the camp?"

"We haven't got enough mounts for more than that, and the longer we're out there, the higher the risk. You take charge of moving the camp."

Ratin put his hand gently to her arm. "Aika, you're being reckless. What if they capture you or, worse, kill you?"

"You've so little faith in me, cousin."

"I'm just not sure the risk to save the man is worth *your* life."

"Ricard's our ally, and he's brilliant on the battlefield. We'll need him." She peered at Nudus and then back to her cousin. "Lock this one up until we can—"

"What right do you have?" Nudus seethed. "You're going to arrest me on what charge? A suspicion? Your father had more sense—"

"My father's dead. He also despised you. The only man that knows the truth is Ricard. He can clear this up when we bring him back."

Nudus's face hardened, but he didn't protest further.

"Get your weapons," Aika said to Xander and Haro. "We leave in thirty minutes."

CHAPTER 51

The forest was eerily quiet that evening, and the undergrowth was damp from an earlier downpour. The moon traversed the sky behind the blanket of ominous clouds, and the subdued hum of the trees away from the camp spoke only of hurt. Fear of the vines had pervaded through every settlement of locals and invaders alike, and on so bleak a night, not a soul dared a stroll in the open or a conversation louder than a whisper. None except for Xander and her party of hunters.

The unwillingness of the critters and humans and bugs to venture out had allowed Xander and the others to travel unimpeded for close to three hours. Still, they were on edge and wary of even the slightest of rustles.

They followed Aika's tracker. A man who, with the slightest sniff or look at a broken twig or ruffled bush, could pinpoint the direction Ricard's captors had taken and the time since they had passed. It was a fascinating skill they were again witnessing in action.

Xander buttoned the collar on her jacket to protect from the chill. To her surprise, this particular fork in the road had stumped the tracker for longer than usual. Aika stood beside him, assisting however she could. The man was especially keen on a set of footprints to the right, which Xander was craning to see. That is, until a light snore drew her attention. She glanced down at Haro, who had fallen asleep on her lap, wrapped in a tiny blanket.

"How in Anemoi can he sleep at a time like this?" she thought to herself, and looked back up just as the tracker pointed down the path to the right.

Aika nodded and motioned for the rest of them to follow. As they were about to proceed, a loud rustle sounded from nearby, causing them to tense.

"What do you think? Vine or bug?" Haro whispered dazedly with one eye open.

Xander didn't respond and instead put her finger to her lips. He shrugged and shuffled around in search of greater comfort. After several minutes, Aika turned to them and, with a nod of her head, beckoned them on.

The group pushed into a wary trot, scanning the obscure horizon as they did. Even at that pace, Aes's powerful muscles rippled under the grip of Xander's legs. With every stride the pair expertly navigated the winding, dangerously uneven path, their movements synchronised and thoughts seemingly as one.

Gliding through the undergrowth like a family of shadowy ghouls, the tracker ground to another halt twenty minutes along.

"What's it this time?" Haro said impatiently, stirring from his sleep.

One of the soldiers gave him a side-eye, visible even through the dim light.

"They've veered off," the tracker said quietly, and he pointed into the bushes, away from the trail.

"How long ago?" Aika asked.

He sniffed the air and shrugged. "Ten minutes, perhaps."

"I recognise this area," one of the soldiers whispered. "The humans and bugs set up a small camp around here a couple of weeks back. A resting station for their messengers. It'll have mounts."

"Security?"

"Watchtowers and a handful of men. Ratin had just given the order to move the camp farther south, so we didn't sack it. The vegetation is thick. Should be easy for us to get close and take out their sentries."

"Thanks." She motioned to her soldiers to demount. "Stay with the horses," she said to one of them.

"Aes will keep an eye," Xander interrupted.

Aika nodded, and they entered the trees, leaving Aes to mind the mounts.

They moved in two groups, with Aika, Xander, Haro, and five others to the right and the tracker and the remainder moving parallel some thirty metres to the left. Carefully they climbed through the bushes, determined not to give up their approach.

With the camp in sight, the two groups split off completely. Aika's group moved up along the right flank and the other group along the left. The settlement was larger than they had anticipated, and there were a dozen human and bug sentries spread across four watchtowers. The interior was obscured, however. The two groups met on the other side of the camp.

Aika looked to the tracker. "Sneak into the camp and make note of what you see."

He nodded and then, without a word, disappeared silently into the bushes. It was an anxious wait, with all of them wary of being caught unaware by a vine or a sentry. Five minutes slowly transitioned into ten, then fifteen. But just as Xander found herself fretting for the man's well-being, he returned as quietly as he had left.

"There's a small building in the centre," he said quietly. "Ricard's scent carries into it. There are two large stables on both ends of the camp and a couple of tents with no one inside. Other than the sentries in the towers, there are no soldiers in the open."

Aika put her finger to the man's cheek and then looked at her fingertip.

"Blood," Haro said of the barely visible smudge.

Aika raised an eyebrow. "You wet your knife?"

"Like I said, there's no one in the tents."

"Xander," Aika said. "How different is your accent to these soldiers?"

"Pretty different," she responded, perplexed by the question.

"But you can imitate it if you need to?"

"I guess—what's this about?"

"Okay. Four groups, one on each tower. Once neutralised, we check the stables. If the alarm isn't raised before we clear those out, we position ourselves around the building. Xander, I want you to call out as if you're in trouble once we're ready. Should be easy for us to pick them off when they run out."

"I'll try my best."

They split into the four squads and dispersed to within shooting range of the four towers, though still far enough to remain concealed within the shrubs. Bugs and humans in sight, each group took out its target. With the watchtowers neutralised, they did a sweep of the stables. But for a single soldier in one, there was no resistance.

Quietly and speedily, they surrounded the hastily constructed building in the centre. It wasn't too different in style to the two-story inns in Nhata, barring the very tiny windows that exuded a faint orange glow. With the archers in position, Xander got close. She peered to Aika awkwardly, a tad embarrassed by the request. Aika simply lifted her thumb, the signal to proceed.

Xander cleared her throat, as if preparing to orate, and then bellowed in as deep a voice as she could muster, "The bastards are attacking! The damn bastards are attacking! Get out 'ere now!" She banged on the door for good measure and then repeated the warning as she ran into the shadows.

Silence. Xander looked at Aika, and they both shrugged.

"Look," Haro whispered. There was movement in one of the windows. "Maybe try—"

A dart pierced into the back of one of Aika's men, knocking him to the ground, just as the forest behind them came alive with the flap of bug wings. Aika and the soldiers on that side of the inn instantly swivelled on their heels whilst in a crouch and began to release arrow after arrow into the dark. Each projectile unleashed an anguished scream as it found its mark. Moments later, the archers on the other side of the building skidded towards them and joined in with deadly efficiency.

"Can't see a thing!" Haro said nervously as he climbed onto Xander's shoulder to garner a better view of the shadows.

The pair tensed as the inn door creaked behind them, and they jerkily turned around to see a handful of Zylencian soldiers pouring from the building. Xander dashed towards a man about to stab one of Aika's men in the back, and she blocked his sword with her blade. In a counter too fast for the attacker, she then jabbed it into his chest, instantly killing him.

The other soldiers stopped in their tracks and turned to her, suddenly forgetful of the squad of archers keeping their bug allies at bay. The men's expressions were wrought with anger. Determined to teach the girl a lesson, they charged at her. The pair didn't hesitate, however, and Haro swiftly launched from Xander's shoulder into the nearest, cutting through the man's throat before he could be swatted away.

Xander parried the sword aimed at her head, ducked, and then rammed her blade into the owner's thigh, forcing him to keel over. About to finish him, as Dogner had taught her, she rolled to the side as another soldier swiped at her neck. She was vulnerable as she scrambled to stand; it was Aika's arrow that dispatched the man as he came in with an overhead swing.

"Get Ricard!" Aika yelled as she and the tracker killed the remaining Zylencian soldiers with their arrows.

Xander turned to the inn in time to see Haro withdrawing his sword from a man's neck.

"Ready?" he said nonchalantly, and ran and jumped into her hand.

She placed him on her shoulder and rushed towards the door. The interior was cooler than outside, and it smelled of dank and mud. They cautiously entered a room with a long wooden table carpeted in bowls filled with steaming slop.

"Nothing here," Haro remarked, and they entered the two other rooms on the bottom floor. "Empty. He must be upstairs."

The flimsy stairs creaked awfully loudly as they sped up, but there was little need for subtlety, given the ruckus outside. The upper floor was a single room lined with bunks on both sides. But for a single torch at the entrance, the light was scarce.

"Ricard," Xander called, ready for any soldiers lurking out of sight.

"About time you caught up," Ricard's voice came from the other end. "Don't worry. None of those bastards left in here."

Xander grabbed the torch, and she and Haro walked over, their guard up.

"You've looked better," Haro said as Ricard came into view.

He was sitting on the floor; his hands were bound behind his back, and his face was bruised. "Well, you just going to stand there and stare, or you going to untie me?"

Haro jumped down and cut the ropes.

"Any idea where they stored your kit?" Xander asked as Ricard stood up and stretched his back with a grunt.

He stumbled over to a nearby bunk and pulled his axe from under the mattress. "The only kit that matters." He peered outside through a small slit of a window. "The man probably should've used it. Might've done him some good."

Haro climbed back onto Xander's shoulder, and the pair, too, peeked outside. Aika and her soldiers were no longer firing into the void. Three lay dead, but the others were uninjured, though they still watched the shadows with keen eyes. Aika called an order to four of them, and they ran out of sight towards the two stables, whilst two others marked their dead with motions of their hands.

"Was drunk off the mushrooms when the vermin got me," Ricard continued as he hastily made for the stairs. "They wouldn't have stood a chance if I was half awake."

"A rare occurrence indeed," Haro whispered into Xander's ear as they bounded after him.

"Glad to see you still live," Aika said to Ricard as they stepped outside.

"And you, Princess," he responded gratefully.

Moments later the four men returned, guiding a stream of mounts.

"Let's get out of here," Aika said. "There were plenty of Damain's minions alive when they retreated."

As if spurred by her words, the grating buzz of the insectoids' wings sounded from not far off. The group mounted and disappeared into the forest, emerging minutes later on the path where they had left Aes and the horses. Xander swiftly transferred onto the stag, with Haro still clinging to her. Quickly pushing into a trot, the tracker took the lead, Aika the centre and Ricard the position just in front of Xander, Haro and Aes, who were at the rear.

A minute along, Ricard turned around. "You're looking pretty cosy up there," he jested to Haro.

Haro pointed forward. Ricard turned around to see one of Aika's men motioning for the big man to be quiet.

Ricard was about to tell the soldier to push off, but he abruptly lunged forward, to the man's confusion, and swung his axe into a bug charging from the trees. His axe passed cleanly through the creature, splattering thick blood over those in the front. Not a heartbeat later, the entire forest came alive, and a swarm of insectoids converged on the column from all sides. Fending off the creatures with bows, swords, knives, and fists, the front of the column pounced into an unordered gallop in the hope of shaking off the threat.

In the mad scramble to reform the line, Xander, Aes, and Haro were left trailing some metres behind the rest. Three times in less than a minute, they were accosted by swathes of bugs from above or from the shroud of the woods, all of them attempting to kill Aes or grab Xander. But Haro was fast, and Xander faster still, and each time the pair fended off the attacks with blindingly vicious parries and jabs and swipes, killing scores of the vermin in the short period of time.

To their unspoken worry, however, the three of them could feel the pursuers growing more desperate and erratic. The bugs no longer sought to simply kill or capture. Their collective intention was to inflict a painful death.

"I can't see the others," Xander managed as they sped forward.

Haro looked up at her. "Good thing it's Aes we're riding, then, isn't—"

Xander leant to her side and cut into a bug coming at them from the flank, dismembering it.

Provided a clear view of the rear, Haro's eyes widened with panic. "Spears!"

Xander threw herself forward and to the side, with her sword hand wound in Aes's fur, and her right foot gripped to the ridge of his muscular back. She just glimpsed the two spears as they flew overhead and hit a bug coming at them from the front.

She righted herself and got ready to take out the bug that had thrown them, but to her surprise, it flew off.

"Weird," Haro muttered.

A faint call reached them from somewhere ahead.

Haro cupped his ear, straining to hear. "What did they say?"

"I don't—"

This time it was a scream that reached them, though whether it was a bug or one of Aika's men, they couldn't tell.

"Vine!" Haro suddenly roared. "Vine on the path!"

Aes abruptly veered into the foliage. Expertly weaving through the bushes and trees, he tried his best to keep pace, but the multiple choruses of screams coming from the trail and bushes ahead soon had him second-guessing.

"The vines are everywhere." Haro spoke nervously. "Take us deeper into the bush, Aes."

Xander didn't say anything as the stag adhered and drove deeper into the woods until nothing but the whimpers of the trees and the thud of his hooves against the mud filled the void. Alone but undiscovered, they continued like that for thirty minutes before finding the path as it meandered in front of them.

"Is this the same one?" Xander whispered, unable to distinguish it from any of the others they had come across that night.

"It looks like it." Haro spoke cautiously.

"What?"

She followed Haro's gaze to a thicket at the base of a young oak on the other side of the path.

"Hi there," Haro called, and a little mouse poked its head out.

The mouse glanced both ways down the path and then looked up at them. "You lost?"

"We're looking for our friends. A dozen men and women of the Lizard People on horseback. They were being chased by a bug squad."

The mouse pointed down the path in the direction that led back to the camp. "You missed them by about ten minutes. They were having a rough time, by the looks of it. There were two other lots of the bugs after your friends passed. They were looking for someone. You, I presume. Best keep off the path if I was you."

"Thanks, friend."

"You're most welcome. Stay safe. And keep an eye out for those vines. Place is crawling with them. Hard to sleep with the buggers all over." At that, the mouse withdrew into its thicket.

"We should hurry," Xander said. "There's still a chance for us to help them."

"No. It'll be too dangerous. We need to stick to the undergrowth. We'll have a better chance of surviving the night."

"But—"

"The bugs want you. I think that's pretty clear now. Let's not give them what they want. Sound reasonable?"

She nodded acceptance, though she felt guilty leaving the others to fend for themselves.

The trio quickly left the path and continued parallel to it at a distance. The route was cumbersome, with thick vegetation, downed logs, and broken ground all barriers to easy flight. And though the undergrowth remained quiet and lifelessly still, the hum of the trees seemed to brighten about an hour into their trek. Reluctant to stop and rest, despite the assurances of safety from the trees, they sped onwards in silence. It took them nearly four hours to breach the outer perimeter of the camp, just as the haze of the weak morning light meshed with the persistent nocturnal shroud.

Ratin's men were everywhere, determined to deter any attack targeting the civilians tearing down the camp. Two hundred were perched in the canopy along that section of the camp alone. It was a level of security that provided the knackered trio some much-needed respite as they made their way to the pods.

Even before the trio reached the first pod, they could hear Ricard's angry shouts disturbing the sombre quiet. Closer approach revealed five men gripping him by the arms as he struggled for his horse. A number of villagers had stopped packing and instead watched the commotion, amazed by the man's strength.

"You lied to me, woman!" he roared at Aika. "You told me they were safe! That they'd be back by now!"

"I wasn't lying," she responded calmly, though her demeanour betrayed her worry. "The bird—"

"You mean that bird we bumped into two hours ago? Have you gone mad? Anything could've happened since then."

"The route they're taking—what?"

Aika followed Ricard's stunned gaze to see Xander and the others stood at the pod entrance. There was a moment's disbelief before she sprinted over and hugged them. Ricard pulled free of the guards and followed suit.

"You're alive, kiddo!" He laughed emotionally. "And you, you damn rascal!" he said to Haro. "I was fully ready for your wife to kill me once I told her."

Aika pulled away from the embrace and looked Xander in the eyes. "I'm so sorry. We tried to wait when we realised that we'd lost you, but they kept coming at us. Again and again. We couldn't—"

"It's fine, Aika," Xander said. "We're safe and you're both safe." She glanced guiltily to the men that had accompanied them on the mission. Only seven remained, including the tracker, and all were slumped on the ground in an exhausted heap. "So few made it back."

Aika straightened. "Not your responsibility to worry about. I gave the order."

Ricard cleared his throat. "It's not yours either, Princess. Nor mine."

"I don't understand."

"It's the rat's." Haro spoke up.

"Nudus?" Aika queried. "You're sure?"

"You think I just happened to stumble upon that mushroom patch in the middle of the bush without a bit of direction?" Ricard said, eyebrow raised.

"You do have a keen nose for the stuff," Haro remarked with a grin.

"Not this time."

▲ ▲ ▲

"You can't prove it," Nudus said to Ricard, straight-faced and sitting on the edge of Aika's bed.

Aika was also in the hut, as were Ratin, Haro, Leila, and Xander.

"You invited me to that damn patch, Nudus!" Ricard raised his voice. "You handed me the mushroom that nearly knocked me out."

"You saw me pull it from the ground, you idiot!"

"You gave me the most potent of the bunch, I bet."

"You're a drunkard, Ricard. And a fool. You know as well as any that when you're trying a new variety, you don't gobble the whole damn mushroom in one go."

Ricard's cheeks reddened, but he wasn't done. "And the humans and bugs just happened to be waiting there to pick me up the moment I lost feeling?"

"It is quite the coincidence," Haro added.

Irritation took Nudus at the interjection, but he held his tongue.

"Or the fact that they had laid a trap at that alliance camp?" Aika spoke.

"Princess, nobody else is foolish enough to risk the forest at night," Nudus said. "And the bugs have eyes everywhere. It's more likely that they knew you followed and, in that moment, decided to ambush you. A tactic you're all too familiar with."

Ricard snickered scornfully. "The man has an answer for everything."

"Not so hard when you're telling the truth."

"What about that 'kick' you spoke of? The soldier barely touched you. Just enough to draw blood. I remember that much."

Nudus shook his head in disbelief. "Again, where's the proof?"

"Here," a voice came from the entrance.

They turned to see Gladis standing there with Oscine.

"Oscine!" Xander beamed. The little songbird flew up, and she hugged him. "How I missed you!"

Nudus shifted awkwardly. "Oscine. Certainly is good to—"

The songbird pulled from Xander's embrace and, hovering in midair, dove into a series of whistles and chirps that had them all, except Xander, wide-eyed by the culmination.

"Then it's true," Aika said.

"You're going to listen to a damn bird?" Nudus growled, standing up.

Haro put his sword to Nudus's neck, and the critter sat back down, his expression no longer sure. Xander looked at Ricard, inviting explanation.

"Right! Sorry, kiddo," Ricard said. "Forgot you're not conversant in bird tongue. The day Oscine left, he saw Nudus conversing with three bugs a short distance from the camp. He didn't think too much of it, given Nudus's usual shady practises."

Nudus grumbled. "I object to that—"

"Oh! Shut up!" Gladis snapped at him.

Ricard continued, "Anyway, on his way back to camp this morning, he and his squad ran into a lone scout. The scout was the same bird that spoke to Aika and told us of your location several hours back. The bird was scouring the woods behind us on Aika's instruction when he bumped into Oscine. Long story short, turns out the scout had seen Nudus talking to three bugs of a similar description yesterday morning, a topic that arose when, together, he and Oscine spotted one of the bugs trailing us this fine morning."

Nudus scoffed. "That's your proof? Two birds seeing a resemblance in a bug? All the pests look the same. You can't rely on that. Especially not if they spotted it from way up there."

"They've got keener eyes than us."

"Doesn't matter. If that's your proof, you've got nothing on me."

"And why were you talking to the bugs?" Gladis asked.

"Does it matter?"

"We're at war," Aika said coldly. "It doesn't look good."

"Does war prevent old acquaintances from rekindling?"

Aika stared at him, her expression unwavering, her posture firm and intimidating. She whistled, and a second later, the tracker popped his head through the tent door. She turned back to Nudus, whose face had paled.

"I can't prove for certain that you orchestrated the attack on them, but your relationship to the bugs makes me uncomfortable. Please confine Nudus until this war is over or until I say otherwise," she instructed the tracker.

The man nodded and, without a word, walked over to Nudus and grabbed him in his hand.

"Put me down, you sack of filth," Nudus spat, and tried to bite the man's calloused finger.

"Put you down? Really?" The tracker unsheathed his knife with a grin. "If you say so."

"I don't mean that, you idiot!"

"Careful now. I've got the knife."

Nudus tried to pull free of the man's grasp but had no luck.

"You going to behave?" the tracker asked as if talking to a child. Nudus's shoulders slumped in defeat, and he simply nodded. "Good boy," the tracker said, and walked out with the little critter.

"You know…" Haro spoke. "It probably was him that set it up. The critter will do anything for a penny."

Aika walked over to the table. It was littered with Xander's sketches of the Great Tree's interior. She opened the drawer and grabbed a fruit, then offered a second to the others. Only Leila raised her hand.

"Probably, but we can't prove it," Aika said as she lifted Leila onto the table and cut a sliver of the fruit small enough for the tiny woman to hold. "At least this way he can't cause more mischief." A loud thud came from outside. "The camp will be fully dismantled within the hour. You all should get your stuff."

"What destination have you got in mind?" Ricard asked.

"South to the mountains."

"That far?" Xander blurted.

"I'll still take you to the Great Tree when the time comes, but for now—" Aika began sympathetically.

"I can't, Aika. Every second I'm away from my aunt and friends is a second something bad could happen. I can't come with you."

"It's too dangerous to be up here on your own. I told you, when you find something on that map that we can use, I'll take you," Aika said, pointing to the sketches on the table.

"Are these drawings of the Great Tree?" Leila spoke with a mouth full of fruit. "They're beautiful and really well drawn."

"How would you know, woman?" Haro piped up. "You've never been."

"And does that mean I can't comment?" she responded defiantly. She lifted one that caught her eye, but a light gust tore through the tent and blew it from her hands.

Slowly it drifted across the tent until it landed on the floor at Gladis's feet.

"You drew this, Xander?" Gladis said as she tilted her head. She began to trace the outline with her steps.

"Yes. It's the way to the lower level."

"But both Ratin and I have been there," Aika added. "There's no way down."

"Fancy that," Gladis mumbled, her gaze still locked on the drawing. She stopped tracing the outline and looked up at them. "Pass me your gauntlet, Xander." Xander obliged and placed it beside the little woman. "Now can you place me on the bed?"

Xander lifted her to the bed. Gladis looked down to the drawing and gauntlet. A warm smile took her cheeks.

"The puzzle piece. Look, the outline of the broadleaf emblem fits the area exactly. Every little divot. Every surface." She peered up at them excitedly. "I think the leaf I gave you is a key. I think it'll take you to that lower level."

"How can you be certain?" Haro asked.

"What? Is the coincidence not enough for you? Is the leaf still in the tent, Xander?"

"It is," she responded.

"And at any point when you were reading that map, did you have the leaf in your hand?"

"Never."

"Well then, do you want to try?"

Xander rushed out of the tent and nearly knocked over Ratin as he sought to enter it. She sprinted through the disassembled pods with renewed vigour and then stumbled clumsily into their tent. She rummaged through the bag and pulled out the map, then grabbed the leaf from the pot.

With the leaf in hand, she unfurled the map. Excitedly she flew through the dimensions of the special parchment until she found the area within the tree that she was looking for. Her eyes brightened. For the first time, the lines and shades of the visualisation were multicoloured and the detail precise enough that she could've sworn she actually stood there. Every blade of grass and every marking on the tree's interior wall were all visible.

She honed in on an indentation that stood out amidst the myriad of markings. The marking's shape was a perfect fit to that of her family's emblem, and it glowed a light gold, like a gold shilling strewn amongst a trove of silver. Just in front of the marking, hovering in the air, she could make out a green broadleaf. The same that adorned her gauntlet. The same that she held in her hand. Then, quite suddenly, the visualised broadleaf interlocked with the indentation.

Disbelief took her. "The leaf *is* a key."

CHAPTER 52

Xander looked around the large command tent that had yet to be pulled down, even if nearly every other structure in the camp had been dismantled. It was bare except for a dozen squat chairs positioned at the far end. Sitting on the chairs were the elders, and immediately in front of them was Ratin, standing with his captains. A dozen hardy men and women that had clearly seen combat. Xander stood near the entrance with Ricard and Haro, watching as the groups talked nervously amongst themselves.

"Where is she?" Ricard asked.

"She said she needed more information," Xander said anxiously, aware that the men and women in the tent felt vulnerable, knowing the bugs watched a camp on edge, a people wary of the slightest provocation. Those gathered were growing increasingly eager to begin the move south.

"This will work against us," Haro murmured. "Too much time to discuss their insecurities won't bode well."

"What insecurities?" a voice came from the door.

They turned around.

"Aika," Xander said excitedly. "Did you get what you need?"

"I did." She walked to the front of the tent, and the onlookers fell silent. "I can feel your worry. We'll begin the move south as soon as this meeting's done." There was relief. "But I'll need at least a hundred of our elite soldiers—"

Confused chatter did the rounds, and one of the elders stood. A lanky woman with a crooked nose.

"You'd deprive us of our best? Why?"

"Something has come to my attention," Aika began. "Something that could help us win this war. A war that will spread across the whole of Anemoi."

"The rest of Anemoi is not our concern." The elder spoke bluntly.

"Nevertheless, this weapon will protect us all. As you know, I very recently had the opportunity to meet our enchantress—" Barring Ricard and Xander, everyone in the tent marked themselves superstitiously. "The circumstances under which we met were painful and not how I would've imagined it, but she gave me hope. She told me that the future of our people and the Great Forest is intertwined with my companionship to the bearer of the Rose, Xander. It's why you accepted my terms upon gifting me my father's mantle."

"We have not forgotten."

"Well, Xander has located a fragment of this weapon. With our soldiers, I will help her to retrieve it."

"And where is this fragment?" another elder said curiously.

"In the Great Tree."

Surprisingly, the elders didn't erupt into protest. Several looked at one another with unease, but they remained silent.

"And your plan?" the lanky woman asked.

"I just spoke to a group of our scouts that had eyes on the Great Tree not more than two days ago. It's heavily guarded at the base by humans, regular-sized bugs, and bugs temporarily shrunken by the Rite. But in the branches on the upper levels, the troop presence is light. If we use the Rite to shrink ourselves and then come in from the sky, concealed by the fog, we should be able to reach the gateway on the uppermost level before we're discovered."

"And then what?"

"I will enter with Xander, her friends, and my tracker. Ratin will return with the soldiers to ensure the security of our people."

At this the room did descend into chaos, and even Ratin, who hadn't been made privy to Aika's full plan, looked at her with disbelief.

"It's too dangerous to leave you alone in there," he said, drawing the attention of the room.

"Get me in, and I'll take Xander to the lower level. Our sources say the bugs won't enter into the tree beyond the upper level. They're scared. We won't need the soldiers, and because it'll take us nearly half a day just to get to that level, it's too risky for you to wait. Keep a scout in the air. Once we've got the fragment, we'll signal from the upper level."

"I don't like—"

"I think your proposal has merit, though the risk to you is troubling," the lanky woman interjected. "But if what you say is true regarding the weapon, I will not protest. Provided you do not occupy those soldiers or Ratin for longer than what's necessary."

"Agreed." Several others spoke up.

"This is madness," Ratin responded angrily. "We can't leave the princess to enter the tree alone."

"And we can't leave our people deprived of you and a hundred of our strongest for so long," the lanky woman retorted. "It's risky enough with both of you journeying up there."

"Then I'll stay with the camp, and we can let her keep the soldiers."

"No." Aika spoke before any other could. "She's right. Even on the best routes, it'll be a three-day round trip, and our people are better served right now if the soldiers return. And if the situation turns ugly up there, the soldiers will need your leadership. It has to be you to take us there and you to bring them back."

Ratin gritted his teeth, his frustration clear. "Then just take more soldiers into the tree with you and stop being so stubborn."

"I'll take another," Aika said. "That'll make six of us. Trust me, cousin, I know that tree inside and out. The fewer of us there are, the faster we'll be."

His apprehension was evident, but he nodded his head stiffly in acceptance.

"Then it's final," the lanky woman said. "When will you leave, Princess Aika?"

"We'll try for this evening. I'll not leave until our people are on the road."

▲ ▲ ▲

"Let's hope this map of yours doesn't play tricks," Ricard said as he climbed into a sleeping sack concealed within the undergrowth.

Though the camp had picked up and moved south, Xander, Ricard, and Haro had remained in the vicinity with Aika, Ratin, and a hundred soldiers. They also had with them an army of birds and the rare flying mantises, the group's chosen mounts for that evening's adventure. On little sleep, and eager for rest, the trio had set up makeshift beds whilst the comparatively fresh elite soldiers prepared and guarded the temporary encampment.

Ricard yawned. "Would hate to get all the way to that lump of a tree and find we've wasted a journey."

"Especially as it'll be Oscine doing the wing work for you," Haro jibed.

"It doesn't play tricks," Xander said confidently as she pulled a tattered blanket over herself.

"Call it a hunch?" Ricard said, looking at her with a grin. His eyes were bloodshot and carried dark circles.

"Call it a hunch."

"Then let's hope this hunch of yours also doesn't play tricks. By the way—" He stifled another yawn. "I am curious to know why your aunt, the evil one, decided to up and leave back to whatever sewer she came from."

"She has the bugs doing the dirty work." Haro spoke up.

"Which has me confused," he said, sitting up. "Why did those Guardians attack the human soldiers at the river that day? If they're allies—"

Haro interrupted with an exaggerated sigh of exasperation. "The Guardians can confront an imminent threat, with or without Damain's influence. They could've been in cahoots from the beginning, and we'd be none the wiser. Any more of your silly questions?"

"Why the alliance?"

"I'm going to sleep. Wake me when it's time. And if my wife shows, having ignored my request for her to stay put with the camp, please send her on her way without bothering me." At that, Haro put a blanket over his face and fell asleep.

"Well?" Ricard said to Xander. "What does your hunch reckon?"

On her back, she stared into the thick clouds. "She wants the shard. Damain offered his help. And now he guards the tree while she's away. In return, he gets the forest."

"You got all that from your hunch?"

She didn't respond. She was tired, and her everything screamed for rest. She closed her eyes and, seconds later, drifted into a slumber devoid of the usual dreams and nightmares that regularly sought to plague her sleep.

CHAPTER 53

Septembrix 9, 476; Borealis, Borlencia; four days before the fall of Borealis—
Xander gripped the horse's reins with her left hand and used her right to
wipe the dust from her eyes. She reopened them and peered to her right,
where her father and Ricard chatted away. She then glanced behind to three
of Carolus's elite guards positioned at the rear.

On horseback, the group was heading at a slow trot towards the East
Gate of Borealis, and though they were still a full kilometre outside the city's
perimeter, the massive city wall and its shadow were already an impressive
sight.

"Three, two, one…" Xander counted, and not a second later, the afternoon sun dipped behind the walled horizon, ushering in the frigid cool of
evening. "She's not going to be happy."

Carolus and Ricard stopped their conversation, knowing full well what
Xander spoke of.

"The girl's right," Ricard said to Carolus. "I'll tell you what—if you go
missing, I'll be sure to question Alya first."

Carolus grinned. "If I go missing, you'll not be far behind." He turned
to Xander. "We'll be back soon. How you holding up?"

She shrugged. "I'm good."

"I'm glad," he said, and returned to his conversation with Ricard.

In truth she was tired, and her thighs were sore from the ride. They had ventured out to the point where the sands of the Ignis Desert meshed with the rocky base of the Ouran Mountains to the east. Though there was no real purpose to the outing other than to explore some of the terrain and hope they would stumble upon the ever-elusive desert rose. It had been an exciting little adventure, albeit a slightly sombre one, given that Lawrence's sarcastic charm was sorely missed. And now the thought of her mother being a worried mess was certainly a concern; granted, it was Carolus and Ricard that would incur Alya's disapproval, not her.

Xander rubbed again at her eye as a grain of sand caught its corner. Trying not to let the tiny intruder scratch the delicate surface, she gently removed it. But as she regained her vision, movement at the base of the city's walls caught her attention.

"Look," she said, pointing ahead.

The two men stopped talking and stared to the dust cloud coming towards them at pace.

"Riders," Ricard remarked. "They coming to us?"

"Looks like it," Carolus said cautiously.

Without prompting, the three elite guards rode out several metres in front.

Carolus looked at Xander. "Get behind us."

"Why—"

"Just do it."

She could feel her father's angst. It was a persistent worry that had enveloped him in the preceding months. But it wasn't just him. The same apprehension had taken large swathes of the city. And not only Carolus's supporters, but even those who had little interest in who governed their lives. Petty crime had risen in blatant fashion. A handful of ministers and reputable merchants had been attacked in broad daylight by street thugs. And more recently, there had been reports of cloaked men prowling the city at night, watching the port and barracks, and in several instances, following politicians to their homes.

"They're ours," Ricard said as the sortie of riders neared.

"Careful," Carolus cautioned.

"Always." Ricard moved his horse beside the three elite guards and then bellowed, "What news have you?"

The sortie ground to a stop, and a lone soldier approached. He, too, was one of Carolus's elite guards.

"It's the lack of news, sir," the man answered sternly.

"Lack of news?" Ricard queried.

"The chief merchant reported two caravans from Nasdir as late."

"Late? I don't see how—"

"They're three days late. Carrying gems and spices."

Carolus kicked his horse forward, and Xander followed closely behind.

"Those are big caravans," Ricard remarked. "Not like them to be late."

"Dust storm, maybe?" Carolus spoke up.

"It's possible," the soldier replied. "The chief's worried something foul has happened. Some of the families are mirroring that sentiment. They're worried sick. The chief's asked that you swing by and have a chat. He says it's urgent."

Carolus looked weary but nodded his acceptance. "Ricard, when we get to the gates, will you see to it that Xander's home safe?"

"Make sure the little one's safe? Absolutely. And what about me when your wife guts me?"

Carolus chuckled lightly, though his features lost none of their burden. He looked at Xander. "You'll keep him safe, won't you?"

"Of course!"

"Good girl."

CHAPTER 54

Novembrix 12, 484; the Great Tree—For all of living memory, the Great Tree had been a towering beacon of enchantment amidst a sea of colourful lushness, a distinct advantage from which to watch over the domain as a shepherd watches over his flock; and though the malevolent blanket of grimness that had befallen the forest had thrown the Great Tree into partial obscurity, the giant still made little work of striking awe into Xander as she and the others traversed the sky's edge far above it. And it was an awe that would only compound, for closer approach revealed the giant's unfathomably thick trunk that was capable of housing the littlest of human hamlets and the sporadic torchlight of settlements dotted across its entire surface, the homes of thousands of tiny critters who had not succumbed to the deterioration of Bronte's Law.

Aika motioned downward from the lead point of the small sortie of riders and their mantises and birds, and the party dove silently towards the tree. Skilfully directing them through the uppermost branches to a platform at the base of a particularly thick branch, she let fly three deadly arrows into the guards concealed in the shadow of the tree's unlit gateway and then signalled the group to land.

With the wary soldiers on guard, Aika and Xander jumped from their mantises and started for the gateway. But as the others sought to dismount and follow, the danger hidden within the tree's dark foliage suddenly exposed itself, and a cascade of panic reverberated through the group. The riders were quick to release their arrows into the avalanche of bugs, but the effect was inconsequential against the vastly superior numbers, and hand-to-hand combat quickly ensued along the group's fringes.

The swarm of bugs converged on them from all sides and from above, bombarding them with spears and darts. On foot and separated from the group by a short distance, Aika and Xander braced as a wall of minions charged at them from the direction of the gateway. But just as they verged on being swallowed, Ricard, atop Oscine, leapt in front of them and killed two of the bugs with a single swing of his axe, causing those nearby to stumble.

Behind them the tracker, too, dismounted, though Haro and the other soldier assigned to enter with them were nowhere to be seen. Like fish swimming upstream, the four of them pushed towards the gateway through the frantic chaos of the two lines colliding around them. The deadly dance of Aika and the tracker was a complement to the brutish swings of Ricard's axe and the efficient attacks and parries of Xander's blade.

Pushing and pushing until all that stood between them and the gateway was a handful of bugs engaged with two of Ratin's men that had found themselves too far advanced. Ricard launched into the commotion and swiftly downed the bugs, freeing the soldiers to enter back into the fray.

"Get into the tree!" Ricard shouted at the others as he turned to face any attempt on their rear.

In the front, Xander headed for the entrance when two sickening thuds sounded from behind her, followed by pained grunts. She turned around just as the tracker slumped to the ground with a spear protruding from his chest. But her immediate horror rapidly transitioned into panic as she glimpsed the spear that had pierced Ricard's shoulder.

Instinctively she rushed towards him, but Aika gripped her arm and shoved her in the direction of the gateway.

Another spear flew at Ricard, but it missed him as he dropped to his knee. He turned to Aika. "Get her into the tree!" He then ripped the spear out of his shoulder and threw himself into a group of bugs coming at them.

"Get in the tree!" Aika shouted at Xander, her eyes livid with adrenaline. "We'll never get this close again."

"The others!" Xander said, unable to peel her gaze from the big man ferociously downing the minions by their twos and threes.

"Ratin will lead them away."

Xander gritted her teeth with indecision, torn by the mayhem that had engulfed the others. Reluctantly she turned and ran into the entrance, with Aika close behind.

The corridor before them was lit by torches, and the air was moist and surprisingly warm. But they were barely inside when a furious roar emanated from the platform.

"Ricard!" Xander squirmed, desperately wanting to backtrack, but she continued on, heavy under a blanket of guilt.

It took several minutes for the pair to travel the lengthy tunnel of the gateway, whose exit led them directly into the hollow interior of the tree.

Xander's guilt rapidly gave way to shock at the sheer breadth and height of the gigantic tree's interior. "It's enormous!"

"You have no idea."

"Does the tree still live?"

"Of course!"

"How's this possible?" Xander uttered in disbelief. "Was it your people that carved it out?"

"The tree's been this way since before my people arrived. I don't think anybody alive knows how the inner chamber came to be."

They jogged across the plane of yellow-and-green grasses to the edge of the airy expanse that traversed the central length of the tree and connected the very top of the inner chamber to the very bottom with an unimpeded line of sight. Xander's eyes followed the vast platform on which they stood as it circled around the open stretch in gradual descent of the tree's massive trunk.

She gawked. "It's like a spiral staircase, but with an empty drop instead of a central pole."

The tree's inner chamber was illuminated seemingly by the glow of the moon, as if the starry night sky penetrated its thick bark, and the sound of running water and the smells of blossoms and sweet fruits filled the air. Across the spiral platform that gradually descended the length of the tree, a colourful forest of miniature proportions dominated the landscape, and on their level, no more than a couple of metres from where they stood, a cluster of wooden houses snuggled into the initial boundary of the forest.

Again Xander peered down the breezy centre of the tree. "I can hardly make out the bottom."

"Come on. Let's get into the forest. We'll walk the edge of the spiral platform to the bottom."

As they began to jog towards the tree line of the miniature forest that made them feel normal in size, Xander pointed to a patch of worn grass at the edge of the platform. "What's that?"

"You know how I said we've not been able to access that lower level? Well, it wasn't for lack of effort. We've tried flying, jumping, climbing, even sacrifices back in the day. Whatever we try, none of it works."

"You jumped?"

"A few times. And that patch is usually where you land when you do it."

Speechless, Xander simply followed Aika into the forest, her mind a melting pot of emotions.

CHAPTER 55

Novembrix 13, 484; inside the Great Tree—"How are you holding up?" Aika asked.

Xander took another bite of the fruit Aika had scoured for them and then squinted up from the edge of the platform through the many levels of the spiral. The central point of the tree's ceiling was now a mere blur of a speck in the distance.

"I'll survive," she said solemnly, her nerves still wrought with worry. She opened her mouth to say something else, then let it close.

"What?"

"When we entered the tree near to midnight, the forest inside was lit by the white glow of the moon, and now, after so many hours walking, we see the first signs of sunrise. It's as if the sun, the stars, and the planets are contained within, or perhaps the skin of the tree lets nature's light in… though I think it's probably the first, given the shroud that's swallowed the forest outside. It's surreal."

"It is."

They walked from the edge of the spiral platform into the eerie depths of the forest towards the wall of the tree's chamber. Barely visible birds rummaged the top of the trees' growth, and thick ferns and nettles carpeted the dark-reddish ground from where the long, bare trunks stretched to the underneath of the sloped platform above.

"I feel like we're being watched," Xander said after several minutes.

Aika glanced around and then abruptly grabbed her neck. "Ouch!"

Xander simultaneously cursed as a pellet took her in the back of the head, and the bushes around burst to life with mischievous assailants no taller than younglings and all donned in green-and-orange garments made from the forest itself. And still more pellets found their marks, the girls unable to find cover from the little stingers projected from slingshots and crafty fingers.

"With me!" Aika shouted, and they hastily continued the course, quickly outrunning their pursuers with the advantage of their long legs and the sticks on their hinds.

"What in Anemoi was that about?" Xander puffed when they eventually stopped.

"Runaways and layabouts from the villages in the Great Tree. Always up to no good," Aika responded, gently touching a welt on her cheek.

"Will they keep after us?"

"Unlikely. I've never seen the rascals near the area we just entered. Where they attacked us, that's the farthest."

"They're spooked?"

Aika turned to Xander, her eyebrow raised mischievously. "Are you?"

Xander let slip a light chuckle and brushed past her into the small grassy grove that held back the forest on one side and bordered the chamber wall on the other. "This is it," she said in awe, recognising the area from the visual the map had shown her. She began to rummage through her sack for the leaf.

Aika approached the wall and brushed her hand over the marking of the broadleaf. "It's been so long since I've been here," she said solemnly. "And it hasn't changed."

Xander pulled out the leaf and walked up to the marking. "Here we go," she said, and fit it into the indentation.

They stepped back with their eyes locked on the wall.

"What now—"

The grassy floor opened beneath them, and they landed with a thud on the level below.

CHAPTER 56

Aika peered up from the flat of her back and frowned as the trapdoor slammed shut. "How far we dropped, and nothing but a bruised bottom." She winced.

"It's the grass. Feel how soft it is."

As Aika got up and brushed herself off, Xander blindly reached for her shoulder whilst gaping ahead at the small wooden door wedged into the centre of an angular masonry arch set against a walled backdrop of grey stone. The keystone, worn but intact, was none other than the broadleaf.

"Beautiful," Aika whispered.

"How odd it is to think we're still inside the tree."

Between the high stone walls on either side of the grassy stretch of court-yard and the tree's inner chamber wall to their backs, rays of sunlight from seemingly nowhere wove past the flutter of yellow-and-white butterflies and pierced the lush ground. Two behemoth trees covered in moss and ancient bark rose formidably from the stretch in front of them as if on guard.

Silently Xander started forward with Aika close behind, and together they climbed the stone steps to the wooden door. Nerves wobbly and heart erratic with anticipation, she opened the door, and they entered a much larger courtyard, and though it was not too dissimilar in layout from some of the more ancient ones that dotted the palace in Borealis, it was almost ghost-like in its absence of bustle and purpose. A clear stream traversed the middle of the courtyard, appearing from one lofty, moss-covered stone wall, only to disappear into the next, and a small, intricately decorated bridge showed to be the only throughway to the five doors on the other side.

"It's surprisingly well kept for a place that probably hasn't been touched in quite a few centuries," Aika observed quietly.

"That you know of. Come on, we should—"

"Don't even suggest it."

"What?"

"We're not splitting up."

"What made you think I was going to suggest that?"

"Gut feeling."

"Perhaps you're wrong."

"Am I?"

Xander chortled as she took out the map. "You are. I'll just use the map to find out which door." She unfurled the parchment and looked at it. She gasped. "It's mapped out this entire structure. Everything. Rooms, floors, corridors…it's massive!"

"Whoever hid the shard must've explored it all. And what of the doors?"

"It shows the farthest on the left."

They walked to the one on the left. Xander reached for the knob and opened it, and they both gawked at what they saw.

"It—it leads back into this courtyard," Aika stammered. "Check the map again."

"It's showing the one farthest on the right now." Xander approached the door and reached for the knob but had barely brushed the worn metal with her fingertip when the map's markings shuffled. "It switched!" she said, and she jumped to the middle door as per the map's new layout. Again it changed at her touch. She slowly reached for the second door from the left, but again the door on the map switched at her approach and now showed the second door from the right to be the way ahead. "This is getting ridiculous. None of the doors want to let me in."

"Try one that's not highlighted by the map."

Xander did that, and again the door opened back into the courtyard. She huffed with frustration.

"What about the stream?" Aika queried.

"What about it?"

"What does the map show?"

Xander peered at the map and frowned. "It cuts off. I'm guessing the last bearer didn't jump in."

"Ah," she said disappointedly. "Then maybe there's another marking. Something we missed."

"But perhaps we should try."

Aika shot her a confused glance. "Try what?"

Xander shrugged, her desire to bathe after the roughness of the forest now bordering on desperate. "The stream." She sealed her sack and swung it over her shoulder. "It's not exactly a tough current. We can cling to the bricks."

"I don't know about this."

"What's the harm? The doors aren't working, and I don't see any markings," she said, taking in the immaculate surfaces of the walls.

Aika hesitated.

"It's fine. I'll go and check it out," Xander said.

"And I'll assume that if I don't see you coming back through the stream's mouth or one of those doors in five minutes, you've either drowned or found yourself lost."

"That's nice of you," Xander retorted sarcastically, and peered over the bank into the clear liquid. Excitedly she jumped into the frigid water and swam with the flow through the small opening in the wall, only to reappear seconds later through the opening on the opposite wall where the stream entered the courtyard.

"Now that's something new." Aika gaped.

Xander climbed onto the grass and lay there in bafflement. "At least I got to cool off," she said, her hair and clothes sodden.

Aika slumped on the neat grass beside her. "Five doors that keep changing, one stream, walls too high to climb, and no discernible markings to show us where to go. Exciting little conundrum."

Epiphany, or some semblance of desperate hope, took Xander. "What if I leave you nowhere to jump to?" she said, referring to the door on the map that refused to stay still and let her enter.

She got up, walked over to the doors, and quickly opened every door but the one indicated on the map. All revealed a different perspective of the courtyard in which they waited, with Aika and their kit strewn on the ground, and Xander stood before them, unable to hide her eureka moment.

"You really think the door highlighted on the map won't jump to an already opened door?" Aika called over.

"Any other ideas?" Xander called back.

"Nope. Just wondering."

Xander breathed excitedly through pursed lips and approached the only unopened door. Ever so cautiously, as if the slightest movement in haste might upset her scheme, she reached a solitary finger to the cool brass of the doorknob and laughed. The map remained constant, but not wanting to tempt fate, she abruptly opened it. Joyous relief took her at a sight other than the courtyard staring back.

"I knew you'd do it," Aika whooped.

"Shall we get a move on? Don't want to be here all day."

The door opened into a long hallway, the walls undecorated except for the same monotonous pattern along the centre crease and the floor padded by a maroon carpet that stretched the length.

"Who lit the torches?" Xander whispered of the flaming splints lining the corridor.

"Yeah, not creepy in the slightest…"

They exited the corridor into an elongated courtyard with two levels. On the ground level, the same neatly kept grass carpeted the surface and was intersected on the left end of the courtyard by a stream flowing from the building they had just exited into the building directly in front; beside the stream's exit stood a second door. To the right of the courtyard, a stone staircase climbed to the third and final door on the upper level.

"The map shows either way as possible, and no switching of the doors this time."

"Let's stick with the lower level," Aika said warily as she took in the shadowy windows on the upper level. "I'm not familiar with the palace or temples of Borealis, but I'm thinking the living quarters are probably not on the ground floor, and I'd rather not disturb our phantom hosts as they slumber."

"Second that." Xander laughed nervously, and the two followed the map through the maze of corridors, courtyards, staircases, and rooms, both bedrooms and living rooms, all hugging the ground floor, each one's presentation as spotless and eerie as the first.

"It's getting late. The sun's nearly set," Aika observed as they entered a triangular-shaped courtyard with no door except for the one they had just come through at the base of the triangle.

Streams entered from the central point of each of the three walls and met in the centre of the courtyard, where they encircled and then vanished under a small island. On the island lay a heavy stone tablet also in the shape of a triangle, with each of its corners unevenly angled to those of the courtyard.

"No shard and a dead end!" Aika added in confusion.

"It lies ahead of us on the map, still to the north but well beyond the markings of this room…the markings end with the top corner of this courtyard."

"And the streams?"

"Same as you see. They all flow to that central point."

They walked curiously to the edge of the moat and then jumped onto the island. The same monotonous design they had encountered throughout the complex was etched into the tablet, but the triangular tablet also carried twenty-eight holes drilled along the edge, nine on each of the two sides, ten on the base. Carved into the centre was an ancient caricature of the moon.

"Interesting," Xander said. "I think each of the holes symbolises the moon."

"And you concluded this how?"

"Twenty-eight holes, the orbit of the moon."

"Right! And you know what else is interesting? This is the only room we've been in with something out of place."

"The tablet?"

"Exactly." Without prompting, Aika heaved the triangular tablet into alignment with the courtyard.

Almost immediately the sky turned purple, and the streams glistened with moonlight.

"Look how the water shines with the light of an absent moon," Xander said, entranced by the sudden change in ambience.

"Not absent." Aika pointed to a small white globe creeping from over the stone wall to the right.

"Rises in the east and sets in the west," Xander whispered. She glimpsed a marking carved into the same stone wall beside the stream and hurriedly leapt off the island towards it. "It's the broadleaf…and look. Small grooves have been cut into the stones all the way to the top of the wall."

Then, without caution or a second thought and nearly slipping in the process, she climbed the stone ladder to the wall's peak and stretched out for the small globe that had already shifted towards the centre of the room.

"I can't reach it. I'll have to jump," Xander called.

"Be sure to aim for the water!"

"Of course!" She then threw herself at the moon and just managed to touch it with her sweaty hand. It was enough to break its orbit, and both she and the glowing ball of white fell into the stream, where she swiftly retrieved it.

"Your gambit paid off," Aika remarked. "Now what? Put it in one of the holes?"

"I think so, but which one? A triangle that aligns exactly with the sides and corners of the room, the moon in my hand, and twenty-eight moons on the tablet depicting its orbit."

"So we need to determine which day of the moon's orbit we're on." Xander nodded.

"Well, the Moonlight Festival was fifty-four days ago, which means we're on day twenty-eight of the orbit," Aika said.

"And I think the starting point is this hole in the base of the triangle," Xander said, brushing her finger on the fifth hole from the right. Unlike the other holes, it had a small groove etched onto its edge. "The same side of the room we entered from. And look, the top corner of the triangle faces north, and because the moon rises in the east and sets in the west…"

Xander held the frosty ball over the hole depicting the twenty-eighth moon immediately to the left of their starting point and then dropped it in with a clunk.

"Nothing," Aika said disappointedly after several moments. "Maybe we got—"

The island shifted, and nearly throwing the girls into the water, it rose a metre into the air to reveal a plunging hole into a cavern below.

"Well, bearer, though I like to lay claim to an unmatched knack for diving blind into the abyss of reckless danger, I think I'm going to let you do the honours," Aika said as they peered down the hazy drop into the obscure pool below, the noise of the streams hitting the water audible even from there.

"Not keen on getting wet?" Xander chided.

"More so I don't know how shallow that pool down there is, but sure, whatever it takes for you to be the bird in the mine."

"Sensible!" Xander said, eyes intent on the drop. Then, taking a deep breath, she swiftly suppressed all thought into the vacant recesses of her mind and set impulse into motion by throwing herself off the ledge into the hole.

CHAPTER 57

The momentum of the drop into the chilly cavern lifted Xander's stomach into her throat and invoked in her an uncomfortable breathlessness that seemed permanent in its suspension. But despite the fact that they had yet to encounter any hostiles since entering the structure, she held the urge to groan and had released only the softest of gasps when the icy water knocked the wind out of her on impact.

Still desperate for breath, she frantically lifted her head in search of reprieve, only to dive back down and re-emerge under the waterfall upon hearing the faint noise of a violent skirmish nearby. She looked up, hoping to warn Aika not to cry out and make known their uninvited presence to any unseen ears, but the girl was concealed by the haze.

"What a thrill!" Aika suddenly whispered from her side. "And look, no broken bones."

"That's a relief! Listen," she said, cupping her ear. "I heard something. It sounded like fighting, but I can't hear it now. Did you hear anything?"

Aika shook her head and then peered to the grassy shore, the way ahead illuminated by a natural light seemingly born from the rock. "Looks clear. Must've come through there." She pointed to a stone archway at the end of a lone path leading from the water.

They swam cautiously to the shore and then froze as the sound of fighting rang out again.

"It doesn't sound like men or critters," Xander said.

"No."

"Any ideas?"

"Your guess is as good as mine. What do you think? Wait it out?"

"The noise is already fading. I say let's check it out," she said, and unsheathed her blade.

"Okay," Aika agreed, unslinging her bow.

"It works?"

"The bow? Of course. Why wouldn't it?"

"It's wet."

"Not the string. See? We harvest the wood from the bark of the Great Tree and the string from the silkworms of Dekor. The bows are versatile and can withstand harsh heat and cold, as well as water. No need to cover the string from getting wet."

"Perhaps I should invest."

"Not an easy learn."

"You underestimate your ability to teach."

"No, just your ability to draw the string."

Xander smiled a mischievous grin that invited competition. "When we're out of here, we'll have to draw up terms."

"You didn't strike me as a gambler."

"Who said anything about gambling?" she retorted with a wink, and they jogged to the archway.

The path trailed alongside a narrow river etched into the length of a tunnel naturally carved into the rock, a monotonous continuation of indistinguishable bends interrupted only by the duo's combined shock of what lay before them several minutes into their cautious wander.

"It's a Guardian…" Aika whispered.

"I thought they fell in the first wave against the humans."

"They did, but this one looks different. It's more colourful. And miniature."

"And certainly leafier."

They edged towards the broken carcass, careful to keep their distance.

"The leaves. There's something growing on them," Xander observed.

"It's a fungus."

"But I don't think that's what killed it. See here. It looks like something tried to break it in half."

A loud crash sounded from ahead, and curious to spy the culprit, they raced to the end of the tunnel and peered into the next chamber. Five bridges, drawn from five entrances, traversed a body of water and connected to a pentagon-shaped island in the centre of the chamber. Torches dotted the island's five corners, and the closest bridge on the left was shattered in the middle. Their gazes fell on the farthest bridge, where two Guardians fought an unseen foe, and it was only when one of the wooded creatures was viciously hurled into the cavern's wall and rendered unresponsive in the water did Aika mutter a curse.

"A forest critter!" Xander said.

The critter was similar in appearance to Haro and Leila but heavily muscled and as tall as the Guardians. It was topless and wore a thick helmet reaching down to its chin. Xander immediately recognised the similarity between its features and one of the critters etched into the ancient tree from Aika's coronation.

"Yes, one of the Gigas. They're very strong and usually very peaceful."

The Guardian swung its club at the Giga's armoured head, and as if to prove Aika's point, the Giga grabbed the club, tore off the Guardian's limb, and broke its body over its knee.

"It saddens me to see this one betrays the forest." Aika sighed, but barely had she finished her breath when another three Gigas emerged from the entrance to the right. "Something's amiss."

"On their skin. It's the same fungus that covered the Guardian."

"Wait! I know this fungus."

"Dammit! Ready yourself. They're coming for us."

"The fungus obliterates the mind, leaving it open to control. There's no coming back from the damage," Aika continued, then smoothly unleashed an arrow into the nearest as it rushed them, but the arrow snapped against the Giga's armoured head, and it took a second and a third into its bare chest to bring it down.

Aware of the threat, the first Giga quickly divvied the broken carcass of the Guardian to the other two, and the trio charged with the makeshift shields held out front. It was enough to render the next half-dozen arrows futile, and Xander found herself engaged with the first one whilst Aika took the other two.

Xander proved unable to land a blow against her assailant's massive frame, the length of its reach and the resilience of the improvised weapons all too much for her and the blade. And though some of Aika's subsequent shots hit true against her foes, she was swiftly overpowered and knocked unconscious, leaving the other two to join the fray.

Ganged up on and on the back foot, Xander gave up the fight and, barely evading the charge, launched herself over the collapsed bridge into the darkness of the next cavern. From there she continued through countless others before fear and adrenaline finally gave way to respite as the grunts and calls of her pursuers dissipated.

CHAPTER 58

"What chance did I have? And still, I can't leave her with those monsters… and neither can I leave without the shard," Xander said in anguish, weighed by her escape whilst her friend lay unconscious and at the mercy of the Gigas, or whoever controlled them. Slumped on the cold, damp ground beside a body of dark liquid placidly content in the trough of a particularly spacious cavern, she peered across the chamber's walls and ceiling, interested as to the origins of the weak glow that radiated from the rock. "It must be something on the rock itself."

Her thoughts drifted to the first chambers immediately after the collapsed bridge that had shown evidence of ancient developments long ago succumbed to the wear of time, and the system of undeveloped caverns through which she now crawled. There was no indication of previous occupation in this undeveloped system, though to her surprise, it was etched into the map.

"I wonder why those critters didn't follow." She shuddered at the thought of something more frightening lurking in the depths of the cavern's lake.

An obscured voice suddenly simmered over the water, causing her muscles to tense and goosebumps to painfully traverse the skin on her legs. It called again, and she squinted ahead to the vertical cavern wall on the other side of the lake from where it emanated.

Again it called, but instead of fright or caution, Xander found herself calmly drawn to the murmur. Casually she threw her pouch to the ground and dove into the icy water with only her blade for company. Throughout the swim, the unseen depth of the frigid lake played havoc on her mind, and it was with no small relief that she began her ascent of the cliff face using a series of small indents knocked into the rock. Halfway up she came across a horizontal tunnel carved into the cliff.

Though the tunnel was generous in width, its ceiling was low—so low, in fact, that she had to remove her sword and sheath and push them along as she crawled through the space, the weight of the rock above always heavy on her mind. Unspoken curse words blessed the tip of her tongue with each jar of a finger or knock of the head, but after what felt like a solid twenty minutes on her front, she saw a faint white glow at the end of the tunnel.

She breached a small chamber no bigger than her room in Nhata and just high enough to stand. The walls were covered in a moss of sorts that glowed the same fluorescent white as the chamber from where she had entered, though the moss was far more abundant in the tiny room.

Her eyes fell to the chest in the middle of the room, and her heart pounded with a sudden longing and sense of familiarity. She wiped her hand across the broadleaf carved into the wood.

"It can't be the shard. I would've seen it on the map."

She undid the latch, threw open the cover, and reached inside.

The circular shield was very light, and the smooth face was a continuous wooden surface as if cut whole from a tree, with only the familiar ancient caricature of the moon dyed into the centre for decoration. She put her arm through the two straps and tried to cut the edge of her blade into the face of the shield that was as wide as her arm was long.

"Not a mark. Even the carcass of the Guardian had some damage."

She cut harder this time.

"And still nothing. How remarkable! We may not withstand a cloud of arrows, but I do fancy our chances against everything else."

CHAPTER 59

Crouched behind a fallen pillar in one of the chambers not too far from where she had left Aika, Xander held her breath as two Gigas walked past. Both were unarmed, and neither was from the earlier brawl. With the Gigas out of sight, she emerged from the rock and continued into an adjoining tunnel at a cautious jog. She felt less vulnerable with her newfound shield strapped to her back and more at ease with the impulsive decision to abandon her friend. It would have done neither of them any good if they had both been captured. At least, she hoped Aika was still just a captive and not worse.

She continued unimpeded until she reached the chamber with the pentagon-shaped island. There were no Gigas in sight. Still concealed, she unfurled the map and took a look. The bridge where the two Guardians had originally engaged the unseen Giga was the bridge she needed to get to the shard. On the other side lay a large complex structure of chambers, rooms, and corridors that stood between her and the reason that they had risked it all.

"But what about Aika?" she thought, dismayed by the prospect of searching every crevice to find her friend.

She looked at the map and scanned the systems connected to the other two unexplored bridges. One connected to a very long corridor with a single, gigantic room at the end, and the other led to a small complex with three floors, a series of small spaces, and several dozen rooms.

"Easy wins," she said quietly, and confident that the chamber was empty, she took a step back and then ran and jumped onto the island.

She crept around the wrecked remains of the Guardians littering the floor, picking up three unbroken arrows as she did, and crossed the bridge into the long corridor with a giant room at its culmination. The tunnel was lit by torches on the walls, and it took her a full ten minutes to traverse its entire length. Standing at the end was a wooden door twice her height. On edge from what she might find, she gripped the heavy metal handle and opened it.

Nothing. There was nothing on the other side, just a massive room illuminated by torches on all the walls. A sense of being watched suddenly took her, and she gently closed the door and ran back the way she came, frequently throwing glances behind her to make sure she wasn't being followed. She crossed back onto the island with some relief.

This time she crossed the bridge leading to the small complex. Immediately on the other side of the bridge was a single room at the base of a flight of stairs. She peeked inside to see a small desk with a lit candle on top. She glanced down to the empty chair. It was leaning back slightly, as if someone sat on it. A barrage of goosebumps traversed her spine, and she quickly and quietly ducked out and up the stairs.

She emerged onto the next level but had barely made it two seconds along when a Giga rounded the corner with something in hand. She slipped into an open room before it could see her. It wasn't alone. Heart racing, she could hear multiple footsteps coming her way and the scratchy sound of something being dragged.

She braced as the footsteps reached just outside the room in which she hid, and then she jumped as the footsteps stopped and the sound of a scuffle broke out. Moments later, two Gigas walked past with a rope extended behind them. Then came the shocking sight of a third Giga being dragged along the ground, its face bruised and bloody.

With the critters out of sight and earshot, she cautiously exited the room. There were five empty rooms in total on that level, and she was quick to suss out the next flight of stairs and move on to the third and final level.

The third level was much, much larger than the previous one. Ahead of her was a sizeable square made of colourful tiles. Houses and small buildings encircled the space, and in the centre was a fountain with running water. If not for the ceiling of jagged rock above, she swore she could have been in any nondescript market square in any of the dozens of towns in the centre of Borlencia.

Over her initial fascination, she crept up to the first house on the right and peered inside through a pristinely clear window. Excitement took her. It was Aika's bow and her kit. She opened the door and cautiously entered the house. It was warm and the furniture cosy. Careful to dull the noise of her footsteps, she made her way into the back. There was a kitchen with a lit stove, and though she could see no food or ingredients on the counter, the scent of bread hung in the air. There was a third room with a bed, but it was empty.

Disappointed, she made a mental note of the location and then left without Aika's gear, not wanting to overburden herself. With growing impatience she explored three more buildings on the right of the tiled square to find only the same eerie scene of an empty structure that was still seemingly occupied.

As she was about to enter into the fourth, a light "hey" reached her ears. She turned around and looked in the direction of the source, then smiled at the face peering from behind a barred window on the other side of the square.

CHAPTER 60

"You took your time," Aika jibed as Xander opened the door. "Oh! And look. You found yourself a new toy. Very stylish," she said of the shield. She stood beside a set of torn binds, and in her hand was a small dagger.

"Thought I'd take some me time and explore what this fantastic destination has to offer. That and I had to navigate a myriad of tunnels and rooms whilst dodging a small army of brainwashed serfs."

"That bad?"

"The maze or the army?"

"Both!"

"Wasn't easy."

"And I take it the map was of no use?"

"For the shard, yes. For you, not so much."

"Well, sorry to have inconvenienced you," Aika said, and kicked the binds against the wall.

"Not at all! Maybe just try a bit harder next time to not get caught."

"Wouldn't worry about that. They removed an untainted Giga from in here a short while ago. Couldn't make out all the screams, but pretty obvious what they had planned for it."

Xander shuddered, recalling the prone Giga being dragged by two of its own.

"So how far is the shard from here?" Aika asked.

"Not far, and I know where they've got your kit."

They crossed the square, grabbed Aika's gear and tracked back the way Xander had entered. In the chamber with the island, they crossed the bridge into the maze of the tree's cellar that would lead them to the shard.

Unlike the areas adjoined to the other bridges, this complex was far, far busier. Gigas roamed every corridor, and more than once, they stumbled across dozens of Guardian carcasses battered and broken and left to rot. Still, despite the minefield of brainwashed critters, they managed to skirt through the rooms and corridors undiscovered until they reached the chamber on the map that was marked by the location of the shard.

Apprehension and excitement took them both as they crept to the breach of its crooked doorway.

"At every turn, we've encountered the Gigas. Why not here?" Aika whispered.

"Maybe the shard keeps them at bay."

"Or whatever controls them."

"And I don't see either."

They wandered cautiously into the massive, perfectly round chamber. In the centre sat a circular stone platform with nine torches lit along its edge that appeared to keep at bay the persistent film of mist that clung to the rest of the chamber's floor.

Aika looked up and gasped. "We're at the central point of the tree!"

"It's as if we're looking through a telescope," Xander said, amazed, pointing to the very top of the tree's inner chamber. Between them and the tiny speck were the many levels of the spiral platform and the wooded paradise it supported. "Though it feels as if time hasn't moved," she said of the nocturnal glow of the moon.

"Or another night is upon us."

A scratching noise sounded from behind them, and they slipped farther into the chamber in cautious fright.

"What in Anemoi was that?" Xander muttered.

It sounded again, but this time it was more threatening and grating in its production, and it caused the girls' nerves to spasm and their faces to scrunch.

"And the stench! So vile!" Aika winced, eyes intent on the entrance.

"On the wall—it's huge!"

"Biggest snake I've seen!"

"I don't think it's a—" Xander swiftly raised her shield, and three long darts the length of spears shattered against it.

She tried to peer at their attacker but withdrew her head as another three slammed into the shield. Aika suddenly jumped into the mist, pulling Xander with her and out of the way of a dart launched from the side.

"It's a damn vine!" Xander hissed as they climbed to their feet and slowly backed onto the platform where the thickening mist refused to linger.

"Those darts are massive!"

The obscure ground around the platform grated with the coarse skin of the vine, and so uncertain were they of where the head began and the tail ended that they huddled back-to-back, with Xander watchful of the front and Aika the rear.

"I saw something," Xander whispered.

"As did I. It's all around us."

"No, something different. Not green. A yellowy pink, almost."

Aika let loose her arrow and then another at the same thread of colour, but they clattered clear of the mark. "I saw it, but it was too—"

The force of the Giga's surprise swing knocked Xander into Aika, causing the latter to fall over, but as fortune had it, the stumble was enough to shift Xander partially out of the route of a giant dart aimed at her throat, and the projectile instead glanced off the edge of her shield and fell to their feet.

Invigorated by the girls' distraction, the Giga, carrying the carcass of a Guardian, swung for Xander's head, but her reflexes were too quick. She ducked and then punched the face of her shield into the brute with such force that it and the carcass were thrown violently to the ground. Momentarily dazed from the impact, Aika launched the still-intact dart into the Giga's chest, and it immediately slumped from the vine's poison.

"To the side!" Aika cried, and Xander stepped off the platform and repeated the action against another Giga, hurling the critter into the mist.

But amidst the obscurity of the cloud, Xander had left her right flank carelessly unprotected. The vine detected the opportunity and swiped its tail viciously against her unshielded arm, causing her to drop the blade, her limb numb and unresponsive.

Aika walked forward, firing arrow after furious arrow into the exposed vine, but its hide was too thick, and half the projectiles were instantly rendered unusable, whilst the others stuck only superficially. She grabbed the fallen blade and then took cover with Xander behind the shield.

"How is it?" she asked as they pulled back to the platform, their eyes wary of the faint flickers in the shroud.

"I can barely lift it!"

"Lucky that shield's as good as a weapon."

"Over there!"

"It's too quick."

"And too strong."

Aika cursed. "I'm running low on arrows. At this rate we'll have no choice but to cut it."

"Good luck getting close."

Another Giga rushed them from the mist and heaved a longsword at Aika's head. She flicked Xander's blade up but was pushed onto the back foot by the force of the intercept, and as the critter came in with a surprisingly quick successive strike, Xander lunged forward and punched the shield into the critter, shattering its chest cavity.

"Perhaps the torches keep the vine at bay," she panted.

"Doesn't like fire…" Aika said. She pulled a vial from a pouch on her waist and dipped her last four arrows into it. "Fire oil," she said in response to Xander's quizzical stare.

"Thought we'd established it's too fast."

"Sure, when it's not distracted."

"You're kidding."

"Any better ideas?"

Reluctantly Xander crept a small distance into the mist and waited cautiously whilst Aika stood watch not far behind with a torch at her side.

Two more Gigas appeared abruptly from the mist, their attack violent and swift and nearly successful in its desired purpose. But despite her impediment, Xander was frightening in her agility and strength, and in rapid succession broke the body of the first with a blow to the arm and decapitated the second with a gruesome punch of the shield to its neck.

Suddenly aware of the vine's approaching strike at her distracted posture but unable to match its speed with a counterstrike, she could only watch and hope in dreadful anticipation that the orange flash piercing the mist would strike true before her undoing.

Her hairs stood on end at the vine's agonising shriek, and she was quick to stumble back into the protection of the platform and Aika's cover. From there, they watched the fire arrow glide through the obscure room before Aika lit another and hit beside the first. The vine raised its head through the thickness of the mist, and for the first time, they glimpsed the flowery head of the leafy serpent and the pain etched across its beautifully alien expression that was understandable even to them.

Still there was no hesitation in Aika's actions, and she swiftly lit another and fired it directly into the colourful flower. The display was both exhilarating and horrific as the creature's head imploded in a flash of fire and sparks, a display not too dissimilar to the firecrackers the naughty kids in Nhata used to explode, much to the indignation of the neighbours.

"Well, that was eventful," Aika said weakly after several moments as they observed the mist slowly subside.

"How very odd it was. It's the first time I've seen one with a head. I wonder if it's related to the others outside the tree," Xander said as she gripped her arm.

"Whatever it was, it's not from the Great Forest. None of the vines are."

"Makes you wonder what else Bronte's power kept at bay," Xander said solemnly, her gaze suddenly distant.

"You okay?"

"I'll live," she muttered, and glanced around the room. "Let's get the shard and get out of here."

"Maybe there's another door or insignia," Aika called, and began a circuit of the room.

Xander followed suit and scoured the walls and floors in the opposite direction until they both connected on the other side of the room.

Aika shrugged. "Except for the corpses on the ground, there's nothing that looked even slightly out of place. You're sure it's in here?"

"Positive."

"Was afraid you'd say that," Aika retorted. "Another loop?"

"We don't really have a choice."

At that, the pair searched every mark and crevice on the walls and floor, upturning stones and shifting broken tiles. A full forty minutes elapsed before they made their way back to the centre of the chamber and sat down in a frustrated heap, their exhaustion catching up.

"This is irritating," Xander muttered, looking at the map. "It clearly shows it in this room. Maybe behind a stone we missed, or hidden in the torches."

"I checked the torches."

"Then buried in the dirt."

"Wouldn't be very secure buried in the dirt, would it?" Aika chimed. "More likely it'd be locked up somewhere safe, away from prying hands."

"I wish the map would give us more. We'll just have to keep looking."

Aika yawned long and hard. "Give me five minutes, and I'll get back to it." Sluggishly, she lay on her back and rested her head on her hands. Marvelling at the many levels between them and the uppermost point of the tree, her tired eyes closed.

Xander peered at her friend and held her chuckle. She, too, could feel the need to pause taking hold, but it wouldn't do for both of them to drop their guard in that place. Forcing herself to continue, she peered around from their position, again hoping for a glimpse of anything that might betray the location of the shard. To her annoyance, nothing in that room looked even remotely revealing.

A snore escaped Aika's lips. As Xander looked down at her dozing friend, she locked on a dirty crease etched into the middle of the otherwise undamaged stone Aika rested her head on. Xander reached her good hand over and fingered the dust away to reveal a perfectly circular indent a half inch deep. Her eyes drifted across the platform and then upwards towards the roof of the tree. The indent was in the exact centre of the tree.

Intrigue took her as she caressed the perfectly placed groove that was the width of her finger, and then an idea struck. For every lock there must be a key, or in this case, a key the width of her finger. It was too much of a coincidence.

Holding her breath, she slid the ring from her finger and placed it in the indent that was a flawless fit. The white light that emanated from above her was pure and otherworldly, and without hesitation or doubt, she stood up, and she reached her good hand into it and grasped the cold, metallic corner of the shard. The next thing she knew, they were both slumped on the beaten grass at the top of the tree.

CHAPTER 61

Novembrix 14, 484; the Great Forest—Through the haze of the unrelenting twilight, the camp at the base of the Great Tree teemed with disarray. Absent any sort of protective barrier along the perimeter closest to the wooded giant, Xander and Aika had been able to sneak right up to the thorny bushes a stone's toss away from the chaotic sea of tents and huts. It was a suitable spot from which to observe unseen.

"What do you suppose happened?" Aika whispered from her crouch as the human soldiers and Damain's minions scuttled about with an evident lack of cohesion, though the army's collective lust for answers shone clear.

"I couldn't tell you, but it looks like they're searching for something or someone."

"The others?"

"You think they'd have lingered?"

"Wouldn't put it past Ratin to have disobeyed to make sure I get out okay."

Voices emanated from nearby, and the girls were quick to hush and sink deep into the shadow of the forest floor.

"Whatever it was, the bugs' commander is a right mess. Cold and blue and bloody, they say," a guttural accent echoed.

Xander's ears perked, but her enthusiasm was swiftly torn by Aika's unchanged expression and the soldiers' continued observation as they plonked themselves directly in front of the girls' hideout, their stench a horrid blend of sweat, nerves, and general lack of hygiene.

"Damain and his filth—"

"*Its* filth, not his, you cretin. *Its*!"

"Right! Damain and its filth are convinced it was deliberate. All sorts'a talk about a witch or demon. They think the damn camp's cursed now. As if it wasn't before," he muttered, and spat something foul into the bush. "At this rate, the bug'll gut all the prisoners before sunrise just to be sure it weren't none of them that conjured no spirits."

"Well, what I 'eard was it was a spider, nothin' more, nothin' less. There's nothin' demonic about no spider, if you ask me."

"Right, superstition, that's all."

"And what ya expect from a bunch of bugs? They're nothin' like us sensible folks. Even the cretins from the tree and the man they was with, ya know, the damn traitor to his kind, they's all—"

"Shut it! Did you 'ear that?"

"I didn't 'ear nothin', ya paranoid whatsit. Now, what was I sayin' before—" A gurgled muffle of a cry tried to escape his lips as Aika cruelly and stealthily cut short his life and the other's with two precisely placed strikes from her blade.

A pang of guilt took Xander. She was no longer a stranger to the ambush, but that didn't mean she didn't struggle to swallow the unexpected death discreetly handed to lone, duty-bound soldiers afforded no opportunity to counter their unnatural demise. Necessity and exposure didn't necessarily entail unquestioning acceptance.

She cleared her throat. "So what now?"

Aika hefted off a boot from the first and lobbed it to her.

"Disguise."

"With half the camp alive? And I thought I was the rash one."

Aika pointed up. "The sky's changing. I can already feel the shroud lift. And you heard him—Damain may kill the prisoners, and I can only assume the man he was referring to is Ricard."

"And yes, rescue him we must, but we don't know—"

The bush behind them rustled, and they jumped to the ground.

"I can't see anything," Xander whispered, and then Aes and Oscine appeared out of the shadows.

Aika grinned. "Like a homing pigeon."

"Which one?"

"Both."

"Come on. Let's move farther into the bush. A stag, an overly friendly songbird, and two girls are hardly inconspicuous."

Away from their previous hideout and the stripped bodies of the guards expertly disposed of in the undergrowth, the girls deciphered the fractured happenings of the prior two days through a combination of motions, visuals, and thoughts, courtesy of Oscine and Aes.

"Poor Ricard," Xander said sadly. "He must be heartbroken."

"He might not be much use to us if he's that far gone. But Ratin—we can use him and the other prisoners."

"How few survived."

"Be thankful it wasn't in vain."

"I am, and all the more reason to return the risk."

"Agreed."

Aika looked Xander up and down.

"What?" Xander retorted.

"The shield looks awkward beneath the soldier's cloak."

"And the bow doesn't? Anyway, I'm not going to be much good without it. My arm's still limp. Doubt I can swing my blade."

"Right, it'll do. There's still enough shroud, and the camp hasn't lost its raucousness."

The girls skirted the edge of the camp with Oscine as their guide, and Aes hung back in reserve to avoid detection. At the point farthest from the

Great Tree, they veered towards the camp with as much swagger and implied masculinity as they could muster in an attempt to throw off suspicion of the ill-fitting garments.

The guards' presence was marginally denser in the woods that side of the sprawling settlement, with a handful of bugs dotted up and in between the trees surrounding the camp. To the pair's relief, however, their new garments were convincing enough to fool the sentries still unaccustomed to the men of Anemoi, and they were able to approach the boundary unimpeded.

Nevertheless, even though the air still hung heavy with darkness, it was evident that some of the more acute bugs knew the unnatural shroud bordered on dissolution, and thus the charade may not last once within the cramped quarters of the enemy base.

Stepping from the thick greenery of the forest onto the levelled clearing immediately on the camp's edge, they both stammered. The perimeter on that side, though without a wall, wasn't completely exposed. Instead, it was marked by dozens of wooden cages filled with critters and what was left of Ratin's men.

"How odd that they would keep the prisoners on this side of the camp, so open to rescue and with a light guard," Xander whispered.

"Better the prisoners be the first to incur the horror of the swamp vines, methinks," Aika remarked angrily.

Oscine beckoned from his vantage point atop a lofty wooden hut on the camp's makeshift boundary, and the girls crept forward warily. Concealed by the hut's shadow, they rounded the structure and stopped where the light from a firepit cut into the darkness. From there, they peered into an open space that was lined with tents on the one side, and three cages on the side facing the forest. The glow of the fire was enough to make out the figures being held captive.

Ratin was there, bruised but otherwise seemingly strong, as were a number of his men, some of whom were in less stellar condition. Xander's stomach tensed, and the air caught in her throat at the sight of Ricard slumped inside the cage that did little to shelter him from the elements. The man appeared broken, hollow almost, and how she suddenly longed to reach out and soothe him. She turned around to see Aika had disappeared.

"Where did she go?" she uttered nervously, and peered up to Oscine atop the lofty roof. The incredibly faint sound of a foot traversing the shadow drew her gaze down in time to see Aika reappearing as stealthily as she had left.

"I count five guards. Three stationed in the opening," Aika said, motioning to the clearing. "And two doing the rounds."

"Bugs?"

"Humans."

"You think you can get the two doing the rounds?" Xander asked.

"Depends. You think you can perform well enough to draw those three in?"

"We'll find out. Oscine, find the tent I told you about and report back."

Aika slid back into the shadows of the camp, and Xander limped towards the opening, aware of the curious stare that bore into her, not from the guards who appeared oblivious and uncaring to her approach, but that of Ratin as he picked apart her disguise with little fuss.

"Oi! Look what I found," she barked gruffly to rouse the guards' attention, though she was suddenly unsure of the itchy leather cap she wore and its ability to hide her soft features and long hair, even in the dark.

"What ya think it'll fetch back 'ome?" she continued, unslinging the shield.

"Well, it ain't nothin' special, is it?"

"Yeah, ordinary piece of wood by the looks of it. Could make that myself, I reckon," another chimed in.

A dull thud rang from behind the tents on the other side of the opening.

"I reckon it'll fetch a pretty penny in Zyphyr, never mind what you lot say." She quickly spoke, drawing back their attention.

The first guard shot a glance at her and then the others.

"Zyphyr? Didn't think anybody from the city was in this regiment. No grunts, anyway. And you say you're from there?"

She cleared her throat.

"No, no, just outside." She laughed nervously, then swung the shield at the nearest, hurling him into one of the cages with such force that he collapsed the door.

And before the others could protest, Aika's arrows had swiftly silenced them.

"Took your time," Xander chided, and rushed to open the nearest cage.

"There were two others we missed," she panted.

"Getting sloppy, cousin," Ratin jibed as Aika pulled open his cage.

"Quiet, you! Come on, swap your clothes."

He tilted his head, puzzled.

"I'll explain later."

Xander made towards Ricard and hesitated. His gaze did not deviate from the ground.

"Hello, kiddo," he managed as she broke the door.

"Ricard, I'm sorry—"

"Let me stop you there. No need."

"But—"

He held up his hand with his eyes still sunken. "What happened to your arm?"

"Long story. Ricard, can you make for the bushes? Aes is waiting out there. We'll be right behind."

"Not going to happen," he said defiantly, and rose from his stupor, vengeance etched in his eyes.

"Not a good idea if he comes," Ratin muttered as he dressed. "He'll endanger whatever plan you've thought up. He's not right in the head."

One of Ratin's men knocked through into Ricard's cage and dumped a soldier's body donned in the garments of the Lizard People.

"There's none left for you, Ricard. Take the others back to where Aes is waiting. If we need you, we'll call," Aika said sternly.

He looked at her for a moment and then sighed. "As you wish, Princess."

"Can we trust him?" Aika asked Xander as Ricard walked towards those not partaking.

"I don't know, but we can't dwell," she responded, concerned.

Oscine flew into the opening and motioned for them to follow.

"He found it," Aika said.

"Found what?" Ratin interrupted, his new disguise odd looking but passable.

"Damain."

"Too dangerous!"

"It must be done."

"Not now and not here."

"Now is the best chance we have."

"And I guess now you'll explain to me why my men and I wear this nonsense."

The girls stifled grins as they took in the disguised assembly and proceeded to explain whilst several of Ratin's men kept watch.

"Very risky," Ratin said. "They might not buy it."

"Worth a try," Xander said.

"At the princess's expense?"

"Enough, Ratin," Aika said. "This is happening, and your presence will only help our chances."

He nodded after several moments, and Xander felt nothing but respect for his unwavering duty to Aika and her well-being.

Adopting a blend of apprehension and purpose similar to that carried by the camp's inhabitants, the group made its way through the maze of tents towards the camp's centre, and much to their surprise, despite the lifting shroud and their collective awkwardness, they weren't noticed.

"I'm guessing humbleness is not in the Dragon King's lingo," Xander observed of the structure situated in the camp's centre.

"The monster's not too dissimilar to my father when it comes to grandeur," Aika commented, and then nodded to the right, where a swarm of bugs congregated, content in their avoidance of the humans.

Xander returned the nod and started towards the congregation with Ratin and his men on her hind.

Comfortably sitting in the centre of the royal tent, the Dragon King admired a parchment rolled out on the floor. The tent was big and extravagant in its relative design and was flooded with talismans and patterns, both inside and out, all of which were thought to ward off curses.

"That damned witch and her rat. Who do they think they talk to with such disdain!" Damain tore the document and then smirked wickedly. "We'll see her tone if I leave her men to the likes of the forest without my—"

The bug's antennae perked.

"What do we have here?" Damain snarled quietly, looking at the wall as if it were transparent.

The Dragon King was about to summon the guards, when calls of panic and the sudden clang of metal on metal stole its attention in the opposite direction.

"The bugs attack!" cried several voices in that guttural tongue of man Damain so loathed, and the next retorted, in the bug's own tongue but with an accent and tone too similar to the first, "The humans did it. It was the humans!"

"They're playing us!" Damain panicked, and emerging from the tent with spear in hand, the Dragon King cursed in disbelief at the scene of chaos erupting like wildfire throughout the camp, a scene where humans and bugs unquestioningly cut one another's throats.

Weeks of pent-up resentment and disgust had been abruptly and unforgivingly unleashed in an inglorious and bloodied frenzy, and that frenzy now showed little sign of curtailment. Indecision swiftly befell the Dragon King and then cruelly blinded it to the real threat: the drawn bow concealed on its flank and the smirk of the bow's owner as she loosened her retribution into the side of its head with a crack.

Aika breathed long and hard, content with the long-desired deed, and then she slipped through the turmoil of the camp to the predetermined rendezvous. Her arrival coincided with what was left of those who had accompanied Xander, and with the match lit over the tinderbox, the group made it into the woods where the others waited, all except for one.

Ricard was missing.

"We have to go!" Aika urged. "It puts us all in danger to wait."

"She's right. We must go," Ratin added in indignation.

"We can't!" Xander had begun to protest when Ricard knocked through the bushes, much to their fright, his hands covered in blood, both human and bug, and his axe slung across his shoulders.

"Couldn't leave my axe."

"Get your fill?" Aika asked dryly, aware his motive was rooted in a need for blood.

He ignored the quip and started into the growing light of the forest. "Shall we go?"

"The man's a beast. A reckless beast," Ratin muttered as they followed, irate that Ricard would trade the safety of the prisoners to satiate his own lust for vengeance.

CHAPTER 62

Novembrix 12, 484; two days earlier, the top of the Great Tree—Outside the tree's gateway, Ricard hefted one of the fallen minions into his line of sight as a volley of spears skimmed through the air towards them. Pushed onto the back foot by the impact, he threw the slain minion at another that lunged at him from the side. Effortlessly he then pulled a protruding spear from one of Ratin's downed men and launched it at the bug that led the swarm.

By the skin of the bug commander's jagged teeth, the spear glanced off its wings and knocked it awkwardly to the side. Ricard grabbed his axe from the ground and roared again, the ferocity and anguish enough to make the minions that made for the gap cower in fright and present a defenceless crop ready to be reaped. And though his left shoulder screamed in agony from the remnants of the spear that had caught him at the onset of the ambush, he ploughed through the crop with nowt but the brutish swing of his battle-axe and the commander in his sight as his overwhelming impetus.

Each blow exterminated two or three of Damain's bugs and inched his unwieldy form ever closer to the vermin, but it was not enough to stem the collapse of Ratin's men under the continued onslaught or make a dent in the swarm they faced.

"We need to get out of here!" Ratin shouted from above as his mantis sidestepped a jab from an overzealous bug, and he stabbed his dagger into its back. "Aika and Xander are in. We must leave!"

"Not without him," Ricard roared again, and decapitated two bugs with one swoop.

Ratin cursed and dove into the melee with his dagger, his quiver long ago empty. The man's movements were elegant and almost hypnotic, and he danced with a deadly style similar to Aika's, though more aggressive in its manner.

"Come on!" Ricard boomed aggressively, red in his sight.

He leapt into the group wedged between him and the prone figure strewn across the ground, but amidst the distraction of his newest victims, the opportune bug commander threw its bloodied spear unchecked and nailed the big man in the thigh. Ricard shuddered and fell to his knees. He quickly attempted to stand before a dull crack rang through his head and left him limp on the ground beside Haro's torn body.

▲ ▲ ▲

Night of Novembrix 13, base of the Great Tree—"Ricard? Are you okay?" Ratin called across the wet expanse from behind the makeshift prison that contained him and the remnants of his men.

Ricard ignored the concern and continued to stare, broken and distraught, into the heavy rain that pelted their unsheltered bodies.

Glumly and with horrid reluctance, he looked down at the small, lifeless body of his friend that was now the size of his hand and the devastated widow whose agonising grief shook his very core. He silently cursed the impulse that had pushed her to follow them and make certain of their well-being. How he pitied her and how he hated himself, both grateful and firm in his belief that he deserved the guilt that wreaked havoc on his being and deprived him of a moment's peace.

How he wished Haro had not followed him up that tree, willing to risk himself for a cause that was only partly his own, and more so the whim of an old man reminiscing. An old man determined to make live a promise made to an old friend long ago removed from this world and that friend's daughter, who had appeared in their lives less than a blink ago. And all the same, how he desperately wanted Leila to stop crying and exasperating his hurt.

As he slept on the rough, muddy ground of his cell, his sleep was burdened with replays of a life cursed by the loss of life. His ears tickled and his mind cried for his waking attention, the murmurs that trickled from reality into his dreamy slumber both disturbing and vile.

"Leila," he muttered groggily. "What do you do?"

She knelt against Haro's body and whispered into nothing, but it was clear what she called, the curse she beckoned, but at what cost, he did not know.

"You must stop!" he muttered harshly. "This is not the way."

But she did not hear, or chose not to hear, for she grinned a grin of cunning and vindictiveness at the ten-legged Gandal spider that pierced the skin and crawled out of the one she loved, so vicious and so eerie in its appearance. Its purpose was clear to the man that watched on in horror.

"Leila, you mustn't. You'll be undone. Everything you are and that you stand for will be undone. Please, I implore you!"

But still she did not listen, and the spider made haste into the wet of the night, its purpose no great distance from where they huddled.

The cries of chaos that woke the camp and the exhausted man told of success and confirmed the actuality of the events earlier in the night that Ricard had so hoped were the results of his unconscious mind.

A death in the camp. The bug commander, Haro's murderer, had been dealt its final, agonising breath during the vulnerability of its slumber, but it was at a price far too dear. A soul for a soul, for no curse was without a cost.

He peeled his eyes from Leila's limp body, her pale skin drained of its life. It was a price far too dear, but one which was ultimately not his to prevent. How he hurt and how he despised his resistance to an inevitability that seemed so generous in providing for those he had loved. How he hurt and how he feared for those he still loved.

CHAPTER 63

Novembrix 16, 484; temporary home of the Lizard People, seventy kilometres south of the Great Tree; the Great Forest—"What about this one, Xander?"

Xander looked down to the forest floor, where Gladis was standing amidst a jungle of twigs and brambles. The little woman held a smooth jade stone over her head. Xander's bruised arm was in a sling, so it was with some awkwardness that she knelt down and took the stone from Gladis. She straightened and then held the stone up to the light. A faint green glow emanated from it.

"Will it do?" Gladis asked.

A sad smile crept across Xander's face. "It's perfect."

"I'm glad! Shall we head back then? It's unbearably chilly this morning."

Xander slipped the stone into her pocket with the other they had found an hour earlier, then crouched down and picked Gladis up. The little woman got comfortable on Xander's shoulder, and they began walking back to camp.

"Do you think he'll like it?" Xander asked.

"I think he will. Have you decided when you will give it to him?"

"I don't know. I guess when the time feels right."

"You're nervous."

"Dreadfully so."

"The man loves you like a daughter. It'll mean everything to him."

"I know—it's not that I'm worried about. I'm nervous that he won't get over this. That it's all been too much."

"Perhaps. But it would've been much, much worse if he had lost—you know. He may be broken, but it's not unrepairable. And when you leave this forest, he will be there by your side."

A glimmer of hope took her. "He's told you this?"

"He didn't need to. I know it to be so. He will recover, Xander. He may just need a little reminding that not all has been lost, that's all."

"And what of you?"

Gladis chuckled. "I care about you, Xander. But I'll have to miss you from afar. The world out there is no place for us little folk."

A whistle emanated from above, and they looked up to see Oscine perched in the tree, watching them.

"Or a songbird," Gladis added. "We'll be watching from afar, wishing you the best on your journey."

▲ ▲ ▲

Evening rolled around, and Xander sat alone in her tent with a single candle for light. Unlike the previous camp, this tent was solely hers. A lonely reminder of all that had transpired in so short a time.

In her hand was one of the jade stones, though it no longer resembled a stone weathered by the elements but a figurine of someone she held dear. A teardrop blurred her eye. She wiped it away and then placed the figurine on her bed next to its mate.

"Goodbye, Haro. Goodbye, my Leila. I miss you sorely."

She wiped her tear and turned to the tent door as a rustle came from outside. A familiar voice entered her mind. It was Aes. She got up and went outside. The camp was quiet, and not a shadow or voice stirred. She put her hand to Aes's neck and felt the warmth of his being course through her.

"I missed you," she said aloud. He got onto one knee, and she climbed clumsily onto him.

Like a bird taking flight, they glided through the camp and into the forest. The moon was high and no longer obscured by the nightmarish fog that had blanketed the region in darkness for so long. For thirty minutes, they passed seamlessly through the undergrowth, navigating nature's obstacles with ease, stopping only when they reached a small grove of untrampled grass.

"This'll do." She spoke silently into her friend's mind.

They waited until their hearts calmed and their breathing had regularised, and then together they reached out with their minds. Searching and calling, determined to find Evia. They did this for an hour, until their heads ached and Xander's hands and feet had numbed from the cool.

"It's no use," Xander said, disheartened. "Why can't we find her? You really think it's because we're too far south? I hope you're right, Aes. I really do."

Though worry gnawed at her, Aes's confidence gave her some hope. Silently they headed back to camp.

CHAPTER 64

Septembrix 13, 476; Borealis, Borlencia—Xander stirred from sleep as a dull thud pierced the early morning quiet. Groggily she opened a single eye and waited for the blur to dissipate. Her room was dimly lit with nature's light, and a comfortable cool abounded. She listened for another thud, unable to tell if the noise had been a figment of her dream world or reality.

The house was silent. She reached her arms overhead and stretched, then closed her eye, eager to continue her slumber. Another thud rang out, louder than the last. This time she wasn't the only one to stir. She heard her mother, or maybe it was her father, emerge from their bedroom and move through the corridor to the front door.

Xander could hear hushed voices from the front of the house, and moments later, footsteps came back through the corridor and into her parents' bedroom. Curious, she got up and entered the hall. At the front door were two of Carolus's elite guards, their expressions stern. One of them spotted her, and he smiled and waved. She returned the greeting and swiftly went back into her room with rosy cheeks, aware she still wore her sleeping garment.

She closed her bedroom door and then pressed her ear against it. Her parents were talking, though she couldn't discern what was being said, and then a minute later, she heard someone depart their room and cross back through the hall with a heavier step. She opened her door a crack and peeked out. It was Carolus. Donned in his work robes, he strode with haste and not a moment later had entered the street with the two guards and closed the door behind him.

Though curious as to what could be so urgent to pull him from sleep, Xander knew it was only a matter of time before she would find out. She closed her bedroom door, reached her arms overhead, and stretched again. She had a busy day ahead of her. Her mother had unfinished work she needed to attend to at the palace and had promised to take her along. Of course, Xander had no intention of sitting idly by, not when there was a palace to explore and guards to toy with. And what good would it do her to not have her fill of rest? She yawned and climbed back into bed, content to doze until her mother woke her for breakfast.

CHAPTER 65

Novembrix 17, 484; temporary home of the Lizard People, the Great Forest—Ratin turned from Aika and peered at Xander, his expression one of exasperation. Wrapped warmly to protect from the cold, they were in Aika's tent and sat on the chairs. All three still carried the cuts and bruises of their journey to the Great Tree. But despite the closeness that had grown between them, the air was tense.

"Her people need her," Ratin said to Xander. "Please don't deprive us."

"It's not her decision." Aika spoke up.

"The bugs have regrouped. They've got vengeance on their tongues. Now is not the time to leave."

"I thought they'd scatter with Damain's death," Aika admitted.

"The monster's simply been replaced, albeit with a less vile and less cruel lieutenant. They've fought too hard to give up their winnings. This war is not over, and now's not the time for you to abandon your people."

"You know why I must leave. All that I've seen, all that I will see. It must be done. It's the right decision; I can feel it. I can't expect you to understand if you still remain unconvinced, Ratin." Aika got up, walked over to him and rested her hand reassuringly on his shoulder. "You remember what my father used to tell us: 'If in doubt, trust your intuition. If without doubt, consult your intuition.' He taught us that intuition is an ally in leadership and should be consulted even if the situation appears black and white because you never know what it may uncover or how it may affect the design of the decision."

"How can you lead your people if you're halfway across Anemoi?"

She removed her hand and sat back down. "That's why I have you, Ratin. You knew this was coming the moment the elders agreed to my request. Now it's time. Do you doubt your leadership?"

"You know I don't. But we'll need you. That, and I doubt your safety. You're asking me to let you leave without my protection. I was tasked with your life by your father."

"And how I've made yours so difficult."

"I'm sure you've removed a few years from my life with your ability to disappear and reappear without notice."

"Well, let me do you a favour. As it's in my power, I remove you of that charge. Your responsibility is solely that of our people and the removal of the scourge from our home."

"Doesn't change the facts. What about—" He shot Xander a guilty glance.

"Ricard?" Xander responded.

"He's—not sound of mind and yet is intent to follow you. At least that's what I've gathered from the three grunts he's given since we arrived at the camp. I think he's dangerous and will put both of you at risk." He leaned forward, his features soft and sympathetic. "Speak to him, Xander. He needs you. But if he gives you any impression of anger or instability, don't take him. If Aika's insistent on following you, please do this small ask for me."

▲ ▲ ▲

Xander dropped a small basket of fruit outside her tent and peered across the pod to the grove she had seen Ricard enter that morning. She inadvertently

412

caressed the two figurines in her pocket.

"He's still in there," a voice brought her to. It was Gladis. She stood at Xander's feet. "Missed breakfast and lunch. Much more of this, and he'll wither away."

"I don't know what to do."

"Just speak to him. He'll not ignore you."

"What if he does?"

"Then at least you tried. Don't deprive yourself of that."

Xander took a deep breath. All she wanted was for her friend to be okay. A sign or a whisper that he would pull through. Decided, she crossed the pod and entered through the trees.

Ricard sat on the dirt with his back against a rock, staring at a pond in the centre, one of his arms also in a sling. He picked up a stone and skimmed it across the water into a cluster of luscious trees on the other side. Each ripple was a sparkly cascade of reflected sunlight and a welcome reminder of the vanquished evil that had sought to collapse the Great Forest into a blanket of forbidding shroud and the dangers it wrought.

He looked over to her. "Hey, kiddo."

"Hi, Ricard," she said softly. She walked over and sat next to him, then picked up a stone. "Five shillings says I can hit the small tree on the right."

"One arm in a sling and you'd make that bet?"

She nodded.

A sad smile crept across his face. "In that case, make it ten."

She lifted her good arm and skimmed the stone. It bounced on the water three times before missing its mark. "Guess I owe you ten shillings."

"Ha! You don't owe me anything, kiddo."

They sat silently for a number of minutes, watching as the ripples in the pond subsided and the surface found tranquillity.

"Ricard?"

"Yes?"

"I have something for you."

"Oh yeah?"

She pulled the two figurines out of her pocket and placed them in his palm. His eyes began to glisten. He clasped his hand shut and put it against his heart. "Thank you," he managed.

"I want to help you."

He wiped the tears from his cheek and recomposed himself. "This is more than enough, kiddo. Your presence and a sprinkle of time will be my healer. I just need a bit more of the latter."

She nodded and the grove fell silent. Minutes passed and then an hour, bringing with it a bitter cold not usually welcomed in the woods that far south. Ready to seek out the warmth of the tent, she stood up.

"Xander."

"Yes?"

"I think I'm ready to tell you about your father. If you want to hear it."

A wave of adrenaline rushed through her, and she sat back down, the cold no longer a bother.

"You don't—" she began.

"I do. Because the opportunity could be taken away from us at any moment," he interjected, and looked at her adoringly. "This is not just my own account but what I've been able to piece together from other survivors. Men I'd trust with my life." He put his hand on hers. "Now it's my turn to ask. Are you sure you want to know this?"

"Every detail."

His face hardened, and he withdrew his hand. "Then despite the pain it'll undoubtedly cause us both, let me tell you about the final moments of the bravest man I've ever had the pleasure of knowing…"

CHAPTER 66

Septembrix 13, 476; The Battle for Borealis—Ricard peered up from the crudely drawn map of the known enemy positions and took in the commotion that emanated from the far side of the square. It didn't take him long to identify Carolus's arrival; the crescendo of cheers that followed the shuffle of the crowd was an expected reaction from the city's soldiers as they caught sight of their champion.

"Good of you to join," Ricard said boisterously, locking arms with Carolus as they met in the centre, the pair a formidable sight even amidst the sea of armed men.

"Couldn't leave you here on your own. No telling what you might get up to."

"And the girls?"

"At the river with the civilians. I gave Alya orders to clear the harbour and reach the fleet."

"You know, I was half expecting her to appear on your hind. She will be missed, her and that sabre."

Carolus smiled softly, momentarily oblivious to the danger that still approached, and then he glanced over the gathered soldiers, their collective expression wary but eager.

"What is the latest on the enemy positions?" he asked, though the echoed thump of the drums and the timed step of the attackers might have led one to assume they were already in the city.

"Same as before. Their main force faces the North Gate, and the two smaller forces approach the East and South Gates." He shot Carolus a worried expression.

"What is it?"

"The banners—they're completely black and have no insignia. And the speed of the horse contingent and the army's mysterious appearance from the desert is unlike anything I've seen. What kind of foe marches without colours and avoids detection right up until the last breath?"

Carolus stared into Ricard's eyes, and bafflement took the burly man.

"You know whom we face…" Ricard said in astonishment at the lack of surprise evident in Carolus's sharp features.

"I can't be certain, but—"

The rustle of the rain-sodden soldiers abruptly died down in tandem with the halt of the enemy's march, the drums now all that filled the air, the calm before the storm stark in its sudden arrival.

"Sir, they've halted their advance," a wiry soldier shouted to the commanders from atop the gate.

Carolus hurriedly climbed the steps to the top of the ramparts with Ricard close behind. Darkness had fallen swiftly, and the thick line of sinister shadows now dominated the stretch of the horizon. He shuddered at the sheer size of the mysterious army that stared back across the plains and could feel the same worry reverberate through the men.

"They wait," Ricard muttered under his breath.

In one last bid to find weakness, Carolus took in the men that lined the stone walls, a deadly combination of spearmen, archers, and axemen prepared to meet enemy ladders and siege towers. In the square below, his battalion of five thousand men, including his own elite guard, stood ready to repel any breach of the thick, battle-scarred North Gate.

"The riflemen?" he asked, perplexed.

"Positioned in the courtyards to cover a retreat…rather than clutter the front line," Ricard responded cautiously.

Carolus frowned for several moments and then nodded in agreement. He understood the burly commander's reluctance to use one-shot volleys in such tight quarters, though he valued the rifle's effectiveness in hindering a determined charge. He turned back to the horizon and had been about to query the attacker's pause when the thump of the drums stopped. The forced silence was eerie and at odds with the number of armed men that had congregated on both sides of the wall, and a sense of unease shot through the ranks.

Shouts suddenly rang out from farther along the wall, and instantly the call of contact was on the tip of every soldier's tongue who was within earshot. On cue, a warning flare rose silently into the air, followed by another half dozen, a solid confirmation that the enemy had reached the walls. The faint light of the flares illuminated the ground below, and the line of soldiers that manned the wall visibly faltered at what was revealed beneath the shroud of darkness.

"Where did they come from?" Ricard spat in disbelief as he hoisted his giant axe in his thick hands. "Not a damn sound!"

Carolus's grip tightened on his spear, the urgency of the situation apparent. He had turned to the nearest signalman, ready to bark his first order, when he found himself hurled violently to the stone rampart. The nearest section of the wall, no more than a hundred metres to the east of the North Gate, blew into the air in a torrent of fire and rock, and the ranks of waiting soldiers on the ramparts and in the square below collapsed like dominoes from the force. The intensity of the blast was so powerful that it shattered the windows in the closest neighbourhoods and set alight half the buildings in the northern part of the city.

Still struggling to rise, Carolus felt a hand grasp his arm and lift him to his feet. Ricard's dirtied face stared back at him. "We need to cover the breach in the wall," he shouted over the racket of confusion and panic that had taken hold of the soldiers, the sudden gap in the city's defences a dangerous invocation of terror.

Carolus nodded in agreement and then shot a glance towards the horizon. The barely visible line of the enemy had shifted, the rumble of footsteps, hooves, and siege weapons on the plains a giveaway to what approached.

"To the breach!" he bellowed down into the square. The men not incapacitated had only just righted themselves but were quick to adhere to the command and start towards the gap. "Ricard, reform the defences on the wall. I'll oversee the defence on the ground."

On the brink of his descent into the fray below, Carolus's mouth dropped, and dread took his focus as a series of explosions erupted from the western perimeter of the city by the water.

"They're in the city?" Ricard blurted in shock.

"The river!"

Aware of Carolus's thought process, Ricard swiftly intervened. "Your place is at the wall. Let me see to it."

Carolus hesitated at the offer, but the blatant ring of metal on metal that emanated from the breach tugged at his sensibilities. "Send the riflemen and two contingents of spearmen with their messenger boys," he blurted finally. "If they're in the city and this is more than an attempt to block escape, have the boys relay the message to the nearest captains."

He disappeared into the river of men that pushed towards the contact whilst Ricard scrambled to pass on the order. As Carolus drew near the breach, he shuddered at the scale of the damage, and despite the defenders' instinctive reaction to plug the near-fifty-metre gap with a filler of armoured bodies, the line soon faltered and concaved a dozen metres into the city.

The press of bodies was a hindrance to swift movement, and Carolus's poor vantage point and the dark cloth and warped masks of the attackers meant he was still unable to confirm the foe. From afar he saw the men on the ramparts commence their attack on the enemy soldiers that filled the breach, a downpour of shafts and boulders.

He grabbed the nearest captain, a man with long blond locks. "Re-form the line five men deep, then empty the oil pots into the breach and set them alight. We need to push them out."

He scanned the vicinity for his elite guard whilst the captain rushed off to relay the order. He nodded proudly. Even without his presence, his guard held the left wing of the melee, the unit's banner a call to arms for the regulars.

The attrition of the two lines was fierce, and in mere minutes, hundreds of men on both sides had been cut down, including a notable portion of his elite troop. The masked assailants clad in black were fast and fought without reservation or care for their own lives. And for every man he skewered with his spear, two took his place, their focus clearly intent on his presence, his banner a target for would-be glory hunters.

Through the mess of weapons and bodies, he felled three men in rapid succession with his spear and had ducked a swipe from a fourth before one of his guards cut the man down. Barely recovered, a brute of a man a foot taller than the next stepped forward through the fray, a club thicker than a man's thigh in his hand. The man's leering grin evident even through the mask, he speedily flung his club at the commander. Carolus instinctively dodged the vicious jab but was subsequently knocked to the ground by a well-placed armoured fist. With Carolus dazed and momentarily incapacitated, the brute grabbed his limp ankle and began to drag him towards the breach, his masked comrades ready to fend off any intervention.

In spite of the soldiers' thus-far-unsuccessful struggles to repel the influx of masked men, the sight of their commander's predicament served as an elixir for bravado and vigour, and his unit and the others rallied ferociously and pushed the attackers onto the back foot. Within seconds they had slaughtered dozens, and the brute, momentarily distracted by the devastating onslaught, did not see Carolus's spear penetrate his chest and render him lifeless.

Carolus was free of the man's powerful grip, and as he struggled to his feet, a handful of his men pulled him back into the protection of the line. He breathed heavily from within the press of bodies, shuddering at the close call and the reek of blood that had smeared his armour and enveloped the confined killing space.

"Commander!" a voice called from behind the line.

Carolus spotted the same captain and a messenger boy and struggled over to them. "What is it?" he gasped.

"News from Commander Ricard." The captain spoke. "The explosions—they came from the ships. The evacuation's been cut off."

Terror took him, and desperation and fear for his family's safety began to steal his resolve. "And the civilians?" he managed.

"Some have taken refuge in the city buildings. The rest have made for the East and South Gates."

"Assuming we still hold them."

"Sir, that's not all. The northern wall has been overcome here, here, and here." The captain spoke urgently as he pointed to a crumpled map that highlighted three positions west of the North Gate. "There are reports that they are also attempting to circumnavigate the marine defences on the northwest corner of the city."

Carolus looked up at the men holding the massive breach in front of him. The attackers had shown no reprieve since the battle had begun, and now a third of the defenders lay dead. They could not hold much longer without support.

"Where is Ricard?"

"He oversees two of the other positions and has none left to commit to the evacuation, let alone support you."

Carolus frowned. He had no idea if the East and South Gates had been taken or the whereabouts of the civilians and his family. He turned from the noise and commotion of the battle and observed the previously packed square. Men ran back and forth with the relay of messages, but other than for a few wounded, he, too, had not enough soldiers to launch a renewed defence of the breach.

In the distance, he could just make out the attackers that now held part of the rampart and one of the towers to the west of the North Gate. The masked men pooled into the streets below with Ricard's men being pushed back. He did not doubt that a similar scene would be replicated at the other two confirmed positions the captain referred to, and any un-bloodied men that remained on the walls and who still waited to engage would soon be tied up.

"We don't have enough men to hold the wall," he muttered angrily. "Boy!" He beckoned the young messenger. "Relay the order to Ricard and the other commanders to fall back to the river on my mark. When the signal is given, we will re-form on the bridges to the south of the city. We can hold them there. In the meantime, have the riflemen secure the crossings and the two contingents of spearmen usher the civilians south."

The messenger nodded and was about to disappear when shock took his face. Carolus followed his stare to the breach, and weariness enveloped him. "Now!" he barked at the confounded messenger.

Carolus and the captain looked back to the melee and the fight that had ensued between his elite unit and the heavy horsemen that had wormed their way into the battle. Supported by the arrival of siege towers on ei-ther side of the breach, these men were bulkier than the foot soldiers and fought with an impetus and speed that made their contemporaries look amateurish. The fatigued defenders faltered from the arrival of fresh, elite troops on horseback, and though the focus of the attack was against the left flank, the renewed drive of the enemy line began to precipitate the collapse of the centre.

"Damn this! We're done!" a scrawny soldier in the rear of the centre screamed, the determination sand ferocity of the attack suddenly too much for his senses. "We're all done! Stay and die if you want, but not me!"

He turned to flee but had barely made it a metre when Carolus grabbed him by the cuff and threw him to the ground. "Then do something about it!" he shouted with an authority and presence that beckoned the attention of the nearest panicked soldiers as they, too, verged on reckless fear. The man stared back at him with a measure of shock and shame, both at his commander's action and his own weakness, and then he nodded subtly and climbed to his feet.

"Form on me!" Carolus called to the rear. "Form on me!"

He held his spear high for all to see. Soldiers that were, moments ago, ready to flee quickly rallied to him, and a renewed resolve discovered their worn faces. The rigidity of the line hardened, his call and his renowned armour and spear a rallying point for the men, and the aura he exuded an invocation of infectious hope and courage that swiftly spread through the ranks. A roar erupted from the defenders of Borealis, and the centre of the line reverberated around him. So invigorated were the men that the line began to creep forward against the sheer weight of the attack.

Goosebumps prickled the captain's skin at the turnaround he was suddenly witness to, but before he, too, could join in the cheer, Carolus pulled him close and whispered into his ear, "When this line collapses and these horsemen enter the city, they'll cut off the retreat and slaughter everyone. Ricard and the others must pull back to the river. Make sure it happens!"

The futility of the rally was etched in his eyes; it would not be enough to save the wall or the city, only enough to buy Ricard and the others time to save themselves. Carolus turned his back to the captain and drove forward in unison with the march of his men. About to protest, the same realisation dawned on the captain, and with a shameful sadness, he ran off to sound the retreat, his message a sure death sentence for the man who had captured his and much of the city's admiration for an age.

⋏ ⋏ ⋏

"Spit it out!" Ricard hissed, his patience wearing thin with the exhausted messenger boy.

"Sir, the commander—he gave the order to retreat from the wall and hold the bridges south. He wants us to get the civilians south and out of the city."

"And what of him and those who still man the breach?" He eyed the boy dangerously. "Well?" he growled at the messenger's hesitation.

"He rallies into the enemy," the recently joined captain interjected, to the messenger's relief. "He draws in the attack with his spear. He insists the wall cannot hold—"

"Keep your voice down, boy!" Ricard whispered harshly, dragging him in close.

"Sir, he does not believe the wall will hold. He wants you to sound the retreat before his line collapses." The captain spoke in a more hushed tone.

"Like hell I will. Santos, ready the elites. The commander needs us," he called to his second, a rugged man born in Nasdir but raised in Crowton. "Captain, relay this message to the other commanders. Stage retreat through this bastard maze of a city to the river on my signal. Make these bastards work for every street corner!"

"And the civilians?" The messenger boy sounded nervous.

"All civilians en route are to be escorted."

"Just those en route?" One of Ricard's men spoke up in disbelief.

"If Carolus is right, we're running on borrowed time…I've made the call; I'll bear the responsibility." Ricard threw his plumed helmet on and hefted his battle-axe. "Let's get our commander," he roared.

Carolus's banner wavered clumsily in the thick of the melee against the brunt of a sustained attack by men on horseback, and both dread and hope took Ricard. The line was dangerously thin in spots, and he swiftly ordered several of his units to buffer the flimsy pockets whilst the rest followed him towards the banner. The worn and weary men of the line showed renewed hope at the sight of Ricard, but it was short-lived as again they were thrown to the back foot by the influx of the attackers. The stench of blood and sweat, the crumple of bodies and the clamour of fighting men invoked an overwhelming sense of claustrophobia and revulsion, but Ricard's desire to ensure his friend's safety gave him the strength and impetus to glide through the thicket with fresh armour, ready to take the fight.

"Where's the commander?" Ricard bellowed to a captain of Carolus's elite unit as he neared the chaos of the left front. The bloodied man looked to him, uncomprehending. "The commander?" he barked again.

"In the centre. He fights alone," the captain shouted back. "Every time we try to shift our position, they cut us off, and now we're too few."

"Dammit!"

"It's like—" The captain quickly lunged forward and knifed a masked soldier through a sudden gap in the line and then withdrew back to the position as several of Ricard's men filled the gap. "Since the beginning, they've targeted him. It's like they've known all along the armour he wears and the spear he carries," he panted. Ricard felt his stomach knot. "They know who he is, and they want him." The captain turned to several of his men and shouted orders, then returned his gaze to Ricard.

"When I give the order, sound the retreat. Make sure my messenger boys over there see it." The captain looked relieved. "We make for the centre," he said to Santos, and beckoned his soldiers to follow, much to the dismay of the exhausted men they left in their wake.

From afar, Ricard could make out Carolus and the men who fought by his side, their collective movements laboured from fatigue. But as he and his retinue neared to assist, the enemy line reverberated as his group's intentions became apparent. Abruptly a wedge of masked assailants drove towards his position, determined to cut him off from Carolus. Ricard wasn't having it.

Without reserve and without thought for his own well-being, Ricard launched himself at the tip of the wedge and slaughtered them by the twos and threes with each swing of his axe, his own soldiers having already made space for the Battle Ox. Bones crunched and limbs severed with each swing, and the horror of his brutality quickly collapsed the wedge. Enraged, he turned to Carolus's position and roared, "To the commander!" for every soldier near and far to hear. Even Carolus heard, and reprieve lit his face at the sight of his friend making for his position.

"Sir, twenty metres ahead!" Santos cried.

Another contingent of heavily armed horsemen powered towards Carolus with little care for those they trampled underneath. The man at the front, vicious and powerful looking, did not wear a mask, and though Ricard could not make out the man's features, the look of apprehension that struck Carolus's face spoke volumes.

"We can't make it!" Santos spat, and skewered another.

"We must!" Ricard screamed in desperation as another wedge made for their position. His heart raced as he drove through the melee, cutting enemies and throwing his own out of the way, but the man without a mask had reached Carolus's position and had jumped to the ground with a wicked smirk and a razor-sharp blade in hand.

Time seemed to slow as the mysterious man donned a purple mask, as both Carolus's regulars and the opposing horsemen readied themselves for the slaughter to come. Then, as one, both sides charged and clashed in a violent collision.

Every desperate metre Ricard made towards Carolus was met with fierce resistance, with swarm after swarm of attackers throwing him back in an attempt to cut off his path. Increasingly panicked, he sneaked a glimpse at his friend after each man he killed, and every glimpse brought only dread. The horsemen were making quick work of Carolus's soldiers, and the masked man's speed was unfathomable, even for a soldier with Ricard's experience. Carolus, exhausted as he was, couldn't keep pace, and as the masked man cut Carolus's spear in two and threw him to the ground, Ricard almost cried.

Every moment from that point was a blur. The collapse of the line at the sight of Carolus's severed head and his broken spear held high for all to see. The rage and blood that enveloped Ricard as he slaughtered dozens in some mad attempt to reach the assailant, only to be dragged back by his own men as they retreated. The chaotic withdrawal of the remnants of the battalions as they pulled back through the maze of courtyards and streets, with each block a brutal fight for survival. The small contingents of enemy soldiers that had overcome the riflemen and hounded the battalions from the river and the bridges. The utter exhaustion and sheer quantity of dead before they retook the bridges and covered the evacuation long enough to save some small portion of the city's inhabitants, themselves included.

CHAPTER 67

Novembrix 17, 484; temporary home of the Lizard People, the Great Forest— Xander lay on her bed with a second blanket to keep the warmth, fondling the newly found shard in her hand. The sun outside had set, and though the cold was biting, she could hear movement within the camp.

She had known the rough details of her father's end, but Ricard's retelling had brought the event into a new light, one that she was both proud of and shaken by. Anger coursed through her, threatening to spill, and despite Ricard's assurances that Carolus was targeted simply because he was the garrison's commander, she couldn't help but feel that there was more to it. That everything was linked. The angst and political strife in Borealis in the months leading up to the attack, the campaign against her father, and then the fall of Borealis itself.

She dropped the shard to the ground and turned onto her side, careful not to jar her bruised arm. She sighed. Her longing to see Evia and Dogner and Joseph was unbearable and on par with the anger. She craved the reassurance that their company could bring. The reassurance that everything would be all right. But instead she was faced with a hole of uncertainty as to whether they were safe or not. A hole that could only be satiated by the knowledge that they were okay.

Her mind flicked back to the friends she would leave behind when she eventually left the forest for Zyphyr with Ricard, Aika, and Aes. To Gladis, who seemed more like a protective aunt than a newly minted friend. And Oscine, the songbird that had reunited her with Ricard. And then to Haro and Leila, the two she never got to say her goodbyes to.

"Poor Ricard," she said sadly.

Though she, too, had experienced loss in her father, mother, and brother, she knew that no two people's grief was the same, for there were a myriad of channels that could feed into its manifestation, moulding both its severity and longevity. She hoped that he would find his way before they left the forest. That the change of scenery and the busying of his guilt-ridden mind would spur his healing. That Gladis was right, that the company of Carolus and Alya's daughter would stave off the complete rupture of his will.

She closed her eyes. She could see Hemish's blurred face, a common visitor in her more sombre moments, and the imagined features of her wicked aunt, Erzse. A cruel woman that surely deserved what was coming to her.

Another sigh escaped her lips. Her exhaustion was complete and all too much to bear. Abruptly and swiftly, she drifted into slumber, the images of the living and the passed imprinted in her mind, ready to resume their nightly performances.

End of Book One

Thank you for reading!
If you enjoyed *Scourge in the Woods*, please consider leaving a short review.
It makes a real difference and helps other readers discover the story.
Xander's journey continues in *A Hand for an Eye*.

AUTHOR BIOGRAPHY

Born in the United Kingdom to a Guyanese mother and an English father, Haydn spent his formative years hopping between the Pacific Islands, Middle East, Central America, and the Caribbean to the tune of his father's job. Now based in New York City, Haydn has found the inspiration to write from his fascination with, and ability to become lost in, the worlds of fantasy and sci-fi. It is the perfect escape from his career in corporate finance.